THE GRAVITY OF ELENDORAS

SPACE MARAUDER CHRONICLES
BOOK TWO

LORENA PARA

To the person I was before I started writing this book.
We did it. Thank you for not giving up.

eBook October 2024
Paperback October 2024

Book design by Lorena Para
Cover Image by Ronnie Jensen
www.tegnemaskin.no

ASIN (eBook) B0D3ZZBHN6
ISBN (paperback) *978-1-7375253-1-8*

Get a free bonus story at
TheShortWriter.com

CONTENTS

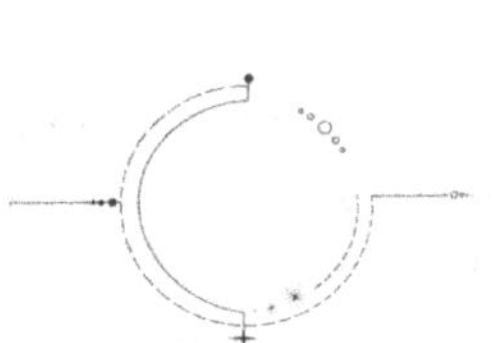

*D*umalth was the first real planet Orinthia Anton set foot on since leaving Earth. Condensation dripped down the side of her cup as she tipped its contents into her mouth. The amber liquid burned her empty stomach. It had been months since she last enjoyed a stiff drink, a lifetime ago. Her current captain, Kos Rogue, wanted to be sure they were not followed by their former captain, Ahto of the *Fera*.

The Fera, she thought. A cold hand gripped her chest and squeezed. Orinthia took another long sip. She felt she deserved every drop in her glass, and the two glasses that followed it.

The bar she sat in smelled of damp bodies, cooked meats, and sour alcohol. Two dozen patrons filled the seats, less than half of which were human looking. Most were the stocky orange natives of the water planet Dumalth. Their aqua-rebreathers bubbled over their gills and hissed periodically.

The promise of adventure and riches led to heartache and poverty, Orinthia continued her line of thought. Her mind wondered back to the med bay of her former ship. The sound of blaster fire ripped through her memory. Her arms ached to reach out through the past to stop her brother from being hit. The nerves on her neck tingled as she willed herself to force a different outcome. One that did not end with a gaping hole in Uri's chest.

A flash of hot rage replaced the chill in her chest. She did not know how, but she would find a way to make her sister pay for what she did Uri.

Conversations of drunken tales and card games triggered the humming in Orinthia's head, drawing her from her deep memories. Though the drink helped to dull the sound, it was impossible to ignore. She eyed the two men beside her and focused on their exchange. The taller of the two and closest to her was her captain. Kos's dark hair skipped over the top of his shoulders as he spoke to the Vronian barkeep across from him.

"Five thousand credits, that's the lowest I'll go," Kos said, swirling his drink but never sipping.

The reptilian creature laughed, exposing his tiny, razor-sharp, and venomous teeth. "Now, don't be hasty, Rogue. Everyone here knows you're no longer under Ahto's protection."

"But without me, Ahto can't navigate his way through a star nursery," Kos said. He released his cup and leaned both elbows on the bar. "And he definitely can't deliver your ship-ment in the time you're asking."

"How about three thousand credits and I don't hail the *Fera* as soon as you walk out of my saloon? I've been fixing to retire, and that kind of bounty would do nicely." The barkeep nodded to the comm relay at the end of the bar.

Without missing a beat, Kos stood and extended his hand. "I hope you find someone to move your shipment, Killian, but it won't be me. Not at that price."

Orinthia threw back another swig of her drink as she

watched Killian stare at Kos' intricately tattooed palm. She could see him working out the offer, judging if Kos was bluffing. Her mod had hummed, detecting his deceit, but she already knew they needed the money. Three thousand credits might as well have been a million. Their food rations on their ship, *Freya*, were about to run out, and they had practically landed using fumes.

Freya, Orinthia thought. *I still don't understand what that thing is. She's an AI that controls the ship and the ship itself? Even as much as Kos tries to explain it, I don't get it. He talks about her like she's a person. I've started doing it now, too.*

"You cheat me, Kos Rogue, and I'll add another bounty to your head," the reptilian man said. His voice rumbled low in his chest and his thick tail flicked tight curves behind him.

Kos grinned and dipped his head to the side. "You can't afford to pay a bounty for me," he said with a wink.

Though he looked at and addressed Killian, Orinthia could feel her cheeks getting warm as she attempted to mask it with the last bit of liquor.

The Vronian lowered himself behind the counter. Faint beeps sounded, followed by the thump of a lock disengaging. He reappeared with a handful of credit chips. "You get half now, and the rest when you load the shipment."

Kos' eyes twitched toward Orinthia, who touched her glass to the counter and swirled twice. Her mod said he was telling the truth.

"I'll have my sons meet you at the docks in the mornin'," Killian said.

"We'll be there." Kos held out his hand again.

Killian grumbled then sighed with a hiss before dumping the colorful credits into Kos' upturned palm.

With his free hand, Kos pulled a velvet pouch from his

coat and filled it with their earnings. They jingled and clacked together as they fell in.

Orinthia knocked the bottom of her glass against the counter to get Kos' attention. He retrieved a red credit from the pouch and tossed it at Killian. Without speaking, Orinthia got to her feet and followed Kos out the door.

The heels of her boots made a muffled thud against the wooden dock. She stood beside Kos and let the cool sea breeze fill her senses. A gentle roll of waves beat against the pilings supporting the pier. Her head seemed to sway, and her stomach churned with the sound. Speeder boats bobbed up and down and their tethers creaked with tension. She let her mind wonder what it would be like to live on Dumalth; to wake up every morning and watch the tide from her window as she ate her breakfast. *Maybe Uri and I can come back once he's fixed,* she thought. *A place like this could use a good surgeon. And I could—*

"Let's get some provisions before heading back," Kos said, stealing Orinthia from her thoughts. "I'm sure Thrutt is pacing a groove into *Freya*'s floor by now."

"Can we make one more stop first?" Orinthia asked. Her cheeks were flushed, and she felt light. She tightly shut the door on the memory of the *Fera*.

"We can't go on a shopping spree," Kos said. "This has to last us a while."

"I just need one outfit that fits me." Orinthia spread her arms and the sweater she wore parachuted around her. "If I have to wear this one more day, I'm going to start going naked."

"Fine," Kos said, clearing his throat. His bronze face turned a light shade of pink beneath the stubble of his newly grown beard. "But only one outfit."

Orinthia smiled and clapped her hands together. "There is

a shop just over there. I saw it when we came in." She bounced on the balls of her feet and led the way. The suns were setting over the horizon, cutting long twin shadows through the honey-colored light.

The door chimed as the pair stepped into the store. A grey, two-headed cat sat on a shelf at the back of the room. It lifted one of its heads, swished its three tails, then rested back on its paws. The air was warm inside and smelled of perfumes mixed with the chemical sting of dye. Gentle music played overhead.

A plump shopkeeper walked in through a curtain near where the cat was lying. A crown of bright red horns pushed through her short, curly onyx hair. The woman's solid black eyes followed them as she waved them to enter. She rested an arm on the counter. The other was replaced entirely with steel. Wires and tubes showed through the cybernetic attachment and connected at the end where instead of a hand, she had needles and hooks of various sizes.

"How'do?" The woman greeted them with a smile. Her voice was strong and came from deep inside her chest. "Looking for new garb?"

Orinthia stepped forward. Emboldened by the alcohol in her system she said, "Yes, I am. See, we're on our honeymoon." She glanced back to see Kos flare his nostrils and give a long blink. Years of deciphering lies made her their master. Her heart thumped with pride at her ability to improvise a story on the spot. "My husband is a sailor, and we are planet hopping. Somehow, we completely managed to forget my luggage on Holbroo. I've been stuck wearing his clothes for days. But he's promised me *three* new outfits. Right, sweetie?"

"Anything for you, sweetie," Kos emphasized the last

word. He forced a smile and gave her an almost unnoticeable head shake.

"Isn't he wonderful?" Orinthia batted her eyes at Kos and gave him an overly done grin. Then, she turned back to the woman and said, "Anyway, we are an adventurous couple. I'm going to need things that are durable and easy to move in. Oh! And maybe a coat, with pockets inside. Something in the pastel family would be best and cut at the waist."

The shopkeeper came around the counter and measured Orinthia as she continued to describe her ideal outfits. The metallic arm split in two and took notes as she worked. When she was done, the woman moved back to the counter and examined her notes. She typed the information into her tally machine before saying, "Right'o. I'll have it ready by the morning. It'll be three hundred fifty credits, paid in full."

Kos groaned as he took the pouch from his coat. He pulled out the money and handed it to Orinthia, who gave it to the seamstress.

"Thank you so much," Orinthia said with a smile. "I'll be back first thing tomorrow." She rejoined Kos and took one of his hands in both of hers.

Kos' warm hand stiffened and fingers twitched in between hers.

The woman thanked them, and they exited back onto the pier.

"Why did you do that?" Kos asked, removing his hand from Orinthia's when they were out of sight from the shop.

"Don't be upset," Orinthia said. She rolled her eyes and crossed her arms. "Saying you're my husband was easier than explaining that I left all my things on the *Fera* after we mutinied."

"I'm more upset about the two other outfits," Kos said. "We agreed just one. It's coming out of your portion."

Orinthia scrunched her nose. "Thrutt wouldn't have complained."

"You should have married him, then." Kos sighed and added, "Let's go find food, *sweetie.*" He shoved his hands in his coat pocket and stuck out an elbow for her to take.

Orinthia slipped a hand through the gap and pinched her lips together to hide a smile.

2

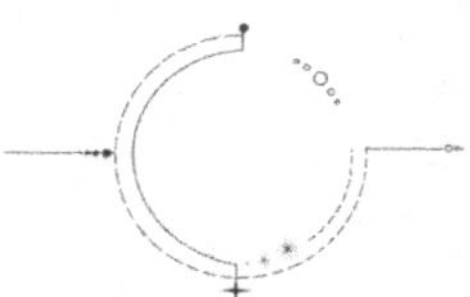

*E*mpty boxes littered the floor of *Freya's* galley as Kos and Orinthia filled the cupboards with their trove. They had purchased sweets, protein orbs, vegetable powder, four cases of hydro-spheres, and an array of dried meats with the thousand credits Kos budgeted for. He wanted a buffer in case Killian decided to back out last minute.

Thrutt, who stood nine feet tall, took the last crate of hydro-spheres from Orinthia as she balanced on her tip toes and tried to reach the highest shelf. He slipped it in with the rest before securing the latch.

The three each took their portions and moved to one of the tables. Orinthia rested with her back against the wall and pulled her legs against her, tucking them into the oversized sweater. She opened her meat stick and listened to Kos explain their plan to Thrutt.

"I'll map out a route before we turn in," Kos said between sips of his hydro-sphere. "Killian is only giving us two day-cycles to get his shipment to his brother-in-law on Vron."

Thrutt made a sound with his mouth. The table creaked

under his weight as he sat down beside Orinthia. "That's not a lot of time for detours if it gets messy."

"No, it's not," Kos said. "Which is why I want to leave as soon as his cases are loaded."

"After I get my clothes," Orinthia added through the side of her mouth, careful not to spit food everywhere.

"Oh, so he took you to get some?" Thrutt asked. "I told you he would."

Kos looked between the two sitting across from him and shook his head. "You conspired together?"

Thrutt waved a diamond hand to dismiss Kos' accusation. "I only suggested she ask."

Orinthia did not need the humming of her mod to know he was lying. It was his idea to begin with. She had complained to him several times about not wanting to wear the same four articles of clothing, two of which did not fit her.

"I think it was my threat of going around naked that pushed him over," Orinthia said. She rested her head on her knees.

Thrutt gave a chuckle. "I think he'd actually pref—"

"We have a little over one thousand credits left from what we got paid today," Kos interrupted. He threw Thrutt a side-long look and pulled a maroon-colored, leather-bound book from his pocket. The spine cracked as he opened it on the table. "As long as Killian pays us the remainder, we'll have six thousand credits, including what I had left over from the last *Fera* job. Now, I'll have *Freya* refueled in the morning and then put some aside for emergencies. We'll each split the remainder with fifteen hundred credits." Kos tilted his head toward Orinthia and pointed his scribbler at her. "Except Thia, who already spent part of hers."

Orinthia shrugged. "I would have spent those credits either way."

Kos returned his attention to the book and wrote down numbers. He then flipped a page and wrote more numbers under a page entitled "Thrutt." He did this for Orinthia and his own pages before closing it and replacing it and the scribbler in his coat. The book was like the one he made Orinthia sign on their first meeting, when she agreed to their marauder code. That, like everything else they owned, was long gone, left on the *Fera*. And though he was a captain on *Freya*, Kos still held his quartermaster duties tightly.

"I'm going to chart those routes, now," Kos said. He stood and took the rest of his meal with him. "Maybe run a few scenarios with Freya, too. There's half a galaxy between us and the Delvrin system and I don't want any surprises."

In the two months of living on the ship, Orinthia had only been in the cockpit once; the day they escaped. She avoided *Freya* at all costs, though she knew the ship's AI listened to everything going on inside her walls. More than once Kos shouted commands to her from different locations around the ship. Thrutt, on their first day together, even informed Orinthia that *Freya* was the ship. However, since the control room was the only place where Freya as the AI could interact with others, Orinthia made no habit of going in there.

"I guess I'll turn in, too," Thrutt said. He stood and his bald, stone head almost touched the ceiling of the small galley.

"Night," Orinthia said. She lifted her head but stayed seated at the table and picked at a loose thread on her sweater.

"Unless you want me to stay?" Thrutt added.

Orinthia feigned a smile and shook her head. "I'm fine. Just not ready to go to bed yet."

"Come get me if you need me, kid." Thrutt tapped her shoulder with a large, diamond finger.

"I'll be alright. See you both in the morning."

Kos gave her a long look and a half wave before walking into the corridor. Thrutt ducked his head and followed him out.

Immediately, the room went silent. *Freya* had no need to run full power when they were docked on land. No life support or motors ran loud like they did when in flight. The noise was something Orinthia grew used to. Back on Earth, silence was welcome. Her empty apartment was a sweet escape from the daily buzzing in Orinthia's head. But on *Freya*, her quarters were less empty though just as quiet. She spent as much time as possible in the galley or top deck. The silence only served as a painful reminder of her ever-present roommate.

Orinthia's palms began to sweat, and she ran them over her knees a few times. She stretched out her legs, popped her knuckles, and rotated her shoulders before running out of ideas on how to waste time. With a long sigh, she stared at the galley door and pictured what was on the other side. Unable to avoid it any longer, she rose and entered the corridor, switching off the galley's light as she did.

She stopped and examined the dent in the ground just below the ladder. Thrutt had put it there the last time they were on the *Fera,* when he jumped straight down from the top deck. To the right of the ladder was Thrutt's and Kos' quarters. At the end of the corridor, Orinthia could see Kos standing in the brightly lit control room. He had an arm tucked under the other and his palm out in front of him. A holographic map hung in the air above his hand.

Orinthia turned left and entered her shared cabin. She tapped her foot to the floor as she examined the room. A soft orange glow came from a lamp outside the window above her bunk. She stood in the opening and unzipped her white leather boots, removing them and tossing them to the side. They were the only things left from her old life. Them, and Uri.

She moved through the room and walked by the bed where the lifeless body of her brother lay. Orinthia stopped at his head and looked down at him. "We got the job," she said in a hushed tone. The exposed gears in his chest, more noticeable than when *Freya* was running, whirred beneath the covers. "We're leaving in the morning. After we make the delivery, Kos will contact his tracker friend. He says we should have enough saved up to get to Elendoras."

A pang of anxiety pricked at her heart, but she pushed it away. "I wish there was another way to bring you back. But, for you, I'll face Father. I'll do whatever it takes to make him fix you." She brushed a bit of his dark brown hair with her fingers.

The alcohol had almost worn off, and a headache settled in its place. She left Uri's bed and moved to her own. Her blanket spilled over the side of her bunk and half of it rested on the floor. Orinthia bent down, her head spun as she did, and picked it up. Without changing, she rolled into the bed and pulled the blanket around her.

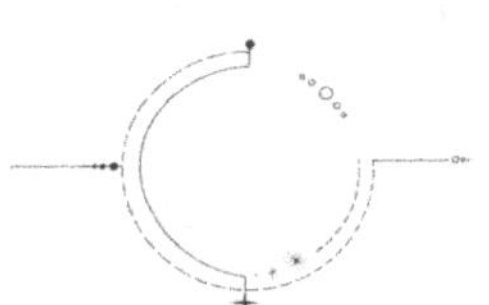

3

*O*rinthia tossed for an hour while the headache grew from annoying to painful. Her tongue stuck to the roof of her mouth. With a grumble, she shifted to her back and stared at the underside of the bunk above her. Though the fourteen stains she counted made her wish she had not. Unable to ignore the pounding in her head, Orinthia rose out of bed, wrapped herself in her blanket, and stepped into the corridor.

She glanced toward the cockpit, a dim blue light shone through the opening. Kos' long legs were draped over the arm of his seat, and he tapped a shoeless foot against the bottom of the seat next to him.

As quiet as she could, Orinthia went to the galley and ran her hands along the wall, not wanting to turn on a light. Her shin was the first thing to contact a bench, followed by her hands as she caught herself from falling forward. She mashed her mouth closed and muffled a yell. Her right hand found the edge of the table as she ran the other down her leg to make sure it was not bleeding. Satisfied with her inspection, she straightened herself and used her fingertips to guide her through the galley to the back counter. She waved her hand through the darkness until she found the hydro-spheres Thrutt left out for the morning.

With her prize in hand, she followed the same route back, careful to avoid injuring any other appendages. Once in the corridor again, she could see Kos' silhouette lean out from the cockpit, looking in her direction. He raised a hand above him and beckoned her to come closer.

Orinthia slouched and regretted getting out of bed at all. She thought about ignoring him, but the idea of taking another inventory of the stains made by who-knows-what pressed her toward her captain. The blanket hung around her feet as she walked.

The room was small with only enough space for three chairs. In front, beneath a window that spanned from wall to wall and up to the ceiling, was a panel of lights, switches, and buttons. Screens blinked and a blue line of radar spun in a slow circle. Behind Kos was a seat that faced another wall of switches and knobs, half of which lit up and faded in and out. Between two control shifters was an unpowered screen. To Orinthia's right was the last chair, the one Kos had tapped with his toes when she saw him before.

"What are you doing?" he asked in a not-so-hushed tone.

"I was getting something to drink," Orinthia said as she sat in the seat beside him. It swiveled so she could face him.

"I think you've had enough to drink," Kos said. He gave a playful smile but quickly straightened his face when Orinthia did not respond.

She knew he most likely meant it as a joke, but it stung anyway. Though he was probably right. *I overdid it again,* she thought. On Earth, she drank to escape the humming and make time pass quicker. But that was not needed with her new crew. Kos and Thrutt shared a pseudo-familial relationship and had no need to lie to each. Orinthia was happy to be with them, and under different circumstances, would have called things good.

"Were you limping?" Kos asked. He shifted in his seat and straightened the hem of his shirt.

Orinthia lifted her pant leg to reveal a thin gash across her skin. "I ran into the bench," she said. Her previous investigation misled her, for a dark, wet line of blood caught the light.

Kos stretched himself and leaned over her. He pushed under the console and a compartment opened. Several items sat inside, only one of which Orinthia recognized. "Thrutt won't mind if we use this," Kos said as he extracted a silver vial. It unstopped with a pop. "Give me your leg."

Orinthia swung her leg toward him. Kos placed a hand under her calf and set the heel of her foot on his knee. He tipped the vial and out slid two blue drops. The liquid cooled the wound and dried the blood. In moments, the cut closed and vanished before them.

The contrast of soothing from the salve was met by the burning of Kos' hand on her skin. When she first felt his temperature, she thought it was because she had disobeyed an order, which had resulted in him killing the man she was supposed to. But later, once they were away from the *Fera*, Thrutt explained it was his body overheating from the mods.

"He's taken in too many," Thrutt had said. "Sometimes, I worry he'll end up like his mom. But he doesn't want to hear it. Honestly, I'm not sure he notices it."

Orinthia wanted to pull away from his searing touch, but she left her leg where it was. Though she would not admit it to anyone, not even to Uri's unhearing ears, she had grown fond of him. Every day that passed, the fondness grew into something more. Something different than what she felt for Thrutt and Uri. Thrutt was more of a father to her in the few months that she knew him than her own father had ever been. And Uri was Uri, her devoted brother. They were her family.

But not Kos. He was outside that circle, and she found herself making excuses to be near him. More than once, she caught herself staring at him longer than casually acceptable. Then she remembered the wink at the bar.

"Does it still hurt?" Kos asked. He ran a finger over where the cut had been and examined it closer.

Orinthia became aware of her breathing that came in short bursts. "No. I haven't slept yet, so I'm tired." Though it was partially true, she was glad he did not have the same mod she did.

Kos nodded and rested back in his seat. "I don't sleep much, either."

The two of them sat in the dim blue light without saying anything for a while. Orinthia stared at her foot on Kos' lap, keenly aware he had not pushed her away and, in fact, mindlessly tapped a finger to her ankle. Kos, with the side of his head resting on his headrest, looked out the massive window into the night.

"Do you miss it?" Orinthia asked, moving her eyes to his face.

"Miss what?" Kos asked, not looking away from whatever he was fixed on.

"The *Fera*. Marauding."

Kos rolled his head to look at her. His hair fell over part of his face. "No." He did not offer any more on the matter.

He was not outright lying, she felt he was holding back the whole truth. He and Thrutt learned how to skirt around her mod. And though she disliked it, she understood their reasons.

Orinthia did not push the issue further. Part of her felt it was her fault they were in their current state. If she had not joined the *Fera*, her brother would not have been shot, and they would not need to fly across the universe to find *her* father, and…

"Hey," Kos whispered. His warm hand stroked the top of her foot. "What's going on?"

Orinthia pulled her leg back to herself. "I think you're right. I had too much to drink." She stood, gathered the edges of her blanket around her, and took her hydro-sphere with her. "We have an early morning. I should try to get back to bed."

Kos moved to stand, but before he could respond, Orinthia was out of the cockpit and halfway to her room. Safely inside, she let herself feel the anxiety built up inside her. It rushed over her like a wave, cooling and warming in rhythms. Her legs trembled as she walked to her bed. She gripped the blanket tighter and laid down, placing her face into the pillow. With a deep breath, she silently screamed into the fabric, releasing the tension from every muscle in her body.

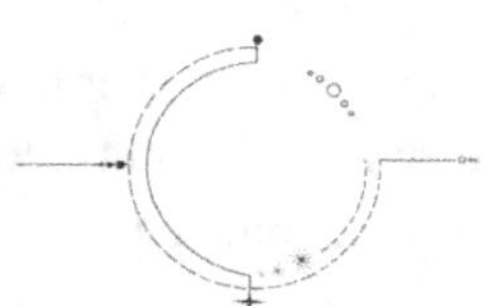

rinthia woke up to the rumble of engines igniting. At first, it meant nothing to her. She swung her arm over her face to block out the sunlight. Her mind wandered through the plan for the day. Then, her heart halted for an instant as she tossed off the blanket and the panic sent her flying out of bed.

Her bare feet slapped the cold floor as she ran down the corridor and up the ladder. The rungs dug into her arches. Bursting through the opening to the top deck, she saw Thrutt at the entrance of the hold. He tugged on a large crate.

"We can't leave yet," Orinthia told him. "I haven't picked up my clothes."

Thrutt turned his head and looked her way. His face was scrunched, but he did not answer.

Orinthia crouched down beside one of the seats and peered out a window. They had not begun preflight yet. If she hurried, she could open the hold before *Freya* took off.

"That's not your box there?" Thrutt asked.

Orinthia looked at him and followed the direction of his diamond finger. In the front row of seats sat a light blue box.

A wave of relief rushed over her, cooling her nerves and settling her heart rate. She walked over and removed the lid to find the outfits she had ordered. Her shoulders relaxed and she lifted the box.

"Is everything settled, up there?" Kos' voice called over the speakers.

Thrutt pressed a button near the ladder and replied, "Just about. We are buckling in, now." He tossed a chin toward Orinthia as he joined her.

They sat beside each other, and Orinthia set the box at her feet. She clicked her restraints together and pulled the box into her lap. A moment later, she took out the top item and examined it. The blush pink fabric was cool in her recycled-air-chapped hands. She set it aside and removed three pairs of slacks, one black, one navy blue, and the other white. Thrutt took them from her and set them across his legs.

"Did you pick these up for me?" Orinthia asked, taking a white cap-sleeved blouse from the box.

"No, I thought you had," Thrutt answered. "I didn't see you at breakfast, so I figured you were getting these."

"It was a rough night," Orinthia muttered.

The floor beneath them rumbled louder than before, then for a few moments, gravity pressed against them as the sloop lifted from the planet's surface and angled toward the sky. All of the windows slid shut, blocking out the blurred world.

Orinthia held down the box and leaned her head against the seat. Her empty stomach seized, causing nausea to creep up on her. She clenched her teeth and breathed deeply through her nose.

In a few short minutes, *Freya* won the battle against gravity and Orinthia's hair lifted gently around her.

"Artificial gravity initiated in three, two, one," Kos announced. Exactly as he said, everything fell back to where it was before. The windows slid open, and the black expanse of space became visible.

Orinthia unbuckled herself, gathered the clothes she had removed from the box, and stood.

Thrutt untethered himself as well and moved out of her way.

As Orinthia approached the hole to descend the ladder, Kos emerged before her.

"Good, you found your box," Kos said as he cleared the last rung and stood in front of her. "I wasn't sure where to leave it so you'd find it."

Orinthia looked at his shoulder instead of his face when she said, "Thanks."

"You're welcome." Kos rubbed the back of his neck, then straightened and tugged the sleeves of his deep blue coat.

The easiness of conversation from the night before was replaced with awkward tension. Orinthia felt a flush of embarrassment at her hasty exit from the cockpit and the fact that she had overslept. She was trying to do better, to be someone they could be proud of and depend on; someone worthy of trekking the galaxy for. It was taking longer than she anticipated.

"I set out a few protein cubes for you in case you got up while I was gone," Kos said. He cleared his throat and scratched the back of his leg with his foot. "I put them away before we took off, but they should be loose in the cupboard above the stove."

Orinthia looked at the box in her hands, though it was only to avoid his eyes. "Thanks," she repeated.

Thrutt came closer to the pair. "Go eat, then try on your things," he said.

Kos stepped aside and made space for her to reach the ladder.

Without saying anything, Orinthia dropped the box down the hole and swung a leg after it, climbing down the ladder. Once she reached the bottom, she stretched out her foot and pushed the box out of the way to avoid stepping on it. She picked up the box, dropped it off in her room, and rushed to the galley.

With lights on this time, she easily made her way to the cabinets and found the food Kos told her about. She set them on the closest table, along with a sweet roll and hydro-sphere, and started to eat.

Her head throbbed and the churning in her stomach grew with every bite. On the *Fera*, they were not permitted to drink, and the hangover she fought was evidence of her forced sobriety. She wished she had enough control to have stopped at one, even two drinks at the bar on Dumalth. *Stupid*, she scolded herself.

Twenty minutes passed before she finished her last bite. It took effort to not get sick over everything. Still tired, but with less fear of throwing up, she set her head on her arms and rested on the table for a minute. Though it was her normal routine, she hated being jolted awake. It was much nicer to wake up naturally, something she had not done since before losing her job as a Galactic Marauder Hunter.

Someone knocked on the wall at the entrance to the galley. Orinthia slowly lifted her head and blinked to clear her eyes. Kos leaned against the door with one arm at his side, and the other holding his coat over his shoulder with two fingers.

"How is your leg?" Kos asked. He chewed his bottom lip and his eyes moved around the room.

Orinthia vaguely remembered what he meant. "Oh, yeah, it's fine. That blue stuff works great. We should probably get more for Thrutt since I'm sure I've used up half of it by now."

Kos did not respond for a moment. He fixed his eyes on the table where her head had been.

Orinthia inhaled to give her thanks again, but before she could get out the first word, a red light pulsed above them.

Kos shot his head up, dropped his coat to the floor, and spun away from the wall. His shoes pounded against the steel as he ran down the corridor to the cockpit.

Orinthia stood and leaned over to see what was happening. Immediately as Kos reached the controls, the ship rocked from colliding with, or being hit by, something. Orinthia gripped the edge of the table, but the jostle from a second collision caused her to slip and stumble to the side.

Another two objects smacked the hull of the ship.

Thrutt slid down the ladder and landed with a thud on the floor, no doubt increasing the depth of the indent. He rushed to Kos and ducked out of sight.

Orinthia moved from the table and ran out of the galley. She scanned her room and saw Uri halfway off the bed. Another toss and he would be on the floor. With great effort, she pushed him back straight and yanked two sheets off the bunk beside his. Tying them around him, she strapped Uri to the bed. With a final tug, she patted the knot and moved toward the door again.

Another crash, bigger this time, knocked the ship. Orinthia slammed against the bunk and scraped her shoulder on the metal. She braced herself and waited for another hit. When it did not come, she ran to the hall, closing her quarter's door behind her, and made her way to the cockpit.

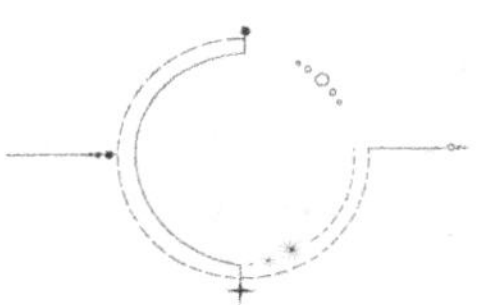

5

"What did we hit?" Orinthia asked. She looked over the screens, unsure of what she saw. The blue radar spun, but instead of an empty screen, a dot blinked at the edge of the circle.

Kos stood at the panels and pointed to the dot. "That hit us. I'm guessing bounty hunters."

Orinthia briefly remembered Killian mentioning a hefty bounty for Kos that he would have liked to have collected. She glanced over at Thrutt, who sat in the chair that faced the wall. He held the turret controls steady and stared at the lit screen. Stars twinkled in all directions, but she could see nothing else. Thrutt moved the display around until a frigate came into view.

"Captain Rogue," a female voice spoke. The disembodied voice, silvery and soft unlike any mechanical sound Orinthia ever heard, filled the room. "We are being hailed by the *Kalumarion*. Should I accept?"

Kos straightened himself and brushed a hand over his sleeveless tattooed arms like he was trying to brush away something. "Accept, Freya."

An image appeared on the window, taking up a quarter of the viewing space. It revealed a purple female Galoric dressed in lavish robes. Silver chains wrapped around her left shoulder and hung lower than the screen could show. Half her face was scarred in every direction, and a metal plate covered from under her left eye to her upper jaw. It was poorly fastened in, and the skin around it had begun to grow over it.

"Rogue," the Galoric said, tilting her head slightly down and raising an eyebrow. Her words were rough. "I never thought I'd see the day you left your commander's side."

"Ahto and I no longer serve the same mission, Captain Aiko," Kos said. He stood stiff with his hands behind his back. Orinthia briefly glimpsed the sailor he once was. "Though I'm sure that's not how he put it."

Aiko twisted her face into what could have been mistaken for a smile. She had more teeth missing than attached, and most of those were chipped into sharp points. "Does it matter how he put it? A bounty is a bounty and I plan to collect. You are outgunned and out armored. Power down and prepare to be boarded."

Kos stood at attention but did not respond. He held his chin high and stared the woman in the eye.

Orinthia looked between the two captains, her palms sweating with anticipation. The nausea she had earlier crept up again.

"Cannon charged," Freya announced.

The opposing Galoric did not react, almost as if she did not hear the report.

"We will not stand down," Kos said. "Let us pass and we will leave you unharmed."

Aiko's skin shifted indigo, and she let out a cackle. "Your tiny vessel cannot match the strength of my *Kalumarion*." She turned to someone off-screen and shouted, "Fire."

As if she was speaking to him, Thrutt slammed his hand on the controls in front of him. On the screen, a silver orb jutted across toward the frigate.

At the same time, Kos ordered, "Freya, helm." Simultaneously, the communication ended on the window, and compartment doors slid apart. A semi-circular steering wheel rose from the opening. Kos planted his feet, took hold of the handles, and ripped it to the left.

Orinthia did not need the blue radar to show her how close they came to getting hit by the *Kalumarion* again. *Freya's* silver charge met its mark, however, and hammered against the opposing ship's port side. A similarly colored force rippled over and around it.

"Fire again," Kos ordered.

Thrutt obeyed and sent another round through space.

A second attack came from the *Kalumarion*.

"Freya," Kos said, turning the helm so she faced away from the projectile. "Strengthen the rear shields and boost the thrusters. Immediately after the next impact, make a jump."

Orinthia gripped the door frame and braced herself. No sooner had the ship rocked did the view in front of her blur and morph into a stream of colors. She only saw a second's worth of the warp before she forced her eyes shut. Her stomach turned and she clenched her jaw tight. The small space around her spun and she slid down the wall beside her. Her mouth filled with saliva and her chin quivered. She tried to swallow, but the motion made her sick. With a heave, she threw up.

Gasping for air, she wiped her mouth on her sleeve, still squeezing her eyes closed. Her ears rang and her body shivered.

"Exiting jump in three, two, one," Freya said. "And will *someone* clean up that mess?"

Orinthia could hear Thrutt's chair squeak as he stood, his heavy feet pounded the metal floor as he moved. His cool, diamond hands grabbed her arms and lifted her to her feet. "I'm not sure if she's talking about you or the floor, but I'll start with you." Thrutt led Orinthia from the hall to the washroom inside her quarters.

The movement almost forced her to be sick again, but an acidic burp floated out instead.

"That's why she closes the windows when we go to warp," Thrutt said. He sat Orinthia on the toilet and turned on the sink. "How do you feel?"

"I'm cold and light-headed," Orinthia breathlessly answered. Her tongue felt fat in her mouth and her jaw quivered, threatening to throw up again.

"It's warp sickness," Thrutt said. He put a wet cloth in her hand. "And maybe a little bit of a hangover. You'll get used to it like us. Clean your face and I'll get you something to change into."

Orinthia did not risk opening her eyes for a few minutes. Despite already feeling chilled, the rag was nice on her skin. It helped settle her enough to draw her back to normal breathing. Her nose burned from the smell of sickness. It still turned her stomach to swallow, but everything stayed where it was supposed to.

There was a knock on the door. "I'm decent," Orinthia said. Her voice was scratchy. As it slid open, she stole a look up and expected to see Thrutt on the other side. Instead, Kos stood in front of her. She wanted to shrivel up and be sucked into the toilet, tossed out into space and float away.

"Are you okay?" Kos asked. He pinched his lips together and avoided looking her in the face.

Before she could answer, Thrutt shoved his way by Kos and held a few of Orinthia's new clothes. "I haven't dressed girls since my daughters," he said and lifted the pink shirt and a pair of black slacks. "We'll leave you to change in peace."

Kos's eyes widened and looked away as if Orinthia had already started to strip down.

Thrutt shook his head and pushed Kos out before closing the door behind him.

Orinthia wiped her face one more time and carefully peeled off her dirty clothes. She rolled the bottom of her shirt into itself, attempting to contain the sick and avoid getting it in her long hair. Once it was off, she tossed it in the sink and turned on the wash cycle. She used the rag to clean the feeling of sticky dampness off her skin. Though a shower was preferred, Orinthia decided her stomach could not handle such stirring.

The clean clothing provided comfort and helped her feel normal. They did not hang off or weigh heavy on her body. She could feel the pants against her skin, but the fabric was so soft and breathable, she may as well have been wearing nothing at all.

Back in her room, she took a moment to inspect Uri. Her homemade harness worked, and he had not moved during the skirmish. "I'll leave you like this for now," she told him and patted the knot closest to her. "There will probably be more moments like that to come."

6

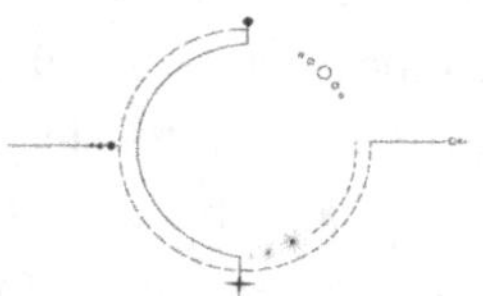

Kos and Thrutt were in the galley when Orinthia found them. Neither of them looked at her when she entered. A blue holomap hung in the air above Kos' open tattooed palm.

"We went too far in this direction," Kos said. He pointed at a spot on the map. "Freya is running a diagnostic to see how much damage we took. If everything is working well enough, we can make a jump to here—" Kos pointed at another spot, a large planet across the map, "—make our way across this sector, then follow a transit lane toward the Delvrin system. I was trying to avoid the star nursery, but now it seems like we don't have a choice."

"How much time will that add?" Thrutt asked.

"A half a day-cycle," Kos answered. His tone suggested he was not entirely sure. "We'll still make it in time, but if we hit any more detours, that window will quickly close. Once we get into the nursery, I'll have to fly manually. It's too unstable for Freya to predict a course."

"Could we go under it?" Orinthia suggested.

28

The two men finally looked at her, almost surprised to see her standing in the room with them.

"Sure," Kos said, turning his hand toward her so she could see it better. "Just not in the time we have. My original plan was to go around it entirely. But now we are in a perfect line with it." He gestured to the spot he mentioned to Thrutt. "I charted for us to go this way, but we were ambushed here. The *Kalumarion* blocked our path, and I used the propulsion from their cannon to give us a boost to get us away faster. Unfortunately, it was in the wrong direction."

Orinthia was as impressed as she was concerned. The GMH rarely used manual mapping. All their travel was done by nav computers, and they did not take any routes they did not know. Kos was the master of his craft.

"Is it dangerous in the star nursery?" Orinthia asked.

Kos closed his fingers over the tattoo on his palm and recalled the map. "It would be if anyone else were flying. But I've used nurseries to hide the *Fera*, so I'll have no trouble getting *Freya* through it."

She could not help but notice the tilt of his head and the shift in his voice. He was boasting, but even in her limited time with him, she knew it was well-earned.

ORINTHIA MADE sure to stay away from any of the port views while *Freya* made the first jump. Though the other windows outside the cockpit remained closed, she did not want to risk another incident. It took almost eight hours to get to the Monchi system where the nursery was.

She and Thrutt ran drills on the top deck. They dueled

with swords; her with her arm blade and he with an elegant saber. The hilt of Thrutt's sword was inlaid with a dozen gems of just as many colors. The blade itself was etched with deep purple lines made when the blade was quenched in waters from the ice planet Haillyon.

There was less room to move than when they practiced on the *Fera*, but Thrutt said it was better to practice in close quarters anyway. After an hour of swordplay, Thrutt had her recall her blade.

"You won't always have access to your mod," he told her. "If you're ever in a situation where that happens, I want to make sure you know how to get out."

For another hour, Orinthia threw punches at a mat Thrutt held out in front of him. He would dodge and weave, pin her against a wall, and force her to work her way out of holds. It brought back memories of her teen years, well before joining the GMH. Not all of them were pleasant, but it felt good to move forgotten muscles.

By the end of it all, she was exhausted. Her arms were weak at her side, and she lay spread out on the floor. Through it all, her clothes moved well with her, and she decided it was worth getting them dirty. The elbow length, bishop sleeves of her new blouse served nicely to keep from snagging on her sword.

"Thia, Thrutt," Kos called over the intercom. "We're out of the warp. Come to the cockpit."

Orinthia forced herself up and shakily climbed down the ladder. She kept her eyes low as she entered the control room, just in case, but immediately picked her head up once inside. Clouds of pink, blue, purple, and many more colors she had no definition for spanned across the space she could see. Lights of various sizes, from tiny specks to the size of small moons dotted the clouds. It was the most beautiful thing she had ever seen, and probably would ever see.

"This is the Monchonian Star Nursery," Kos explained.

"How many stars are in there?" Orinthia asked.

"No one knows," he answered. "The biggest ones are thousands of years old. Ones like that—", Kos pointed in the direction of a tiny ball, the relative size of their ship, "—probably as old as you. There are gasses in the clouds that feed the stars. As they grow, they expand farther out and eventually will move so far away, that they will create their own star systems. The universe is always growing and will forever be uncharted, waiting for travelers like us to explore."

Orinthia had no words. Her mind could not comprehend the beauty, let alone the idea of space expanding and changing. "How are we going to get through?"

"Slowly," Kos said with a twist of his mouth. "Because of the number of stars, gravity wells ebb and flow, sometimes pulling stars in together. If we get caught in one too long, we'll be split apart between whichever stars are competing."

Orinthia took an involuntary step back.

"Freya can detect when we get too close," Kos said. He put a hand on her back. As quickly as he had done so, he pulled away and shoved his hands in his pockets. "She'll warn me before we run into one and I'll navigate around it, right Freya?"

"Of course, captain," the woman's voice said. "My survival depends on yours, so I have a vested interest.

"Also, if anything happens to the ship," Kos added, "there's a hatch under my seat. It leads below the deck to the engine compartment and skiff storage. We'll be snug, but the skiff is enough to get us to the nearest planet."

"I think we've stared at the beautiful things for long enough," Thrutt said. "Maybe we should make a move?"

Kos shot a warning look to his friend before saying, "Freya, helm." Once again, the semi-circular steering wheel rose from the panel. Kos turned to face it and placed a hand on either side. He leaned forward and eased the ship in the same direction.

Orinthia sat in the seat she had the night before and watched colors and lights move by them.

"Freya, let me know if our shields get compromised at any point," Kos said. "We don't want to fry."

"Aye, captain," Freya said.

"Thrutt, keep an eye on the course reader on the nav computer," Kos instructed. There was no strain or harshness to his voice. He was in his element, and though the Navy molded him into this position, it was where he belonged. "If I veer too far off route, let me know. We need to keep the heading."

His talents were wasted as quartermaster, Orinthia thought as she watched him. *He should have commanded his own ship long ago.* She let herself smile for a moment, unable to shake the feeling she was where she belonged, too.

Before he was shot, Uri had demanded to go with her instead of returning to Earth with the twins. She tried to picture him as a marauder, plundering and fighting his way across the galaxy. Though, she knew that was not what he would do. Instead, he would stay on the ship and patch up any wounds they might receive during their escapades. There would be lectures thrown in about how reckless she was and swear the next planet they landed on would be their exit, knowing full well he would never make her leave. They would be a family and a crew, but more importantly, they would be together.

Though living on the run was not the life she wanted for her brother, and one she knew he would not want for her, she wondered if he would really stay. Or if Kos and Thrutt would even want them to stay. She was not sure and had never asked about what life would be like after Uri returned. In her mind, *Freya* was where she wanted to be. The time would come, hopefully soon, when she would know if her friends had the same idea.

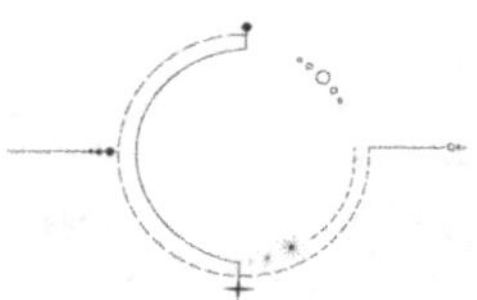

7

*A*n hour passed before Kos made his first course correction. A gravity well swelled in front of them, and he used all his weight to lean sideways on the helm. *Freya's* engines whined, but just as Orinthia thought they were going to crack in half, they made it through. Kos still had his body against the helm, and the ship shot away, abandoning the course he set. It took a few minutes to dodge debris and return to the right path.

This cycle continued for another two hours. Orinthia fidgeted in her seat the entire time. The beauty of their surroundings lost its awe-factor and the need to move overtook her. At first, she walked around the cockpit, examining the different indicators, switches, and knobs. When she ran out of things to look at, she hovered behind Thrutt and watched the nav computer. Thrutt took several glances back at her before she picked up the hint.

"I'm going to grab something to eat," she said, flopping her hand against her thighs. "Anyone want anything while I'm gone?"

Thrutt shook his head, but she noticed his shoulders ease slightly.

"I'll take a hydro-sphere and protein cube, if you don't mind," Kos said without looking away from the window.

Orinthia walked out of the room to the galley. She thought about checking on Uri but knew there would be no changes from the last time she saw him.

In the galley, she collected an armful of hydro-spheres, sweet rolls, and protein cubes. She lifted the hem of her blouse to create a makeshift basket and set her treasures inside.

Compared to growing up in the desert city of The New Cruces Republic, space was cold. But as she turned to leave the galley, Orinthia wiped a bead of sweat from her forehead. The fabric of her shirt felt damp against her biceps, and she realized the room was warm.

"Get back up here," Kos shouted from down the hall.

Orinthia gripped the food tight inside her shirt and jogged back. Lights flashed across several indicators and Thrutt stood beside Kos pressing and turning anything he could touch.

"What's going on?" Orinthia asked. She set the food down in her seat and tried to decipher what she was looking at.

"Another solar flare inbound, captain," Freya said.

Kos gripped the helm and threw himself to the left. A bright flash engulfed the ship. Orinthia smashed her eyes closed as an intense wave of heat washed over her. When she opened them again, the light in the cockpit was dim.

"Engine's failing," Freya said. "I advise turning off all auxiliary power."

"Agreed," Kos said. His knuckles were white and the

muscles in his arms were taut. He looked to Orinthia for a brief moment, then back to the window. "Go grab the blankets from your room. Then come back and wrap up as tight as you can."

"What's going on?" Orinthia asked again.

"The solar flares caused an energy disruption," Kos answered. His voice was strained. "Our shields are failing, so I'm going to turn off life support to provide as much power as possible."

"Uri," Orinthia said. Her hands tingled and the sensation traveled up her arms, gripping her chest tight.

"He'll be fine," Kos said. "I have my armor, Thrutt is stone, but you're the one who needs protection. Go, now."

She disliked the idea of leaving Uri on his own, but she enjoyed the idea of freezing to death even less. As hard as it was to leave her brother, she did as she was told and dragged four blankets from her room back to the control room. Thrutt stood by her chair when she returned and held a cylinder with a nozzle in his hand.

"Take this and give me those," he instructed. Orinthia and he traded. Thrutt placed two blankets on her chair and motioned for her to sit. "Put this end in your mouth and breathe in like normal." He pointed to the black, U-shaped nozzle.

The extra padding from the blankets made sitting in her seat awkward, but she shimmied her way in. Thrutt folded the rest of the covers around her and strapped the belt over her. He pulled part of one of the blankets over her head and left only her eyes exposed.

Kos cast a sideways glance at them before calling his armor with a swipe up of the tattoo on his left arm. In succession, the metal plating formed over every inch of his body, sealing shut with the visor over his face.

"Freya," Kos said, his voice muffled by the helmet, "divert all power to the shields and thrusters."

"Aye, captain," Freya responded.

Though she was covered from head to toe, the skin around Orinthia's eyes chilled as the life support shut off. She realized, too, why Thrutt had strapped her down. Kos activated the mag-boots on his armor and secured himself to the floor. Even Thrutt's weight was no match for zero gravity, and he strapped himself to his seat.

Orinthia took deep breaths through the rebreather, the bottled air left a tangy taste in her mouth. She took uncomfortable swallows of saliva that pooled in her mouth and tried to focus on what was going on around them.

With one hand on the helm, Kos called the palm map and examined it.

"There is another gravity well two klicks to the right," Freya warned.

Kos closed the map and veered in the opposite direction. The ship whined as he forced the thrusters to their limit and avoided being drawn in. But as he straightened out, another bright flash crossed the window.

Orinthia squinted her eyes but did not close them all the way. In the distance, she could see a massive explosion.

Kos cursed. "Two stars just collided," he yelled. "Freya, give me everything you have. We have to get out of here now." Without any other warning, Kos sent the ship into a dive. Alarms blared as a wave of radiation shot through the clouds toward them.

Orinthia's teeth dug into the mouthpiece. Every nerve was alight with adrenaline and her muscles seized. The blast grew closer.

"We're going to have to warp," Kos said. "Freya, shoot for Vron."

"Captain," Freya said. "There's a possibility we'd hit a star."

"Do it," Kos ordered.

It almost sounded like Freya groaned as the engines geared up. The wave of radiation grew to extend beyond the width of the window.

Orinthia concentrated on closing her eyes so tightly she forgot to breathe for a moment. Her lungs trembled for air, and she took in a large breath.

The alarms continued to sound, and it was difficult to focus on anything else. Everything was loud and chaotic at once.

Then, the room was silent. Orinthia risked opening an eye and was greeted by the blackness of space. Stars and planets blinked through the vastness.

"Status, Freya," Kos said. He sounded winded, standing hunched over the helm.

"There's enough power for one more jump, but shields are almost gone," Freya said.

Kos stayed silent for a minute. He took one hand off of the helm and placed it on the side of his helmet. "Move all shielding to the front of the ship," he said. "Find the closest transit lane and take us through that way."

"You want to warp through a transit lane?" Freya asked. "With other ships?"

"I can do without the remarks," Kos said. "It's the shortest distance between us and Vron."

"Aye, *captain*," Freya said.

For the third time, Orinthia closed her eyes. She wondered how long it would be before she could open them again. Or even how long they had been inside the nursery. She felt disjointed in time and had no bearing on where or when they were. And though there was no actual weight from the blankets around her, she felt confined and almost trapped. Each movement she made, rubbed against the fabric and served as a reminder of their presence.

No one said anything for the next two hours.

At one point, Kos' captain's chair made a noise, and Orinthia assumed he had sat down.

Throughout the journey, in the darkness of her mind, Orinthia choked back bouts of nausea as thoughts of colliding with an unseen ship reeled around her head. She pictured it in her mind's eye. It would not take more than an instant, and in reality, she knew there would be no warning nor feeling to it, but the fear gripped her nonetheless.

Her head dipped several times as she weaved in and out of consciousness. The sensation of the rebreather slipping from her grasp continually brought her back to reality, though she was careful not to risk opening her eyes.

An alarm tolled around the room. Kos shifted in his seat and his mag boots dragged against the floor. From somewhere near where he was came a beep followed by the whirring down of the warp engines.

Orinthia slowly opened her eyes and lifted her head. The light reflecting off the planet below them stung and she blinked several times before she could focus. She was greeted by more shades of green than she had ever seen before. For a moment, she forgot about the danger they were in and took in the sight of another new world. *I'll never get tired of this,* she thought.

"Welcome to Vron," Kos announced.

Landing in the port was the least eventful part of their trip. They drifted slowly to the ground and landed on a port at the edge of a large village. Kos chose a spot at the end of the dock and lowered the landing gear. With a bump and some jostling. *Freya* was safely on solid ground.

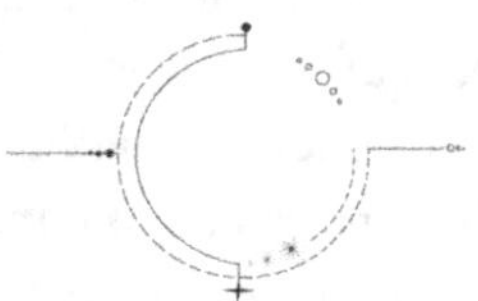

8

wo Vronians approached the three marauders as they exited *Freya's* hold. Their long tails swished behind them; the tips flicked in sharp movements as they stood in the late afternoon sun.

"You Rogue?" One of them asked. His voice was rough like Killian's. Bits of slimy saliva stretched between his jaws as he spoke.

"I prefer to call it freelancing," Kos said. He grinned. When his joke did not receive appreciation, he swallowed hard and answered, "Yes, I am."

"Run into a bit of trouble, did ya?" The other Vronian asked. "The shipment make it okay?"

"Everything is the way it should be," Kos answered. A breeze picked up and tossed some hair into his face. He took a tie from the pocket of his coat and fastened it at the nape of his neck.

Orinthia took in full lungs of air. Aside from only breathing in recycled, canned air for more hours than she cared to count, the trees that surrounded the village provided the freshest oxygen she had ever experienced before. She looked around as the others spoke amongst themselves.

There were a few dozen people walking in the area, and five other ships docked nearby. The immediate vicinity was clear with enough space to land most types of ships. But half a mile from the port, surrounding them for as far as she could see, rose trees taller than some buildings Orinthia had seen back on Earth.

And they were green.

Of course, she had seen green before, but in the desert, it was a hard color to come by. Especially when most of that desert was covered with steel and concrete. After a summer rain, the dried plants absorbed as much moisture as possible and returned to life for a brief time. But the colors were muted and dull, and hardly the lush foliage that surrounded her on Vron.

The two Vronians moved closer to *Freya* and a lev-cart followed behind them. Kos led them to the hold. Thrutt pulled Orinthia to come after the others. She wanted to refuse, not eager to return to the ship they were trapped inside a short while before, but instead obeyed.

They each loaded two boxes, except for Thrutt who moved six without a struggle. Once secure on the cart, the Vronians thanked Kos and left with their hoard.

Kos stepped outside and examined the ship. He shook his head and touched the hull. "She's not that bad, but it's going to take some work to get her going again," he shouted.

Orinthia sat on the edge of the ramp and swung her legs back and forth. Kos was more interesting to watch when he was not paying attention. He moved with ease and purpose. The way he doted over his ship was endearing, like a child with their favorite toy.

"I'm going to make sure she's okay," Kos said as he stepped onto the ramp. He stopped beside Orinthia's hand. "Thia, do you want to come with me?"

Surprised at his invitation, she almost forgot to answer. "Sure, why not." Orinthia kicked her legs to the side and climbed to her feet.

"I'll just be here," Thrutt said in a mock overworked tone, "cleaning up this mess."

"Don't forget to color coordinate the straps," Kos said.

Thrutt made a rude gesture at Kos as they walked by.

Orinthia loved the banter between the two friends. In her childhood home, gestures and rude remarks like that were not so lighthearted.

She and Kos climbed down the ladder, and he waited for her at the entrance to her room as she checked on Uri. The makeshift straps had done their duty. Uri was safe and looked no worse for wear. She rejoined Kos and together they went to the control room.

"Freya?" Kos called out when they made it to the cockpit. "You did a good job. Thank you for keeping us alive. I think you should power down to rest. Initiate stasis for the night and I'll reactivate you in the morning to discuss repairs."

"Thank you, captain," Freya responded. "Goodnight." The lights in the cockpit lowered and a steady blinking orange light flickered in the middle of the panel.

Orinthia opened the compartment beside the chair she had sat on to return the rebreather. The food she had brought before fell out. She bent down to retrieve it and Kos moved to his knees to help her.

"I was wondering where all that went," Orinthia said.

Kos stowed it back in the compartment. "We'll keep these here in case of future emergencies."

Her blankets were still piled around the chair, and she pushed them off to sit down. The orange light caught her attention and she focused on it. "Do you think she dreams?"

Kos made a sound with his mouth closed. He also sat in his chair and kicked his heels onto the console. "I never thought about it."

"Uri doesn't dream," Orinthia said. Her voice was low as she thought. "Or rather, my father implanted a chip that overwrites his dreams as they happen. He used to scream in the middle of the night almost every night for a year. After the first month, Desidario gave up and stopped going to him. Uri's screams would travel across the hall and fill my room. I took over and started going to him as soon as the fits would begin. After I'd get him to calm down, he'd lay his head in my lap, and I stroked his hair until he fell back to sleep. In the morning, he'd have no memory of what frightened him so bad. My father said it was something with his cybernetic connections sending crossed signals into his brain. Like phantom pain from parts of his body and brain that no longer existed."

Orinthia took a shaky breath. "Then, one day they went to Desidario's lab. From that night on, he never had another dream."

Kos put a hand on her shoulder. "How old were you?"

Not old enough, she thought but did not wish to say out loud. "I hope he's not dreaming now," she said instead.

"We'll do everything we can to get him back. Once I patch up *Freya,* I'll contact my friend. If anyone can find Desidario, she can."

Unable to stand the prickly feeling that crept up her spine, Orinthia stood. Kos' hand fell from her shoulder. "I'm going out for some air," she said.

"Alone?" Kos rose up.

"You and Thrutt are great." Orinthia offered a half smile. "But I've spent more time on my own than with people. Lately, and especially after the last day we had, I find myself missing it."

Kos raised his hand, flared his fingers, then put them back to his side. "Be careful."

"I'll be fine," Orinthia said.

Though he did not look put at ease, Kos nodded. "At least take a comm." He reached into the compartment, dug around the food, and pulled out a small, circular communicator.

Orinthia reluctantly took the device from him and put it in her pocket. "Thanks."

"Are you sure you want to go alone?" Kos offered a second time. "I could look at the part shops while we're out."

His gesture made her heart thump quicker, but she declined. "When Thrutt offered me the job on the *Fera,* he promised I'd be able to see new places. I'd like to enjoy this without feeling rushed."

"Call me if you run into any trouble," Kos said.

Without saying anything else, Orinthia turned and left him standing alone in the cockpit. She returned to her quarters and retrieved the credit satchel from the bed nearest the door. Before leaving, she stopped at Uri's bed and stroked his hair. "Don't wait up."

She turned into the hall and went up the ladder to the upper deck. Thrutt kneeled on one knee near the exit, wrapping the straps together. He placed them in their storage compartment and looked back as she emerged from the hole.

"Going somewhere?" he asked.

"Just going to stretch my legs for a bit," she answered. "Kos already gave me a comm," she added as he opened his mouth.

"Want company?" He offered.

"Not really."

Thrutt stood and rolled his shoulders. "Stay away from seedy places."

Orinthia let out a laugh. "We're marauders. We make places seedy."

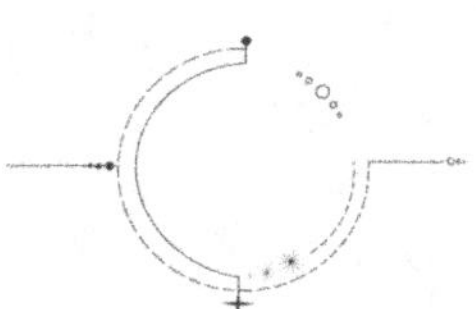

$\mathcal{A}$ pale yellow sun lowered on the horizon behind the building. It cast long shadows around the port. Orinthia exited the ramp onto the mossy stone and slung her credit satchel across her body. She gripped the strap with both hands.

There were shops along the row across from the docking area. The street went roughly half a mile in either direction. Orinthia chose to go right and looked through the storefront windows. A few of the first shops she peered into had displays of trinkets, dried meats, and baked goods. Others without windows had large hand-painted signs in different languages, announcing what was offered inside.

A savory scent caught her nose, and she followed it around a corner and through a narrow alley. She walked past chattering villagers who ignored her. It did not take long to find the source of the smell. Orinthia stopped in front of an eatery with its door wide open. Humid air rolled out from inside, carrying the odor of cooked food with it.

Few of the seats were taken by locals, and some others

were obviously visiting sailors and tourists. But, for the most part, the restaurant was empty.

The walls of the dining area were painted a deep grey and matched the color of clouds before a storm. Large saucers with amber lights hung from the ceiling. Warmth radiated from the lamps as she passed under them. Beneath her feet, the floor was made with smooth stones, grouted with dark brown clay.

Only the Vronian behind the counter looked up at her as she stepped inside. He waved a three-clawed hand at her, signaling to come to him. As she approached, she could see his skin was a lighter shade of green and smoother than Killian and his brother-in-law's from the dock.

"What'cha," the young reptilian man said as Orinthia took a seat at the counter. "Fair winds have brought you in. Travel far today?"

"As far as I had to get here," she replied. "Do you have a menu I can look over?"

"Of course, of course." The waiter ducked his head down below the counter and emerged with a datatab. "Give a shout if you have any inquiries. Or, when you're ready to order, just tap the item and I'll bring it out when it's done." He handed her the tablet and moved out from behind the counter to tend to his other customers.

Orinthia scrolled through the list. Her translator mod decrypted speech, not written words. And only half of the menu was in a language she could understand. Not wanting to talk to the staff more than she had to, she decided on something and selected it. *Whatever this is,* she thought, *I'm sure it's going to be better than protein cubes.*

She set the datatab on the counter and waited for her meal. Periodically she could hear the low hum inside her head, but whoever was speaking was too far away for her to make out their words.

The server moved back and forth, carrying meals to the other patrons. But no one else joined her at the counter. Though she enjoyed the company of her new crew, she missed being on her own and with her thoughts.

Are they more than just my crew mates? Orinthia thought.

Thrutt was her friend, she knew that for sure. He was kind and patient with her. The only times he judged her were when she overstepped her boundaries and needed to be put back in her place.

She wondered if she could call Kos her friend, however. They grew closer in the few months they were on the run. True, he was helping her find her father, but she did not know if that constituted friendship. He was her captain and as such it was his duty to care for her wellbeing. Whatever the case was, she did not have a simple label for their relationship. Then, there was when he absently stroked her foot in his lap. *What was he thinking about?*

Deep in her own thoughts, Orinthia had not noticed her waiter place the food in front of her. She flinched at the sound of a mug tap against the wooden bar. Translucent blue liquid moved in the cup, and she stared at it.

"I didn't order that," Orinthia said.

"Complimentary," the waiter replied.

"Is it strong?" Orinthia leaned over and sniffed it. It had a sweet scent with a hint of floral notes. "Alcohol?"

"By the trees," the Vronian exclaimed. "No, no. Only juice from the mori fruit. It grows wild all over our village."

Normally, Orinthia would have welcomed a stiff drink, especially a free one. But after her sick incident on *Freya,* she decided it was better to stay away from it altogether, at least for a while.

"Please enjoy." Her host gave a short bow at his shoulders and left her to eat.

Orinthia picked up her utensil and poked at the food before her. A brown loaf of mashed meat sat in a pool of orange sauce. She placed the tip of her utensil into it and pulled off a small piece. Iridescent, clear liquid trickled from the hole. The texture was soft in her mouth and gave a little chew between her teeth. It had a smokey flavor, followed by the sensation of salt on her tongue. It was not unpleasant to eat. The sauce was mild and earthy, and it complimented the meat nicely.

The humming in her head grew from dull pulses to a steady stream of noise throughout her meal. A few customers had come and gone while she sat at the counter, but she could not tell where the deceitful person was in the room without looking around. She tried to focus on her meal and ignored the annoying sound.

Orinthia took the mug and washed down the last few pieces of her entree. The liquid had a viscous feel, but overall was sweet. She sipped the drink until the mug was empty.

The humming was nonstop by the time she finished her meal. Orinthia, fed up with the sound, slammed the mug to the counter and looked behind her. She watched every mouth and tried to weed out who it was that was spewing lies like a fountain. Slowly, she moved from right to left until, at the last table near the left side of the entrance, she saw the culprit.

Her heart banged in her chest, and she struggled to keep down the food she just ingested. Their eyes met. She had hoped to never see that overstuffed head ever again.

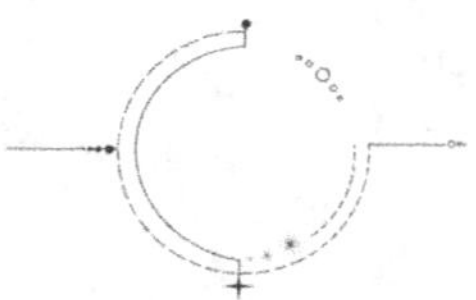

"Errol," Orinthia said quietly, forcing herself not to shout across the room. She slammed her fist on the counter. The utensil clattered and splashed bits of sauce onto her shirt. With shaking hands, she reached into her satchel and retrieved a credit, tossed it next to her plate, and walked to Errol.

"What are you doing here, you creepy little worm?" Orinthia asked. Her arm was braced across her chest, ready to activate her sword if she needed to. Errol, with his tubes and wires protruding from his large, squishy head, was no threat on his own. But she knew better than to underestimate him.

"Tell me a story," Errol said with a grin. His voice jingled. "I'll share my information if you do."

"I'm not giving you anything," Orinthia said. Her legs wobbled beneath her. "Except maybe the chance to walk out of here alive."

Errol's grin widened, exposing more of his jagged, brown teeth. He leaned forward and stage whispered, "This is the path I had hoped you'd take."

Orinthia's head swayed a bit, and she shook herself clear.

"And what? You've come to spectate on my life? To mock me?"

"Have you learned the truth, yet?" Errol asked, ignoring her question. His smile nearly split his face in half and his pudgy legs wiggled in delight beneath the table. "No, I suppose it's still too early. But soon. Soon you'll know."

"The truth about what?" Orinthia said. Her words felt heavy in her mouth. "How did you even get here? I thought no one left Rust Rock."

"Give me a story," Errol repeated like a child asking for sweets they were not allowed to have. "Tell me a secret and I will tell you anything you want to know. You've come so far and yet have not gotten any closer to finding Desidario."

Orinthia took a second to think about his statement. It was true. They had been gone from the *Fera* for two months and had not even begun looking for her father. Kos swore it was to gather credits and information, but they had only done one job and not spoken to anyone about finding her father.

I could ask Errol anything, she thought. *He wouldn't dare lie to me. And even without his machines to sequence with, he wouldn't have come without knowing what I'd ask for.*

She looked over the sickly old man, if one could even call him that. *What could I trade? What is worth enough to Errol that he would give me what I want?*

One idea crept to the surface of her mind, like a ghost from the shadows. A secret she stowed away and was forced to never reveal. She debated whether it was enough, and decided it was all she had to offer.

"When Adoracion Anton, the founder of the Galactic Marauder Hunters, was nineteen, she deactivated the auto drive on her hover car while drunk. There was an accident with another hover car, and she killed a family of four. Two children and their parents. Desidario Anton covered it up."

Orinthia breathed out a long sigh and had not realized the weight that secret had left on her body.

"Antons." Errol gave a squee and wiggled in his seat. "Sounds like your family is trouble to be around. Now, your question."

Orinthia's arm grew tired, and she leaned it against her chest. "I'll show you trouble if you try to lie to me. Remember, I will know." She worked out the best way to ask her questions to get the most useful information out of Errol. Her mind was cloudy, and each blink took longer than the one before. "How do I find Elendoras?"

Errol chuckled before answering. "You need to trust her."

"What kind of answer is that?" Orinthia, enraged, tried to toss out her arm, but it was weak, and she did not use enough force. "I gave you what you wanted. Give me more."

The sequencer slid out of the booth and leaned closer to her. "I've given you everything you need. Trust her. You'll find your father."

Orinthia reached out with her arms and lunged for his neck. "You slimy dung eater. Tell me how to find Elendoras." She moved too fast and too far forward. Her footing slipped and she stumbled. The unforgiving stone did not give way as her knees crashed against them. She caught herself with her hands and breathed hard.

Errol took a step forward and whispered, "Here is a bonus. You're not going to like what you find on Elendoras. Sweet dreams, young Anton. Until we meet again."

With the last of her strength, Orinthia took a swipe at him. Her nails caught the exposed skin of his lumpy arm. Bright red lines formed where she tore his flesh.

The other arm that held her up trembled and collapsed under her weight. Her face hit the tile and she watched the man wobble out before the room faded to darkness.

"How long have you been out here?" Thrutt asked.

His booming voice sent Orinthia's head spinning, and she threw her eyes open. She blinked a few times before she realized where she was. A lamp post lit up the dock and she saw Thrutt and a black sky full of stars above her. The back of her head rubbed against the stone ground beneath her as she moved her head to look around.

Thrutt lifted Orinthia to her feet. The motion made her nauseous and she threw herself forward, bracing on her knees. "Whoa," she said, placing the heel of her palm on her forehead. Cool beads of sweat formed on her skin.

"Are you drunk?" Thrutt asked with an accusatory tone.

"No," Orinthia answered. She scrunched her face and tried to look at him better. "What time is it?" It was not the first question to come to mind. That would have been, *how did I get here?* But her head could not hold a thought long enough to follow through.

She tapped her lips with one finger and attempted to recall the events that led her to where she was. *I don't think I have a teleportation mod,* Orinthia thought. *Unless I was given one without my knowledge. Are there teleportation mods? I'll have to ask Kos, he'd know. Wait, no. Focus.*

Orinthia ran a hand down her chest. The satchel was still attached to her, and the weight was what she remembered it to be. *I wasn't robbed,* she thought. *But why am I here instead of, well, wherever I just was? Whenever I just was, too.*

"It's late enough that Rogue and I got worried and decided to look for you," Thrutt answered. "Why didn't you answer your comm?"

Orinthia slowly straightened up again and tried to remember what she had asked him to make him respond that way. *The comm.* She reached into her pocket and found the device Kos gave her before she left. "I was eating, I think." It was not actually meant as a direct answer to Thrutt's question but served as a waypoint to trek through her memories. "The Vronian gave me a drink on the house."

"So, you *are* drunk?" Thrutt asked.

"No, stop." Orinthia swatted at him as she continued to think out loud. "He said it was mori juice or something. I made sure it wasn't alcohol. And hello, human lie detector here. I'd know if it was." She leaned forward again. The side of her head ached like she had been punched.

"Let me take you inside," Thrutt said, grabbing her elbow. "I'll call Kos and let him know you're back. Though he's not going to be thrilled to see you like this."

"I'm not drunk," Orinthia shouted. Her ears rang and she gripped Thrutt's arm to keep from tipping over. She took a steadying breath through her nose and added, "I just can't remember what happened."

Thrutt held out his free hand in defense. "Kos can scan you when he gets here. Please, let's go inside. Whatever *this* is, you need to lie down."

Orinthia let the frustration leave her as she followed Thrutt up the ramp. Her feet were as sluggish as her head.

"Do you think you can climb down the ladder?" Thrutt asked as they neared the hole.

Orinthia shrugged.

"I'll go down first. That way if you fall, I can catch you."

She watched Thrutt descend to the lower level and copied him. Before she could reach the middle rung, her foot slipped, and she slid down. Thrutt caught her in his stone and crystal arms. "Thanks, Space Grandpa," she muttered and rested her head against his chest.

Thrutt carried her the rest of the way to her bunk and laid her down. He unzipped her boots and set them on the floor. "I'm going to get you a hydro-sphere. Stay here."

Stay here, she repeated in her head. *Where else am I going to go? Everyone is either dead, missing, or hates me. I have nowhere else to go.*

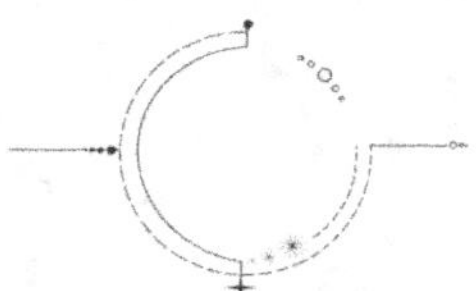

11

*O*rinthia lay on her side with a hand tucked under her pillow. Thrutt sat on the floor between her bunk and the one beside it. He was too big to fit, but he shoved his legs under her bed.

Flashes of memories crossed Orinthia's mind as the two of them sat in the dim silence. She could remember seeing someone she knew, but not who it was or if they had talked. Thrutt helped her verbally retrace her steps to the restaurant, but she could not find where it was in her mind.

His questions and her lack of answers made her angry. Frustration tears trickled down her eyes more than once, and Thrutt gave up on pushing her more.

Kos stepped into her room through the already open door. "Where have you been? We searched half the village looking for you."

Thrutt held up a hand. "Slow down, Kos."

"No, Thrutt," Kos said. He was almost shouting. "I told her to be careful. Maybe I should have told her not to get wasted, too."

"I'm not wasted," Orinthia said, forcing herself to sit up

on her elbow. "And I was careful." *Careful*, she thought. The sound of the word loosened something in her mind. She repeated it several times, taking it apart by syllable. "Errol. It was Errol at the restaurant."

Thrutt and Kos looked at each other, then back to Orinthia. Immediately Kos straightened his stance. He moved to sit at the foot of her bed and spoke with softer words than he had before. "Did you talk to him?"

Orinthia closed her eyes and dug as hard as she could. "I think so, but I'm not sure. Though I must have. Somewhere I can remember feeling angry, like I wanted to hurt him." She opened her eyes again.

"Were you drinking?" Kos asked.

"No." Orinthia sighed and laid back down. The impact made her head throb again.

Kos pressed two fingers to his temple and the visor shut over his eyes. He looked her up and down. Then, without saying anything, he stood and left the room. A few seconds later he returned with a pin and a tiny glass vial.

"I'm going to poke your finger," Kos said. He gently pulled her hand into his and turned it so the palm faced up. With the needle, he poked at her index finger and squeezed four drops of blood into the vial.

"Freya will test this and find out what's in your system," Kos said. He jumped from the bed again and moved for the door.

"She's sleeping," Orinthia said, sticking her finger in her mouth. "Don't wake her."

Kos stopped at the door and looked back. He stared at her for a moment, then said, "I'll do whatever I have to to make sure you're going to be okay." Without another word, he disappeared into the corridor.

Orinthia looked at Thrutt through the side of her eye. Thrutt looked wide-eyed at anything but her.

"I'm going to get you another hydro-sphere," Thrutt said. He pulled his legs out from under her bed, braced himself on the bunk behind him, and stood.

Orinthia's mod hummed, but she did not have the energy or capacity to think of why he would lie. In the moment, she did not care. Her body felt loose and heavy at the same time, like an unraveled cord piled on top of itself. The sheets around her were warm and inviting, which was a nice change from the chill that normally clung to her. She curled up and rested her eyes. Her breathing slowed and she could feel herself drift to sleep.

Just as she was seconds from unconsciousness, a hand shook her. "Stay awake," Kos said.

Orinthia opened an eye to see him standing above her. His eyebrows were pulled together, and his mouth was turned down.

"I just need a nap," she said. Her voice was airy.

"You need to stand up." Kos pulled off her blanket.

Orinthia protested and unsuccessfully clung to it. "I'm so cold."

"I know, it's the toxins. We have to get them out of your system."

His words were gentle but did not make sense in her ears. "Will you hold me?" she asked.

Kos did not answer. He pulled at the blanket again.

This time, she let him. "You're so hot." She placed her feet on the frigid metal and attempted to stand. The room spun around her. She sat back down and put her head in her hands.

"I don't know how to respond to that," Kos muttered.

Orinthia, with her head still down, said, "Your skin. It burns to the touch. That'll keep me warm."

"You can keep your blanket," Kos said.

"Afraid I'll bite?" She feebly snapped her teeth in his direction.

Thrutt stepped in.

Kos eased Orinthia to her feet and together with Thrutt, they walked her to the door. "We have to keep you awake long enough for the poison to wear off," Kos informed. "If we don't there could be lasting effects."

Before they reached the ladder, Kos released her and went to the galley. The cupboards opened and closed, and he returned with a hydro-sphere. "Take this. It's an anti-toxin. It'll bind to whatever Errol gave you and flush it from your body."

"My hero," Orinthia breathlessly said. She took the pill Kos offered her and placed it in her mouth. The cool water from the sphere sent a shiver through her body.

Thrutt wrapped Orinthia tight in her blanket and lifted her onto his shoulder. He climbed the ladder and set her down on the top deck.

Kos joined them and held Orinthia by the elbow, as best he could through the fabric, and began walking laps with her. He and Thrutt took turns doing the circuit. Occasionally, they would let her stop and rest to drink something. The pattern continued for more hours than Orinthia could comprehend. White rays of sunlight poked through *Freya's* portholes by the time Orinthia felt back to herself, albeit worn out.

"I'm sorry," Orinthia said to Kos on their final loop. "First you had to search out there for me, then you've stayed up all night because of me. I didn't mean to upset you or cause these problems."

"You're okay," Kos said. He had one arm firmly around her back, as she had ditched the blanket an hour before. "None of this was your fault. What mattered was making sure you were safe. I don't sleep anyway, remember?"

Orinthia stopped walking and set her head on his shoulder. "Thank you." Her voice came out in a whisper.

Kos took in a sharp breath but did not move. "You're welcome. I think it's safe enough for you to sleep. Thrutt can take you to bed and I'll check on you in an hour."

"An hour isn't long enough for you to rest." Orinthia lifted her head and frowned at him.

"It's longer than I'm comfortable leaving you unattended, though. Don't worry about me. I promise I'll be okay."

Exhaustion set in, but Orinthia did not want him to let go. She wanted to place her head on his shoulder again and have him hold her close. A long yawn escaped her mouth, and she turned her face away. The power to argue evaded her and she surrendered with a nod.

Kos released her and grabbed her blanket off the floor. He handed it to her and set her in the seat closest to where they stood. "I'll get Thrutt," he said.

Orinthia laid her head on her hand which was propped on her knee and watched Kos descend the ladder. A few minutes later, Thrutt appeared, alone.

"How are you feeling?" he asked.

"Like I've walked the length of the ship a million times," Orinthia half teased. She handed Thrutt her blanket and, with unstable legs, lifted herself to her feet. All energy had left her body, and she was genuinely surprised that she stayed conscious.

"You can rest now, so let's get you tucked in and you can sleep as much as you need." Thrutt lifted her over his shoulder again and climbed down to the bottom level. He set her right at the base and nudged her toward her quarters.

Orinthia's feet slapped the floor as she waddled to her bed. Without much effort, she rolled onto her side into the bed. Thrutt was behind her and placed her blanket around her. "Sleep well," he said as he tucked the fabric around her.

Before she could respond, she passed out and fell asleep.

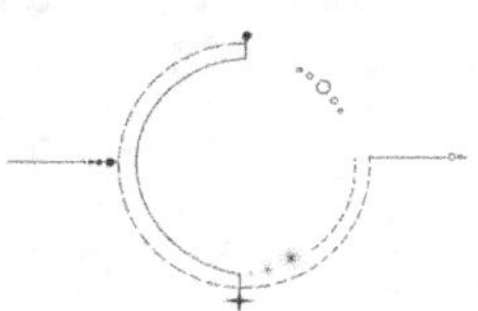

12

Other than to use the washroom and shower once, Kos and Thrutt refused to let Orinthia leave her bed. They worked for two days to repair the damages done in the star nursery. Any parts Kos did not have on hand, he was forced to buy which ate into their credit reserves.

Though the pair visited when they could, Orinthia spent most of her time alone. Any time she was not asleep, she kept her back to Uri. It was one thing knowing he was there in the dark, but it was another to have his lifeless body be her constant companion for days.

On the third morning, Kos allowed her to go outside. The fresh air greeted Orinthia like an old friend. The coolness of the autumnal season wrapped around her and filled her lungs with clean, non-filtered oxygen. Being in the white-gold sunlight and stretching freely made her feel better than the rest she had up until that point. She and Kos did three slow laps around *Freya* before she needed to sit.

Outside the ship, nothing had changed. The trees were still trees, ships came and went, and the sky was as blue as it had been before. But Orinthia felt different, disconnected from her surroundings. After spending nearly seventy-two hours locked in her room, being out in the open felt almost foreign to her.

The poison was out of her system, Kos checked twice a day to be sure. But her stamina was zapped. Her muscles were weak from being sedentary and she could not remember a time she felt as poorly as she did.

Kos crouched beside her and pulled a protein cube from his coat pocket. "Eat this. Then we'll go another round or two before heading back in."

Orinthia retrieved the food from his hand and unwrapped it. It was warm, almost too warm from being pressed against his body. The cube had an odd texture at that temperature, but she chewed a piece anyway.

Still low beside her, Kos looked at their surroundings. He moved his head with a bird that flew overhead.

"Have you thought about leaving marauding completely?" Orinthia asked. She set her hands in her lap, cupping one under the other.

Kos let his gaze fall toward her. His eyes lingered on hers but was slow to answer. "Occasionally. I lived a brief life between retiring from the Navy and joining the *Fera*. The EC gives you skills for one task and one task only. Anything I was remotely qualified for as a civilian was oversaturated with other veterans looking to start over." He paused and rested his backside on the ground.

"My aunt left me some money when she died," Kos continued. "With it and the retirement from the Navy, I bought a little restaurant along with the cheapest, most abused droids I could find. I taught myself how to rebuild them, and used whatever parts would fit. I even programmed the hostess-droid to run everything autonomously. It's still there, back in the town where we picked you up. Maybe someday I'll go back and run it properly."

Orinthia smiled and recalled the day Thrutt offered her the job that changed the course of her life. "Thrutt took me there when we met."

Kos' expression lit up and he opened his mouth to say something. Thrutt's heavy footsteps cut him off.

"Comm link for you, Rogue," Thrutt said. "It's Nakahara."

Kos unfolded his legs and stood with a stretch. "Make sure Thia walks a couple more rounds, then you both can come inside." He trudged up the ramp and back toward the ladder.

"Who is Nakahara?" Orinthia asked Thrutt.

Thrutt shifted on his feet and held his hand out to help Orinthia stand. "Mimi Nakahara. The contact who is going to help find Desidario."

"Do you know her?" Orinthia asked. She set the protein cube on the edge of the ramp and dusted her pants. Neither of them spoke about their other friends. She tried to picture what a friend of Kos and Thrutt would look like and imagined a tall, thick woman; every inch of her strapped with weapons and covered in military tattoos.

Thrutt nodded and avoided looking in her face. "The three of us served together." He was quick to get his words out.

Orinthia sensed there was more to his statement. She tilted her head and set her jaw. "What aren't you telling me?"

Thrutt tapped his fingers against his leg. "Let's take that walk now. I'm sure you're eager to be done and back inside."

Orinthia planted her feet and crossed her arms. She stared at Thrutt until he glanced at her.

"She's our friend. If you want to know more, then you

need to ask Rogue," Thrutt said. Without offering any more, he moved away from her and walked toward *Freya's* nose.

Orinthia gave a huff and followed him. She had to take longer and quicker steps than she did with Kos. But she guessed Thrutt was purposefully keeping out of her reach to avoid more questions.

They did the two laps Kos prescribed. By the end of it, Orinthia was winded. Her head felt light, and it was difficult to catch her breath. Thrutt had moved so fast, Orinthia jogged to keep up.

"That wasn't fair," Orinthia said between gulps of air. "I've been lying in bed for two days straight."

Thrutt continued to hop in place at the base of the ramp. His heavy stomps sent tremors through the ground. A group of passing sailors gave sideways looks at the nine-foot-tall stone man. They whispered to each other as they moved by.

"You need it," Thrutt said. "None of us have been as active as we should. In fact, I think you and I will spar after lunch."

Orinthia made a noise in the back of her throat. "I'm not doing that."

"We'll have plenty of time for drills," Kos said from the top of the ramp.

Startled, Orinthia looked back at him. He stood with his hands on his hips and feet spread. His eyes were squinted as he looked from the shaded ship to his crew standing in the yellow sunlight. The white sleeveless shirt he wore accented his tan skin and his black tattoos were wrapped tight around his thick arms.

Orinthia pressed her tongue to the back of her teeth and had to avert her eyes before either Kos or Thrutt caught her staring. She did not know where to place her gaze but was suddenly thankful for the workout to mask her breathing.

"Mimi said to meet her on Sarv'on," Kos said. "I've already set *Freya*'s nav computer to take us straight there and it's a three day-cycle flight. If you're feeling well enough, I can teach you some new moves, too."

Thrutt made a choking sound and lost his rhythm. He regained his footing and stopped his exercises.

Kos threw his hand over his armor tattoo and repeatedly wiped it down like he was trying to remove it from his skin. His face flushed behind his beard. "I'm going to start preflight." He all but ran away from the entrance of his ship.

A breeze picked up and blew Orinthia's hair forward as she ascended the ramp after her captain. The smell of cooked meats that enticed her before followed with it. She halted at the entrance of the hold and stared through time to that night. Errol's voice filled her memory. *You need to trust her.*

13

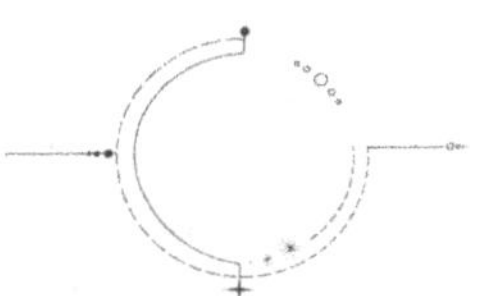

The first day of warp was quiet. With Kos' help, Orinthia convinced Thrutt to let her rest one more day before sparring. Eager for a change of scenery, she spread out two blankets on the top deck floor and made herself a comfortable spot. The few days she spent in Uri's ever-present company was more than enough to last her a while.

Kos saw her lug things up the ladder and offered to join her. He brought a small buffet of food with him to share. They ate together, but neither of them said much for a bit. Kos stared into the distance, but Orinthia could not see what he saw. His eyes were fixed somewhere outside of the ship, probably outside of time. She had seen him go blank a few times during their time together. Thrutt told her he was reliving moments of the war. None of them spoke about what those moments were, however.

After a few minutes, he blinked back to reality and quickly focused on the tattoo on his hand.

"When we were still with the *Fera*, Thrutt told me you always wanted to be a sailor," Orinthia said. "Why?"

Kos set his hand down and tapped his thumb against the

blanket but did not look at her. It took him a minute to answer. "My dad was my hero when I was a kid. I was four when the war started, and he enlisted a few years in. He came home twice on leave during that time, and when he did, he told me about the amazing places he'd been. I loved listening to him talk about his adventures and wanted a piece of that life."

Kos paused and took a deep breath. "It wasn't until I was in his shoes did I realize he told those stories to hide the truth. He didn't want to talk about the things he saw, the friends he lost, or the nightmares he faced every time he closed his eyes. I don't blame him for running away."

"I never saw war," Orinthia said. She held her head down and looked at her own smooth hands. "Desidario was an EC-funded scientist, and he was my only connection to that world. Outside of his occasional explanations of experiments and the closed-door meetings he hosted, I never even thought about it."

The war was far away for her, but for Kos, it was in his home. It was in his heart.

"I'm sorry, Kos," Orinthia added softly. She moved her eyes to the side of his face, tracing the fine lines his short but stress-filled life created.

"Don't be." Kos met her gaze and gave her a pinched smile. "I regret a lot of things about my time serving in the Navy, but I'm solid in who I am. There have to be people like me in order to have people like you. I'm glad you don't understand war like I do. I wouldn't want you to. And that's why I wanted to be in the Navy." He tapped his index finger to his knee for emphasis.

Orinthia pictured the selfless young man he once was, before the Navy changed him. Thrutt would have warned him about the horrors of war, of course, but he offered himself as a sacrifice for the comforts of others. Her stomach turned with acidic anger. Though she would have never met Kos if he had not become the version of the man he was before her, she hated the EC and the Navy for breaking him.

"Well, that was depressing," Kos gave a half-hearted laugh. He took a sweet cake and shoved half of it in his mouth. His lips barely closed over his teeth as he chewed.

The Kos who sat in front of her was different than the quartermaster of the *Fera*. There, he had been under the command of a sadistic killing machine who wielded him no different than the EC. Ahto made him kill and pillage, and Orinthia saw firsthand the damage it did to him. As captain of *Freya*, Kos was his own man. He was in control and chose the path he wanted. He could not be the Kos before the war, but the new man was healing.

"What about you?" Kos asked. "I can't see being a Hunter as your dream job."

Orinthia rolled her eyes. "It wasn't. But when your sister founds the organization and you're *gifted* with a mod like mine, you're more or less conscripted in."

Kos' mouth popped open. "That I didn't know."

"With connections like my father's, it wasn't hard to do. The EC made Arsenio commissioner of the GMH and Adora is the fleet admiral. And there I was, their disappointing embarrassment. In the four years I worked there, I never made it above officer."

Kos shook his head. "You're not a disappointment or embarrassment. Not letting you rank higher was a mistake on their part, though I'm sure the lack of obedience on your end did play a factor." He chuckled.

A warmth rose inside Orinthia's chest. She let it fill her and she smiled.

"But really, what would you do if you weren't a Hunter?" Kos asked.

Her smile faded. Orinthia avoided his eyes and looked at the tattoos on his arm. She studied the details as she spoke. "I started drinking young; the one thing Adora and I did together. I did it to dull everything around me. She did it because she hated everything and everyone, especially herself. We'd end up coming to blows. It was the only time she allowed me to fight back, and I'd usually win. By the time I was eighteen and I got my swords, she started taking me to NCR District 6 to do underground fighting. She was making good money betting on me as my unofficial manager, and I thought about going on my own and earning enough to get out."

"What stopped you?" Kos was intently staring at her.

"Uri," Orinthia said. "I had a lacerated kidney or something I don't remember, and it was way beyond any street chem fixes we normally used, so we had to go to him. To say he was livid would be an understatement. Uri never told Desidario, but the things he threatened to do to Adora…" She let her voice trail off as she fondly remembered that night. "Shortly after that, the war ended, marauders came about, and I became a Hunter."

She lifted her eyes to meet Kos'. He stared at her with his mouth ajar.

"It was over six years ago," Orinthia said with a shrug. "I got into a few marauder fights while a Hunter, but they weren't the same. Even dueling Thrutt doesn't bring the thrill I used to chase."

"So, I guess there isn't anything I can teach you," Kos said. He curled his lips in between his teeth.

"Oh, I don't know," Orinthia said. She set a grin on her

lips and tilted her head. "I've never fought a captain before. But I wouldn't want to hurt you."

Kos' look of admiration quickly turned smug. "Are you challenging me?"

Orinthia thought through her options. Her body had regained some sense of normalcy after resting, and she was less fatigued than earlier. Also, Thrutt had wanted them to practice and be more active. Kos seemed like he was willing, and though she knew he would not take it as far as her old fights, he could sustain a few good hits before she'd back down.

"Yes," Orinthia said.

Kos was first to his feet. He moved to the entrance of the hold and did a few stretches.

Orinthia gathered the blankets and food and set them out of the way on the seats. The snacks she ate weighed heavy in her stomach, but she ignored it. *The fight won't last long enough to throw up,* she thought. *And at least I'm sober this time.*

She took her place a few feet in front of Kos and held a stance with one foot planted behind her and the other ahead. Her fists came up to her center and she inhaled a few lungfuls of steadying air. Tucking her chin into her chest, she signaled to Kos she was ready.

Her pulse quickened and she waited for Kos to make the first move.

As soon as he stepped forward, she rushed to meet him. Though they were almost the same height, she was able to get lower and move quicker. Kos swung and she ducked, sending her fist into his ribs.

He grunted and jumped back. Orinthia took the opportunity to lunge forward and jab at his face. Kos dodged and kicked her leg.

With a thud, she hit the ground with her side.

Kos froze, and a flash of concern crossed his face. Using the distraction, Orinthia curled her legs behind Kos and knocked him back. As he fell, she jumped up and readied for him to get up.

Kos scrambled to his feet. He threw a punch that Orinthia blocked. She tossed his arm out of the way and jabbed him twice on either side of the face. Her knuckles seared against his skin.

Kos swung again, knocking her in the mouth. She fell back and shook it off, but it was too late. Kos dove forward and swung again.

Quickly, she rolled to the side and his fist slammed into the metal floor. He threw a look at her, but his face was not the same as it had been before the fight.

Blood dripped down from the corner of his eyebrow where she had hit, and his eyelid started to swell. His pupils were fully dilated, and his teeth clenched so hard they might have snapped under the pressure. The realization that their friendly spar had gone too far hit her, right before she dodged another one of his punches.

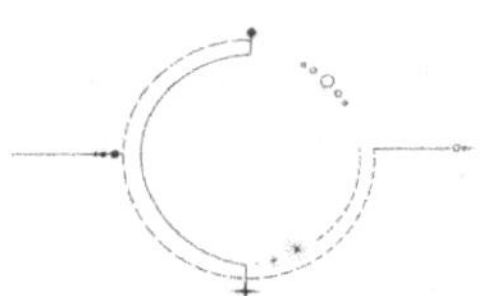

14

The same eyes that looked at her with fire and hatred on the *Fera* bore into Orinthia on *Freya's* top deck. Kos was transformed into the killer he had been in the Navy. He was fighting for his life and only one of them would walk away from it.

Orinthia pulled her legs against her and kicked both of them out into Kos' stomach. Kos flew back a foot. There was enough space for Orinthia to get to her feet. She held her hands open in front of her in defense and tried to defuse the fight she started. "Kos," she said in a low tone. "I concede. Fights over."

Kos came forward, one fist back, and threw himself at her.

Orinthia moved and jabbed him in the gut. She used his momentum to come behind him and grab his arms. "Listen, it's done. Come out of this."

Kos struggled, but Orinthia put her foot on the back of his knee and forced him to kneel. He reached back with his free hand, but Orinthia pulled it into a lock and moved his hands up his back toward his shoulders.

"I yield," Orinthia said. "You win. I'm not going to fight you."

He squirmed and yelled. Orinthia used all her weight to keep him down.

"It's okay, Kos," Orinthia tried to say as calmly as she could. "You're safe. No one is going to hurt you again. I'm sorry."

His chest continued to rise and fall rapidly, but the tension in his shoulders dropped. He slowly lowered his head and stopped struggling.

Orinthia risked releasing him and jumped out of his reach. She moved back toward the ladder but did not descend. It was only to put space between them and make for a quick exit if she had to.

Beneath her, she heard Thrutt's heavy steps approach them. His stone feet clanged against the rails, and he climbed the ladder. He took one look at Orinthia and then at Kos.

"What is happening up here?" he asked.

Orinthia brushed the hair from her face. A few strands caught to her mouth, and she saw crimson streaks in her silver strands.

"We were sparring," Orinthia said. She touched a finger to the crease of her lip and felt warm blood.

Thrutt rubbed his face with both his hands and moved to Kos who was still kneeling where Orinthia left him. "Rogue?"

Kos shook his head but did not say anything.

Thrutt glanced back at Orinthia and tossed his head toward the ladder. She took it as a signal to get out and complied.

The bars dug into her bare feet as she went down to the lower deck.

Once in her quarters, she closed the door and went to examine her face in the washroom mirror. A purple bruise already formed on her chin. She took a cloth from the cabinet and wet it. The fabric stung against the cut, but the water cooled the skin.

That has to be one of the dumbest things I've ever done, Orinthia thought as she held the cloth to her face. *Just as he was starting to see me as a friend, I had to pick a fight with him. What is wrong with me?*

There was a knock on the washroom door. Orinthia thought about ignoring it but decided against it.

Thrutt stood with his hand against the frame and leaned in. His face was unreadable, but Orinthia could tell what he was thinking. He was working out a way to scold her without making her shut down. She was his wayward child and needed constant correction.

"I—" Orinthia began to say, but Thrutt held up a hand to cut her off.

"Rogue knows better than to fight unsupervised," Thrutt said. "He hasn't had an episode like that since—"

"The EC sailor." It was Orinthia's turn to interrupt.

Thrutt nodded. "What were you two thinking?"

Orinthia pushed by him and went to her bed. She sat on the edge and cupped her forehead in her hands. She gave Thrutt the details, from her history as a back-alley boxer through the moments prior to him finding them. Before, she had been proud of her skills, but in the fallout, she wished she had never brought it up.

Thrutt groaned. "Kos handles most things well. But there are times when he needs extra care. He's done and seen things that he won't tell even me about. Those are where he goes when he blacks out."

Orinthia placed her hands on either side of her legs and hung her head back. In her mind, being away from Ahto would have made him better. "Is there anything I can do to fix it?"

"No," Thrutt answered. "He'll come out of it eventually, but right now he needs space."

ORINTHIA SPENT the rest of the flight to Sarv'on in her room. She only left to get food and bring it back to her bed. Neither Thrutt nor Kos came by. Once again, it was her and Uri alone in the silence.

She distracted herself by exercising and rebuilding the stamina she lost while poisoned. Sprinting in between the row of beds, push-ups, and stretches. Technically, she won the fight against Kos, but he was a few good hits away from taking her out. She shadowboxed and imagined scenarios in her head. It did not count as the real thing, but she put as much effort into it as if it were. Her muscles were slow and sore, but they remembered how to move like they did before the GMH.

Waking up on the morning they were due to arrive at Sarv'on, Orinthia showered. She stepped into the washroom. With a flat palm, she pressed the control beside the sink and the toilet rolled into the wall, swapping places with the shower head. Instantly, warm water poured from the spout and steam filled the small space. Orinthia removed her clothes and set them in the sink. With a tap of two buttons, the sink began to fill with water and agitated her clothing.

While her garments washed, Orinthia stepped into the steamy water. She stood in the downpour unmoving for a minute and let it soothe her muscles. Though she had been in space for over half a year, she could not get used to the cold. New Cruces was an arid desert and even the coldest winter nights never reached lower than sixty degrees.

Orinthia pressed another button and the shower head retreated into the wall. This time, the wall spun and reappeared with six grated tubes protruding out. As hot air blew from them, a fan spun above her, sucking away any moisture as she dried.

She ran her fingers through her long hair and detangled what she could, though the under section of her hair had a large clump of knots. Once she was dry, the fan and blowers stopped. With her clothes also dry, she redressed and opened the washroom door.

The room smelled of sweat and dirty sheets. Orinthia stripped her bedding and threw them in the sink to wash.

A trill sounded over the speakers with the proximity alarm. Orinthia waited for the alarm to stop before she stepped out of her room and went to the cockpit.

In the distance shone a planet that resembled Earth. The difference was, large brown tinted rings orbited around it.

"Is that Sarv'on?" Orinthia asked Thrutt as she stepped in.

He stood alone at the controls. "Yep. We should land in about an hour."

"Why did we come out of warp so far away?" Orinthia asked.

"Freya?" Thrutt said.

"Too many factors," Freya's voice answered. "Traffic, debris, trajectory. In this instance, the town we are due to land in is in the southern hemisphere, but our current path would lead us to the equator."

Orinthia sat in the seat beside Thrutt's and looked over the various screens. Kos had tried to explain what they meant.

Most of them she forgot, but the radar she remembered. A small dot blinked at the edge of the screen. It was not blue like when the *Kalumarion* attacked, but red.

"What's that?" Orinthia asked pointing to the dot.

Thrutt followed her hand and stared at the screen. "Get Rogue."

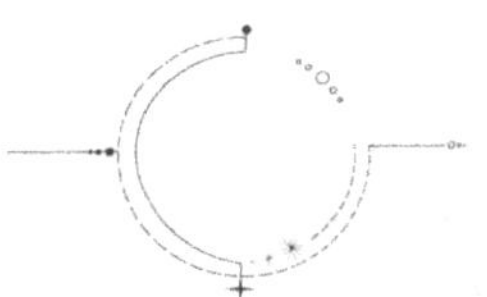

15

*I*t was only two words, but the urgency was clear. Orinthia rushed to Kos' quarters and slapped the door multiple times.

Kos opened and looked at her. His bruises had not healed and were shades of green and yellow. The swelling on his left eyelid had gone down, but it was noticeable enough.

Orinthia briefly wondered why Kos had not used a med-pack to heal his wounds. "Thrutt said to get you," she said. "There's something on the radar."

Kos shrugged on a coat as he slid his way by her and took long, fast strides to the cockpit. He and Thrutt were talking to each other before she could join them.

"The shields will hold," Kos said. His voice was raspy, like it was the first time he had spoken in a while. "But we can't jump, not when we're this close to Sarv'on. We'll overshoot it. It's even too close for the hyperdrive. We would punch right into the planet."

"Given the *Fera's* proximity to us," Freya said. "Landing anywhere on the planet would pose a risk."

Orinthia's body shook. She had hoped to never see that

ship, or its captain, again. The three of them had not left on the best of terms and she was not ready to make a repeat of their last meeting.

Kos swiped at the tattoo on his palm. The holographic map rose up before him. "We could skip to the Telnavi system, then to Relea, and come back to Sarv'on from the other side. He wouldn't be able to detect us through that many jumps."

"If you're trying to blow my warp drive and leave us all stranded in the middle of space, just say so," Freya said. "It would be more effective to just detach the whole thing and jettison it towards them."

Kos chewed his bottom lip and tapped his finger to the console, then shook his head. "I can't replace that as easily."

"I thought the *Fera* wasn't able to be detected?" Orinthia spoke up. "Isn't that why it's made of asteroid metals?"

Kos and Thrutt turned to look at her, and it seemed like they had not noticed her until that moment.

"Does she not know what I am?" Freya said. "I've commanded fleets. I've—"

"The *Fera's* operational base code is integrated into *Freya's* system," Kos interrupted. "Any other ship would see space junk, sure, but *Freya* can detect the difference. On the downside, even though I've rewritten our tracking signal, the *Fera* has our base code as well and can find us if we are within range of their radar."

Orinthia's head spun with the information. Most of what he said made sense, but it was too technical for her to fully understand. What she did know, however, was the *Fera* was close and they were probably spotted. *But how did they find us to begin with?*

Thrutt and Kos argued about what to do. Orinthia focused on the screen. A small dot blinked toward them.

"Cannon fire inbound," Freya announced.

Orinthia closed her eyes and placed her back on the wall. The other two held onto the console.

Seconds ticked by. Nothing.

Orinthia checked the radar, the blinking dot was behind them and moved out of range of the screen. "Did they miss?"

"There is no way they would have from that distance," Kos answered. "It was a warning shot."

"Captain Rogue," Freya said. Her voice, if it was possible for a ship, was uneven. "Captain Ahto is attempting to hail. Shall I accept?"

Kos hung his head over the panels. The skin on his knuckles was white from tension. He took a deep breath, then straightened himself. With a tug of his coat sleeves, Kos answered. "Accept."

An image blinked onto the center of *Freya's* window. Ahto's human form appeared before them. Not a single thing about him had changed. His crisp, navy-blue EC uniform stood out against his ghostly grey skin. "Rogue," Ahto's cold steel voice said. He curled his upper lip and showed his too perfectly straight teeth. "You look... worn. Mutiny hasn't been kind to you, has it?"

Kos shifted his stance and placed his hands behind his back. "It was only mutiny because you went against the oath. We protect civilians."

"You are a civilian," Ahto said, emphasizing each word. His eyes flashed to his slatted snake eyes then back to normal. "They don't care about you."

"What do you want," Kos asked.

Ahto tilted his head back and looked down his nose. "A trade."

"I have nothing," Kos said. "We left everything on the *Fera* when we left."

"Not, everything. Her." Ahto moved his eyes to focus on Orinthia and pointed.

Kos and Thrutt looked at her, too.

Orinthia froze. *Me?*

"Why?" Kos asked for her, facing Ahto's image again.

"Did you think I wouldn't find out? That Desidario Anton's daughter was aboard my ship, and you took her? Give her back and I will call off the bounty."

"No," Kos said. His voice solid.

Again, Ahto's eyes flashed. This time, his face morphed slightly with them. "I will not fire another warning. Refuse and you will be disabled and boarded. There will be no mercy."

"I've never seen you give mercy, so I'd expect nothing less," Kos said. His shoulders were pulled down and he held his chest out. "Every marauder that sets foot on my ship will die."

"You'd kill your brothers and sisters?" Ahto was losing his grip. His voice was not cool like before, but high and loud. More and more snakelike features rippled over him as anger poured from him.

"If that's what it takes," Kos answered. His demeanor was the opposite of Ahto's. The harder Ahto pushed, the more-firm Kos stood.

Ahto's composure broke. In an instant, his snake body rolled free and attacked the console in his command room. Sparks flew on his side of the link and the screen went black.

"Freya, strengthen forward shields," Kos announced. "Fire two cannons at the *Fera*, then head toward Sarv'on at full speed."

As quickly as Kos had ordered, the ship obeyed. Two yellow orbs flew from beneath them with a jolt and flew in the *Fera's* direction. Half a dozen red flares erupted from the

Fera, pulling a yellow orb away from its target. The second orb kept the course and found its mark on the port side. An electrical current curled around the hull and dissipated halfway through.

Orinthia stood helpless at the entrance to the cockpit and watched Thrutt take his seat at the weapon computer. He turned the ship's laser turret until their enemy came into view. Another cannon fire came toward *Freya*, which showed both on the screen and out the window. Thrutt jammed the controls and sent a rapid fire at it, making contact just before the collision.

"Freya, helm," Kos said. He took hold of the semi-circle wheel when it appeared and steered.

The *Fera* was becoming larger in the window as the ships came closer together. A light burst through an opening in the hull as a second, smaller ship exited.

"There's another sloop," Orinthia said.

"I see it." Kos's voice was strained as he threw himself to the side and dodged three torpedoes. "Strap in."

Orinthia did as she was told. She wished for something she could do to help.

A fourth torpedo slammed into the starboard side of *Freya*, rocking the ship. The sound hurt Orinthia's ears.

Thrutt fired at the sloop with a hail of ion blasters from the turret. It weaved through a good portion of them, but more than half were true. Explosions erupted around it. A second wave of blaster fire followed. The opposing sloop had no time to evade and caught each one of the shots.

Through the debris that chunked off the hull, they returned fire. Kos dove forward onto the helm and pulled to the left. One of the blasters hit *Freya's* tail with full force. If Orinthia had not been buckled, she would have been tossed across the room.

Kos, who was not secured to anything, slid across the deck. His head smacked against the console, then the steel floor with a slap. He did not get up.

The stars spiraled around them. Orinthia released the clasp from her belt and leaped for the helm. She pulled to the right and straightened the trajectory. "Kos is out," she yelled. Her ears rang. The blood in her veins felt cold.

"Take the turrets," Thrutt said. He moved her out of the way and they swapped places.

Her body quaked with a combination of fear and being tossed around. She reached out to Kos and turned him over. The cut above his eye had reopened and a steady stream of blood flowed across his face. She dragged him to the side, her muscles straining from the weight, and placed him against the wall out of the way.

"Thia," Thrutt said. "You need to get on the controls, now."

Orinthia sat in Thrutt's previous seat and latched her belt before grabbing the handles. She moved the viewfinder and searched for either ship. The sloop came into view. A red indicator pulsed on the screen and, suspecting Thrutt had already primed a weapon, she pressed it.

Freya jolted twice as two energy missiles launched from her cannons. Five seconds later, according to the timer on the computer, both hit the sloop. A fireball puffed out of the ship as the oxygen inside made contact with the flames of the torpedo and ignited. The ship blew apart into pieces and rocketed in every direction.

Orinthia stared at the screen, unsure of what she saw. She could not move. Her mind detached from her body and was looking at herself from the outside.

"We need cover fire," Thrutt yelled. His voice was distant. "Concentrate on the *Fera*. I'm going to take us in."

Orinthia's hands acted on their own. They turned the viewport to the *Fera* and held down the buttons on the controls. Red streaks shot across the screen in rapid succession. She moved the controls to follow the image as *Freya* flew beneath it. They were past it.

"Freya, strengthen rear shields and put everything into the boosters," Thrutt ordered. "Once we're through the atmosphere, set for the coordinates Mimi gave."

"Aye chief," Freya replied.

"Thia, you can let go of the hammer," Thrutt said. "Only fire again if they come closer or send more attacks our way."

Orinthia released the depressor and watched the screen. She slowly came back to her body with a chill. Her hands trembled and her stomach felt hot.

The *Fera* shrunk on her screen. The blackness and stars were replaced by a bright orange glow of flames. Her heart jerked and she looked back at the windshield. To her relief, they were not blown up, but breaking through the first layer of Sarv'on's atmosphere.

The windshield dimmed to protect their eyes from the light. The air around the room warmed a few degrees, almost to the temperature of a summer night in New Cruces. It helped alleviate some of the chill that grew over Orinthia, but she continued to shiver.

Sarv'on's surface broke through the flames as *Freya* applied the airbrakes to slow their descent. Landmasses took clearer shapes and became recognizable. They switched to cruising speed, flying away from their entry point and over open water.

Orinthia looked back at the turret computer and scanned the sky around them. No one followed and they were alone.

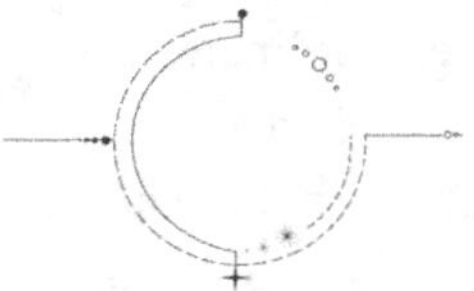

16

*K*os groaned in the corner Orinthia had left him. He rolled from his side to his back and pulled his legs into an angle. He blinked one eye, the other was covered in blood. A deep red splotch formed around the injury over his face. His skin was marked with purple, blue, and burgundy.

"We're not dead," Kos said dryly. Still, on his back, he rubbed dry blood from his eye with the back of his sleeve.

Neither Thrutt nor Orinthia answered. Orinthia had left the turret controls and returned to her seat beside Thrutt. She had her knees pulled against her chest. Her chin rested against her folded arms, and she stared out the window at the sunset as they flew toward their destination. She glanced at Kos when he first moved, but went back to looking out.

Her mind was full of a myriad of thoughts. She had no way of knowing how many marauders were on the sloop. How many lives were ended at her hands? Some she most likely knew from her time on the *Fera*.

Thrutt had tried to console her. "Ahto promised no

mercy," he told her. "They would have shot us out of the sky if they had the chance. You saved us."

She had not responded or said anything since the dogfight. *That's what Kos said when I killed Neve*, she thought. *I killed her, and I killed whoever was on that ship. Saved us. Saved him. Death doesn't change just because the reason is good, does it? I killed them.*

Movement caught her eye and she watched Thrutt go to Kos and help him up. His gigantic body covered Kos and blocked him from her view. She focused back on the twilight. Stars poked through the darkening sky.

Kos was on his feet and shuffled his way to the captain's seat. He lowered himself and stretched his legs in front of him. He laced his fingers over his stomach and rolled his head to face Orinthia.

She took a long blink and placed her eyes on Kos'. They stayed fixed on each other. Orinthia could not tell what he was thinking, his face was as blank as she hoped hers was.

Thrutt stepped out of the cockpit. The door to his quarters opened and then closed again.

"Thank you." Kos broke the silence.

"Don't," Orinthia said. "You were right, this isn't the place for me."

Kos' eyebrows pinched together. He took in a sharp gasp between his teeth. "What are you talking about?"

"On the *Fera*, you said I don't have what it takes to be a marauder." Orinthia leaned her back against the seat and placed her feet on the ground. "After Uri is fixed, he and I will leave. If he'll even be able to stand me after what I just did."

Kos spun his chair around and bent closer to her. He touched her knee with his fingertips. "You're going to be okay. It's a shock, I know. But—"

"You're not okay, are you?" Orinthia shoved his hand away and stood. "I killed them, Kos. I. Killed. It makes me sick. That's not who I am. This has all gotten out of hand and I feel so lost. None of this would have happened if I stayed on Earth."

Kos rose and took her in his arms. He smashed her tight against his chest.

Orinthia broke down and sobbed into his shirt collar. Emotions swirled through her. She wanted to push him away and scream. She wanted to hold him and never let go. She wanted to run to her room and not look at anyone again.

Kos stroked her hair and hushed her. "I know. I wish I could take it from you."

A door down the corridor slid open, and Thrutt's stomps came closer to them. "I have your med-pack," he said as he stood outside the control room.

As if releasing a wounded animal, Kos slowly let go of Orinthia. He took the pack from Thrutt and cracked it over his knee. It hissed for a second, then he placed it over his eye. "Get her some water and something to eat." He looked at the nav computer then back to Thrutt. "Keep her close. We should be there in about half an hour. I'll come back after we land."

Thrutt moved a diamond hand to Orinthia's back and ushered her out the door. He led her toward the galley and placed her on a bench. The cabinet doors knocked about as Thrutt did as he was instructed. Then he set a hydro-sphere and a package of dried fruit on the table in front of her. "Do you want to talk?"

"No." Orinthia took the hydro-sphere and drank half of it in one shot. Her eyes itched from drying tears. She mashed the heels of her palms into her face and rubbed hard.

The bench on the other side of the table creaked as Thrutt

sat. He placed his elbows on the table and rested his chin in his hands. As talkative as Thrutt was, he knew when to keep quiet. The pair sat without saying anything for the remainder of the flight.

A SHORT WHILE LATER, a thump beneath her told Orinthia the landing gear was activated. She stood and stretched her body in different directions. The numbness she had before lifted slightly, but her chest was heavy.

The ship rattled around them as they touched ground and the thrumming of the life-support system died down. Orinthia's ears rang from the lack of noise. She stole a look down the hall and saw a misty pink sky from out the front window. Dawn was breaking and she wondered how long a day-cycle lasted on Sarv'on.

Kos moved from his captain's chair to the hall. He paused for a moment, then went forward to meet Thrutt and Orinthia.

"I had to set her down a few miles south of where we're supposed to meet Mimi," Kos informed them. "There's no landing pad outside of this village and the marsh would swallow *Freya* if we tried to land anywhere else." His bruises were almost gone, save for a few green spots on his left cheek. The swelling in his eye had vanished entirely, but when he blinked, it was slow to reopen.

"We'll rent a lev-speeder to get the rest of the way," he continued. "Thrutt, you stay with the ship. Get her ready to go by the time we come back. And keep the scanners on in case Ahto sends anyone after us. Freya's running a diagnostic and she'll let you know when she's done."

Thrutt nodded in acknowledgment. "Freya and I will take care of everything."

Kos addressed Orinthia. He avoided her eyes and looked somewhere on her face as he spoke, "I'll meet you on the top deck when you're ready."

When she did not respond, he turned and climbed up the ladder out of view.

"He's a good man who cares too much," Thrutt said, stealing Orinthia's attention back to him. "You've both been through a lot in the last few days. Take care of each other out there, okay?"

"I'll do my best," Orinthia said with a flat tone. She followed Kos up the ladder and met him at the entrance to the hold.

Kos examined the map on his hand. Orinthia did not understand how he always had a map of every location they were at. She made a mental note to ask him when she felt more like talking.

A puff of moist air burst in through the doors as they opened before them. Almost immediately, Orinthia's clothes clung to her skin. The air was thick and hard to breathe. It smelled of soggy wood and rotting vegetables. It took every-thing in her not to gag.

Kos, on the other hand, took a deep drag in through his nose and closed his eyes. "Wetlands," he said. He let out a sigh and looked through the fully open door. "Come on. We only have a short time before the sun sets again."

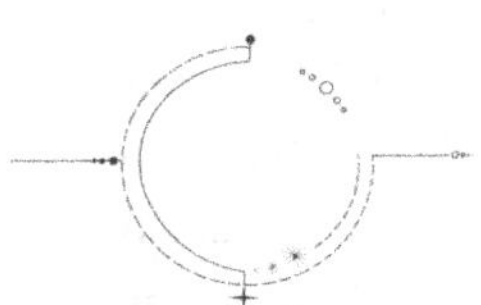

17

Orinthia held tight to Kos' coat, pressing her cheek to his back as they rode together on one speeder bike. They left the clearing where *Freya* was docked and drove a mile into a thick, swampy forest. Mossy green plants blurred by them, and branches smacked her legs. She vaguely wondered how long it would take for the branches to cut through her new pants.

Before she could find out, the trees opened, and they were surrounded by patches of grassy mounds that seemed to float around them. The speeder had no trouble adjusting from solid ground to skipping over the black water. Orinthia gripped tighter to Kos, lacing her fingers together around his middle. She did not know what creatures could live in that environment, but she did not want to meet them.

Kos navigated smoothly through the maze. His visor was down, and it displayed the direction to take. They traveled for fifteen minutes before they reached a second village. Kos popped the speeder at an angle and brought it up a wooden ramp. He slowed to a crawl and parked in front of the first shack on the dock.

Orinthia climbed off, her legs were damp, and her white boots were streaked with mud. The wood beneath them groaned as they walked. Chunks of boards were missing every few feet, so Orinthia made sure to watch where she stepped.

The humming in her head began before they stepped in through the doors, and Orinthia did not need to be told what type of place they were meeting Mimi. Kos went in first and held the door open for her to follow. The smell of sweat and half a dozen other bodily fluids hit her nose as she entered. A thin layer of green moss covered the walls and white smoke hung in the air.

Orinthia opted to breathe through her mouth instead of her nose, though the taste was almost as bad as the smell. She kept her head low and looked over the faces of the patrons. A few caught her eye, and she recognized them from holo-posters in the GMH headquarters.

Kos nodded to open seats at the bar and led the way. He ordered a drink, but Orinthia declined one for herself.

The sound of trapped bees in a jar filled her head. She could not remember why she ever liked to hang out in bars to begin with. Maybe it was the quietness of *Freya* that made her forget what the real world was like. Whatever it was, she found it hard to concentrate on anything else.

It was not until she felt the pressure on her ribs that she realized someone was behind her. "Get up," a woman's voice said in her ear.

"Kos," Orinthia said, trying to keep still. She glanced down and saw a pink revolving blaster jabbed into her side. Her eyes moved to Kos and noticed a blunderbuss against his ribs as well. There was not enough space between the three of them for Orinthia to activate her sword. Her mind raced trying to find a way out of the situation.

Kos turned his head slowly to the woman and set his drink down.

"I said get up," the woman repeated.

Orinthia did as she was told and faced the woman. She could feel the metal scrape her skin through her shirt. The woman was short and did not reach Orinthia's shoulder. She had light tawny skin and bright pink bobbed hair which poked out the sides of her hood. Her long bangs hid her eyes from view.

Kos, too, was on his feet. He slowly slid a hand down to his hip and pressed it. A pocket opened with a hiss, and he laced his fingers around the grip. Before he could retrieve it, however, the woman lifted the blunderbuss from his side and smacked him across the face.

Orinthia used the distraction to swing her arm up and out, activating her sword. She shoved the woman with her normal arm, causing her to stumble back. She pulled her arm up and readied to slash, but the woman leaned back and kicked Orinthia in the knee. It hit and Orinthia toppled forward, landing on her face.

By the time Orinthia scrambled to her feet, the woman had one blaster pressed to Kos' head and the other trained on her middle.

The fight was over. Orinthia, with her sword still active, lifted both arms in defeat.

Every eye in the bar was on them.

"Move into that room." The woman waved her blunderbuss to somewhere behind Orinthia.

Orinthia made eye contact with Kos. He nodded at her to follow the demand. Slowly, she turned and walked where she was ordered.

A door stood ajar at the back of the bar. Orinthia,

followed by Kos and their attacker, walked in. The woman closed the door behind her.

The smell was not much better inside, what Orinthia could only assume was, the utility closet. A window above them let in light and spore-like particles hung in the air. There were boxes, a broom, and spare glasses and plates on shelves.

"Is this really necessary?" Kos asked, dropping his hands to his side.

"There were two more bounties added to your head this morning," the woman said. She flicked the safety on each of her blasters and holstered them to her hips. "You're lucky I got to you first."

Orinthia saw the opportunity and made to charge at the woman. Kos put his hand in front of her and blocked her movement.

"This is Mimi Nakahara," he said, waving his free hand at the woman.

Mimi pushed her hood back and smiled at them. "It's been a while, Rogue. I'm glad to see you're finally out from under Ahto's thumb." She was nothing like who Orinthia had imagined. Mimi wore a pair of black shorts that stopped at the top of her thighs and exposed the smooth connection of skin to the metal that made up the majority of her left leg. Orinthia's reflection looked back at her as clearly as if she were looking in the washroom mirror.

"How many other bounty hunters are out there?" Kos asked.

"Only two, but I made sure to get them pretty wasted before you got here," Mimi answered. "They shouldn't put up much trouble, and that's if they can even remember their own names."

Orinthia looked between the two. They could not have

been more different in demeanor. Kos stood stiff and straight-backed. Mimi leaned against the door with a leg propped behind her and her arm tucked under the other at the elbow. She did not look like someone Kos would make friends with.

"So, how did you plan on getting us out after that show?" Kos asked.

"Hey, that was part of the plan." Mimi waved a hand behind her. "If I didn't make it look like I was collecting, I'd lose my reputation. And that's not something I'm willing to sacrifice, even for you."

Mimi lifted her waist-length leather coat to the side and pulled out a pair of cuffs. "Put these on," she said, shoving them toward Orinthia.

Orinthia stepped away. Her back pressed against the wall. "Those are mod dampeners." She recognized them from her time in the GMH. They sent out negatively charged pulses, hindering the use of mods while worn.

"If we don't commit to the act, someone will notice and could make an attempt at claiming the bounty for themselves." Mimi did not drop her hand. "Ahto has half a million credits on Rogue. The GMH has a hundred thousand and a pardon for anyone who brings you in."

The news hit Orinthia like a meteor. Every time she heard the bounty mentioned, she had assumed it was only for Kos. It never occurred to her there could be one for her, too.

"What for?" Orinthia asked. She tried to think of all the things the twins could have pinned to her. *Marauding is illegal, sure,* she thought. *But to offer a pardon?*

"Murder," Mimi answered.

Orinthia was thankful for the wall behind her to hold her up. The tips of her fingers tingled and her head felt light. "Excuse me?"

Mimi dug through another coat pocket and pulled a holo-display. She pressed a button and scanned through several images before she stopped at Orinthia's. "Orinthia Anton. Wanted for marauding, kidnapping, and second-degree murder of Uri Anton," Mimi read.

No longer trusting her legs to hold her up, Orinthia reached for Kos and gripped his shoulder. She knew the twins hated her; it was never a secret. But to go as far as accusing her of murdering their eldest brother and putting a bounty on her head was out of the realm of belief. She looked at Kos with tears in her eyes. "Adora shot him." Her voice broke.

"I know," Kos said, softly. He placed a hand on hers and patted them. "But this is why we are here. We need Mimi to find Elendoras first, then we'll take care of everything else."

Orinthia nodded, but her heart ached.

"We have to go," Mimi said. Her words were quick. "We've been in here too long and someone is bound to come looking. Put them on and I'll get you both out."

The strength to recall her sword almost failed her, but she managed and took the cuffs from Mimi. Kos helped her place them on her wrists. No sooner had they clamped closed did the room go silent. Not the room, she realized, but the sound in her head. The tears she fought back poured down.

Kos' eyes widened and went to remove the cuffs. His hands fumbled with the lock. "What's wrong?"

"Lie to me," Orinthia said.

It took a second for him to register what she meant, but then he said, "Thrutt is my real dad."

Silence. A smile broke through her tears. "I can't hear it."

"She's deaf?" Mimi asked.

Kos shook his head and replied to Mimi without looking away from Orinthia. "It's a long story, but she's fine." His top lip moved between his teeth. He kept his gaze on her face, his pupils dilating as they stood in silence. He looked like he wanted to say more, but whatever it was he kept it to himself.

"Let's go. Now." Mimi pulled her blunderbuss and aimed it at the back of Kos' head. With her other hand, she grabbed the link between Orinthia's wrists and led them back into the bar.

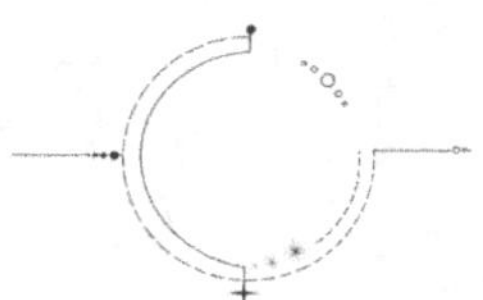

18

A glass shattered somewhere in the back of the room. Shouting followed it. Chairs toppled over and the thuds of fists against flesh filled the air. But Orinthia's head was silent.

Some patrons turned their attention from the fight to the group that emerged from the closet. Kos cursed at Mimi and threatened her life. Orinthia, on the other hand, had no intentions of contesting her restraints. She had no memory of a time when her head was so quiet while in a crowded space, and she wanted to hold onto every moment.

Mimi dragged Orinthia to the exit, shoving Kos when he stopped walking, and out onto the dock. She led them to the back of the shack and pushed them into a lev-car with no roof. No one followed them, but Mimi did not wait long before placing the vehicle in drive. They left Kos' rented speeder bike and moved down the ramp back onto the water.

Kos pulled his comm from his coat and called Thrutt. "We have Mimi and are coming back, now."

"Good." Thrutt's voice was faint over the sound of wind rushing around them. "There's been nothing on the radar, but

I'd like to put a few systems between us and here as soon as we can."

"See you in a bit," Kos said and closed the comm. He moved to his knees and turned to face Orinthia. His ponytail slapped him in the face. "Let's get those off."

The cuffs came undone as Kos placed a key into the slot. "You okay?"

Orinthia nodded as she rubbed her wrists.

"So, where are we headed?" Mimi asked. She had to shout over the wind.

The blue map appeared in front of Kos as he swiped at his tattoo and sat down simultaneously. "*Freya* is over here." He pointed to a spot. "It shouldn't take us more than ten minutes."

Mimi took several glances between the twisting rows of water and the map. "Okay, got it."

Kos curled his fingers over the map and it disappeared.

The ride was quiet, save for the rushing of air and rippling water beneath the car. The sun was completely overhead and reflected white spots over the dark pools. They cut back into the trees and turned down a wider path than the one Orinthia and Kos had taken previously.

Orinthia watched Kos from the backseat. He repeatedly moved his bottom lip between his teeth and fidgeted with his hands in his lap. Neither he, Mimi, nor Orinthia spoke for the rest of the ride.

Freya's nose appeared in the clearing and grew larger as they approached. Orinthia could see impact marks from the previous battles. Paint chipped off in some places, revealing patches of bone-white metal. The ramp was already lowered and Thrutt stepped out to greet them.

Mimi slowed the car and parked at an angle in front of the ramp. She jumped out first and walked to Thrutt. Kos helped

Orinthia climb out, though he let his hand linger on hers a moment longer before releasing her once she was firmly on the ground.

"Thrutt," Mimi shouted, throwing her arms wide open.

"Heya, Mimi," Thrutt said. The two embraced. He lifted her off the ground and gave her a friendly shake.

"I haven't seen you since the divorce," Mimi said as she let go of the giant man. She was tiny beside him, even more so than most people compared to his size.

The word *divorce* struck Orinthia funny. She noticed Kos shove his hands in his pant pockets and shuffled his feet as he walked toward the pair on the ramp.

Orinthia stayed by the car and watched the three interact. Mimi spoke rapidly about the events at the bar. Thrutt nodded as she did and made faces in between story breaks. Kos chimed in when he had something to correct in her embellished version.

Orinthia could not help but feel like she was getting a glimpse into the past when they were sailors sharing post-battle tales. She had not, until that moment, given any thought or realization to the fact she would have to share her new home with someone else. *The room is a mess,* she said to herself and slipped by the others to clean up what she could.

She looked at Uri in his bed. The space they shared was about to change. *How is Mimi going to react to seeing a practical corpse? Is she going to find it disgusting to share a room with him?*

The thoughts continued to flow through Orinthia's head as she replaced her freshly clean sheets back on her bed.

Thrutt stepped in through the open door. He carried a large suitcase under each arm. Orinthia watched him pause in the center of the room and look at the bunks. She guessed he was trying to decide a place to set Mimi's things.

Not once in her life had Orinthia shared a room with anyone. She did not count Uri who might as well have been part of the furniture.

Thrutt chose the bunk closest to the back of the room, catty-corner from Orinthia's, and set the luggage down.

Orinthia dodged his gaze and went back to moving a pile of clothes into the footlocker by her bed.

As if he read her mind, Thrutt stepped closer and said, "It'll be different for a while. But Mimi is a sweetheart. You'll get to like her."

With a forced smile, Orinthia looked at Thrutt. "I'm fine. This is what we've worked toward. Now I can get Uri to Desidario."

"You know, you'll always have a place here," Thrutt said. "I know you think you don't fit in, but you do."

"I don't—" Orinthia could not finish her sentence. The faint sound of blaster fire came from outside the ship. She and Thrutt stared at each other for half a second before they both ran toward the ladder.

Thrutt reached it first and, skipping rungs, climbed through the hole. Orinthia followed behind him. Before he left the hold, Thrutt tossed one of his blasters at Orinthia. She caught it before it hit the ground.

It took a moment for her eyes to adjust to the light when she was on the ramp, but Orinthia could see Kos and Mimi crouched behind Mimi's speeder. They shot over it into the trees. To the left of the ramp, Thrutt had taken cover behind a tree and fired in the direction the others did.

Orinthia jumped off at the middle of the ramp and squatted behind it. A bolt of energy sparked off *Freya's* hull where Orinthia had stood a second before. She looked across the clearing and tried to find where the attack came from. A handful of bolts flew back and forth through the air.

In the distance, Orinthia could make out three figures. She focused on one of them and watched him fire repeatedly at the car. The thought of shooting him made her stomach tighten. *I can't do it again.* Her hands shook and the blaster was heavy. A bolt went over Kos' head, missing by inches. *But I have to do something.*

She placed an elbow on her knee and aimed at the tree where the man shot from behind. With several quick pulls of the trigger, she laid cover fire. Pieces of the trunk splintered off the tree, sending charred wood flying.

A second blaster bolt hit the ramp. The bolt would have pierced through her if her cover was not there. Orinthia ducked her head back and recentered herself. Her chest pounded and her body trembled.

When she was ready, she stuck her head out again and looked over the clearing. The man behind the tree she shot at took a bolt to the chest and flew to the ground. She watched to make sure he did not get back up. When he did not move, she scanned the area for the others. Just as she found the second one, a bolt from behind the car struck the attacking woman in the middle of her stomach. She fell forward, her arms wrapped around herself.

Blaster fire ceased from the opposing side. Movement caught Orinthia's eye across the way.

Kos must have seen it, too. He leaped over the hood of the lev-car and sprinted into the woods after the last man.

Without thinking, Orinthia moved out from her covered position and ran after them. Rays of light cut in through the branches. Orinthia strained her eyes to keep Kos in her sight. She ran as hard as she could, her boots pounding into the soft soil.

Kos pulled ahead and she could not see where he went. She tried to look at the ground for his tracks. A single blaster fire split through the air. The sound almost made her trip. Her feet pressed hard in the direction of the firing. *No,* she thought. She begged it not to be Kos. *I could have prevented this. I could have shot him from where I was. If Kos is dead...*

The thought cut off as she saw a figure standing at the edge of the woods. An orange glow cast over the water. The grassy mounds looked like they were on fire in the evening light.

Orinthia slowed her pace and stopped just before the line of trees ended. A second set of footsteps, which she had not heard until then, stopped behind her. She glanced back to see Mimi.

Kos stood over a body, his shoulders heaved up and down. The golden blaster in his left hand caught glints of light at his side.

Mimi and Orinthia called out to him at the same time. He did not move.

"Kos, listen to me," Orinthia coaxed. She handed Mimi her borrowed blaster and reached her hand out to Kos. Daring to move closer, she took a single step forward.

He snapped around and aimed his blaster at her face. A dark shadow laid over his blazing eyes. They were the same as during their fight.

Orinthia planted herself and spoke gently. "Kos, this isn't you anymore. You've done your duty, and you can choose your path. Please come back."

Kos' breathing slowed to a normal rhythm and the shadow faded. His face softened like he was coming out of a trance. He blinked hard then looked at Orinthia's outstretched hand. Without looking away, he holstered his weapon and moved toward her.

Mimi placed a hand on his arm when he joined them, but

Kos did not take his eyes from Orinthia's. Embers of the previous flames smoldered.

"Let's get back to *Freya*," Mimi said.

Kos nodded and stepped between the two women, letting Mimi's touch fall.

Mimi looked at Orinthia with a long stare before they both fell into step behind him.

19

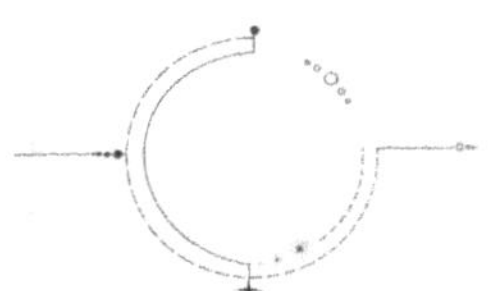

Thrutt already started *Freya's* preflight by the time the three others arrived. The engines gave a quiet but high-pitched whine as they idled. Mimi closed the ramp when they were aboard, and the airlock sealed shut.

Orinthia followed Kos down the ladder. To her surprise, he did not go to the cockpit but to his quarters instead. The door closed behind him. She stared at it, wishing she could see inside or even better, morph through.

Mimi squeezed by her and went to the cockpit where Thrutt stood at the controls. They talked briefly about why Kos did not join them.

The ship shook as it lifted from the ground. Orinthia rushed to the gunner's seat and strapped herself in. She mashed her eyes together just as they angled up and launched toward the sky.

No one said anything until they were out of the atmosphere and cruising.

Mimi was the first to speak. "I didn't know he had gotten so bad."

Orinthia risked opening her eyes. She looked back at the

windshield and saw they were in normal flight through the emptiness of space.

Thrutt tapped one of his diamond fingers on the radar. There were no signs of the company anywhere nearby. "He doesn't sleep either. I think he lives on cortis-chems."

"Should I talk to him?" Mimi asked. "It took me a while to climb out of the hole, but I did. He seems to still be so far down there. I'd hate to see him go the way of the others."

"You can try," Thrutt answered. "Just not now. He's had a lot happen in the last few days. Speaking of, what went on out there?"

Mimi took another long look at Orinthia then back to Thrutt. "We were chasing after the guy. Rogue got to him first and laid a shot into him. When we finally reached them, he was just standing there, staring at the body. It was hard to watch."

She paused and shook her head. "This one got him out of it, though. At least enough to come back."

Thrutt smiled at Orinthia. He placed a heavy hand on her knee and gave her a pat. "Thanks for bringing him home."

Orinthia nodded, unsure of what to say. Her mind was on Kos. She needed to know he was okay.

"I want to put some distance between us and this place," Thrutt said. "We're going to make a jump. Take Mimi to the galley and tell her everything you know about Desidario."

The pit of her stomach lurched up. Though it was the reason they needed Mimi, Orinthia suddenly did not want to talk about her father. Everything felt more real in that moment. Before, it was abstract, an idea of finding him. But, hopefully, with Mimi's help, that would soon become a reality.

Nevertheless, Orinthia rose to her feet and led the way to the galley. She stared at the ground and did not dare look toward Kos' room. *He needs to be alone,* she told herself. *There will be time to talk to him later.*

The door to her room was also closed. She was not ready to introduce Uri to Mimi. Doing so would take almost as much courage as talking about Desidario.

Orinthia stepped into the galley and walked to the pantry. She took two hydro-spheres out and offered one to Mimi, who took it and sat on the edge of a table. They stayed silent for several minutes. Both took long sips of their drinks and stared in different directions. Orinthia tried to guess how Mimi was taking their first meeting.

"Rogue, Thrutt, and I served together in the Navy," Mimi said, setting her sphere in her lap and drummed the sides with her forefingers. "It's not much of a secret what they did to us. The EC gave us mods and reshaped us into weapons that served whatever purpose they had at the time."

"I'm a tracker," Mimi continued. "One of the mods I was given allows me to memorize anything. I'm sure someday it'll start overwriting old data, but that hasn't happened yet. New information gets run by what's already up there and it knits patterns together, seeing connections between things most people can't. So, the more details I have, the faster I can get the job done."

"What do you need to know?"

"Well, it's not a deal breaker, but do you have a picture?"

Orinthia shook her head. "Although when he went missing, my sister put together a profile for him on the net."

Mimi chewed the corner of her lip. "I'll look him up when we're done, then. Now, when was the last time you saw him?"

The last conversation Orinthia and her father had was constantly simmering below the surface of her mind. "Over two years ago, on Earth. We lived in District One of the New

Cruces Republic. During the war, he was a weapons designer for the Earth Confederacy, but continued to freelance after."

"What kind of weapons?"

"Experimental stuff," Orinthia said. She rubbed her thumbs together on the table. "Mostly mods. And Ahto."

Mimi sighed and placed her hand on her forehead. "Of course he did. That's why Ahto's looking for him, makes sense now."

"Ahto sent us to an information broker, a sequencer named Errol on Rust Rock. He told us he was on Elendoras."

A single, harsh laugh came out of Mimi. "No, he isn't. It's gone."

"I can't tell you anything other than what we were told. But Errol wasn't lying."

"You got played." Mimi swung her legs around the table and sat facing Orinthia. Her voice was firm. "I knew people who died during that battle. The Mod Bleyers blew up the planet and took multiple ships with it."

An ember burned inside Orinthia's chest. The anxiety she had moments before melted. "Ask Thrutt or Kos about it. Kos might even have kept the data chip. But I know he wasn't lying. Kos said you would find Elendoras, but if you can't, fine. I'll search every system alone if I have to."

Thrutt stepped in through the door and looked between the two women.

Orinthia realized she was on her feet and leaning over Mimi with her fists clenched. She did not wait for a response before storming out of the room. Thrutt grabbed her arm to stop her.

"Don't touch me," Orinthia shouted.

Hurt shot across his face. A wave of guilt hit Orinthia, but she did not apologize. She pulled her arm free of his grip and went to her room.

Inside, Orinthia went to Uri's bed and sat beside him on the floor. She pulled her legs close to her and rested her forehead on her knees. With a muffled yell, she wished for a way to be at the end already. To have Uri back and be past facing Desidario.

The door to her room opened, then closed again. Orinthia did not lift her head. She listened to the footsteps move closer to her.

"Hey," Kos said.

Orinthia put her chin on her knees and saw him crouched in front of her. His face was weary.

"What?" She snapped her voice.

"I'm sorry," Kos said. His words were light and breathy. "I should have been there with you to help navigate things with Mimi. But she's going to have to know everything. We can't keep your mod secret."

"At what point do I get to stop telling people?" Orinthia asked. "I've had it used against me my whole life. Can you just vouch for me?"

"Do you trust me?" Kos asked.

Orinthia lifted her head all the way. They locked eyes. The anger fizzled out of her body as her shoulders lowered. The knot in her stomach loosened. Kos had not given her a reason not to trust him. He went back for her when she was shot. He asked her to go with him to stop the *Fera* from attacking the cruise ship. They were traveling across the galaxy together to find a fix for her brother. She knew the answer without a doubt. "Yes."

"And I trust Mimi. So, take a moment to cool down, and we'll try again. I'll be there with you, but we have to give her *everything* she needs."

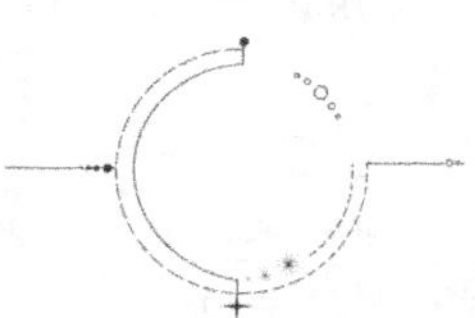

rinthia took a long time to work up the nerve to walk to the door. Even when she had, she stood with her hand hovering over the switch. It trembled. The sound of the air recycling through the vents seemed louder than usual. Even the vibration of the engine was more noticeable. Her fingers brushed against the switch and the door slid apart. "Hello?"

Mimi, Kos, and Thrutt moved from the galley into the corridor.

With a toss of her head toward her room, Orinthia stepped back and stopped in front of Uri's bed. She waited with her hands clasped in front of her. "This is Uri," she said as they joined her. "I did not do this to him. My sister, Adora, shot him three months ago when we were trying to escape the *Fera*. He's not dead. When my brother was twelve, he and my mother were crushed in an accident. My father saved his life by recreating most of his damaged body and made him into a cyborg. That is the only reason he is still alive, as much as we can call it that."

She paused and looked at each of the faces before her.

Thrutt gave her an encouraging grin. Kos held her eyes, his face was soft like he was desperate to hear every word she said. Mimi's gaze darted between Orinthia and Uri.

"Drunk with success and driven by the grief of losing my mother," Orinthia continued, "Desidario reimagined the rest of us. The twins can communicate telepathically with each other. I can decipher the truth from lies. It's never wrong. I don't care what anyone says about Elendoras, Errol was telling the truth."

The seconds after her confession dragged on. Orinthia's ears rang from her blood pressure ticking up. She concentrated on breathing normally and not giving away the fact her insides wanted to burst out of her. Another person was in on her secret, and she once again gave it up at someone else's orders.

"I need maps," Mimi said.

Kos motioned to activate his mod, but she stopped him.

"I need old maps. Prewar. There used to be a collector on Mos Kaanan. It's been a while since I've had contact with her, and the last I heard Warton Clan had taken over the system."

"Whatever we need, I'll get," Kos said. He gave a sharp nod.

Mimi leaned on her heels and squinted at Orinthia as if she were studying her worth. She tossed her eyes to Kos and gave him the same scrutinizing gaze. Whatever she saw she must have agreed with because she said, "Alright, I'm in."

Kos fanned his hand and held his arm out toward the door. Mimi stepped into the corridor, and he filed out after her.

Thrutt, however, stayed behind. He crossed his arms and gave Orinthia a warm smile. "I'm proud of you."

Weak, Orinthia all but collapsed beside Uri again. She

stretched her legs out in front of her and ran her sweaty palms over her pants. "I wish this was over."

"I know," Thrutt said. "It will be. You just have to get through it first."

Orinthia moved her hands to her face and pressed her fingers against her skin. Moisture built up around her temples and she wiped it away. She let out a long stream of air and rested her head against the wall behind her.

A question she fought to keep out of her head crept up. Part of her did not want to know the answer. She would be better off not hearing it. But a larger part knew if she did not ask, the speculation would eat her alive. "Whose divorce?"

Thrutt did not answer right away. His silence told her more than enough. "Mimi's," he said. He almost whispered it.

Orinthia met his eyes, and he did not try to avoid it. "And Kos'?" she asked.

"I told him he needed to tell you before we got to this point." Thrutt made a clicking sound in his mouth. "And I already advised you to ask him about her, too. It was six years ago. That's all I'm going to say on it." He crouched down the best he could in the tight space. "Just know I trust Mimi with my life, as much as I do you. She'd never do anything to hurt us and is as loyal as they come."

"Can't be that loyal if they got divorced," Orinthia muttered.

Thrutt made the face he gave her when she crossed the line. It was too familiar of late. "Don't judge too harshly, Thia. You've only been part of our lives for a short time and don't understand what it was like before."

Orinthia placed her head back again and sulked. She thought she knew them better. That the three of them had been open with each other. Though she knew they did not lie when they mentioned Mimi as a friend, she found it mildly disgusting they would skirt around her mod like that.

Thrutt grazed her foot and stood. "No matter what their former relationship was, it doesn't change the fact that Kos brought Mimi here to help you. Be kind to her, to both of them. Take a few minutes to feel whatever you're feeling, then join us in the cockpit so we can plan out what comes next." Without another word, Thrutt stepped out of the room and went left to find the others.

Trust her, she thought.

Orinthia leaned against the frame of the open door to her room and peered toward the cockpit. Though they were far from her, she could hear the others talking and listened closely.

"We have to remember Ahto is looking for Anton, too," Kos said. "We've already wasted months to get to this point and any more time we spend searching is more time for Ahto to get there first."

"Or come back after us," Thrutt added. "We made it out last time, but just barely. I don't think we can take too many more fights like that."

"Once we're all seen together, word will get back to him that I'm helping," Mimi said. "There's nothing stopping him from following us if he really wanted to. There are other trackers out there he could hire or kidnap and force to work for him."

Orinthia had enough of listening to them squabble. She left her spot and went to the cockpit. Thankfully, they were out of warp. A cluster of purple and pink gases swirled around the front window. Stars glinted beyond it. "He can have Desidario when we're done with him. I don't care what happens after he fixes Uri. But bickering isn't going to get us there any faster."

They turned and gawked at her.

"I don't want to fight Ahto every step of the way," Mimi said. She placed her bottom on the console and lifted herself to sit on the edge, bracing herself with a foot on Kos' captain's chair. "He's a super-processing computer wrapped in synthetic flesh. We need to figure out how to stay ahead of him."

"I will face Ahto a thousand times if it means getting Uri back," Orinthia said. She tried to keep her voice at a normal volume. "This is not the end that man deserves."

Kos took a step toward Orinthia, but she matched him and moved back. She was not ready to forgive him. His shoulders slumped.

Orinthia took a deep breath. *Trust her*, she repeated. Though Errol was not her first choice of advice givers, she knew in her heart this woman was the only way to get to Elendoras.

"You're holding all the chips, Mimi," Orinthia said. She bit down her pride and found the words to say. "This is why you were brought here. If you want to make the plan, do it. I only ask that you get us where we need to go."

Thrutt and Kos exchanged wide-eyed looks.

Mimi raised her eyebrows and pressed her lips into a thin line. "We start at Mos Kaanan, then. I need to see when Elendoras was last shown on a map. I also know someone who was at the battle. We'll have to talk to him, too. If your mod is as good as you say it is, you'll be able to tell me if he's telling the truth."

Orinthia nodded in agreement. "Fine."

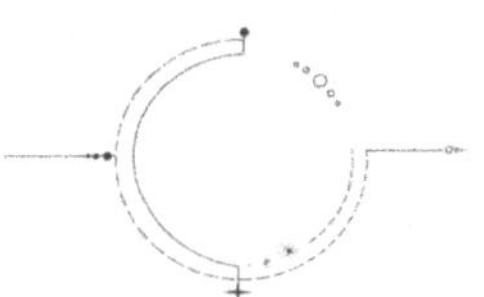

21

The top deck was quiet. Orinthia sat alone reclined back in one of the seats. In the months she spent on *Freya*, she had yet to find an easy way to pass the time. And with Mimi invading her quarters, there were few places for her to hide.

She skipped both mealtimes following her secret revelation. Her stomach growled. Grabbing something to eat from the galley would have been easy. It was the thought of running into the others that kept her in her seat. She was embarrassed from letting her temper flare. Upset from being forced to expose herself. And to top it all, the conversation with Thrutt ran through her mind on repeat.

"Thia?" Kos called out to her from the top of the ladder.

Orinthia did not answer and kept her eyes fixed on a spot on the ceiling.

Kos walked softly to her and stopped by the empty seat next to her. From the corner of her eye, she could see he held something in his hands. "I brought you something to eat," he said. "You've been up here a while and I thought you might be hungry."

"I'm not," she lied. Her eyes strained and she no longer saw the ceiling. She was intent on not looking at him.

"Please," Kos said. His voice was low, like he had been wounded and it was hard to speak. "Don't shut me out. I'm sorry for raising my weapon to you. If I could take it back, I would."

His words were shocking enough to force her to face him. He looked as hurt as he sounded. Their time on Sarv'on was already a distant memory to Orinthia.

"Kos, that wasn't you," she said. The back of the seat popped up as she straightened herself. "I've already forgotten about it."

Some light returned to his eyes, and the wound changed to confusion. "Then what is this?" He gestured in a wide circle toward Orinthia.

"Your wife."

Kos sighed and sat in the empty seat. "My ex-wife."

"Your relationship isn't the issue," Orinthia said. "It's the dishonesty that hurts the most. You and Thrutt found a way to lie to me without me knowing. That's what Arsenio and Adora would do."

"Mimi was never more than my friend," Kos said. He pressed the heels of his palms to his forehead, still holding the food. "Yes, we didn't give you the whole truth, but I didn't lie. We met during training. The Navy doesn't only hold your debt for deserters like my dad. They also do it if you're injured beyond repair and can no longer serve. Your time still gets passed down to the next of kin. Mimi's older brother was like that, and Mimi had to take on his debt."

"So, her and I made a deal," Kos continued. He set his hands in his lap and stared at the headrest of the seat in front of him. "But it only worked if we were married. To keep her sisters from being swept up, and my aunt out of another lifetime of debt, we became each other's next of kin. That way if anything happened to either of us, we could take on the extra service."

A new anger burned in Orinthia's chest. It was no longer directed toward Kos, but toward the EC. As a Hunter, there was always a possibility of getting hurt or killed. It rarely happened, but when it did, no one was forced to serve in their place. Kos was not just part of the war; he was a victim of it.

"Kos," Orinthia said. "I'm sorry." She wished she knew a stronger word. It did not cover the extent of what she felt. Sorry for what the Navy did to him. Sorry for the terrible things in his life. Sorry for her harshness toward him. And sorry for making him, even for a moment, relive a time he was desperate to forget.

"I am, too," Kos said. He met her gaze and bit his bottom lip a few times before speaking again. "You're right. I should have told you about Mimi, especially since I made you give up your secret."

Orinthia's nerves went electric at the way he stared at her. She could feel the air move in and out of her lungs. Something else was in his eyes — the longing she felt toward him. Neither of them had the capacity for more than stolen moments, she knew that. Perhaps there would come a time to sort out whatever it was between them.

"I brought Mimi aboard purely to help you," Kos said. "Please don't be upset with her over this. She had no information when she agreed to help us. Honestly, she knew less about the situation than you did about her."

"Don't lie to me again," Orinthia said. It was not a threat, but a plea.

"I won't."

BACK IN THE ROOM, Orinthia found Mimi sitting on the bed Thrutt had chosen for her. Sheets draped over the sides of the top bunk and created homemade curtains. They were pulled back and tied to the posts with lavender ribbons. Mimi looked at home, like she had spent a long time living in cramped quarters. She glanced up from her PortTab at Orinthia, gave her a short eyebrow twitch, then went back to watching the screen.

Orinthia brushed her fingers against Uri's hair as she walked to her own bed. The springs creaked as she tossed herself onto the mattress and stared at the underside of the bunk above her.

The air was different in the room. Not in smell, but in the atmosphere. Like it had less space to move with the extra person and her things.

"How did you manage to get wrapped up in all of this?" Mimi asked. "This is a far fall from marauder hunting, especially for an Anton."

Orinthia rolled to her side and faced her newest roommate. Mimi had her PortTab beside her with her legs folded. She leaned forward and placed her weight on her elbows.

"I wasn't a very good one," Orinthia said. For Kos' sake, she decided to give Mimi a chance. "I broke more of Adora's rules than she liked. Thrutt found me, offered me a job, and here we are."

"Our paths crossed once, mine and Adora's," Mimi said. She leaned back and braced herself with her hands behind her. "It was during the early days of the GMH. We came upon the same mark. Although I got to him first, she pulled some

GMH code and stole him, along with my bounty. Three weeks of tracking dusted."

"That sounds like her," Orinthia replied. "She waits until all the hard work is done before she swoops in and takes the credit."

"If she doesn't get her hands dirty, how'd she get the scar?"

Orinthia smiled. "Not hunting."

For the first time since they had met, Mimi let out a chest full of laughter. It filled the room and made it less suffocating. "Man, what did she do to deserve that?"

The question made Orinthia's smile fade. She had told Kos and Thrutt about her fighting days but was not keen about sharing another secret with Mimi. Eager to change the subject, she asked, "What about your leg?"

Taking the hint, Mimi stretched out her left leg and wiggled it. "Landmine. I was leading a small team on a search for a Mod Bleyer settlement. Lost half my people and my leg."

She took a pause and closed her eyes. After several long breaths, she returned to her story. "The Navy, being the opportunistic parasites they are, used it to their advantage. They took leftover Irelad material and fused this old girl to my body."

Mimi lifted her hand, splayed her fingers open, and flicked her wrist. In one swift motion, starting at the back of her hand, her slender tawny body shifted to a masculine and olive-toned figure. The woman no longer sat in front of Orinthia, but instead, a wrinkly-faced man grinned at her.

"I only have to come in physical contact with someone once," the old man said. Their voice cracked and the creases on his skin opened and closed as their mouth moved. "The nanites don't take more than a few seconds to register DNA and replicate it over mine." The old man twisted their hand again and Mimi transformed back to herself.

Orinthia shot up in her bed and stared, mouth half open. She was equal parts horrified and impressed.

"It's similar to Rogue's armor, but way more sophisticated," Mimi continued. She set her hand back behind her and continued talking like nothing happened. "His nanites form a shield around his body. Mine completely change the structure. On every level, except neurologically, I am that person. Though it gets tricky crossing species. The closer the person is related to humans, the easier it is."

"I don't have anything as unique as that," Orinthia said. "My dad tried to convince me to take in another mod he was working on. That's what we fought about when I last saw him. He doesn't like to be refused. I also used to have two arm blades, but one snapped when we were escaping the *Fera*. Actually, it was part of the reason we had to escape."

Mimi tilted her head and studied Orinthia again. "How did you get him to leave?"

Orinthia lowered her eyes and looked at Mimi's bedsheet. She told the abridged version of their escape. How Ahto ordered the attack on a civilian ship, but Kos refused to go along with it. She and Kos attempted to warn the ship, and when their warnings were ignored, they had to manually disable the cannons themselves. She only briefly mentioned Neve's part in the story, however. Neve was always there, never leaving the shadows and stationed in the recess of Orinthia's mind.

"I tried to get him to leave a few times," Mimi said when Orinthia was finished. "To be honest, I was surprised when he contacted me. We haven't spoken in four years. Mostly because I didn't agree with his devotion to that snake. I'm glad he's found a reason to be normal again."

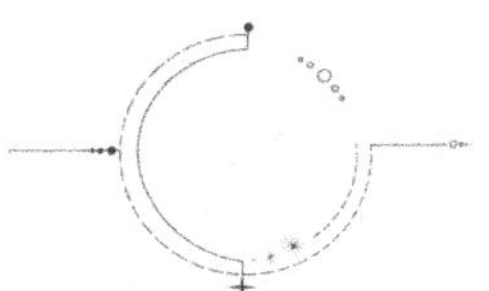

$\mathcal{M}$imi and Orinthia continued to swap stories for the following hour. The comfort level in the room grew from uneasy to enjoyable. They were both laughing by the time Kos called over the speakers.

"We're dropping out of warp," Kos announced.

Taking her PortTab with her, Mimi slid out of bed and made for the cockpit. Orinthia waited a few more minutes to be sure they were out of warp before following her. She slung her credit satchel across her body and hurried to join everyone upfront.

The sun was on the opposite side of the planet from where *Freya* waited in her holding pattern. This served only to enhance the spectacle of Mos Kaanan's surface. Trillions of lights covered most of the planet. It was easier to count the dim areas than those which were lit.

"I've done some research," Mimi said when they were together. She set down her PortTab on *Freya's* console and tapped the screen. The middle of the large window mirrored her tablet. "This whole sector is controlled by the Warton Clan. We need to go here—" the image zoomed in "—to

Caytoo, the capital. It's a major shipping port, and from what I can see on the social nets, my friend is still there."

"How well do you know this friend?" Thrutt asked.

Mimi popped her lips. "A bit. She hired me to find and retrieve EC data disks her partner stole from her a few years ago."

"So, she's a client?" Thrutt rolled his eyes. "Can we trust her?"

"Look, unless we want to waste more time to find a more reputable source, she's the only broker I know who collects prewar maps. The EC has archives, but in case you forgot, she's wanted and he has several bounties on his head. You'd all draw too much attention."

Kos stepped from his spot by the console. "We're here now. If this friend—" he gave Mimi a side look "—doesn't have the information, we'll have to risk the archives."

Thrutt opened his mouth to speak. Kos held a finger to him as if threatening him to keep his comments to himself.

"Right now is the best chance we have," Orinthia said. "We're closer than we've been since we left the *Fera*. I'm tired of waiting to move forward."

"See?" Mimi clapped her hands together and rotated in a semi-circle. "That's taken care of, then. We better get down there before we jam up the lane."

"Freya, take us down to Caytoo," Kos ordered.

"Of course, captain," Freya replied. "I'm so glad to be included in this conversation."

Kos rubbed his eyebrow and lowered his head.

"We better get up top and buckle in," Thrutt said to Orinthia.

Mimi stayed behind in the cockpit while Orinthia and Thrutt ascended the ladder a few seconds later. They were strapped down by the time the windows snapped shut.

"You okay?" Thrutt asked, patting Orinthia's knee.

Orinthia examined the fracture on his knuckles. The memory of him rescuing her and Kos from the cell on the *Fera* crossed her mind. "There is no way I can repay all that the three of you are doing."

"Hey," Thrutt said. He leaned forward to get a better view of her face. "We're your friends. This is what people who care about each other do. You don't repay friendship. You build onto, make sacrifices for, and share it."

"My life has been a constant give," Orinthia said with tears building in her eyes. She was determined to keep them back but could not help the tightness in her throat.

Thrutt gave her one of his gentle smiles. The kind that made her feel warm and welcome. It was her favorite smile. "I know. As long as we're around, you'll never have to fight like that again. I can never replace my daughters, but you and Kos are the closest I have to being a father again. There is nothing I wouldn't do for you two."

The tears trickled through her defenses. "Thank you for rescuing me in that bar."

Thrutt grinned. "And I'd do it all over again if I had to. Now, dry your eyes. You have another new planet to see."

The ship around them rocked and jostled as it came to a stop. At the edge of the hold, the door hissed, and the ramp lowered. An orange glow shone in and illuminated the entrance.

Mimi was the first to emerge from the lower deck. She moved to the ramp and stood looking out with her hands on her hips. Her metal leg reflected the light.

The other three joined her and viewed the surroundings. Orinthia was used to megacities, formerly living in one herself. But Caytoo was on a different scale. Everything was twice as big as New Cruces. The buildings were so tall that their tops were lost in the darkness.

Hundreds of people, human and non-human, crowded the streets beyond the harbor. Droids of every size and color rolled in all directions between the bustling hoards. Speeder bikes lifted off the ground and rose to the sky traffic, joining the stream of hover cars.

The crew exited the ship, sealing it behind them. They walked for twenty minutes, turning down streets and alleys. The farther in they went, the emptier the streets became. Mimi led the way as if she had come to Caytoo every weekend. She stopped in front of a shorter building. The storefront had large glass windows half covered from the inside by maroon sheets. Piles of goods were displayed between the curtains and glass, enticing visitors to come in and check out the wares.

Orinthia's eyes scanned around the cluttered room as they walked in. Paintings hung on the walls. Shelves held up boxes of trinkets and gems. Crates of unknown tech sat along the floor. The air was clean, or as clean as it could be for filtered. It had a tangy smell to it that reminded Orinthia of the air on *Freya*.

A tall, thin human woman stepped out from a back room. Her white hair sat in a curly bun above her head. "Mimi Nakahara," the woman greeted. Her voice was deep and raspy. "It's been a while. What brings you all the way to my part of the galaxy?"

"Vandra, these are friends of mine," Mimi said with a quarter turn and gestured toward the group behind her. "We're looking for hard-to-come-by information, and I could not think of anyone better than you."

Vandra smiled a greedy, toothy grin. She looked at them

as if she were counting the credits she had won at a card table. "What do you need?"

"Prewar maps," Mimi said. "There are faint rumors that Elendoras still stands. We heard they fabricated its destruction to cover the shady stuff the EC was doing. There's supposed to be a lot of leftover material there. A score like that would keep these guys in business for a long time."

Orinthia's head hummed as Mimi spoke.

Vandra studied each of their faces. "Scavengers?"

It was Kos' turn to speak. "Just vets looking for work."

The woman continued to study them from behind her glass counter. Orinthia could hear the filtered air blow in the silence.

"Information like that isn't cheap," Vandra said, crossing her arms. "More than scrappers can afford."

"How about a trade then?" Kos offered. "We do a job for you, and you give us the maps."

The grin on Vandra's tight face widened. "You do a job for me, and I *show* you the maps."

Kos and Thrutt exchanged looks for a second, moving their heads slightly as if speaking in some unknown signals.

"Deal," Kos said, addressing Vandra again. "But we get as much time with them as we need."

"I can abide by those terms." Vandra bent down behind the counter and dug through something in one of the cabinets. There were several beeps followed by a clicking sound. She stood up and placed a black data disk on the glass. "I bought this from a couple of idiots a few weeks ago. They had no idea what it a gem they had."

"Those are Mod Bleyer symbols," Mimi said. She stepped closer and reached for the disk.

Vandra snapped it back. "That much I can make out, that's

why I bought it. But the data is encrypted. There are a few abandoned Mod Bleyer facilities in the neighboring systems. Get me the information from the disk, and I'll get you the maps."

Orinthia watched Kos through the side of her eye. She could see him breaking down the details and working out what to do. "Agreed," Kos said.

Mimi reached for the disk again. "We'll be back in a few days."

"Not so fast." Vandra wagged a finger and pulled the disk closer to her chest. "There is nothing stopping you from taking my disk and selling it yourselves. One of you has to stay behind as collateral."

"I'll stay," Thrutt said before anyone could object to Vandra.

"Nice try," Vandra said. She made a face as if someone had told her a bad joke. "You could overpower me in a heartbeat. No, I'm keeping that one."

Every eye fell on Orinthia.

"No," Kos said. "The deal is off."

Mimi held up her hands and stepped between Kos and the counter. "Give us a minute to talk about it." She pulled Kos to the door and the others followed.

"She's not staying," Kos said.

"I can stay in her place." Mimi rolled up Orinthia's sleeve and wrapped her fingers around her wrist.

"Then there would be two of me and no you," Orinthia said, yanking her arm back from Mimi.

"If we all go outside, I can change into you. Then Thrutt can walk me back and she won't know."

Orinthia thought through the plan. She did not want to stay, especially when they were doing this job for her. But Mimi's skills were more necessary than Orinthia's. "I'm staying."

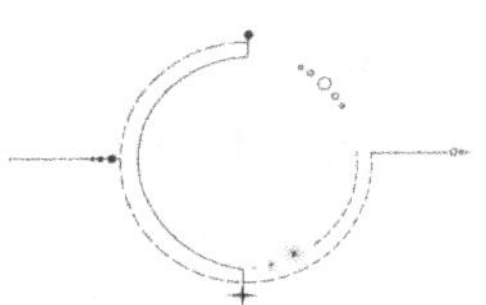

23

The realization of her decision had not fully set in until Mimi and Thrutt said their goodbyes. Thrutt held Orinthia in a long hug and begged her to change her mind. When he released her, he looked as if he would cry, if stones were capable of producing tears.

"It's only for a short while," Orinthia said, though she was not exactly sure how long *awhile* meant. It was just as much reassurance to him as it was for herself. "Take care of Uri for me, okay? I didn't get a chance to say goodbye."

Thrutt nodded. "Don't do anything you would do, got it?"

"That's probably the best advice you've given me so far." Orinthia chuckled.

Mimi shoved him out the door. "She'll be fine. Let's go."

Vandra, Kos, and Orinthia were the only ones left inside the store. The woman leaned against the glass and eyed the pair at the front.

Kos reached into his pocket and retrieved his comm. "Take this. I'll check in often. If anything happens, call me immediately. Leaving you doesn't feel right." He ran his bottom lip between his teeth a few times. The look he gave her after he confessed about his marriage painted his face once again. A mixture of hesitation and desire.

The loaded weight of his gaze made Orinthia's hands shake as she took the comm and tucked it into her coat.

He tipped her chin up with a curved finger and made her look him in the eye. "Please, be careful. I'll be back as quick as I can."

"You always come back for me. I'm not worried." The spot where his finger touched ached, but she did not pull away. She wanted him to stay there for as long as he could.

Vandra had other ideas. "My disk isn't going to decrypt itself. Kiss her goodbye and get out of here."

Kos' cheeks flushed red. He released Orinthia and turned to face Vandra. "If anything happens to her—"

"Threaten me all you want." Vandra cut him off with a wave of her hand. "Get the job done and she'll be fine."

"You have to go," Orinthia said, gently nudging Kos away with a push of her hand.

Kos gave her one last look, then without a word, walked out the door.

The shop was larger with everyone else gone. It was louder, as well. A few bugs tapped against the lights on the ceiling. Electricity hummed from behind the walls. Vandra rapped her nails against the counter.

"Come here," Vandra called out. She moved around the counter and met Orinthia. Without warning, she pressed a device against Orinthia's bicep. It hissed and stabbed something into her skin.

Hot anger rushed through Orinthia. She shoved the woman away, lifted her sword arm to her chest, and swung. There were inches between Vandra and the tip of Orinthia's blade. "What was that?"

"Don't be so dramatic," Vandra said. "It was only a

locator to keep tabs on you and make sure you don't run off. I don't have the patience to keep you alive as a prisoner. The chip will dissolve in a week."

Orinthia glared at the woman. The injection spot stung, but no more than getting a splinter. An image of Vandra stuck to the end of her sword flashed across her mind. It quickly vanished as her heart seized in her chest. Orinthia did not know what frightened her more; the thought, or the fact that she wanted to do it.

"The back room is yours to stay in," Vandra continued, oblivious to the vision Orinthia had of her a moment before. "But don't talk to anyone who comes in. In fact, stay out of the way altogether when I have customers."

Orinthia composed herself and rolled her eyes. "So, you're forcing me to stay here, but you don't want me around?" She threw her arm up and recalled the blade.

"You're collateral. Doesn't mean I have to look at you. Come and go whenever you like. That chip will let you back in if I've closed up for the night. Just don't go into the room on the far end. That's my room."

"Anything else?" Orinthia stepped back and made a mock bow.

"Stay out of the Plo district. The Warton Clan runs dealings through there and I don't need to get wrapped up with them. And feed yourself. I'm not running an inn."

"No, you're running a hostage situation."

Vandra narrowed her eyes and shook her head. "Yeah, yeah. When this is over, we'll both get what we want, and you'll be free to go back with your boyfriend. Now, make yourself scarce before you run off any customers."

Orinthia did not wait to be told twice. Ignoring Vandra's comment about Kos, she walked out the door and back into the alley. The sporadic yellow lights lit up only part of the street. A breeze blew in between the buildings and Orinthia felt a chill pass over her.

For a moment, she wondered if she could catch up to her friends, but realized she was not confident in the way she came. A group of people exited a conjoining alley to the left. Wishing to avoid them, Orinthia took a right. She walked for over two miles, or at least she assumed, before the space widened and dumped into a street.

The lights above flicked and blinked in bright colors. Signs flashed advertisements and business names, none of which she cared to read. Hover car vibrations bounced off the walls. It did nothing to drown out the shouting and laughing of the people around her, however.

Orinthia stayed in the shadows and inspected her surroundings. Her home, District One of The New Cruces Republic, was named so because more than four hundred years before, it was the first city to establish itself in commercial space travel. Even with that as its legacy, its streets had never seen the diversity of Caytoo. More than half the people were of unknown species to Orinthia.

To top it off, the more she watched, the more differences she discovered. On Earth, most people covered their mods and treated them as implants. Almost everyone before her wore them as accessories. It was difficult to find someone who did not have some type of outward modification. And though the EC had outlawed weaponized mods, this lot was not shy about them. She wondered how close to the edge of the EC territory they had gone.

Orinthia looked down at her hand. *I could probably get this fixed,* she thought. With renewed interest, she turned her attention to the signage above the storefronts along the street. Limited to only her native written language, she was unable to read a lot of the names. Eventually, halfway down the row, she found one she could understand.

As Orinthia entered the shop, she noticed a large woman sitting on a tiny metal stool next to a cot. She did not look up from her PortTab when Orinthia walked in. With a puff of smoke flowing from her mouth, she asked, "What you need?"

Orinthia studied the inside. It was stale, but clean. The air was not recycled or even filtered like in Vandra's. A single red light hung above the cot that lit up the room, which barely reached where Orinthia stood. Her eyes fell on the woman. The left side of her body, from her shoulder to her torso, was replaced with machinery. Her arm was a configuration of rods, pipes, wires, and countless sharp objects.

"This ain't a museum," the woman said with a gruff voice. She pressed the PortTab to her buxom chest and tossed her chin to Orinthia. "If you aren't looking to get work done, get out."

"Do you do repairs?" Orinthia spoke up.

"Depends." The woman shifted in her seat. She set her tablet on the cot and squinted at Orinthia. "What'cha need repairing?"

With a quick swing, Orinthia activated both arms. The silver sword looked eerie in the red glow, but the other arm was gone from the elbow down. "Lost this one a few months ago. Broke off."

The woman stood and hobbled toward Orinthia. She took the sword arm in her hand and turned it over, examining the metal. "What's it made of?"

"Martian steel."

The woman scoffed. "No wonder it broke. That's EC regulation. What you need is Tullian metal. It's mined in the deepest part of Tullia's ocean. Won't find much stronger than that, at least not outside the black market."

Orinthia recalled her blades. Her heart sank. *Something that good is going soak me*, she thought. "How much?"

"Very rare," the woman said, hobbling back to her seat. "But it just so happens I have some pickings left over. Only enough for the one, though."

"Price?" Orinthia repeated.

"Thousand credits."

The credits in her satchel hung heavy. She had enough, but just barely. *They'll be back before I need more*, Orinthia thought. "How long will it take?"

The woman scooped up the PortTab and patted the cot. "How long you got?"

24

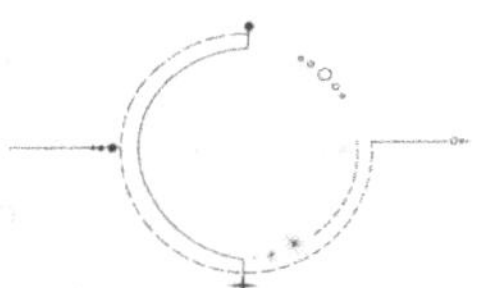

The first step of recreating Orinthia's sword was forging the blade itself. In the back corner of the room sat a waist-high solid stone workbench. It was three feet wide and had glowing blue liquid in the center. Orinthia followed the woman and leaned forward for a better look.

"Better keep your space to yourself," the woman said, placing her fleshy arm between Orinthia and the bench. "That fire is meant to liquefy ore. It'll melt your skin right off before you even know what happened."

Orinthia stepped back and watched the woman work from several feet away.

Into a tall steel canister, the woman dumped in pieces of onyx-colored balls. They were the size of children's marbles and clacked together with the same sound. After it, she poured grey sand of some type and knocked the canister against the workbench, adding more sand each time. Her arm flipped once revealing a torch with a thin line of blue flame. She placed a square lid on the top of the canister and sealed it with the torch.

With a set of clamps, the woman set the canister inside

the flame and held it in place for a few minutes. It glowed orange, then red, and finally when it was blinding white, the woman removed it from the heat. She set it on the stone, flicked her wrist, and hammered the molten canister with the second tool that protruded from her wrist.

She continued the pattern for an hour until the canister was no longer a blocky object, but a slender and ragged bar. It was another two hours before the bar resembled a blade and the woman was satisfied with her craftsmanship. She set it in the liquid one more time until once again the metal was hot. Swifter than Orinthia had seen anyone move, the smith plunged the hot blade into another container. Steam rose and sparks flew out of the top. The woman pulled it from the quench and quickly set to polishing it.

"How often do you sharpen your blade?" The woman asked, leading Orinthia back to the cot when the metal finally looked like a blade.

Orinthia, who had stopped giving all her attention by the time the woman had mashed out the bar, thought about the question. "I don't think I've ever sharpened it."

The woman grumbled. "Well, you better start. I'm not doing all this work for you to not keep up with it." She waved Orinthia to sit back down and set the black blade on a table beside the cot.

It took another few minutes, but the woman moved from the cot to the back of the room and returned with a panel. She plugged in the wires coming from her arm and sat on her stool. Dials and gears moved inside the mechanical arm. She flicked her wrist again and the metal hand spun from five fingers to a single, thin barrel.

"Call up your mod," the woman instructed.

Orinthia obeyed with a quick swing. It was odd to see nothing in its place, though she had done it a short time before. She had kept it as her normal arm since she lost it on the *Fera*, when the blade broke off in Neve's back. Neve, who stood over Kos, ready to strike him. She remembered the sparks that rushed through her veins as she plunged the blade into the marauder and the horror of watching the metal snap from its place. And Kos' voice telling her not to let it in.

The thought had gone on too long, and Orinthia forced Neve back into the shadows where she belonged. Once her mind was clear, she discovered she missed the reconnecting process.

"Better than any Martian steel, I'll tell you what," the woman said. She leaned back on her stool and examined her work with a grin. "How does it feel?"

Orinthia lifted her arm and moved it around. It was lighter than the original. The red light did not reflect off its matte surface, either. "Move back," she told the woman. With a swish, the blade returned to a normal hand. Everything felt the same, no pain, or any noticeable changes.

"You better stock up on some more Tullian steel," Orinthia said with a smile. "I'm coming back to get this other one replaced."

The woman gave a satisfied humph and tipped her head. "Come back with the credits, and I'll fix you up with whatever you want."

Orinthia thanked the woman and left the shop with her credit satchel a lot lighter. But her body was whole again. She would be a better fighter, and better able to protect her friends.

The sun was rising by the time Orinthia arrived on the street. Light did not fully reach the lower levels where she stood, but it cast enough to chase away shadows. The air was cool, and though it smelled like fumes from the various vehicles, it was comforting.

Fewer people filled the street as well. Small bunches of groups roamed together. Hardly the hoards of the night. Looking for the way she came, Orinthia realized everything was different during the day.

Each building led to an alley, with hundreds more connecting through them. None of them had distinct features to lead Orinthia back to Vandra's. The nerves on her shoulders tingled. It was not panic, at least not yet, but anxiety that made her choose the closest alley.

The path was narrow, like the one she had taken to get to the main road, but Orinthia assumed each of the alleys were. She looked for any sign that would trigger a memory. There were none.

Someone stepped from a side alley and blocked her path. Orinthia halted and examined the person. It was as tall as a child, but that's where the similarities ended. The creature was covered in curly auburn fur from its forehead down. Tufts stuck out of the baggy clothes it wore. Its skull, however, was clear, exposing the brain for all to see. And a bundle of wires ran from its nape to its shoulders.

"Where are you going in a hurry?" The creature asked. Its voice was raspy and took in gulps of air every few words. "Looking for some cheap mods?"

"No, I'm not." Orinthia tried to step around whoever this was.

"Come on, I got some great deals." The creature lifted the sides of its coat. Data chips, wires, implants, and even a few mechanical limbs hung from the fabric. "Best secondhand mods you'll find in this district."

Orinthia glared at the creature and tried to stand to her full height. "I'm not interested. Get out of my way."

The creature's face contorted. Two small fangs appeared from behind its lips. "You one of them no-mods?" He spit on the ground, almost nailing one of Orinthia's boots. "There is nothing special about you because you're not like everyone else. Think you're so pure? Holy, even?"

Orinthia thought about calling her new sword. She put her hand to her chest and waited for the opportunity to release it.

"Leave her alone," a second person said from the alley the creature had come out of. A man with a knee-length black coat stepped into view. He looked down his nose at the alien and pushed his coat from his hip. A single black revolving blaster hung holstered. "Take your trash somewhere else."

The hairy creature snatched its coat closed and ducked into the shadows, dashing to find cover.

Without saying anything to the man, Orinthia pressed on her way, faster than she had gone before.

"Whoa, where are you going?" The man called to her.

Orinthia ignored him and kept her arm on her chest.

A rushing sound came from behind her, and before she could look back, the man flew overhead and landed in front of her. Orinthia stopped and stared at the man more clearly in the rapidly brightening alley.

His coat was made of leather, worn and tattered at the seams. He had a faint orange tint to his skin, and it made his chin-length yellow platinum hair brighter. An etched metal patch covered his right eye. His animal skin boots had a slight heel and lifted him two inches taller than Orinthia.

"Celso." The man held out a gloved hand.

Orinthia lifted her chin and gave him the coldest stare she could muster. She did not take his hand, nor reply.

"Come on," Celso said. He tilted his head and grinned. "I can't get a name?"

"No, you can't," Orinthia said. "I need to get back to my ship."

"Well, you're heading in the wrong direction," Celso said. "I can take you to the docks if you'd like."

"I would not like that." Orinthia tried to step around him, but he matched her movements and blocked her way.

"You sure? Warton Clan runs this part of town. Don't say I didn't warn you when you get caught up with them." Celso winked at her.

The pit of her stomach lurched. She did not have enough room between the two for her to toss out her arm. *I need to get a gun from Thrutt,* she thought. With each step she moved back he continued to follow. "You're the only problem I have right now. I'd rather take my chances with them."

"Okay, I give up. I'll see you around, then." Celso thrust his hand out and took her fist. Before she could stop him, he kissed the back of her hand and winked. In one leap, he flew over her. His jets spouted blue flames as he moved over the alley. He turned to face her as he cut through the air backwards and blew a kiss.

Orinthia yelled every curse word she knew at him. Part of her wanted to give chase, but instead, she waited until he was out of sight before lowering her arm. She unclenched her fist to see her fingernails had left dents in her palm. Hot pokers pressed through her nerves and pushed her forward with haste.

It was purely by luck that after twenty or so turns, Vandra's shop appeared before her. The cool feeling of relief washed over her as she stepped into the filtered air.

"Got lost, huh?" Vandra asked as Orinthia walked in. "I told you to stay out of Plo district."

"Were you watching me?"

"You weren't back when I got up," Vandra said with a shrug. "So, I did a little check."

"Thanks for being concerned enough to come find me,"

Orinthia said. She moved from the door to the back of the shop where Vandra had assigned her a place to sleep.

"I have someone coming by in an hour to look at some items," Vandra said, following her through the curtains. "Make sure you stay in here until they're gone."

Orinthia did not respond. She had no plans, nor the funds, to leave the room again. Though her encounters had not affected her enough to be frightened, she did not want to draw any more undue attention. Kos would not be happy if a bounty hunter snatched her while he was gone.

Vandra scoffed at Orinthia's disinterest and left the small room. It was not as much of a room as she had made it out to be. More like a storage closet. A thin mattress with a faded, thin sheet laid on top of a pile of boxes. As Orinthia unzipped her boots, she vaguely wondered if Vandra made it a habit of keeping strangers in her back room.

The bed was stiff and barely had enough padding to be called a mattress. Someone who avoided bathing must have used it last. A puff of body odor lifted when Orinthia laid herself down. The corners of the boxes dug into her back and sides as she rotated to find a suitable position. It took more tries than she liked, but finally, the discomfort was bearable. Her stomach growled. She ignored it and forced herself to sleep.

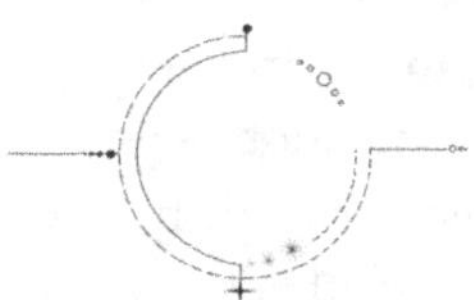

25

*O*rinthia swatted the air in an attempt to silence the constant beeping somewhere to her right. In her haze, she reached farther out than the makeshift bed allowed and fell with a thud to the ground. She groaned and opened an eye. A red light flashed from between her boots.

"Hello?" Her voice was dry, and she cleared her throat a few times.

"Thia, finally," Kos said on the other end. Though the sound came from a tiny device, the tension in his words was clear. "I've been trying to reach you all day."

There were no windows in the room, nor any type of clock. Orinthia did not know how long she was out for, but guessed it was more than a nap. "Sorry, I was asleep."

Kos did not respond. The comm continued to blink indicating the line was still connected. "Kos?" she asked.

"We came out of warp a bit ago," Kos said. He paused like he was distracted by something on his end. "Mimi knows of a facility we're going to check out. It should be done by the end of the day."

"Oh, that was fast." The possibility of being with her

friends again served to wake her up enough to realize she was still lying on the floor. She shifted to her side and pulled herself into a seated position.

"I don't want to leave you there any longer than I have to."

"Everything is fine," Orinthia said. "I have a bed and even went out for a walk earlier."

"Did you eat?" Kos asked.

Orinthia rubbed her eyebrow and scrunched up her face. "A while ago."

"Define a while."

"How long have you been gone?"

"You have to eat," Kos shouted. A bit of rushing air blowing over the speaker told Orinthia he was taking in a few calming breaths. "Did you take credits?"

"I did." Orinthia raised her hand and rotated it in the air. "But I got my sword replaced. Custom Tullian steel blade. It's beautiful."

"Please, get some food and stay put. Don't go exploring anymore, and don't talk to anyone else."

"Careful, Kos. Your Thrutt is showing." Orinthia teased.

Kos made a noise. Orinthia pictured his face, a mixture of annoyance and surrender. "Sometimes he is right." There was a drumming sound from his end of the line. "I have to go. They're waiting to make a landing. I just wanted to make sure you're okay. Please, stay put. I I—" he stumbled over his words, "—I'll call you when we're on our way back."

"See you soon. Please be safe." She tried to lay as much care into her voice as possible.

For a few seconds longer the light blinked then switched off. Orinthia closed the circular device and set it beside her boots. She smiled to herself and spun her thumbs in circles around each other. Her heart fluttered and her cheeks warmed. *He called to see if I was okay,* she thought. *Not because he needed something from me, but to hear my voice. I think can get used to that.*

The door to Vandra's shop slammed shut, drawing Orinthia's attention from her thoughts. She moved to her hands, crawled to the curtain, and stuck out her head. As she approached, she could hear Vandra shout, "I said get out."

A pair of rough-looking people stood at the counter. The one closest to Vandra was almost as tall and wide as Thrutt. He had a blaster rifle slung across his chest. The vest he wore was unbuttoned exposing his bare and sandy-brown scaly skin.

His partner was a humanoid female with thin lines carved into her skin. They stemmed in multiple directions from her temple and ended beneath her shirt. She crossed one arm under the other and licked her pointed teeth in a sinister grin.

"I'm a collector," Vandra said. "Nothing I have will be of interest to whoever you'd try to pedal it off to."

"We're getting paid to shake you down," the tall man said. His voice had a hiss to it. "That's what I'm going to do. So, either you show us what you got, or we'll take a look for ourselves."

Orinthia climbed to her feet and faced the duo. In a fluid motion, she lifted her newly repaired arm and thrust out the black blade. "We're closed for the day."

The first intruder raised his rifle and fired. A blaster bolt whizzed by Orinthia's head. Vandra screamed and threw herself onto the floor behind the counter. Orinthia darted forward and placed her normal hand on the glass. With a shove, she hoisted herself over and slid across the top.

Rifle blasters were terrible for close-quarter fights, and the scaly attacker must have been new to using them. It took longer than it should have to retrain the weapon on Orinthia.

By the time he had, Orinthia slashed up. In bright sparks, the rifle split in half.

The owner hollered and swung a heavy fist at Orinthia's face. Orinthia moved enough to dodge the full force, but he grazed her shoulder and knocked her back a step.

Seeing the opportunity, the woman lunged forward and grabbed Orinthia by her unchanged arm. An electric current coursed through her body. It seized her muscles and not even a scream escaped her mouth. Every atom in her body threatened to ignite. The room had no sound, no air, no matter at all. Dark circles grew around Orinthia's vision.

Then the pain stopped. Orinthia breathed heavily on the ground, her head resting on the thread-worn carpet. As her vision cleared, she noticed a splotch of orange growing in front of her. She followed a line up the scaly man's leg and saw him holding his calve.

"Get out before I aim higher," a familiar voice said.

For a second, Orinthia thought it belonged to Kos, but when she looked past the attackers, she realized she was wrong.

Celso held his revolving blaster out with the hammer cocked, ready to send more rounds if his orders were not heeded. The female took a step forward. Celso fired into her hand. A pink mist flew from the wound and painted her shirt with spots.

He retrained his sights on the man and shot a second round into his thigh. "Your friend is going to bleed out if you don't get him help."

The woman cradled her arm to her chest and hooked the other around her partner's shoulder. A trail of orange followed them as they hurried to the exit.

Celso followed them with his blaster ready and did not lower it until they could no longer be seen through the storefront's window. He placed his weapon into the holster at his hip and approached Orinthia.

Orinthia had gotten to her feet before he could offer his hand and she leaned her back against the glass cabinet.

"Are they gone?" Vandra whimpered from her hiding spot. She rose with trembling limbs and held her hands over her face.

"You okay?" Celso asked, ignoring Vandra's question.

Orinthia flexed her hands. The muscles where the woman had electrocuted her arm ached, but she did not have residual pain. "Yeah."

"I thought you were going to your ship?" Celso asked, with a smirk. He leaned on his leg and crossed his arms. The air about him clashed with the scene of broken glass and puddles of blood.

"I thought you could take a hint," Orinthia said. "What are you doing here?"

"There's been a robbery," Vandra said.

The statement struck Orinthia odd. Everyone in the room was aware of what happened. She looked over her shoulder to see Vandra was not addressing them but speaking into a silver comm relay.

"Send the authorities," Vandra continued. Sobs fell out of her mouth.

Orinthia felt like she was struck by a second bolt of electricity. Her ears rang and eyes unfocussed as she realized what Vandra was doing. The moment a law enforcement agent scanned her, the warrant would be pulled, and she would be arrested.

"Vandra, no." Orinthia rushed to the back room. Her body was light with panic. She shoved on her boots and pocketed the comm. It took all her concentration to not run into the doorframe as she left the closet and rushed to the front door.

"Don't tell anyone my friends or I were here," Orinthia said, turning to face Vandra for the last time. "I'll be back once things cool down." She did not wait to see if Vandra understood her warning. In New Cruces, law enforcement dispatched androids within two minutes after a call came in. There was no telling how swiftly officers arrived on the scene in Caytoo.

Celso followed her and kept pace a step behind.

Long shadows almost covered the alley. It was later than Orinthia had realized.

"Don't like cops?" Celso asked.

"Do you know anyone in this sector who does?"

Celso chuckled. "Fair. Well, I got a place you can hide. We can keep each other company. Or maybe I'll stick around in case I need to save you again."

"If I need rescuing a third time," Orinthia said, "I deserve whatever misfortune happens. Maybe the universe has called my number." Her lungs struggled to take full breaths.

A booming laugh echoed through the alley. "Who am I to argue with the universe? How about dinner then?"

Orinthia slowed her pace and looked at him over her shoulder. "You paying?"

"I offered, didn't I?" Celso answered. He flashed her a grin.

Kos did want me to eat, she thought. *And if whoever this is wants any more than just dinner, I'll know before it's too late.* "Lead the way."

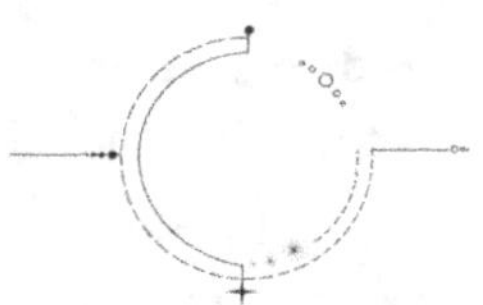

26

Celso led her through the alleys with a bounce in his step. He moved as if he had not assaulted a couple of gangsters a few minutes earlier. Anyone looking at him would assume he had no cares at all.

As the night fell upon the city, the people returned. Crowds formed in the passage and spilled into the street at the end. The sound of the vehicles reached them before the sights. Celso pushed his way through the people and stopped at the edge of the sidewalk. He held his hand in the air and waved at an incoming vessel.

A white hover car lowered itself and landed in front of the pair. Celso opened the back passenger door and made a grand, swooping bow.

Orinthia rolled her eyes and entered the car. The droid driver greeted her with its head turned perfectly at a one-hundred-eighty-degree twist. It gave a second greeting to Celso who joined them, then spun its head around to face forward.

"Tenpenny Street," Celso said, as he snapped the door

closed. He scooted closer to Orinthia and set his arm on the back of the seat, his fingers almost touching her shoulder.

"My pleasure," the droid replied.

The car lifted a few hundred feet into the air and swerved through the sky lanes amongst the other cars. Giant display signs levitated in the air. Bridges and catwalks spanned from one building to another, connecting the upper levels of the city.

It was reminiscent of Rust Rock. *Do they ever leave their towers or are they like those in the Shard?* Orinthia thought.

"I still haven't gotten your name," Celso said. His voice was close to her ear.

Orinthia looked away from the window and inched back from him. "Adora." *Better to have her name than mine floating around this place.*

The gloved hand was offered once again. Orinthia took it by his fingers and gave a half-hearted shake.

"What brings you to Caytoo?" Celso asked.

"Vandra is a family friend," Orinthia falsely explained. "I'm staying with her while I'm between jobs."

"If you need a place to stay, I got room for you on my ship. There's only one bed, but I'm sure we'll make do." Celso winked at her.

Orinthia's face went hot. It dawned on her what a mistake she might have made in agreeing to go with him. "I won't be here long. My friends are coming for me in a day or two."

"Then where are you off to?"

"Is this an interrogation?" Orinthia tested him, unsure of what his true intentions were.

Celso held up his hands in front of his chest. "Just making conversation. Would you rather sit in silence?"

"Yes."

The hover car began a gradual descent and rested on a platform labeled *Tenpenny Street.*

"Guess we won't get the opportunity," Celso said. He leaned forward, tapped his watch to the droid's shoulder, and paid for the ride.

"Have a nice night," the droid said, spinning its head to face them again.

Celso opened the door and stepped out. He held his hand for Orinthia to take, but she ignored it and exited on her own.

The platform was attached to the building by two large steel arms that were parallel to the ground. Each one had railings across it and served as a bridge connecting the platform to the tower. Orinthia stole a look over the edge of the walkway. They were at least twenty stories from the bottom level.

A human man stood on the deck before them. He opened the door and dipped his head as they dismounted the bridge. Celso gave a nod as they walked by him to get into the building.

The inside of Tenpenny Street was not what Orinthia had expected. People stood around talking over thumping music and drinking in expensive-looking glasses. Each guest wore elegant clothes and jewels that caught the lights rotating around the ceiling. A few women looked down their noses at Celso and Orinthia. One of them twisted her body as if she was afraid contact with the outsiders would give her a disease.

Celso tucked his arm into Orinthia's and forced her to walk through the crowd quicker. He leaned closer to her and said, "Don't worry. We're going two floors down."

Orinthia tried to pull away from his grip, but it was a struggle enough to keep up with him without tripping. She followed him to an elevator at the back of the room. Once they were both inside, Orinthia rescued herself back from him. "Don't touch me."

A grin spread across his face. He stepped closer, making her retreat. Her back pressed against the wall. She moved her arms to her chest and began to swing out, but Celso caught both her wrists.

His face was inches from hers. "What about this?"

Orinthia could feel his breath on her neck. Her pulse raced. Her breath quickened. She tried to move her leg to kick him off, but there was not enough room.

Celso's mouth brushed her jaw just under her ear.

Orinthia leaned her head to the side, and with as much force as she could manage in the short distance, knocked it into his. The pain was worth the look of shock on his face as he pressed a hand to his cheek. It served to make enough space for her to get a hand between them and shove him away.

"I'd rather go with the police." The attempt to sound defiant was overtaken by the twisting of her stomach. She had faced men who wanted her dead, that was easy. What Celso attempted frightened her more than the thought of being run through with a blade.

The elevator doors opened to a dimly lit, loud, and smokey bar. She moved to exit first, but Celso beat her. He stood between the doors, forcing them to stay open. "I'm sorry," he said, though his face did not match the sentiment. "Let's eat, and then we can get out of here."

"Are you expecting more than just a meal?" Orinthia prodded him. She waited to listen for the deceit in his words before determining her next move.

"We're holding up the elevator." Celso reached out to her.

"Answer me." Orinthia placed her newly modded arm on her chest.

Celso dropped his hand and sighed. "Right now, I just want to feed you. I'm hungry, too. People are starting to stare. For someone who wants to avoid attention, you're sure bringing on a lot."

"I'm not leaving this elevator with you," Orinthia said. She thrust her hand to the floor selector and pressed the button for the one they arrived on. "Move out of the way."

"You don't want to make a scene in here," Celso warned. He did not obey her order. His gloved hand reached for her again.

"Touch me and I'll take your arm off."

"I believe you would, Orinthia."

All warmth rushed from her body at the sound of her name. She tried to keep her face still.

A wide grin spread across Celso's face. "Don't be so surprised. You haven't exactly hidden yourself very well. I'm genuinely shocked I picked you up first. I thought that mod dealer might have been onto you until I realized he was just hocking his wares."

The elevator dinged, announcing a request from another level.

"You're not going anywhere," Celso said.

A server droid rolled to the pair. "Is there a problem?"

"My girlfriend just got some news she wasn't expecting," Celso said, clamping his hand around Orinthia's wrist. "She needs a drink to settle her nerves."

"Follow, please," the server droid said. It moved from the elevator to a table in the middle of the bar.

"Come on, babe, let's take a seat." Celso yanked Orinthia from inside the elevator and dragged her with him.

Escape options rushed through Orinthia's head. The farther they went from the lift, the fewer those options became.

Celso tossed her into a booth and slid beside her, blocking her in.

"What're you having?" A red electric line danced across the server's face screen as it spoke.

"Two of whatever today's special is," Celso ordered. "Same for the drinks."

Without a reply, the droid zoomed away, leaving the pair alone.

"Now, I'm sure you have questions for me," Celso said, shifting in his seat to face her better. "You'll test my answers to see if I'm lying. I'll skirt around the truth with half answers."

The air failed to fill Orinthia's lungs. *He knows.*

"The real Adora told me all about your mod and how to get around it," Celso continued. "She hired me personally."

Orinthia gave up trying to keep up her charade. Her mod had not hummed at the mention of her sister. She found the strength to settle herself and use the opportunity to get as much information as possible.

"How did you know I was here?" Orinthia asked.

"I've been following you since Sarv'on."

"Why didn't you take Kos and I then? You could buy a small district of your own for what we're worth together."

Celso shrugged. "Adora offered me a pardon. That's worth more than credits. Besides, I don't want to deal with Ahto."

"Then why did you wait until now?"

"I wanted to get you alone," Celso answered. His flirty persona changed to casual. "Back on Sarv'on, the group I hired to attack your ship was supposed to separate you from your friends. When that didn't work, I traced your crew here. Then they left you. That's when I knew I needed to get you to trust me. So, I paid another set of thugs to rob Vandra's shop."

Orinthia shook her head at his answer. His plan would have been more impressive if it had not been used to capture her. And the fact she had not picked up on it before made her nauseous. She played his game without hesitation and lost. Her mind drifted to her friends. They had traveled across the galaxy, risked their lives, and gave up everything to help her.

In one night on her own, Orinthia threw it all away.

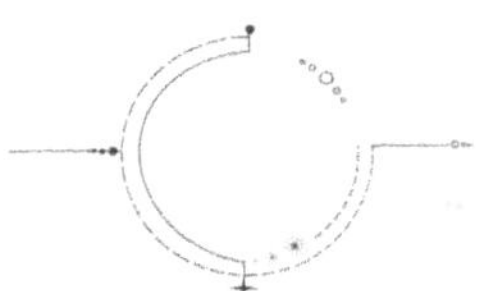

a scent of rich meat steamed up from the plate set on the table. Four dumpling rolls sat piled on top of each other. Beside it was a small dish of sauce and two eating sticks.

Celso took his sticks and used them to pop a dumpling into his mouth whole. He chewed with his mouth slightly open and breathed out to let the heat escape.

Orinthia stared at the food. She did not move. Thoughts of liberating herself ran through her head.

"Make sure you eat," Celso said, sipping his drink. "It'll be a long time 'til you have anything this good again."

The will to be stubborn was lost to the emptiness of Orinthia's stomach. It twisted and gurgled. A headache built up in the back of her neck and her hands trembled from more than just fear. Defeated, Orinthia took a utensil and poked it into a dumpling. A translucent shiny liquid dripped from the holes.

It squished between her teeth and her mouth filled with broth and chunks of meats and vegetables. On *Freya*, they had only eaten shelf-stable foods for weeks. The dumplings were the first true meal she had since Vron.

"You had the potential to be so much more than a rundown marauder," Celso said, interrupting her thoughts. "I always admired your grit."

Orinthia kept her eyes forward and ignored his statement.

"Do you honestly not recognize me?" Celso asked. "Sure, it's been a while. But six months together in the Hunter academy was a long time."

Nothing about him sparked a memory. She dug through the recesses of her mind trying to find even a glimpse of him from her past.

"I guess we're both different now," Celso continued. "Both fallen from that path."

For the first time since Orinthia met him, she could hear his velvet facade slip. She turned her head to him enough to see his face. His eyes were low and looked unfocused like he was watching a memory play in his head.

Then, coming back to their current time, he replaced his veneer. "Tell me, how'd you get into this mess? I think I was the only one surprised when I heard you left the GMH."

"I didn't leave," Orinthia said. "Adoracion fired me. My sister threw me out and left me with nothing. Where else was I supposed to go? It's not my fault the first person I ran into was a marauder."

"Why'd you kill your brother, though?"

Celso's question was worse than a slap to the face. Orinthia had forgotten what the bounty was for. "I didn't do that either. Adora did. She's ruined every good thing in my life. Every word that dribbles from her mouth is a lie."

Orinthia's hand throbbed. She looked down and saw her fists clenched over the utensil, the edges of it dug into her palm. It clattered to the table as she tossed it down. "What good is my mod if I'm the only one who knows the truth?"

"Look," Celso said. He turned and placed his knee between them on the bench seat. "I don't really care what happened between you two. This is the only way I can have a chance at something normal."

"Whatever you're running from, we can help." Orinthia's pleas sounded desperate, even to her. But she needed to try everything she could. "My friends are good at what they do. We'll trade for any favor you ask. But Adora will kill me if you take me back."

Celso shook his head. "I'm sorry, Orinthia. Really. But nothing is worth more than this pardon. Finish your food." His velvet was completely gone as he splashed down the last of his drink.

The food went down heavily and hit the bottom of her stomach like stones. Eating was difficult, and her body fought to take it in. She forced it down, knowing she would need the energy to execute her final plan.

Celso waved for the server droid to come back and handed it a red credit. "Keep the rest."

The droid gave a bow at the wheels and rolled away.

"Time to take you home," Celso said, standing to his feet. As his habit, he extended his hand out for Orinthia to take.

Orinthia slapped it out of the way, but he caught her mid-swing. His other hand came down and closed a cuff around her wrist.

Immediately, the incessant humming ceased. Her heart lurched inside her chest. The plan had to shift.

Celso pulled her to her feet and cuffed her other wrist in front of her. With the gloved hand on the connection between the two cuffs, he escorted her through the bar and back to the elevator.

Neither of them said anything as they ascended to the platform level. They walked along the wall to avoid as many eyes as possible and went out the door. A couple were exiting a sky cab when Celso and his prisoner reached the departing deck. Celso waved for it to wait.

"The docks," Celso said to the driver droid once they were inside the car. He did not let go of her cuffs, even inside the cab. Their hands rested on the middle of her thigh.

Celso looked at her through the side of his eye and smirked. "In another life, this might have been more exciting than it is."

He was handsome, though scarred and damaged. His crooked nose was slender, and his jaw was sharp. Celso was no Kos, but *in another life,* as he put it, there could have been an attraction. However, the move he pulled in the elevator left a poor taste in her mouth. The way he looked at Orinthia made her stomach twist and her dinner threatened to make a reappearance. She was all too aware of where his hand rested on her leg.

"What do you need pardoning for?" Orinthia tried to keep her voice unwavering and match his tone.

"I could tell you anything right now," Celso answered.

"Or you could tell me the truth. I wouldn't know the difference."

Celso gave a chuckle. "True. Though I could just not answer and let your imagination go wild."

An idea flashed through her mind. It was almost as crazy as the other plan she worked on, but she had to try something. Drawing as much strength as possible, she tilted her head down and looked at him through her eyelashes. Her chest was tight as she said, "I could let my imagination go wild if you'd like. These cuffs give me a few ideas."

Celso's eyes widened for a second, he was caught off

guard by her words. As quickly as it happened, though, he regained composure. "Nice try. I don't need your tech to know you're full of it."

Orinthia sighed out the tension from her body and straightened her posture. Truthfully, she did not know what to do if he had taken her advances. He could take advantage of the situation without the offer. His coat had too many pockets to look through for a key in a hurry. On top of it all, they were several hundred feet in the air. She had nowhere to run.

Neither of them spoke for the remainder of the ride. Orinthia ran through her next moves and committed each step to memory. She would not go with him willingly.

The sky cab descended and landed at the entrance of the docks. Celso thanked and paid the driver before pulling Orinthia out of the car.

She followed him for four steps, then yanked her hands down. Celso stumbled back but did not loosen his grip. The glove slipped a little and exposed wires and mechanical joints.

With a second tug, he was pulled back again. This time, Orinthia used his momentum to plant a foot into the back of his knee. Celso fell on his back; his grip broke from her restraints.

Orinthia jumped out of reach as he tried to regain control of her. As hard as she could run, Orinthia darted in the opposite direction into a crowd of people. Her feet pounded the pavement. She shoved people aside and dodged those too big to move. Half a block ahead of her, she saw a parked speeder bike. It was her new target.

The whooshing sound of Celso's jetpack grew louder as he propelled himself toward her. Orinthia listened as closely as she could through her panting. Just as he came close enough to grab her, she threw herself down and slid forward out of his reach. The pavement cut into her new pants.

Celso landed with grunt then yelled, "Stop!"

Orinthia rolled to her feet and used as much power as she could to push herself faster.

Another sound came from behind her. Orinthia allowed herself to look back and jumped over the bola that flew toward her feet. As she came down, she twisted her ankle and fell onto her knees. Through gritted teeth, she forced herself up. Pain shot up her leg. Determined to escape, Orinthia limped as fast as she could. Each step burned white through her mind.

A second bola caught her around the thighs. Her cuffed arms shot up to protect her face as she fell forward. The fabric of her shirt tore, taking bits of her elbows with it.

Celso closed the distance with his jets.

Orinthia rolled onto her back and waited until he was right above her. She pulled her legs back and kicked into his stomach. Both feet put pressure and she yelled with the effort. The momentum threw him into a crowd of people who hollered and cursed at him.

Using the distraction, Orinthia unwrapped the bola's cord from her legs and moved to her knees. As she placed her good foot flat to stand, a hot electric current ripped through her back. She screamed and fell forward. The side of her face scraped the pavement.

Celso walked to her and used his foot to turn her over. He shook his head. Without saying anything, he took her cuffed hands and lifted her up. He placed her arms around his neck, grabbed her off her feet, and pulled her into his arms. The jetpack ignited as he jumped into the air.

As the distance between them and the ground grew,

Orinthia decided against a second escape attempt. She rested in his arms and surrendered.

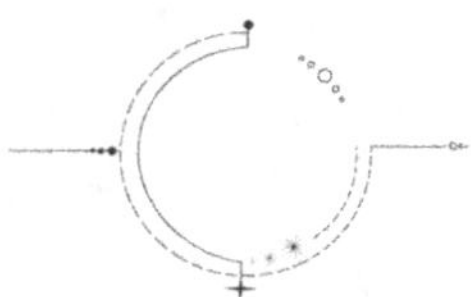

28

*C*elso did not land again until they reached his ship. From what Orinthia could see, there were no weapon mounts. It also was no bigger than a hobby craft. The hull was painted bright orange and had a single yellow stripe wrapped around the side. A ramp lowered and the door opened as they neared.

Pain continued to pulse through her leg as Celso set her down on the ramp.

"That was some fight," Celso said, dragging her inside. She did not have the energy to resist, but she made him work for it. He opened a barred cell and pushed her in. The door slammed shut behind her.

Orinthia moved to face him. His white shirt bore a foot-print from her boot.

"I'm going to search you now," Celso said. He put his hand through the bars, but Orinthia limped out of his reach. He sighed. "You're not going anywhere. This cell is four feet wide. If you let me search you, I'll take off one of the cuffs. Deal?"

There were not many options, and with one arm free, at

least she could fight her way out if she had to. Orinthia agreed and moved toward him. "Try anything else, and I won't need my swords to end you."

Celso did not react to her threat. He put his hand through the bar and into her pocket. He found Kos' comm.

Orinthia's heart sank. One of her tumbles had cracked it in half. It clacked to the floor as Celso dropped it. His heel came down on it and smashed the comm. "We don't need your friends tracking us with that."

Celso finished the search, then left the cell and pressed the button beside the ramp.

"You said you'd take my cuffs off." Orinthia shoved her hands through the space between the bars.

"I lied."

Orinthia shook the bars and let out a string of curses. She threatened not only his life but everyone he ever knew.

Before returning to the front of the ship, Celso leaned against the wall. His jetpack detached from his back with a hiss and stayed on the rack. He walked to the pilot's seat, draped his leather coat over the back of it, and sat down. Lights flashed as he flicked switches. The floor rumbled and engines ignited. A screen to the left of his seat turned on and he typed coordinates into it. Without warning, the ship's motors roared to life. Caytoo's lights out the window streaked, then after a minute disappeared.

The movement knocked Orinthia over and she scooted to the corner of her cell. She closed her eyes, determined to not give him the satisfaction of throwing up on top of everything else.

In true GMH fashion, Celso initiated the artificial gravity before they cut through Mos Kaanan's atmosphere. There was no sensation of the weightlessness she loved. Nothing to tell her when they were in space. She sat with her eyes shut for more time than she could tell before risking a peek. The view was black, dotted with stars far in the distance. They were not in warp, but floated stationary somewhere in space.

Orinthia fully opened her eyes and viewed her immediate surroundings. The inside of the ship was smaller than she first thought. There was only one door, and she assumed it was the washroom since a cot sat across from her cell. Several weapons hung from the walls, including some GMH-issued and a few handmade ones. She was briefly reminded of the studio she left back on Earth. There were no personal items to tell her anything about Celso.

She turned her focus to the man. "My friends will blow your ship apart."

He did not look away from his controls as he spoke. "Yeah, probably. But by the time they realize you're gone, we'll be halfway across the galaxy."

Orinthia wondered how long it would take *Freya* to return to Mos Kaanan. *How is Kos going to react?* she thought. They had Mimi, and if she was as good as Kos and Thrutt said she was, she could find her. But that would not matter if Celso took her to Adora by then. Nothing after that would matter. The farther they flew from the planet, the less likely it was she would see them or Uri again.

Tears pricked at her eyes, but she was unwilling to show weakness. The pain in her ankle and arms served well enough to distract her. She unzipped the white boot. A moment of relief washed over her as she gingerly removed it from her foot and set the boot aside.

"Do you get warp sickness?" Celso asked.

Orinthia ignored him and took off her other boot.

"I need to know so I can close the screen. No need to make a mess if we can avoid it."

"Yes." She hated to admit it to him, but a closed window was better than keeping her eyes shut the entire flight.

Orinthia watched through the side of her eye. Celso tapped a button and the window darkened until it was black. The view outside was replaced by a digital map of their route. She followed the trail, but could not see beyond the sector they were in.

Celso stood out of his seat and walked to his cot. After he sat down, he unlaced his black boots and placed them underneath his bed. He leaned farther forward and pulled out a PortTab from beside his shoes. The screen lit up his face and he laid down with an arm behind his head.

Orinthia stared at Celso and wanted him to burst into flames. The anger was not just toward him, however. Some of it was reserved for herself. She was so wrapped up in being witty and had not seen through his facade. For the first time in her life, she was disappointed in her mod. It had not picked up on his deceit. She had not realized how dependent she had become on it and discovered a limitation she was unaware of before.

The tension was too much to handle. Orinthia let out a yell and slammed her bound fists into the ground between her legs.

"You're already hurt enough," Celso said without looking away from his PortTab. "Don't break your wrists, too."

"I wasn't exaggerating when I said Adora is going to kill me," Orinthia said. "She's been trying for a long time. And now, at least in her own twisted mind, she actually has a reason to get away with it."

"Family drama is not my department," Celso laid his tablet on his chest and turned his head to look at Orinthia. "I'm just doing my job."

"This is a trade," Orinthia said. "You're using my death sentence to gain your freedom."

"Does it matter my reasons?"

"What do you need pardoning for?" Orinthia asked a second time. "Whatever it is, my friends are good. They can help fix it. There is room on our ship. You can join us for as long as you need."

Celso looked away and stared at the ceiling.

"My friends are decrypting a Mod Bleyer disk," Orinthia said. Desperation flowed from her voice. "It's yours if you let me go. Sell it and use the credits to get away from Adora."

"I've made enough bad deals, thanks. I'm seeing this through and that's it."

Orinthia huffed and slid from a seated position to lay on her back. The small space did not have enough space to stretch out, so she had to bend her knees at an angle. Her long hair fanned around her, and she rolled her head back and forth.

"My ankle hurts," she whined. If he would not let her go, she was going to make him regret taking her in the first place. "I'm cold. It's so cramped in here. Couldn't you have put some padding in this cell?"

She continued to complain until she ran out of things to fuss about. Then, she changed gears and started reciting every fact she ever memorized. This went on for fifteen minutes before Celso threw his boot at her cell. It bounced off and made the bars ring.

"Shut up," he said.

"No. And there is nothing you can do to make me. Sure, you could hurt me. But Adora won't pay you if I show up too damaged. She likes to watch Arsenio do that." Orinthia returned to rattle off facts, starting back at the correct way to strip and reassemble her old GMH blaster.

"I was undercover," Celso said with a loud sigh.

Orinthia stopped talking and rolled her head to look at him.

"I served on the *Moonblood* for three years and worked my way up to the first mate of the master gunner. She was the most beautiful Gorain I had ever seen. It wasn't long before we both fell for each other. The next time I met with my handler, I told him I wanted out and that I was going to leave the GMH. He told me the only way I was getting out was with the list of every marauder I served with."

Celso paused. "I was desperate but didn't know how to get him the names without giving up Dashar. I begged him for another way. He refused by pulling a blaster on me. Said it was the list or my life. We fought and I wound up killing him with his own gun. When I tried to get back to the ship, I found Captain Thrownin had me followed. The quartermaster saw the whole thing."

"She took me back to the ship and I was put on trial for mutiny. They voted guilty. Dashar was accused of conspiracy, and we were both sentenced to exile. The quartermaster flew us off the ship the next day. I managed to break free from my restraints, killed her, and we escaped in this dinghy." Celso gestured around the room.

The story was outrageous, and Orinthia had no way of knowing if it was true or not. But the tightening of his face made her believe it was real.

"I turned mercenary just to keep food in our bellies and a roof over our heads," Celso said. "Two years ago, Adora caught me while on one of my jobs and gave me the choice to either work for her or rot in prison."

Celso turned to look at Orinthia. "I know what your sister is capable of. Mostly because I've done it for her."

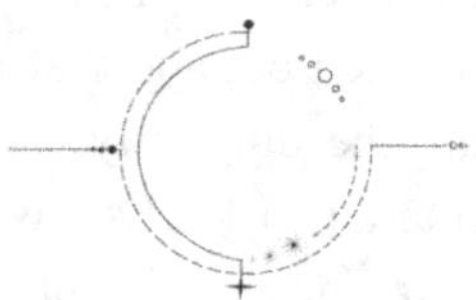

29

When Orinthia was younger, and Adora and Arsenio would beat her, it was Arsenio who dealt the blows while Adoracion called the shots and held her down. Only on special occasions did Adora do the job herself. This fact corroborated Celso's story and convinced Orinthia he was telling the truth. It was a strange feeling, having to rely on logic rather than her mod. Orinthia could not understand how other people had to remember so many details just to know if they were being deceived.

Celso's confession must have been as exhausting for him to tell as it was for Orinthia to hear. He turned away from her and faced the wall shortly after. Within ten minutes, soft snores came from his direction.

The cell was less than ideal for Orinthia to rest in, however. Her ankle had swollen and throbbed with every turn she made trying to find comfort. Sleep did not come for a long time. When she did manage to pass out, it was broken and erratic. There were no dreams, only black unconsciousness.

Time did not exist on the ship, either. During her wake

cycles, she had no way of knowing how long she had slept. Celso did not offer the information, or any words at all. If it was not for the few hydro-spheres and protein cubes left beside her cell when she woke up, she would have assumed he had forgotten about her completely.

When discomfort beat sleep and laying down was no longer an option, Orinthia sat up and sipped the water just to give herself something to do. She watched Celso walk around the tiny space, falling into whatever routine he created for long flights.

In some ways, he reminded her of Kos. Though Celso was not as rigid in personality as Kos, they both moved with the heavy weight of their past on their shoulders. With his mask gone, Orinthia could see the strain on his face. He was a tired man, looking for a way out.

Orinthia's heart ached at the thought, and she turned away. She missed Uri, of course, but she had grieved for so long that this new loss was nothing different. And then there was Thrutt. Her first real friend. The man who said she was as much of a daughter to him as his own children were. He would mourn for her and that alone almost brought her to tears.

Kos, however, existed in the forefront of her mind. Alone, and as the chances of seeing him grew slimmer, Orinthia allowed herself to think about him. It was him she missed the most. His touch burned through her memory. She wished she had kissed him in Vandra's shop, though she did not fully realize it at the time. The word for what she felt was too strong for Orinthia to admit, but she understood why Celso left the GMH for Dashar.

"Give me your leg," Celso said, drawing her from her thoughts.

Orinthia rotated to see him standing next to her cell. He

held a med pack in his hand. Though she wanted nothing to do with him, relief from the pain drove her to react. She stuck her ankle through the bar, and the weight of her foot sent shocks up to her hip.

Celso rolled up her pant leg and placed his cool hand on her blistering skin. Orinthia hissed at the movement as Celso wrapped the pack around her injury.

"Don't be such a baby," Celso teased. "I don't think it's broken. You should be glad I didn't shoot you."

"I've been shot before," Orinthia said dryly.

Celso made a face like he was impressed. "Right on. Was it on the job?"

Orinthia mindlessly pressed her hand to her side as she thought about the incident. Though she bore no scar thanks to the nanites, it left a mark in her memory. "Marauding."

"Ah." Celso leaned down and set her foot on the ground. "I got a few of those." He lifted his shirt to reveal a mesh of wires, servos, and rods that made up his torso. "Scatter blaster. Ripped me in half. The *Moonblood's* medic was a field surgeon during the war. Saved my life."

He returned his shirt to its place, stood, and went to his cot. It made a small creak as he put his full weight on it and sat cross-legged.

"The marauders treated me better than the GMH ever did," Orinthia said with a low tone. "They give each other loyalty and respect. The *Fera* has a code, that if a fellow crewmate dies while protecting another, the surviving party has to avenge their death. I didn't understand it at the time, but I get it now. The crew is a body, and everyone does their part to make the body work."

Orinthia closed her eyes and took in a long breath. "My friends saved me, and not just when we escaped the *Fera*. They changed my life and how I view things. By no means can I justify their previous actions, but desperate people will do dangerous things when given no other options. We as a society helped create marauders by pushing them out and discounting their sacrifices. Their bond was forged through fire. That's something the GMH can't manufacture nor destroy."

Celso threw his other boot at her cell. "That's enough of that. You're going to make me want to release you, and as a desperate man myself, that isn't an option."

Seeing as she struck a nerve, Orinthia pressed her luck one more time. "Take me back to my friends. They are understanding. We can take you and Dashar somewhere Adora can't find you, or you both can join our crew. Either way, we'd help protect you."

Celso's face went dark. He stared at a spot above the cell. "Dashar is gone. She's dead."

His words hit Orinthia in the chest, but she did not understand. "Then why do you stay working for Adora? If you have no one to protect, then her threats would be hollow."

"Stop," Celso said, more firmly than he had spoken to her before. "No more questions and no more stories. We're not friends. You are my prisoner and I'm taking you in."

Orinthia was not sure if he was talking only to her, or also reminding himself of their relationship. What she did know for sure was her luck had run out and her fate was settled. She had nothing left to barter.

Celso walked over to the controls and tapped a screen on the console. The windshield changed from the route map to a video comm connection. It blinked for a minute, then the channel opened.

Blood rushed from Orinthia's head and her heart beat like a small bird trapped in her chest at seeing the woman on the other end.

"You were meant to check in two days ago," Adora said. Her voice was cold and hollow.

Orinthia stayed as still as she could, willing herself to blend in with the walls. She was filled with fear and hatred. At the moment, she was not sure which one was winning.

"I'll be at the Mathias in three hours," Celso informed.

Adora's eyes moved from Celso, across the room, and stopped at the cell. Her thin lips curled into a tight smirk. "Little sister. Flew too close to the black hole, didn't we?"

Orinthia kept her face as neutral as possible, not breaking eye contact with the devil on the screen. She could not think of anything to say in reply, but she refused to let her terror show.

Adora turned her attention back to Celso. "Come in through the main bay this time. I'll send you the clearance codes."

With a nod, Celso disconnected the link. The screen went back to the map. He did not look at Orinthia when he moved to his cot and lay down again. He placed his modded arm over his eyes and stayed still.

Orinthia was done begging. It was time she planned out how she would face Adoracion. If she was going down, she would give the hardest fight of her life.

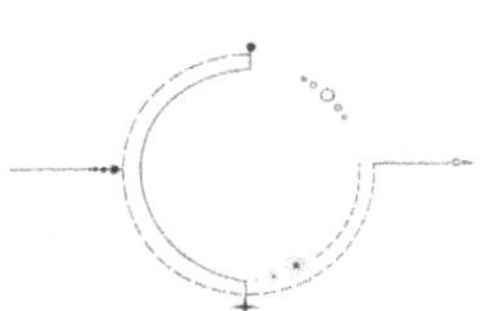

Orinthia spent three hours in meditation. Thrutt had taught her to visualize her plans and move through every scenario she could think of. She used every bit of knowledge she had, on every subject, to do just that. The fear dissipated and she was ready to face Adora.

No sound came from Celso's cot for the remainder of the flight. He did not snore, stir, or even cough. He did not move at all until the nav comm blared its proximity alarm.

Keeping her head down, Orinthia watched him walk over to the console and turn off the warp. The ship's engines lowered to a hum and the visor opened. In the clear window, Orinthia could see the unmistakable details of the MHS *Mathias*. Slightly longer than the *Fera*, it spanned almost two thousand feet and had space to quarter over three thousand Hunters. It rarely kept more than a few hundred at a time, however. Formerly a battleship during the war, the *Mathias* was the largest ship in the Galactic Marauder Hunters' fleet.

Orinthia swallowed hard and forced out any fear that crept up inside her. She was determined to be brave. The main hanger doors of the *Mathias* opened, cutting a rectangular hole into the white hull. Celso tapped on his screen and the smaller ship moved inside on its own.

As the floor rumbled to a stop, Orinthia could feel her resolve crumble. With long steady breaths, she steeled herself and regained composure. Her nerves were afire with anticipation, but she slowed her mind to focus on every detail.

Celso laced his boots on his feet, then stood in front of the cell. He bent down and undid the med pack from Orinthia's ankle. The swelling was gone, and she could freely move it without pain. He did not say anything as he stood back up and unlocked the cell.

Orinthia refused the hand he held out and wobbled to her feet on her own. With a gloved hand back on the link between the cuffs, Celso led her to the ramp and pressed the release. The ship decompressed with a long hiss and the ramp lowered, exposing the insides of both ships.

From where Orinthia stood, she could not see anything but light reflecting off the metal floor. But as they stepped onto the ramp, she was greeted by no less than two hundred Hunters in their grey and teal uniforms. Each member held a blaster ready and stood in neat rows.

In front of the garrison, in their black and teal captain's coats, stood Adoracion and Arsenio Anton. Arsenio trained his blaster on Orinthia as she stepped out of the ship.

The hangar was large enough to house half a dozen sloops *Freya's* size. There were two docked at the far end. A few mechanics were making repairs on one. Tools clacked against the hull and sparks flew up as one of them cut through the metal with a laser torch.

Orinthia's bare feet padded against the cold steel. The sensation kept her in the moment, for which she was thankful. Each time her mind began to fill with panic, she focused on the cold instead.

"Welcome home, baby sister," Adora said loudly as Celso stopped in front of the group. Her red scar was more noticeable than usual. Like she had spent less time in natural light, dulling her already grey complexion. She stepped forward and reached out for the cuffs.

Celso yanked Orinthia behind him. "Credits and pardon first."

Without breaking her gaze from the pair, Adora waved to her twin.

Arsenio lowered his blaster and joined them. The heels of his boots echoed around the bay. He handed Celso a data pad as he said, "Place your hand here."

Celso put his free hand to his mouth and pulled the glove off with his teeth. To Orinthia's minimal surprise, it was human and not artificial like the one that held her restraints.

He placed his palm on the screen and a white light moved up and down twice, scanning the impression. The machine beeped and a light flashed red at the top right corner.

"Your warrants are null and void," Arsenio informed. He tucked the data pad under his arm and motioned for one of the men behind him to come forward. "As for your payment. One hundred thousand galactic credits."

The GMH officer held out the case to Celso. Celso took the glove from his mouth and shoved it in his pocket. With a nod, he instructed the officer to open the case.

Orinthia could see stacks of red credit chips inside. The officer closed it again and passed it to Celso. He traded Orinthia to Adora at the same time.

The first step in Orinthia's plan fell into motion. She planted one foot into the ground and used the other to send a farewell kick into Celso's knee.

Her former captor yelled in pain and nearly fell forward. He regained his balance at the expense of his credits. The case crashed and sent an ear-splitting echo through the hangar.

Adora, who was a foot shorter than her younger sister, yanked on the restraints. Orinthia's leg buckled, and she fell to her knees. Adoracion leaned forward and stared into Orinthia's eyes. Her thin nostrils flared with anger.

Without hesitation, Orinthia drew in a breath and spit in her sister's face.

Adora swung back, and with a solid hit, backhanded Orinthia across the face. The contact sent a bright light across her eyes, and it took a few moments to refocus. She worked her jaw and felt it pop slightly.

Adora stood to her full height and told Celso, "Leave now. I never want to see your face or that ugly ship again." She glanced behind her and addressed the Hunters. "Everyone else is dismissed."

The sound of hundreds of boots marching filled the space. Even though they were leaving, it was intimidating to listen to.

Celso, who retrieved his case from the ground, did not bid Orinthia farewell or give her a parting glance. He turned on his heel and returned to his ship. The Antons were all that were left. None of them said anything to each other. Celso's engines ignited and, before the ramp was fully closed, moved for the bay doors. He passed through the opening just as the ramp sealed.

Orinthia watched his ship grow smaller as *Mathias's* hangar doors closed. She returned her attention to her siblings and lifted her chin so she could stare into their eyes. No matter what they did to her, she was determined not to break.

"You are never going to see the outside of this ship again," Adora said. She yanked Orinthia's cuffs and shoved them into her twin's hand.

Arsenio forced Orinthia to her feet and pushed her forward. Orinthia moved as slow as she dared. She knew where they were taking her, and she was in no hurry to arrive.

As well as being a military ship, the *Mathias* had doubled as a mobile prison, housing deserters and prisoners of war. The twins had not renovated that part of the ship and, when the need arose, used it to transport prisoners of their own.

Stepping through the senior-officer-only elevator, Adora pressed the button to take them to the belly of the ship. The elevator's doors closed. In turn, phase two of Orinthia's plan began.

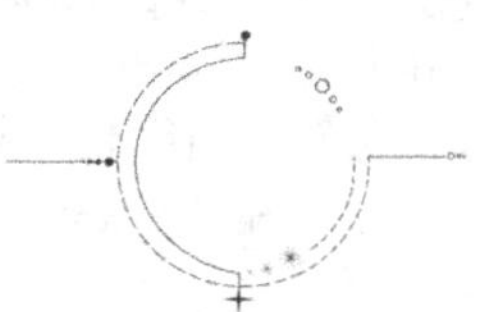

31

Orinthia had no misgivings about escaping. Even if she managed to make her way out of the elevator, she did not know how to fly any of the sloops in the hanger. Also, the escape pods were not made for long-distance travel, and without knowing where the *Mathias* was in space, she would not make it far without being recaptured or blown up.

Her plan was to do as much damage as possible; to cause chaos and bloodshed before she was locked away for good. She watched the light blink indicating descent. On the second level down, Orinthia closed her eyes and clenched her fists. With a throaty yell, she threw herself back into Arsenio and pinned him against the wall. Before he could react, Orinthia swung an elbow into his jaw.

Adora rushed forward. Orinthia leaned toward her and closed the gap, shoulder first. She made contact with Adora's chest. Adora made a sound as the air left her lungs and she stumbled back.

As her sister fought to regain her breath, Orinthia turned her attention back to Arsenio and the mule kicked him between the legs. He tumbled to the ground, clenching himself and moaning in pain.

Adora grabbed Orinthia's hair and pulled hard. Orinthia threw her weight down and landed on the ground. She moved her arms over her head and, using her cuffed hands like a club, she swung around into the back of Adora's knee. Adora fell, and Orinthia rolled to her feet.

Orinthia took her sister, who was clamoring to her knees, by the back of her head and thrust her knee into the center of her face. Blood poured from her nose. Before she had time to react, Arsenio was on top of her with his hands taking hold of her shoulders. Releasing Adora, Orinthia threw her body down and slipped from his grip.

Adora reached out for the panel on the wall and slammed her palm on the emergency alert button. The lights inside the elevator turned red, darkening the blood dripping from her face.

Orinthia squinted and readjusted her eyes to the new lighting. Her heart raced. Her arms were heavy from the effort, but she was not satisfied with the amount of harm she inflicted.

Arsenio, who must have suddenly remembered he was armed, lifted his blaster and aimed for Orinthia. Orinthia ducked down and rushed at his waist, smashing him against the wall again. The blaster fired beside her head and struck the wall. He curled forward and Orinthia swung her knee into his cheek. His eyes unfocused and he fell face-first onto the bloody floor.

Adora reached for Arsenio's gun, but Orinthia pressed her bare foot onto her hand. She leaned forward and forced it down with all her weight, twisting it into the steel.

Adora yelled and punched Orinthia in the ribs with her free hand. Orinthia coughed and the momentum pushed her off Adora's hand. Unrestricted, Adora took the blaster and swung the grip at Orinthia's head. With fatigued reflexes, Orinthia tossed her head back, but the butt caught her in the jaw. For a second time, a bright light flashed across her vision. Her ears rang and she could taste the metallic sensation of blood pooling in her mouth. She reeled back and spit the crimson liquid toward Adora.

The elevator doors opened, flooding the space with white light. Orinthia took her last chance to charge at Adora and tackled her out of the lift. They both fell, hands flying to each other's faces. As Orinthia lifted her clubbed hands to strike again, two metal clamps tightened around her arms. She was lifted off her sister. Her feet flailed as she kicked wildly and yelled out between gasps for air.

Her feet were suspended off the ground as she was guided to a cell. The security droids rolled her to the back of the cell and dropped her to the floor.

She had no strength left to struggle. Orinthia stayed where they deposited her. Her chest rose and fell with deep gulps of air. She worked her jaw, and pain flared through her cheek as her teeth brushed against the cut inside her mouth.

The cell door slammed shut. Orinthia took a second to take inventory of her injuries. Her side ached and was surprised to not detect a broken rib. The skin beneath the cuffs was red and parts had rubbed raw, exposing deeper layers of pink. Her clothes were torn, and she was also covered in blood, but was pleased with knowing not all of it was hers.

Adora and Arsenio joined the two security droids on the other side of the cell. Orinthia shifted to face them. Their normally neatly pressed white shirts were stained with bloody splotches. The sleeve of Arsenio's coat was ripped at the shoulder seam. Both had blood smeared across their faces in an attempt to wipe it away.

Orinthia gave them a gory grin. "I'm not a little girl anymore."

Adora looked down her twisted purple nose and met Orinthia's eyes. "No. You're a dead woman."

Hysterical laughter ripped through Orinthia. "I've taken you on many times before. If it was just the two of us, you'd be dead. But like always, you have Arsenio fight for you. Take these off and we'll see who walks out of this cell."

"Marauder trash," Adora said with clenched teeth. "There is no one left to save you. You are alone and will die here. No one will ever see you again and you'll quickly fade from all our memories."

"I'll never leave you, Adoracion." Orinthia's voice was even. She spoke with purpose and though she was locked in a cell, she knew she had won. "We both know you think of me every time you look in a mirror. No matter what you do, you'll never be rid of me."

Adora balled her fists. Without speaking, she looked at Arsenio. They stared at each other, having a conversation only they could hear. Adora's expression, if it was possible, grew more enraged. She shoved Arsenio out of the way and returned to the elevator alone.

Orinthia looked at her brother who hobbled closer to the cell. She smirked. "She's going to let you have your own voice?"

Arsenio kept his face smooth, though his normally slicked-back hair was not as controlled. "Orinthia Anton," he spoke in his husky tone. His already bulbous nose had swelled from repeated blows to the face. "You are charged with two counts of illicit and immoral acts of marauding, one count of kidnapping, and one count of murder in the second degree. Under the Galactic Anti-Marauding Act of the year 2618, your charges forfeit your rights to representation, counsel, or pleas. According to the Intergalactic Accords, you are subject to the highest authority in open space. I, Arsenio Anton, as Commissioner of the Galactic Marauder Hunters and highest-ranking Earth Confederate official in this sector, sentence you to death."

With the last bit of strength she had left, Orinthia leaped to her feet, ran forward, and squeezed her cuffed arms through the bars. Arsenio tried to move out of her grasp, but his movements were slowed by the injury he received previously. Orinthia took him by the collar and pulled him toward her with all her weight. His face smacked against the bars which rang out.

A security droid stuck a shock pole through the cell. It struck Orinthia in the thigh. She yelled and released her brother. The droid did not remove the shocker until Arsenio was safely out of reach.

Orinthia's leg went limp, and she crumpled to the floor. Her body trembled from the current that had gone through her.

"Add three counts of assault on an EC law enforcement officer to those charges," Orinthia said through gritted teeth. "Just so everyone knows I kicked your—"

"Strip her," Arsenio interrupted. "Put her in a prison uniform and burn her clothes." He turned and, though he tried to hide it, limped to the elevator.

Alone with the security droids, she relaxed her body, and the pain set in. The cell door opened and once again, she was lifted off the ground.

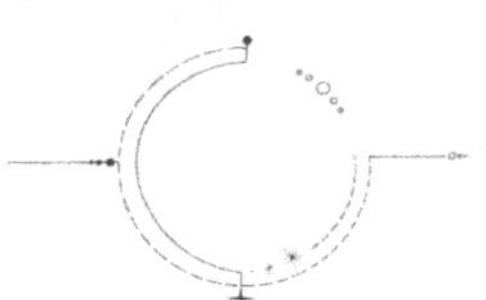

32

The only entities the Earth Confederacy hated more than Mod Bleyers, were marauders. So, the sentence Orinthia received did not come as a surprise. As a former GMH officer, she knew the penalty for her crimes. Truthfully, she had participated in the siege of an EC ship and was complicit in the death of an EC sailor. But that information had apparently not made it to the GMH. Even if she had not been a marauder, the charge of murdering her brother was enough to keep her locked away for the rest of her life.

That fact was evident in the way the two droids treated her. They removed the cuffs and undressed her with stiff and almost violent movements. Orinthia put her thoughts elsewhere. She blocked out the prison from her mind, a technique she developed in her past life, and imagined she was back in Vandra's shop, watching her friends discover she was missing.

In her head, Vandra greeted them, though her voice would be tense. She would say, *"About time. Did you get my data?"*

Kos would pull the disk from one of the various pockets in his coat and show their deed was done. *"Where is Thia?"*

"Disk first," Vandra would say, her eyes darting around to avoid his accusing glare.

Imaginary Kos tossed the disk to the floor and his foot hovered above it.

Thrutt would step in and attempt to smooth the situation. *"Why are you avoiding the question?"*

Vandra's face would go red as she accused them of double-crossing. *"You already took her back. You're trying to cheat me out of my data by pretending you don't know where she is."*

Mimi would come forward, possibly even pulling one of her blasters from its holster. *"If we had her, we wouldn't have brought the disk back. Now, where is she?"*

The room would go silent as Vandra contemplated her words. *"She left a few days ago. Some guy with an eyepiece came for her."*

"And you let her go?" Thrutt would ask. He rarely let his temper flare, but in Orinthia's imagination, he would be furious.

"The place was robbed," Vandra would say, excusing her actions. *"She didn't want to be here when the authorities arrived."*

Orinthia's false reality was broken through by the orders of one of her droid guards. "Step to the wall and turn around."

With laced fingers behind her head, she did as she was told. She had heard the command dozens of times. Up until that moment, Orinthia had always been on the other side of the cell when it closed. The droids rolled back to their docking stations, and Orinthia listened for their locks to engage before she moved again.

Exhaustion set into Orinthia's body and mind. She stepped to the cot and collapsed onto it. Every part of her throbbed with pain. Though it was nice to have somewhere other than an unforgiving metal surface to lay on. *At least there is a pillow*, she thought.

A cold band tapped against her right ankle, and she lifted her leg to examine it. The droids had removed the mod dampening cuffs and replaced them with a similar tech on her ankle. She lowered her leg and massaged the chapped skin on her wrists. Her shoulders ached, but it was a relief to be able to move freely again.

She tried to fight sleep as much as possible, knowing the twins would eventually return. But her body was too worn to resist for long.

When Orinthia woke up, she perceived she was not alone. Her half-open eyes moved around the room and fell on a figure outside her cell. It was too tall to be Adora, and too broad to be Arsenio. Even without those characteristics, the purple skin of the Galoric made it clear who it was.

"Kian," Orinthia said in a raspy tone. She cleared her throat and rubbed her eyes to dislodge the sleep from them.

"I had to come see for myself," Kian said. He leaned against the wall with his arms crossed.

"Last time I saw you, you were given captaincy of the *Daring*." Orinthia swung her legs over the side of the cot and sat up. Every muscle fought to go prone again.

Kian's skin shifted orange, indicating his shame.

A wicked grin spread across Orinthia's bruised face. She pulled back on one side and smirked. "Did you lose it?"

"It was overtaken by marauders," Kian muttered.

"And then you were demoted, weren't you?" Orinthia did not hide her joy. She looked over his uniform and spotted the grey lapel that separated the officers from the captains. "I'm glad to see I'm not the only one who fell out of the blessed Adora's good graces."

Kian's skin shifted green. "At least I didn't join them over it."

Orinthia rolled her eyes but did not respond.

"Or kill my brother," he added with a low tone.

The accusation sent a fire through her body. She moved to her feet and pointed a finger in Kian's direction. "I did not kill Uri. Adora shot him. They can say anything else about me, but I will not let go of that. Why are you even down here, Kian? None of this has anything to do with you."

The Galoric looked away. His skin faded back to purple and took a moment to reply. The words were barely over a whisper when he spoke. "Because I believe you."

Like a splash of cold water spilled over her head, the fire burned out of her chest. Orinthia could not believe what she heard. "Why?"

"I was on the *Fera* that day. I saw Adora and Arsenio return to the ship. She looked like she had seen a specter. After I heard what they accused you of and where you were supposed to have done it… I put things together. I've known you and your family a long time and know you would never hurt Uri, marauder or not."

The floor seemed to fall out from under Orinthia. She fell back on the bed and stared at Kian. His skin was purple throughout his speech. She did not need her mod to know he was telling the truth. Galorics were incapable of hiding their emotions. It was a physical reaction that worked in the opposite way to her mod. Where she could not help but hear the truth, their bodies could not stop from showing it.

"Look," Kian continued. "I can't do anything about your sentence. But it's been eating me up knowing you were framed. I felt it was important you heard someone was on your side."

Orinthia did not know how to respond. She had spent her

whole career as a Hunter looked down upon by those she served with. Each of her fellow officers felt she did not belong and only had the position because of her familial relations. It was not far from the truth but did not hurt any less to be treated poorly by her peers.

Kian, being one of the first Hunters to join the GMH at its founding, treated her no better. They had an unspoken and unfriendly rivalry over the years. Orinthia partly suspected it was supported by the twins, always giving Kian the missions Orinthia wanted. Even on her last day as a Hunter, Kian was assigned the task of backup for the *Mathias* as they searched for the *Fera*.

Yet, despite that, he believed her.

"You could have commanded fleets," Orinthia said. "The twins are intimidated by you, so they refuse to promote you any higher. Don't let them waste your talents."

Kian's skin turned blue. He gave her a half smile. "Don't tell anyone I said it, but I think marauding made you soft."

Orinthia nodded. "Becoming a marauder saved me from myself, for whatever that's worth now."

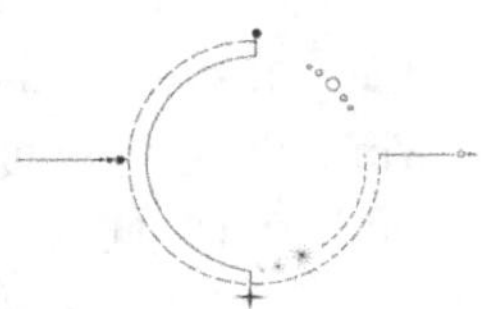

33

Though Orinthia had never seen it herself, she often heard stories about a ship dubbed the *Spectral Scow*. It was not uncommon to find former military ships abandoned and floating aimlessly through deep space. Like shipwrecks of ancient times, space-fairing vessels sometimes disappeared in uncharted quadrants, only to be found by accident. However, the *Spectral Scow* showed on scans as fully operational. The difference was, there were no life signs aboard the ship.

Smaller ships went missing from time to time after reporting an encounter with the frigate. When retrieval teams arrived on the scene, all they could find was debris and chunks of metal from what used to be a ship.

Alone in the belly of the *Mathias,* Orinthia felt she could believe those tales. In the stillness, her mind was alert and aware of every noise. More than once, she swore she saw a shadow dart around a corner.

She mentioned it to Kian during one of his secret visits.

"There is nothing but the droids and you down here," he told her. "Isolation will play tricks on you, so don't believe everything you see. Besides, this ship is old. The metal can cause sound to travel from all over. And you're close to the engines."

His answer did not make her feel better, but Orinthia did not want to waste her visits arguing. Kian became a friend in the few days she had been in prison. The twins did not allow visitors, so Kian snuck down when he could spare time.

"Thank you for risking coming to see me," Orinthia said, dropping the subject.

"It's the least I can do. You don't deserve to spend your last days alone."

The phrase *last days* made her ears hot. No one had confirmed when her sentence would be carried out. Orinthia suspected making her wait was part of the punishment. Kian had not heard any updates, either.

"I'm sorry," Kian said. His skin turned orange. "That probably wasn't as comforting as I meant it to be."

Orinthia gave him a solemn smile. "It's okay. I know my days are numbered. And I'm okay with that." She paused and looked at the ground beside his feet. Her toe tapped as she sought the courage to say what was in her heart. "Can I ask you a question? Or rather, make a request of you."

"I can't let you out," Kian replied. He stood straight off the wall he leaned against.

"No, it's not that. It's probably something almost as impossible. But I have to let someone know and hope it makes its way to them."

Kian rested against the wall again. "What is it, then?"

Orinthia did not lift her gaze. She pictured the faces of her crew as she spoke. "I just want my friends to know I cared about them. And that I thought of them until my last breath. Tell them they were the best part of me, and I would not have traded a single second." She moved her eyes up and looked at

Kian with blurred vision. "Thank them for showing me what love could be."

The Galoric's skin shifted to maroon, a color Orinthia had not seen on him before. "I will do my best to find a way to tell them."

The tears would not stay back, no matter how much she hated the idea of crying in front of Kian. Thankfully, he let her cry for a few minutes before speaking again. "They always painted you as their screwup sister. I wish I had taken the time to get to know you outside of all of this."

Orinthia wiped the tears from her face. "I was a screwup. I still am. Look where I am. Anything good about me, I learned from my friends."

Kian gave her a half smile. "Maybe I'm wrong about marauders, too, then."

"Not all of them are bloodthirsty and crazy. A lot of them are trying to understand their place in this post-war galaxy."

The sound of the elevator doors opening cut off Kian's reply. Both he and Orinthia watched Adora and Arsenio step out and march toward them. Adora's eyes bulged with rage, her lips pulled into a tight line. Arsenio followed a step behind her, still moving with a noticeable limp.

"Commander Kian Roldross," Adora said in a shrill voice. "If you do not wish to join the prisoner in a cell and be held under contempt, I suggest you leave immediately."

"Leave him alone," Orinthia said. She stood from her cot. "He has more humanity and compassion than you'll ever understand."

Without missing a step, Adora yanked an electric prod from the wall beside her and held it in front of her. She moved to Orinthia's cell and stuck it between the bars. The pole stopped an inch from Orinthia's chest.

"You can't scare me," Orinthia said, bracing herself for a

shock. "I'm at death's door. All you can do is speed up the process. I have nothing left to lose."

White lines danced around the tip of the prod as Adora ignited it. She jabbed the electrified spike into Orinthia's chest. It tore through her prison shirt and cut the skin beneath.

Orinthia gritted her teeth as the current tightened every muscle. Even as she collapsed to the floor, Adora held the charge turned on.

Kian begged for it to stop. His voice mixed with the sound of electricity, but Orinthia could hear the desperation.

"You have three seconds to leave before I demote you again," Adora threatened.

The Galoric glanced down at Orinthia's flopping body. His eyes searched her face as he watched. Sorrow and anger rolled off him as his flesh changed from maroon to orange in pulses. He shook his head and left without argument.

Adora continued to light the prod. She stabbed Orinthia half a dozen times before the pain made her yell out. Each time Adora struck her in a new spot and held it longer than the last. The smell of burnt fabric and flesh filled the air.

The torture continued for another ten jabs before Arsenio spoke up. "That's enough. We don't want it to *look* like we tortured her. You're leaving too many marks for it to seem like only a punishment."

Hatred filled Orinthia between the moments of electrifying pain. As long as they never went too far, they could reasonably explain her injuries. It was the same tactic they always used during her tortures. Only with more power came bigger and deadlier tools.

The jabs ceased long enough for Orinthia to pull herself to her knees. She used her hands to brace her trembling body and looked her sister in the eyes. Her hair hung across her face, clinging to sweat. "No, keep it coming. Let everyone know what kind of monster you are. Show them the Adoracion I know so well."

A throat-ripping yell came from Adora as she thrust the stick forward. Arsenio pulled his twin back and snatched the prod from her hands. They stood staring at each other, speaking in a way only they could hear.

Orinthia used the respite to sit and rest her head against the bars of her cell. She watched the pair, and though she could not hear them, she could read Adora's reactions.

Her red scar grew darker, and her face scrunched. She was almost in convulsions over what Arsenio was telling her. It would have been comical if it was not in direct conflict with Orinthia's safety.

The twins continued to stare at each other for several more minutes. Arsenio had taken his sister by the arms and dragged her toward the elevator. They did not make it far before an alarm cut through the air in a three-pulse pattern. Its sharp sound bounced off the walls. Bright red and white lights rotated along the ceiling.

Orinthia covered her ears and squinted. The six security droids activated in unison. They rolled from their crevices and created a barrier at the elevator.

The signal was not a familiar one, but by the look on her siblings' faces, Orinthia had an idea of what it meant. A small fire of hope lit inside her chest.

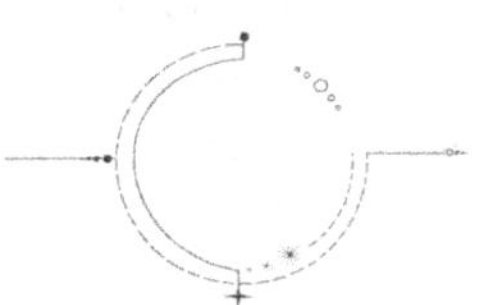

34

*A*dora and Arsenio took turns yelling at the droids who remained as sentries. No amount of shouting or commands changed the unmoving wall. Even when the alarm ceased, they stayed locked in place.

"I am the captain of this ship and the fleet admiral," Adora shouted. She stood on her tip toes and tried to reach the face port of one of the droids. "Move."

"The ship is under lockdown," the droid replied, like the other six times Adora demanded the same thing. "No one is permitted to leave or enter."

Orinthia sneered. "You're just as much of a prisoner as I am."

Adora glared at her. Frazzled hair crowned her head. Her teeth were clenched tight.

"They're coming for me," Orinthia said in a sing-song voice as she pulled herself to her feet using the bars of her cell.

For the first time, Orinthia saw a flash of fear cross her sister's face. "Let them come. I won't have to waste time in hunting them down," Adora said. She had a slight warble to her voice. Her chest moved quickly with short breaths.

"Your armor is cracking. I saw it. You're scared." Orinthia gave a hard smile. Though her body ached with burns, she would show no weakness. Her friends were close. She had to hold out for them.

Adora yanked the prod from Arsenio's hand. She yelled as she rushed forward and thrust it into the cell.

Orinthia had enough time to move back, but the tip grazed her bicep. Her momentum allowed her to break free from the touch. The muscle ached, but she was able to stay standing.

Unhindered by Arsenio once again, Adora continued to attack Orinthia. Her wild movements were not easy to dodge, but Orinthia managed to for most of them. She missed a step once, however, and came in full contact with the poker. It caught her in the center of her thigh. Orinthia screamed and toppled forward, her shoulder taking the full force of the impact.

The strength to get up evaded her and she lay on the cold floor. She took in shallow breaths. Her throat and skin burned. Her nerves were ablaze with electricity. The muscles in her upper body were light and she quaked uncontrollably.

Adora huffed from the effort. She ceased her attack. "Another word and I won't stop until you're dead."

Orinthia stayed as still as she could. She did not know how many more she could take before Adora actually did kill her. *Please hurry*, she said in a silent prayer to her friends.

As if summoned, the elevator door opened. Blaster fire rang out as all six security droids fired on whoever was inside the lift. The sound made Orinthia look up in time to see three droids fly ten feet backward and slam into the wall across from the elevator. Only one of them got back up and rejoined its comrades.

Another two droids flew back. They stayed crumpled with the first two. The remaining guards continued to shoot. Orinthia watched two diamond hands come out of the elevator, take hold of one of the droids, and bring it down vertically on top of the other. The blaster fire ceased.

In reality, it had not taken more than a minute for the fight to begin and end. Arsenio had no time to react to what was going on in front of him. There was barely enough time for Adora to turn and watch the intruder destroy her droids.

Orinthia rolled to her stomach and stretched her arm out to rest her cheek against it. She watched Thrutt's hulking mass exit the elevator. He stepped over the mangled pieces of metal as if they were no more than discarded trash.

Thrutt's face was in a form Orinthia had not seen before. His eyes were narrow, and his head moved with quick jerks as he looked between the humans in front of him. The ground shook as he closed the distance between the scrap droids and the twins.

Adora lifted her hand and shot a dart at Thrutt. The needle snapped and bounced off his stone body. She shot a second one with the same results. Readjusting the prod in her hand, she ran to meet Thrutt and thrust it at him.

Thrutt grabbed the stick and snapped it with ease. He threw the broken pieces to the ground at his feet.

Arsenio took the opportunity to move behind Thrutt. He removed a blade from his belt and tried to stab the stone man in the back. It hit with a clack but did not pierce through.

With his longer arms, Thrutt reached behind him and grabbed Arsenio by the hands. He yelled as he swung the human man over his head. Arsenio crashed nine feet down, straight onto this back. He groaned but did not move.

Orinthia could not help but let out a smile. She knew

Thrutt was thinking of every story he had heard about them. He was showing no mercy.

Adora attempted to go for another prod off the wall. Thrutt caught her arm, pulled her back, and shoved her down with her twin. He grabbed them both by an arm and dragged them to Orinthia's cell. He stopped in front of her and finally spoke. His face softened. "Hey, kid. Grab their badges real quick."

Orinthia's arms shook under her weight as she pushed herself up. It took a moment to still her body before she reached through the bars and searched their coats. Once they were relieved of their escape options, Thrutt moved to the cell beside Orinthia's. He pressed his hip to the lock and the door swung open. In one move, Thrutt threw them both into the cell and slammed the door closed.

The twins laid limp in their new positions and continued to do so as Thrutt returned to Orinthia.

With Adora's badge, Orinthia disengaged the brace on her ankle. At the same moment, Thrutt opened her cell and pulled her off the ground into an embrace. Orinthia gripped him as tight as her damaged body allowed and sobbed with relief. They held each other until the twins stirred.

Thrutt set Orinthia down on her feet and they both faced the neighboring cell. Orinthia held Thrutt's arm with both hers, borrowing his stability.

"You won't get far before my officers shoot you on sight," Adora said. Her voice was weak. She held her ribs and winced as she sat up.

Arsenio used his twin sister's shoulder to steady himself and put a hand to his forehead. Blood trickled from one of his ears. He repeatedly blinked like he was trying to clear something out of his eyes.

"Adora," he said. "My head is killing me, and I can't hear anything."

The smaller woman reeled around and looked at her brother. She held her hands on either side of his face and brought it to her level.

"We have to go," Thrutt whispered into Orinthia's ear.

Orinthia, not trusting her ability to walk after the torrent of electricity that had coursed through her, kept an arm looped into Thrutt's. The pair moved to the elevator and stepped inside. As it closed, Orinthia could hear the threats from her sister. The door snapped shut and her voice was blocked out.

Thrutt moved his hand from Orinthia's arm and placed it around her shoulders. Relieved, Orinthia rested her head against his side.

"Where did you get the badge from?" Orinthia asked.

"It's a long story, but one of the officers gave it to Kos who gave it to me. He told us where to find you and how to use it." Thrutt showed her the badge.

Orinthia traced the embossed letters with her finger and smiled. "Commander Kian Roldross," she read out loud.

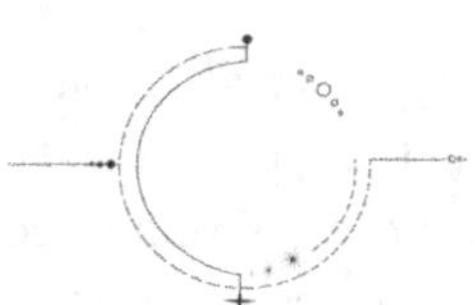

35

The elevator smelled of cleaning chemicals and stung Orinthia's nose. There were dents in the wall from where she had slammed Arsenio. She eyed the blaster burn beside the door. "Where are the others?" Orinthia asked, turning her focus to Thrutt. Her muscles had stopped trembling as she waited for him to select a level on the elevator. She was grateful to be free, of course, but she knew they were not safe until all of them were back on *Freya* and far away.

"Let's find out," Thrutt said. He pulled a short-distance comm from his pocket. The light blinked blue, indicating it was connected to others nearby. "I got her," he said into the device.

Orinthia watched the light continue to blink. It switched to green as a reply came back. "Stay out of the hangar," Mimi said. "They have *Freya* surrounded."

"Copy," Thrutt said. "Where are you?"

"I took a little trip to the captain's quarters," she answered. Her voice was light.

Thrutt pressed his fingers to his forehead. He pinched his

lips together and closed his eyes for a second before responding. "What are you doing in there?"

"Just looking," Mimi said with a dismissive tone. "No one is up here. Besides, I grazed one of the officers on my way through the hangar. I'll just change if I have to."

"Stop touching people," Thrutt said. His fingers slid down his forehead to his mouth. He made a muffled sound and then changed the subject. "Rogue, you out there? You've been awfully quiet."

There was no response.

"Last time I saw him was when he gave you the badge," Mimi said. Her voice was more alert than it had been a moment before.

"Meet on the third level," Thrutt instructed. He dialed the number on the elevator, and it began to lift.

"Copy."

Thrutt placed the comm back in his pocket. Orinthia looked at him. She could read the tension on his face and knew what he was thinking. *Kos has been captured.*

The doors opened at the third level. Thrutt stuck his head out first. He did a quick look around and nodded for Orinthia to follow. The hall was silent, save for the thumping of Thrutt's feet against the metal floor. Orinthia walked close beside him, treading on the balls of her bare feet to stay as quiet as possible. She strained her ears and tried to listen past the sound of their movements.

Thrutt stopped at an intersection in the hall. He held his arm out and prevented Orinthia from moving forward. With his other hand, he drew his blaster before peering around the corner. The gun whirred as he switched off the safety.

Orinthia crossed her arms and waited for the moment she needed to call her swords. The sound of several footsteps came from the joining passageway to their left. Thrutt moved back, forcing Orinthia away. His body blocked her view, but she ducked her head around his arm and watched the group turn in their direction.

The air was sucked out of her chest. Kos was cuffed between two officers who were in the middle of the squad. One held him by the hair and forced his face upward. The two officers broke formation with Kos in tow and rushed back down the hall they had come from.

Orinthia knew the *Mathias* as well as Thrutt and Kos knew the *Fera*. She rarely left the ship when on tour as a Hunter, save for boarding parties. Most importantly, she knew the paths to take to avoid people when she wanted to. With this knowledge in mind, Orinthia ran back toward the elevator and took a left down the hall to a second connecting corridor. She pushed her weak body to go faster, begging it not to fail her.

As she closed the distance, the two officers and Kos stepped into her path. They halted in their tracks and took a moment to register what was before them. The officer to Kos' left released him and fumbled for his blaster. Orinthia threw herself back and slid feet first into his leg. The officer collapsed on top of her, his head colliding into her shoulder. Orinthia lifted him at an angle with one hand and punched him in the jaw with the other.

The second guard yelled and fell to her knees beside Orinthia's head. Orinthia, still scuffling with the guard on top of her, glanced to see the female officer's arm twisted back between Kos' cuffed hands. He shoved her forward and pressed a foot to her back while still holding her arm. The woman screamed, waving her other arm back trying to get her attacker off.

Orinthia's opponent took advantage of the distraction and swung his fist into the side of her face. The room spun and her vision tunneled. Darkness closed around her for what felt like a few seconds. However, when she came to, she heard someone whimpering. She blinked to clear her sight and followed the sound. The female guard was not too far away and cradling a limp arm. Her leg was twisted in a way it was never meant to.

Still, in a haze, Orinthia searched for Kos. She found him at her feet, standing with the first guard's head between his still-bound hands. He had him pinned to the wall and repeatedly slammed the back of his skull into the steel.

"Kos, stop," Orinthia said. Her voice was raspy but carried all the strength she could place on two words.

Kos made no indication he heard her. His face was twisted, and teeth bared. His fingers dug into the man's skin with such force that the tips were white.

"I'm right here," Orinthia said, moving to her knees and propping herself up with one hand. She reached out and touched his leg.

The pounding stopped but he did not release the man's face.

"Let him go. I'm safe, Kos. Please come back to me."

Kos' white fingertips returned to their normal color as he loosened his grip. Slowly, he let go and the man crumpled to the floor. Bruises had already formed on his face where Kos' fingers had been.

Orinthia pushed herself to her feet and held onto the wall for support. "Look at me, Kos."

Kos' expression softened and he closed his eyes. He stood planted where he was. His shoulders slumped forward.

Carefully, Orinthia reached him and placed a hand on either side of his head. She forced him to turn and face her. "I've got you. You're safe now." Her voice was almost a whisper. She placed her forehead on his. "Open your eyes."

Kos moved his head to her shoulder. Through soft sobs, he choked out, "I don't know who I am anymore."

Orinthia wrapped her arms around him and cradled him tight. She stroked his thick hair and felt his body jerk as he cried. "We'll find out together. But right now, I'm here and I'm not leaving again."

They stood together until the sound of Thrutt's feet came from behind Orinthia. Kos straightened himself but did not look up.

"Let me get these off of you," Orinthia said. She reached for Adora's badge and placed it on the cuffs. They disengaged and crashed to the floor.

Thrutt reached them. "Are you two okay?"

Orinthia slipped her hand into one of Kos'. She did not face Thrutt when she said, "I think so."

Kos closed his fingers around hers and looked up. His eyes were rimmed red. The brokenness he kept locked inside had seeped out. Orinthia could see the lost boy struggling to come home.

"We need to get out of here," Orinthia said to Thrutt, turning to face him. "The longer we stay, the more likely they will find the twins."

"How are we going to get past the guards in the hangar?" Thrutt asked.

Mimi, who no one had seemed to notice before, poked her head around Thrutt and grinned. "I have an idea."

THE FOUR EXITED the elevator on the tenth level. Orinthia had hoped to never see it again, but she trusted Mimi's plan and followed the others. Kos, who had not let go of Orinthia's hand, walked in front of her, shielding her from whatever danger lay ahead.

Arsenio was on his back on the cot while Adora used a broken dart to pick at the lock of their cell. She stopped when the newcomers came nearer and stood to her feet. Her auburn hair had fallen out of her bun and hung below her shoulders.

Mimi and Thrutt were the first to reach the cell. The two women were the same height and looked at each other with equally cold stares.

Adora lifted her hand to shoot a dart, but Mimi stepped to the side and grabbed her wrist. She continued to pull until her arm no longer had the length to move. With the cuffs Orinthia had taken off Kos, Mimi secured Adora's arm to the bar.

"Get off her," Arsenio said. He stumbled off his cot and moved to his sister.

Kos opened the compartment in his hip and aimed his blaster at Arsenio's head. "I'd love nothing more than to make you exist only in memory."

Arsenio squinted his eyes and looked between the gun and Kos. He threw his hands up and moved back to the cot. Adora struggled and tried to break free. Everyone watched Mimi roll up Adora's sleeve and press her hand against the exposed skin. A few seconds later, she stepped back and twisted her hand in the air.

Two Adora's stared at each other. The caged one yelled, "Filthy imposter. No one is going to believe you're me."

Nobody outside of the cells responded. Kos let his blaster hang at his side and led Orinthia back to the lift. The others joined them and for a second time, Adora's voice was blocked out by the elevator door closing.

With a deep breath, Orinthia pressed the button for the hanger level. "Everyone ready?"

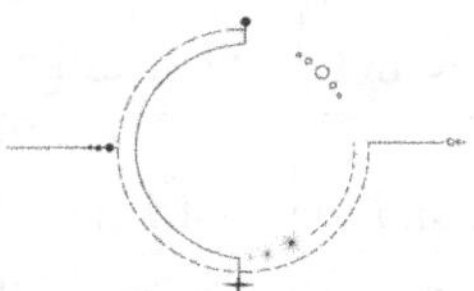

The tip of Orinthia's black blade dug into the side of faux Adora's neck. Though it was lighter in weight than her other sword, her arm shook. The prisoner hissed.

"Sorry," Orinthia said, pulling back a bit. "I'll try my best not to actually hurt you."

"If you do, you'd better make it look good." The faux Adora snapped her words with such accuracy to the real one that Orinthia flinched.

As the elevator door opened, Orinthia took a steadying breath and lowered her eyes. Kos scooted around them and held both his blasters in front of him. He moved with ease, like a ghost gliding over the floor. Thrutt brought up the rear and walked at his full height.

Orinthia shoved the imposter forward and shouted for her to move. Hundreds of officers in the hangar turned to face the intruders. Each of them trained their guns on the group.

"Everyone, get back," Orinthia yelled.

A few shuffled their feet, but no one made significant steps to follow the order.

The blade dug into the skin of her hostage. It made an indent. If she pressed any harder, she would have drawn blood. "I will gladly separate her head from her body. Get back now."

"Don't be stupid," Adora shouted. "Let them pass."

The officers shared uneasy glances but did as they were told.

Kos moved forward and pushed his way through the crowd. Orinthia followed close behind him, making sure to leave no room for anyone to cut her off. Halfway to *Freya*, she turned her back to him and faced the crowd closing in. Thrutt blocked everyone else from getting too close and he too walked backward.

A tall, green-skinned Galoric stepped forward through the crowd. "Orinthia, let her go. This will only bring more trouble for you. Show them they are wrong about you and do the right thing."

Orinthia risked a glance behind her. They were less than ten feet from their ship. "We'll drop her off somewhere uncomfortable, don't worry," she said, facing Kian again. "After that, she's free to contact anyone she wants to pick her up."

Freya's ramp hissed as it lowered. Kos entered first. His steps grew quieter and disappeared to the lower deck.

Orinthia's bare feet grazed the edge of the metal and moved onto it. Thrutt continued to block anyone from following them. He made sure they were inside the hold before joining them and closing the door.

Freya's engines ignited and lifted off the ground. Her door was half open as Mimi shifted back to herself. She waved at the Hunters outside of the ship. "Bye!"

With a sliver left to see out, Orinthia watched Kian's color change to orange. The ramp snapped closed and blaster fire pelted the hull. *Freya* lurched forward, knocking the three over.

Orinthia tucked her sword close to her chest to keep from impaling Mimi or herself. Her body lifted off the ground as they exited *Mathias'* artificial gravity. She was a foot high before, without warning, *Freya's* gravity activated and sent her back to solid ground. Her hip made contact first before she rolled to her back where she stayed for a minute.

It was almost a week she since had last been on *Freya*. The smell of old oil hung in the air. The engines hummed at a low frequency. The cold, recycled oxygen filled her lungs. They all meant she was home. Home with her friends. Safe in *Freya's* hold, she let silent tears roll down the sides of her face.

Mimi knelt beside her and placed a hand on her forehead. "You're okay now. When you're ready, I'll help you get cleaned up."

Thrutt's shadow covered Orinthia as he looked down at her. He gave her a look up and down before offering only a tight-lipped smile. "I'll get the vial and set it in your room." His steps moved to the ladder and down to the lower level.

Mimi stayed stroking Orinthia's hair, putting slight pressure with her nails against her scalp. She stayed silently soothing Orinthia for a while. Each pass of her hand eased the tension in Orinthia's nerves.

"We should get those cuts healed," Mimi finally whispered.

Orinthia took Mimi's arm and pulled herself to her feet. She recalled her sword and climbed down the ladder to their quarters.

The room was dim, but she could make out Uri's figure on the bed nearest the door. Her chest grew tight. She was not ready to see him yet and continued moving to her bed.

In the closed window beside her bed, Orinthia caught a glimpse of her reflection. The grey prison shirt was pocked with black-rimmed holes. They served as frames for the burned and bloody skin on her chest and arms. Shadows of bruises marked her face. She had not realized how terrible it must have been for the others to see.

Mimi touched her elbow and turned her away from the window. "Sit down for a minute. You'll need to take off your shirt so I can get to those wounds."

Orinthia sat on the edge of her bed. Her stomach twisted and a chill clung to her hands. She did not want to be stripped down and exposed again.

Mimi moved to her own bed and yanked a sheet from the makeshift canopy. She returned and folded it in quarters, then held it out for Orinthia. "Cover with this. I'll be quick and only reveal what needs to be taken care of, okay?"

Orinthia wrapped the cloth around her abdomen and gingerly removed the shirt from her body. She winced as some of the fabric tore from her skin, having melted on in a few places.

Able to work freely, Mimi wasted no time in uncorking the vial Thrutt had left on the bed. She worked efficiently and in less than five minutes had resealed the solution. "How are you feeling otherwise? Is there anything else I can take care of?"

"Just sore," Orinthia answered. The pain from the burns faded from her body but did nothing to settle the fatigue in her muscles.

"Let me know if anything hurts or doesn't feel right." Mimi placed the almost empty vial in her pocket. "I can have Rogue scan you just to make sure there isn't anything more serious."

Orinthia gave a half smile. There was still a pain in her

mouth, but she did not complain. "Thank you, Mimi. I'll be better once I get washed and into my own clothes."

"Take your time," Mimi said. She gave a short bow and walked to the door. "Holler if you need anything at all."

Orinthia waited for Mimi to leave the room before she carried the sheet with her to the washroom and undressed. In the full view of a real mirror, she took in the damage. Her face had a round bruise above her jaw. The skin around her middle was green and yellow. Her eyes were puffy from crying and exhaustion. She still had a few burn marks on her legs. There were also fading thin lines from Celso's bola across her thighs.

She turned away from her image and stepped into the warm shower. The temperature helped to ease some of the aches, but it was more comforting to wash away all traces of the last week from her skin.

Once she was clean and dressed, she returned to her room and sat on the floor beside Uri's bed. She laid her head on his mattress and pulled her legs as close to her body as her injuries allowed. In her mind, she tried to imagine what he would say to her. His voice had started to fade from her memory. She closed her eyes and pictured his smile and felt his embrace.

Her week away from him had pushed back their efforts to find Desidario. They were off course by who knew how much, and she had no idea if her friends managed to get the information they needed just to take one more step forward. Hopelessness crept into her chest. She could not see an end to her journey, especially not one with Uri back in her life. Every move felt in vain, as if she were caught in a never-ending cycle. Her life was lived in fragments. Nothing they had done since leaving the *Fera* got them closer to her goal.

For the second time, Orinthia cried.

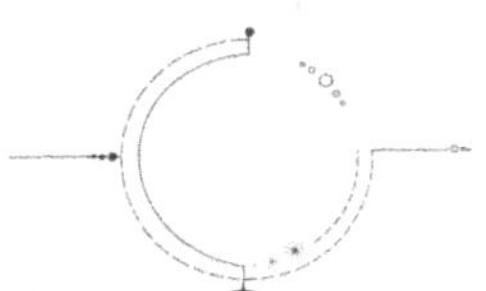

37

The familiar sounds of her room did nothing to relieve the numbness in Orinthia's core. Her clothes had not belonged to her long enough to feel like they were anything more than another uniform. Even the texture of Uri's hand under hers was foreign. In the darkness of her mind's eye, she could still see the bars around her. The ground beneath her reminded her of Celso's ship. Every thought led to another and sent her into spirals of recollection.

Her tears came in waves, draining whatever energy she had left. Tears turned to indifference. Indifference turned to trembling. The trembling grew into nausea. And nausea brought on more tears. Orinthia's emotional cycle lasted for a while as she sat beside her brother in the otherwise empty room.

Voices in the hall grew louder, as if they were moving from one end to the other. They stopped in front of her door. Orinthia could make out the sound of Kos and Mimi's voices, but their words were muffled by the metal. Whatever they were saying was intense as the pitch in volume grew after every pass of phrase.

Orinthia lifted her head and wiped her eyes on her sleeves. She did not have the energy to hold a conversation or answer any questions, but the idea of another warm body in the room served to ease some of the dread.

The door slid open. Mimi stood with her lips pinched and arms crossed. Kos stepped in and looked around the room until his eyes landed on Orinthia. He closed the door behind him before moving forward. "Mimi said I should let you rest, but I wanted to make sure you ate something." Kos crouched in front of her and held out a sweet cake.

The package was warm and squished in her hand as she took it from him. She placed it in her lap and looked at the man in front of her. Kos' long hair was pulled into a low bun and exposed his worn face. He aged years in the short time she was gone. There was no smile on his face, nor emotion at all. Whatever was going on behind his eyes, she could not read.

"Thank you for coming back for me," Orinthia choked out, forcing back another torrent of tears.

Kos rocked forward and placed his weight on his knees. He reached out and took one of her hands in his. "I would have flown into a supernova to get you back. We never should have left you on Mos Kaanan. I will regret that decision for as long as I live."

The dam cracked. Tears pricked her eyes, but she did not blink them away for fear of exposing their presence. *He came back for me*, she thought. *They all could have died or ended up in prison too, but he took them there. Kos Rogue came back for me.*

A tear escaped.

Kos released her hand and scooted between her and the other bed. He put an arm over her shoulder and drew her closer.

Orinthia rested her head on his chest and wept. Kos did not shush her or offer words of comfort. He instead stroked the back of her hand with his thumb. His clothes smelled of fabric soap, but Kos himself did not have a scent. The heat rolled off his body and seeped into her muscles. It soothed some of the aches away.

Her sobs slowed enough for her to calm down. She took in hiccupped breaths and blew air out through her nose.

"Thia," Kos said in a low voice. "I've wanted to hold you like this for so long. Most of the time, it's all I can think about. Losing you made me realize I've wasted too much time not saying so."

Orinthia's mod kept quiet as he spoke. Though it was possible she could have missed it over the sound of the blood rushing through her body at speeds she had never experienced before. Her hands tingled and she was aware of every atom in her body.

"I'm not sure right now is the right time to say this," Kos continued. He gave a small chuckle. "In our lives, the right time probably doesn't exist. We both carry so much damage, and some days will be difficult. I hold no illusion that we can fix each other. But I do know I am a better person when you're around. You've pulled me back from my darkest moments and helped me find the way out. You are not my crutch, but rather a respite from the battle."

Orinthia lifted her head and faced Kos. He looked at her with a piercing stare. His lips ran over his teeth and took short breaths through his nose. "I hope I make you feel as safe as you do me," Kos whispered.

With hands that no longer belonged to her, Orinthia gripped the back of his head and pulled him close. His mouth blazed against her chapped lips. Every crack stung. She did not care. If she burned, she burned.

Several pounding heartbeats passed before they parted. Orinthia fluttered her eyes open to see Kos give her an affectionate smile. His cheeks flushed pink, and he ran his eyes over every inch of her face. It was as if his burdens had lifted, even just for a moment. He was a content man who found a place in the chaotic universe.

Orinthia smiled back. She also knew she was where she belonged. Kos was her safe place. He would protect her, and she would fight for him. Everything in her wanted to be the person he thought she was. She rested her head back on his chest and vowed to prove herself worthy of his care.

"I'm not leaving you again, either." Kos tilted his head down and kissed the top of her head. His heart banged in her ear with such force, she could feel it on her bruised cheek.

They sat in silence together. Kos stroked her hair and rested his head against the wall. His pulse slowed to a steady rhythm. The sound soothed her. Secure in his arms, Orinthia fell asleep.

38

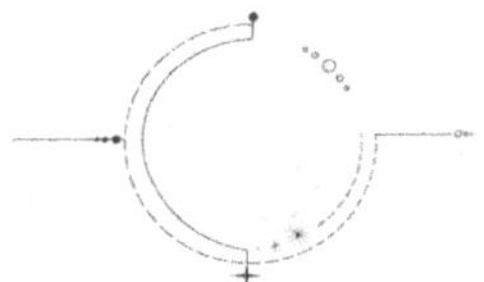

*O*rinthia awoke to a dim room with her head on Uri's mattress. Her neck cracked as she shifted to look around. Kos' faint snores told her she was not alone. He laid on his back with his head in her lap and legs stretched out under the bed beside them. She smiled and gently ran her fingers through his hair.

Kos stirred and he opened an eye. "You okay?" His voice was hoarse and stiff from sleep.

"Sorry. I didn't mean to wake you," Orinthia whispered her reply.

His warm head rolled in her lap. "This is the best sleep I've had in months."

"Go back to sleep, then." Orinthia untangled her fingers from his hair. "We can talk in a bit."

Kos reached out for her hand and placed it back on his head. "I want to hear what you're thinking about."

Orinthia glanced over to Mimi's bed. The canopy sheet she used to cover herself with had not been replaced. Her roommate lay curled under a blanket with her back turned to them. "We'll wake Mimi."

Kos rolled to his side and sat up. His elbows popped as he stretched. He nudged his chin toward the bedroom door and stood, reaching for Orinthia's hand.

In the corridor, Orinthia did not dare look at the cockpit for fear of seeing the warp. Instead, she kept her eyes fixed on the galley and entered quickly. She stroked the wall with her fingers until she found the light and switched it on.

Kos motioned for her to sit. He went to the cabinets and grabbed two of every edible item he could find along with four hydro-spheres. With his treasures in hand, he laid them on the table and sat across from Orinthia. He leaned his back to the wall and crossed his feet in front of him on the bench.

The water from Orinthia's sphere went empty in three long swallows. It cooled her throat and freshened her spirits.

Kos passed her another and asked, "What's on your mind?"

It took a minute for her to reply. In truth, there were a dozen things on her mind. Did they get the information? Did Vandra give them the maps? Could Mimi find Elendoras? There was one question that she thought about the most and decided to go with that. "How did you find me?"

The wrapper in Kos' hands crinkled as he opened a meat stick. He looked away and stared at the wall across from him. His face hardened. "The bounty hunter who turned you in."

"Celso?" A chill went up her back at the sound of his name.

Kos licked his lips and rolled his shoulders. "Vandra told us you left with a man and hadn't returned. Mimi used her bounty hunter access to check security footage around the docks. She saw him take you to his ship. Obviously, I wasn't happy seeing you in a fight, but you put up a good one. We thought you were going to get away."

Orinthia touched her ankle. It was healed, but the memory lingered.

"We were only a day and a half behind you at that point," Kos continued. He fiddled with the packaging of his snack. The side of his shoe tapped the table as he wiggled his foot. "But with all the flying we had done to get to Mos Kaanan both times, *Freya* needed to refuel. I wanted to steal another ship and have the others catch up, but Thrutt talked me out of it."

Orinthia pictured Kos and Thrutt arguing. Thrutt would have agreed with him but knew drawing more attention would not help anyone.

"While we waited, Mimi found Celso's ship ID and tracked down his last pinged location. Unfortunately, it's almost impossible to track a ship while it's in warp, even for *Freya*. We took the chance and followed the trail as best as we could. To our surprise, he was still there."

"At the *Mathias*?" Orinthia asked.

Kos shook his head. "No. Some system at the edge of EC territory. He wired your broken comm into his nav computer and used the signal to automatically open a channel when we got near. He said he didn't have you anymore but sent us the code to get onto the *Mathias*. Thrutt felt like it was a trap, but at that point, I didn't care. I figured he was either telling the truth, or I'd get to send his rotting corpse through the vacuum of space. Either way, it was more than we had."

Orinthia rested her elbow on the table and put her chin in her hand. Celso had repeatedly said he needed to trade her for his pardon. A smile formed at the corner of her lips. *He did keep up his end of the bargain*, Orinthia thought.

"If I ever run across him again, though…" Kos said. His nostrils flared.

Orinthia reached across the table and touched his bare arm. Her fingertips burned as she stroked his skin. A line of goosebumps grew along her trail. "I want to hate him, but he's like me. A former Hunter who turned marauder. He fled that life for his Master Gunner."

Kos moved his hand and laced his fingers between hers. He pulled her hand to his lips and pressed them against her skin.

Thrutt's heavy footsteps trotted closer to the galley. Orinthia tried to take her hand back, but Kos did not let go.

"Oh, good," Thrutt said, looking between the two in the room. "Now we can stop pretending like you two aren't obsessed with each other."

Orinthia's face and ears went hot.

Seemingly unfazed by the pair holding hands, Thrutt moved to the table and pushed Kos' feet out of the way to sit down. "We'll be coming out of jump in about an hour. As far as I can tell, no one followed us. Freya did a scan for tracking devices, too. We're in the clear."

"Where are we headed?" Orinthia asked.

"Neutral space, for the moment," Thrutt answered. "It's a star squid sanctuary. Even if your sister follows us, the EC is vigilant and does not allow larger vessels to enter. We'll be safe long enough to look at the maps and decide our next move."

"So, you have the maps? Vandra actually gave them to you?" Orinthia remembered Vandra had said they could only look at the maps, not take them.

Thrutt patted Kos on the back. "Well, we made a trade. Just not the one originally agreed to. Kos let her keep her life and she let us have the maps and the disk."

Orinthia gave Kos a sideways glance. He stared at a spot

on the table, his eyes low. "Did you decrypt the disk?" Orinthia asked, shifting her attention back to Thrutt.

Thrutt nodded but broke eye contact and looked away.

"What are you hiding?" Orinthia asked.

Kos shifted in his seat and stiffened his grip on her hand.

"There's information on him, isn't there?" Orinthia's palm began to sweat under his touch. "My father was a traitor."

The two men exchanged looks. Thrutt raised his eyebrows and dipped his head toward Kos.

Kos let out a long stream of air through pinched lips. He placed a second hand on Orinthia's and leaned forward. "It's about your mom."

Orinthia's eyebrows scrunched together. "My mother? What does that mean?"

"There were nine names and references on the disk," Kos said. "Mimi worked it out and more than likely it was a Mod Bleyer hit list."

Despite Kos' burning hands on hers, Orinthia's body went cold. Her ears rang as her blood pressure ticked up. "I don't understand. My mom was killed in an accident."

"Who told you that?" Thrutt asked.

She did not need to answer. They knew who. It was the same man who did everything out of self-interest. The same man they were searching for in every corner of the galaxy.

"You were very young when it happened," Thrutt continued. "Memories can be manipulated, especially at that age."

"But even if that were true," Orinthia said, finding her voice. "He spoke about the accident multiple times. Uri did, too. I'd know if they were lying. How does Mimi know it was a hit list?"

"More than half the names were confirmed assassinations; mostly politicians," Kos answered. "Mimi's memory mod filled in the rest. She pieced together the information and crossed it with other reports from the EC. There is no other reason for her name to be there."

The entire ship could have imploded, crushing Orinthia into dust and it would have been easier to process than what she just heard. She knew of only one way to find out what it meant. "We need to get to Elendoras," Orinthia said.

39

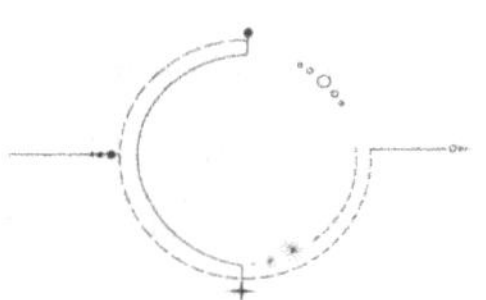

*M*imi set two holo pads on the table with one hand and held her blanket closed around her with the other. She let out a long yawn then spoke. "This is the official Earth Confederacy map of the Burquian system. And this—," she pressed the second holo pad, "—is the prewar map of the system. Right there is Elendoras. According to the EC map, half the system is a no-fly zone and littered with mines." She pressed another button and the image on the first holo pad shifted. The two maps merged together.

"Elendoras isn't the only planet missing from this map," Mimi continued, stifling another yawn. "Provis, Kromin, and Zolot, as well as all of their moons are gone, too. Now, with that many planets having been destroyed, there would be debris everywhere. The whole system would have lost balance and changed the sector itself. Not to mention Zolot is… was? Is a gas giant. One, it would be extremely difficult to destroy. And two, the force from the planet dying would be so strong there would be nothing left in the entire system."

"So what does that mean?" Orinthia asked. Even as Mimi explained it, none of what she looked at made sense.

"It means the EC map is faked," Mimi answered. "I think Elendoras is still there, and someone is hiding it."

"You mentioned a while ago knowing someone who was at the battle."

Mimi nodded and sunk onto the bench. She lifted her blanketed hand and rested her head on it. "Arkady runs a smuggling organization out of Imjumi. I did a job for him a few years ago. He was a friend of a friend, and we struck up a conversation about the battle."

"Then we start there," Orinthia said. "I'm tired of running headlong into nothing."

Kos moved around the table and studied the holo pad images. "I'll have *Freya* set a course for Imjumi while I upload these to my charts." He pressed a button on each of the pads and the screens deactivated. Then, he left the galley.

"I'm going back to bed," Mimi said. She pulled her blanket tight and followed him out.

Thrutt, who stood beside Orinthia, turned to face her. "Are you okay?"

Orinthia filled her lungs with as much air as they could hold, then slowly let it back out through her nose. "I'm just tired. Everything is happening all at once and it's a lot to take in."

"It is a lot," Thrutt agreed. "But you don't have to carry it alone. If you want to talk about your mom, dad, Rogue, or what happened while you were away, I'm ready to listen."

"Back on Vron, Errol told me I won't like what I find on Elendoras." Orinthia lifted herself onto the side of the table and rested with her feet on the bench. "I thought he meant Desidario, but what if he meant the truth about my mom?"

Thrutt leaned against the wall and crossed his arms. "The

trouble with sequencing is how vague answers can be. You currently have just enough information to form speculations. With those speculations in view, everything seems to fit in the gaps, and you believe it's all connected. No matter what we find on Elendoras, I don't think we're going to like it. So, it isn't much of a prediction."

"I guess that's true."

"Don't think about it too much," Thrutt said. "You're going to cook up a million scenarios, most of which will never come to pass. Then you'll be stressed over things in your imagination. Trust me. Nothing good can come of it."

Orinthia did not reply. She knew he was right and was speaking from a place of love. But she did not know how to *not* think about what was crowding her mind. Her head was always loud with thoughts.

Wishing to change the subject, Orinthia asked, "What is a No-Mod?"

"Where did you hear that?" Thrutt asked.

"A dealer in Caytoo called me one," Orinthia answered. It was also the same time she met Celso, but she decided to leave that tidbit out. "I didn't want to buy one of his second-hand mods and he got mad."

"I've never personally met one, but they are a sect of Mod Bleyers who are against modifications of any kind. They believe that mods are an abomination to life."

Orinthia tried to think if she had ever met anyone who did not have at least one mod. Her discolored eyes and hair were side effects of being modified too young. There were a few others like her in the NCR, but after the EC passed restrictions on modifications shortly after the war began, children under fifteen years of age were no longer allowed to be given mods. Other than that, no one came to mind.

"Have you thought about removing your mod?" Thrutt asked.

The thought had crossed her mind after the worst days when she was younger. "As much as I hate it being used against me, I wouldn't know what to do without it. When I was with Celso on his ship, I had to rely on instinct to judge whether he was lying. It was like looking through a dark room with a match and I never knew if I had all the information. That was scarier than being a prisoner. Though I've come to realize I depend on it more than I should."

"Back on my planet, we didn't have mods," Thrutt said. He lifted his diamond hands and slowly spun them in front of him. "Stone is difficult to modify. These aren't considered mods. They are more like prosthetics grafted on. Though I wouldn't call myself a No-Mod, mods were a foreign concept for a long time."

Orinthia touched the crack along his knuckles and thought back to when it happened. The first time she sat in a prison cell awaiting her fate. He rescued her then, too. A lifetime ago.

Kos poked his head into the galley. He was light on his feet and his sudden appearance startled Orinthia. "I didn't want to say it over the speakers and wake up Mimi," Kos said, "but you both need to see this."

A knot formed in Orinthia's stomach. *Who do we have to fight now?*

"It's nothing bad," Kos quickly added. He held out his tattooed hand and waited for her to take it.

His grip was strong but gentle like he was afraid to lose what he was holding onto, while also trying not to hurt it. He led her out of the galley toward the cockpit. Thrutt followed behind them.

The large window came alive with light. Five enormous

glowing creatures floated in the distance. Each of them rotated shades of every color Orinthia could name, and then some. They moved closer, the edges of their bodies rippled as they did. The star squid used the fins on the sides of their heads to propel themselves through the void. Each flap seemed to go in slow motion, swirling like silk in water.

The largest star squid could have consumed *Freya* in one go. Its tentacles were longer than four of her lined end-to-end as well. A smaller one broke from the group and veered toward the ship. It drifted above and out of view.

Orinthia leaned forward to try and get a better look. As she did, the squid came up from underneath the belly of the ship, coming feet from the window. The cockpit lit up with the luminosity of the surprisingly fast creature.

Back on the *Fera,* Orinthia had seen a tadpole galaxy and thought it was the most amazing thing space had to offer. The presence of the space squid made her realize she knew nothing of the universe.

Orinthia saw Kos smiling at her through the side of her eye. She moved back from the panel. "What?"

"I've seen space through the lens of war," Kos said, pressing his arm against hers. "There was hardly time to appreciate its wonder and beauty. Watching you experience it for the first time makes me see it for what it really is."

"When this is all over, we'll go somewhere neither of us have been." Orinthia wrapped her pinky around his. Her throat went tight and her heart raced faster. It was foreign to be so familiar with someone. "Explore the stars until we go farther than even you've gone."

Kos took his free hand and placed it on her hip. He turned her to face him. A tender smile formed on his lips. "I'd like that."

"Can I come, too?" Thrutt asked in a not-so-quiet whisper.

The sound of his voice made Orinthia flinch. Her cheeks warmed almost as much as Kos' hands. She had forgotten he was behind them.

"No," Kos said with a definitive tone.

"It was worth a shot." Thrutt shrugged. "Anyway, I'm going to go... somewhere else. I've had enough *star squid* watching to last me a lifetime." He dipped his head in salutations and left down the corridor to his quarters.

"We need a bigger ship." Kos sighed.

40

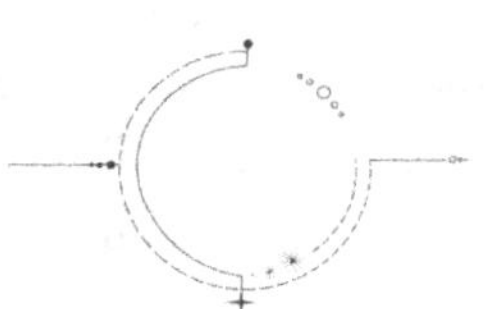

The trip to Imjumi took over two-day cycles of jumping sectors and changing trajectories. Kos mapped out a route that would prevent anyone from following them while taking the shortest amount of time. All the while, *Freya* complained her warp drive would never recover from the amount of system hopping she had to do. Her engines puttered louder after each adjustment, sending shudders through the ship at the beginning of each jump.

They came out of the last jump close enough to orbit around Imjumi. Kos and Thrutt were already in the cockpit when the women joined them. The view out the window was partially blocked by a detailed map of the planet below. There were no continents, from what Orinthia could see. Most of the planet was covered with water. Clusters of islands were scattered throughout deep blue oceans like puzzle pieces across the map. When everyone was together, Kos zoomed in on the image and focused on a large archipelago.

"Arkady runs his smuggling ring from that island," Mimi said, pointing to one of the smaller islands in the chain. "I ran

223

security for a few of his jobs when I first left the Navy. So, unlike Vandra, I know him pretty well."

"What kind of infrastructure does the island have?" Kos asked. "I'd like to refuel and restock the ship if possible. That way, we can leave as soon as we're done talking."

Mimi's eyes lit up. "He's built up the place in the last few years. Nothing like Caytoo, of course, but more than enough for our needs. And there is a nice little armory in the port. I wouldn't mind checking that out while we were there."

"You and Thrutt stock up on ammunition and whatever else can be useful," Kos said. "There's no telling what we will find on Elendoras, and I'd like to be prepared. We—" he pointed to Orinthia then himself "—will resupply the food. We're running low on hydro-spheres."

Orinthia pinched her lips together and curled her bare toes against the floor. The cold metal stung. Her bones ached from the chill. She stared at the map and swayed from one foot to another, taking turns pressing a cold foot to her slightly warmer legs.

Kos furrowed his eyebrows and looked at her feet. "What's going on down there?"

"Nothing, I'm fine," Orinthia answered. "Keep going."

"The archipelago is in the northern hemisphere," Kos said, turning his head back to the map while keeping his eyes on Orinthia until the last second. "It'll take an hour to orbit around to the correct side of the planet. In the meantime, I want everyone to pack up and prepare to land. I'll call over the speakers when it's time to buckle in."

Mimi and Thrutt moved out of the cockpit. Orinthia tried to follow but Kos stopped her with a hand around her wrist.

"Why didn't you say you needed shoes?" Kos asked.

"And ask for another shopping trip?" Orinthia rolled her

eyes. "I don't want to add something else to the growing list of things we have to do."

"This is a genuine need. You can't help it." Kos set her on the chair and crouched in front of her. He wrapped his hands around her feet. The chill left her body with such a force that it was almost euphoric.

"I could have stayed in Vandra's shop and not gotten arrested," Orinthia said, soaking in the warmth.

"Well, there is that," Kos said. "But either way, you can't galivant across the universe without shoes."

"That was a Thrutt word if I ever heard one," Orinthia teased. "But I'm fine. I'll figure something out." In truth, she had a solution in mind. The thought turned her stomach, though. Uri's shoes were only a size larger than hers. He was not putting any miles on them, and with two pairs of socks, the extra space could be filled without much issue. She ran the idea by Kos.

"I think you'd hurt your feet after a while." He let go of her feet and stood. "We'll get you another pair. If it's about the credits, I'll cover it."

"I'm not asking for anything else," Orinthia said. She held her feet out so they did not touch the ground and undo what Kos fixed. "Let me still do some things for myself."

MIMI WAS ADJUSTING a belt on her waist when Orinthia returned to their cabin. A dagger hung in a sheath between her mod dampening cuffs and a brown leather pouch. She saw Orinthia eye her gear and turned to reveal a pink revolving blaster on the other side. On the bed behind her laid her blunderbuss, a handful of throwing knives, several grenades, and an array of weapons Orinthia could not name.

"And I thought Thrutt liked his weapons," Orinthia said with wide eyes.

"Who do you think taught him?" Mimi smirked. "These are only my traveling essentials."

Orinthia gave a whistle and opened her footlocker. Inside were all the possessions she had collected over the few months with her new crew. "Well, this is all I have left," she said, pulling out socks. "Everything else I took from Earth was abandoned on the *Fera* when we escaped. Which wasn't much to begin with."

"The three of you need real jobs," Mimi said. She crossed her arms and leaned against the frame of Orinthia's bunk. "Something that isn't completely illegal and pays well."

"Know anyone who wants to hire a useless marauder hunter and a couple of vets? Because that's exactly why I signed with them in the first place."

Mimi twisted her mouth in thought. "I'll see what I can drum up when all of this is over."

The cold did not penetrate as easily through two layers of fabric, but it was noticeable enough that Orinthia rushed to Uri. The gears in his chest whirred beneath the makeshift straps. She instinctively stroked his hair before moving to and sitting on the foot of the bed. Her hands hovered over his shoes, and it took several mental counts to three to unzip the first one.

I miss you, she thought as she gently pulled the shoe from his foot. His heel popped out with ease. *A lot has happened and I'm not sure I'm making the right decisions. My new friends have made me too trusting and I forgot not everyone is like them.* The zipper from the other shoe caught and she had to tug to get it undone. *I'm sorry I left you for so long.*

And I'm sorry I haven't really spoken to you since coming back. It's hard with so much going on. But this should be the last stop we have to make before we go to Father. Everything will be better after that. I can't wait to hear your voice again.

Orinthia held both shoes in her hands. *As soon as you're awake, I'll give these back.*

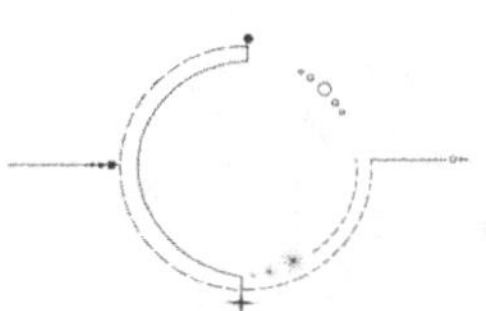

*A*rkady's smuggling island was larger than anticipated. As *Freya* cut through a layer of clouds and came in for a landing, Orinthia watched the land grow closer through the window. In the center of the island was a massive mountain covered in lush green foliage. Thin brown paths snaked around its base, disappearing beneath the trees and climbing higher up the mountain. There were no hover cars flying through the skies like in the bigger cities. Only lev-speeders or pedal bikes could be seen moving around below.

Freya's landing gear thumped the wooden dock. The door decompressed and sounded like the ship sighing with relief to finally be able to rest. It also took longer than usual for the ramp to lower. The journey had put a strain on *Freya* and took a toll on her systems.

Mimi was the first to unbuckle and stand up from her seat. She bounced toward the door and stood waiting for the others. Her light blue tank top revealed a tattoo on the middle of her bicep that Orinthia had not noticed before. It resembled the insignia on Kos' geared arm tattoo. A shield with a vertical sword in the center. On either side of the blade were wings stretched out across the shield in full span.

"Kos has a tattoo like that," Orinthia said joining Mimi. "What does it mean?"

Mimi twisted her shoulder to get a better view of her arm. "It's called Lavin's Shield. We were part of the Guardian Division. It's mostly a military story now, but the Guardians were an ancient human-like species who have protected humans since the Earth was very young. They've almost all died off through the centuries of wars, but those who are left still keep to the old ways. Our former Rear Admiral, Admiral Lavin, is a Guardian. So, we wear his shield."

The Navy was full of traditions Orinthia did not understand. Nor had she ever heard of Guardians. Every day spent with her friends made her realize how little she knew. The universe was bigger and stranger than life inside her bubble. These were the types of stories she hoped to hear when she agreed to become a marauder. And Imjumi was the type of world she envisioned visiting.

Kos and Thrutt emerged from the lower level and joined the others. Like Mimi, Kos wore a sleeveless shirt exposing the detailed tattoos stretched over his tight skin. He caught Orinthia staring and grinned.

"We'll meet back in two hours," Kos said, addressing the rest of the group. He tapped a number into his watch. "After that, I want Mimi to reach out to Arkady. Let him know we're here for more than just shopping, but don't give too much."

"With only two hours, we should get going then," Thrutt said. "See you two in a bit." He not so subtly winked at Orinthia before pushing Mimi toward the exit.

Orinthia blushed and nibbled on her bottom lip. She kept

her eyes on Thrutt's back as he walked away. A fresh breeze blew in from the opening, cooling her warm face. Soft light shone on the floor of the hold casting a defused glow around the space.

"Ready?" Kos asked.

They walked onto the ramp together. Kos pressed the button on the hull, sealing the door. Waves beat against the pier they were docked on, and a light mist drifted through the air. There were several hobby crafts nearby. But it was the cargo ships that caught Orinthia's eye. Most were the size of *Freya* except for two at the very end of the row. The ships ranged from pristine condition to borderline junkers.

Those have to be Arkady's ships, Orinthia thought. *Blending in means different things depending on the type of location they needed to smuggle.* That she did understand. Taking a brand-new ship into an unregulated system would draw just as much attention as a beater in a wealthy one.

Kos tapped his pinky against hers. She looked down and saw him wiggle his fingers. As she slipped her hand into his, a wave of heat rushed over her. It was from more than just his skin. She looked at him through the side of her eye. Kos had an airy look. His eyes were bright, and a smile spread across his lips.

A few children giggled and ran past them as they left the platform and neared the boardwalk connecting the docks to the shore. For a moment, Orinthia let herself think this was her real life. Not a marauder, not on a mission, but walking hand in hand with someone she cared deeply about. They were on their way to do normal morning things as normal people.

The smell of salty sea air mingled with the sweet and savory scents of food. Orinthia's stomach growled. She gazed at the booth closest to them. Bags of snack mixes lined the shelf. Each was filled so high that some of the colorful treats fell out around them. There was a sign for other options such as sandwiches and various meats on sticks.

Kos looked at her and then followed her line of sight to the stand. "Come on, I'm starving for some real food." He pulled her to the stall. The vendor greeted them as they approached.

Being closer, Orinthia read the sign better and chose one of the meats on a stick. Kos ordered one for himself, too, and a snack bag to share. He reached into his pouch and handed credits to the fish-like vendor. Four out of the vendor's six arms worked quickly to assemble their food. In less than a minute, he handed them their order.

Kos released Orinthia's hand, and they grabbed their food. With a "thanks," the pair continued on their way.

The taste of salty meat filled Orinthia's mouth as she bit a piece from the stick. She leaned forward, trying to avoid the grease that dripped down.

Kos chuckled but immediately had to do the same. "There's a bench," he said through the side of his mouth. He pointed to a spot at the edge of the dock.

They sat down and Kos set the snack bag between them. He crossed his leg over his knee and cupped a hand under his chin as he took another bite of his food. Shiny, clear liquid dripped down his beard.

Orinthia grinned over his casual demeanor. The hard exterior was removed and the young man she envisioned sat beside her. It was a side of him she had only glimpsed before.

Kos wiggled his foot on his knee. He looked over the water as he spoke. "You know, I didn't have much growing up. Between the debt my mom left when she died and my dad's desertion, there was nothing left. The Navy took my childhood home and my aunt had to sell her house just to keep us alive."

He turned to face Orinthia. His eyes were not as bright as they had been a minute before, but he chuckled. "What a depressing first date starter. There is a point, I promise. Until we met Thrutt, and a few times after, food was a luxury. Even when I was in the Navy, I ate only rations and sent my aunt every credit I could afford. I've been run through with a blade, had broken bones, been burned and beaten. None of it was as hard or frightening to go through as being hungry."

Orinthia frowned. She had never known hunger like that. Even when her father withheld food as a punishment, Uri made sure she ate. Her heart ached for Kos.

"That didn't come out how I wanted it to," Kos said, nervously laughing. "All of that was just to say that I love food. Good food, especially. It's why I bought the restaurant in the NCR and why I make sure the galley is stocked."

"Thanks for clearing that up," Orinthia half-heartedly teased. "I wasn't sure where that story was going."

Kos rubbed his forehead with his clean hand. "I know. It sounded better before I said it. Being with you like this has my thoughts out of order. We've spent months together, but not alone. And I haven't been on a date since before the *Fera*, so I don't remember what I'm supposed to do."

"This is my first real date," Orinthia muttered. She popped a piece of snack mix into her mouth and looked away from him. Her eyes focused on a spot on the horizon, but she could feel Kos staring. "I've never really had friends at all. This—" she pointed to her head, "—doesn't allow for close relationships. Always knowing exactly how someone feels about you isn't as liberating as you might think it is."

Kos touched her chin with his forefinger. He turned her to

face him and passed his gaze over her face. His lips moved over his teeth like they did when he was deep in thought.

Orinthia's pulse quickened. She wanted to go back to his silly stories and awkwardness. The way he looked at her said he was onto something more serious. His attitude change was jarring. Her mind tried to find a place to hold onto. A puff of sea breeze blew strands of hair across her face. People laughed and spoke loudly around them. A vendor several booths away called out their goods. The pier was alive. She was aware of it all.

"I thought I should wait longer to say this, but now I know you need to hear it," Kos said. He dropped his hand and took the snack bag from between them. Free from obstacles, he inched closer to her. His leg pressed against hers. "We're both adult enough to know what we want. I'm only thirty, but I feel like I've lived a hundred lives. This life is dark and lonely. You've given me the light to find my way. There is still so much more to learn about each other, and I want to learn everything. But I've seen enough to decide there's nothing else out there for me."

Orinthia's hands trembled in her lap. Her heart punched into her throat. Every nerve in her body was on fire.

Kos' breath was quick. "I'm falling in love with you, Thia. And you deserve love. I can give you all of mine if you'll have it."

The air moved in and out of Orinthia's lungs like they were holes in her chest. Her fingertips tingled and her palms were warm. "I don't know how," she whispered.

"That's okay," Kos said, leaning closer. His breath warmed her face. "I'll spend my life showing you." He tilted his head and pressed his mouth to hers, giving her a long, gentle kiss. There was no force to his action, nothing to suggest he expected more. After a moment, he pulled back.

"Don't say anything. This was for you. I can hold onto this moment until you're ready."

Orinthia reached up and placed her shaking hand on his cheek. Kos leaned into it and tucked his fingers between hers. He rubbed her knuckles against his stubble to his mouth and kissed each of her fingers.

"We should finish our errands," Orinthia said breathlessly. "I might forget I have responsibilities."

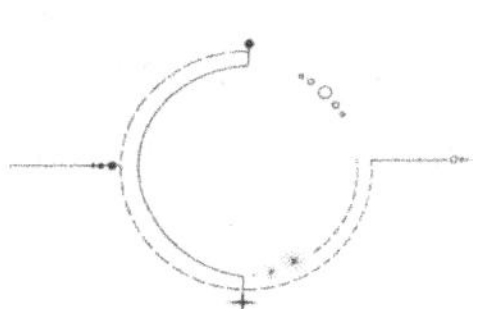

42

*M*imi and Thrutt waited at the base of *Freya's* ramp. Orinthia and Kos returned with a crate full of fresh, locally grown food. The crate rested on Kos' hip as they neared the others. None of the vendors had shelf-stable foods, not that Kos put up much of a fuss over it.

Kos was not the only one who bought something special. A second revolving blaster hung on Mimi's hip beside her pink one. "Look what I found," she said, reaching for the weapon. "I've been searching for a match for years. When we're done with all of this, I'm going to have it painted lavender."

Thrutt walked over to Kos and Orinthia. "The ship is refueled, too. We should be good to go as soon as we get back. But you might want to go check on *Freya*. She was complaining about one of her internal scans."

"Thanks," Kos said. "I'll take the food down and see what she has to say. Hopefully, it's nothing too serious. I used most of our spare parts after the star nursery."

"I still need to contact Arkady, so I'll come too," Mimi said, opening the doors to the hold.

"Do you want to come down or are you good out here with Thrutt?" Kos asked Orinthia.

Orinthia winked at Thrutt. "I'll stay here. Thrutt might wander off and get poisoned by a sequencer or something."

The boards beneath their feet rumbled with Thrutt's booming laughter. Mimi's eyebrows came together, and she shook her head. Kos walked up the ramp and explained the joke to Mimi as they entered the ship.

With the others gone, Orinthia let the weight of reality set in. They had bounced around every corner of the galaxy to end up on Imjumi. Talking to the smuggler was the last piece they needed before jumping into the deep. She was ready to have Uri back. She needed him back. But Desidario was on the other side of the information. Fear clawed up her stomach to her chest. It stroked long, cold fingers across her spine, sending a shiver through her body.

"What's on your mind, kid?" Thrutt asked. He placed a comforting hand on her shoulder.

Orinthia looked at her feet and rocked back and forth on the heels of her borrowed shoes. She confessed her fears to Thrutt then added, "Or worse, what if he isn't there? Or he refuses to help? Or he simply can't fix Uri? I don't know what I would do after everything we've been through to find him. Part of me, as much as it makes me sick, thinks I would have to let go and put Uri to rest."

Ten waves crashed against the pilings between Orinthia's confession and Thrutt's reply.

"Then we'll all do it together," Thrutt said. "If you really want to move on, we would support you. Only you can make that decision. But don't go there, yet. We have just as much information as we did yesterday. Even if this friend of Mimi's doesn't pan out, we're still going to Elendoras. There is a long way to go before you can give up."

Orinthia rubbed her face with her hands. Stars flashed over her vision as she pressed hard on her eyes. "I'm tired, Thrutt. Every second since we left the *Fera* has drained me, and I want to move on with my life. Kos just bared his soul to me, and I can't return it because there is not enough of *me* to go around. I can't help but feel shame in being happy when I know Uri is strapped to a mattress with bedsheets."

"Neither of them want you to feel like that, though," Thrutt said. He lowered himself to her level. "I don't know Uri other than how you talk about him and the brief encounter on the *Fera*, but I would wager he wants you to live your life no matter what he was going through. And Kos can handle whatever you can give him. He hasn't been this grounded since before the Navy. He understands what being with you entails and he's counted the cost."

"What if—" Orinthia began to say.

"You keep putting yourself in places that don't exist," Thrutt interrupted her, shaking his head. "My people have a saying that goes 'mountains aren't created in a day.' We spend our lives growing. Giants roamed the ancient lands of my planet. The oldest of our kind grew so big, they became mountains. But they did not start that way. It took thousands of years, millions of moments, and decisions to get there. You live as though you're a mountain, when in reality, you're only a stone. Focus on what is now."

The truth of his words set in. Orinthia had wasted her time on *Freya* by worrying about what would happen after Uri was back. They had visited several new worlds and all she could think about was what it would be like to return at another time. She missed seeing them for the first time.

"Are all your kind as wise as you?" Orinthia gave a half smile.

Thrutt frowned. "There aren't many of us left. But that's beside the point. Whatever happens next, we face it together."

Orinthia moved in and hugged his neck. "I'd be lost without you, Thrutt. Thank you for rescuing me in that bar."

The stone man returned the hug and wiggled her around a bit. "I'd do it all over if I had to. Someday, when I can no longer move and I lay down my foundation, I will think of these times. You'll live on in my memory. The valley will shake with tales of the human who fought the galaxy to save the ones she loves."

His words brought tears to her eyes. Orinthia released her friend and quickly rubbed them away.

Kos and Mimi emerged from *Freya's* hold. The door closed behind them and the ramp retreated itself into the hull.

"What did we miss?" Kos asked.

Thrutt stood straight and chuckled. "We've decided to run away and start an acrobatics troop."

Orinthia smiled as she wiped the last few tears. She was glad her head hummed. Neither Kos nor Mimi needed to know that confidence in her decisions was failing. *Maybe one day I'll tell him,* she thought. *But not right now.*

Mimi clapped her hands together and rubbed them in front of her. "Arkady is sending a couple of speeders to pick us up. He's eager, albeit curious, to see us." She looked up at Thrutt, who stood almost double her height. "You'll have to go in your own ride, though, big guy."

Thrutt stretched his arms out like he was lounging on a sofa. "Good. About time I get treated like a king."

The four walked to the end of the boardwalk and waited beside the dirt road. Two speeder cars turned a corner from a street and came toward them. Both stopped in front of the group.

Mimi entered their car first. Kos climbed in after, but

Orinthia stayed to watch Thrutt get into his ride. The back of the roofless car sagged almost low enough to touch the ground, and the lev-motors whirred louder as they fought to keep the vehicle afloat.

"Coming?" Kos asked from inside the first car.

Orinthia stepped in and snapped the door shut beside her. Once the door closed, the vehicle jerked forward. There was enough space to fit eight people comfortably in the U-shaped layout of the seats. The driver was partitioned from the rest of the car and had his own separate space.

They were only in the town for minutes before the single-level homes and buildings disappeared behind the trees. Orinthia looked through the window at the thick jungle on either side of the path. The tree trunks were smeared with green and orange moss. Vines hung from high branches. At one point, the land on her side of the car dropped off, and she was met with the sight of a vast ocean as they ascended the mountain.

Orinthia swallowed hard and turned her attention back to what was inside the car. She tried to stay in the moment and not let the what-ifs of falling off the side of the cliff would be like. In an attempt to distract herself, Orinthia asked, "Why couldn't we have landed wherever these cars are taking us?"

A compartment opened on the table in the center of the car as Mimi tapped it. She took out a hydro-sphere for each of the passengers. As she sipped hers, she leaned back and crossed her silver leg over the normal one. "Arkady likes his privacy. He has a strict no-fly policy. This whole area—" she waved her hand in a circle, "—is littered with caches that could potentially be found from the air. That, and he's nothing if not dramatic. I could have pushed the issue and got us clearance, but seeing as we're about to ruffle some feathers, I thought it was best to do things his way."

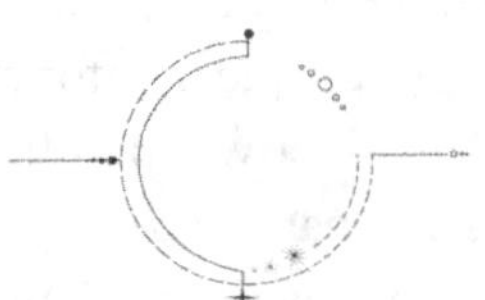

43

The lev-car sped around the mountain for miles, scraping bushes each time the path narrowed. Waterfalls splashed beneath bridges, cutting deep crevices through the rock. It would have been breathtaking if not for the switchback turns that made Orinthia's stomach hot. A ball of tension built up at the base of her skull, and she rested her head on Kos' shoulder. His heat did not relieve the motion sickness, but it was nice to have something solid to hold onto.

Kos tapped rhythmically on her knee. It was not a beat of any song she knew, but it was enough to keep her mind off the world outside of the car. He leaned the top of his head on hers. His arm stiffened to hold her in place whenever the car jerked too fast.

Mimi glanced over to the pair once before taking a long sip of her sphere and shifting in her seat. Her gaze made the nerves in Orinthia's spine tingle. She tried to pull away from Kos, but he did not budge.

After half an hour, the road evened out. Through the glass of the driver's partition, Orinthia saw the black metal gates of Arkady's compound a quarter of a mile ahead. The seams parted and sunlight split the middle. As the car moved through, Orinthia moved her head off Kos to look out her window.

The gate was three times as wide as their car and twice as tall. On either side of the opening were two sets of turrets that followed the vehicle as it entered. Four guards stood on each half of the wall, pacing the length in turns. Built into the corners of the walls were watch towers with windows bigger than the observation deck window on the *Fera*.

Orinthia shrank back in her seat. Arkady was set up better than some of the warlords she had heard terrorized the outer zones of the EC. The uncertainty of her decision to come to him grew. She almost wanted to turn around and take their chances in blindly going to Elendoras.

The others, it seemed, did not share her sentiment. Mimi sat with her legs crossed and looked as if she was meeting a friend for lunch. She shook her foot and stretched her arms behind her on the seat. Kos was not as relaxed as Mimi, but he gave no impression he felt as Orinthia did. He leaned forward and looked out the window. His eyes moved around quickly, taking in everything from where he sat.

Both cars pulled into the compound and stopped at the base of a hill. A platform beneath them activated and lifted the vehicles up a hundred feet. With a shudder, the platform ceased moving and a bridge extended to connect with it.

The driver of the car stepped out and opened the door on Orinthia's side. She exited and took in her surroundings. Across the bridge was a small mansion built into the side of the mountain. Wall-length windows reflected the afternoon sun, making her squint just to see. Behind her was a space that opened to the courtyard. There were hover cars, animals pulling carts, and stacks of crates scattered throughout.

Scores of workers moved around from one side to the other, loading and unloading various goods.

Kos joined her and put a hand on her elbow. She turned her attention toward him, and he nodded his head to the side for her to follow. The group regathered to cross the bridge. Mimi took the lead and led them to a lofty set of doors. Two guards, both holding laser rifles across their chests, stepped aside and opened the doors for them to enter.

Inside was no less impressive. Their steps echoed through the entrance chamber. Light shone in from the windows, making the black stone floors shimmer like crushed jewels. Massive paintings and tapestries lined the hand-carved walls. In between them, across from the main door, was a second doorway that led to a long hall. The frame was at least a foot thick. A pair of blast doors sat half open.

Orinthia's head swam with anxiety and awe. The GMH did not deal with smugglers, and she had no idea it could be so lucrative. Whenever she thought of smugglers, she pictured greasy ships with hapless crews. Not empires.

A male alien of a species Orinthia had never seen before stepped out from behind the second set of doors. His three head-tendrils were tied together with a black leather strap and hung below his shoulders. His blue skin was detailed with thin luminous lines that pulsed from white to yellow in rhythm. The grey short-sleeved suit he wore was pinstriped with black. It clung to his wide, muscular body in a way that accented just enough to make it clear the sizing was deliberate. He favored his left leg as he walked, but instead of a limp, he turned it to a casual swagger. An ornately etched hand cannon hung on a clip at his waste. There was no doubt this was who they came to meet.

"Nakahara," the man said, grinning and lifting a glass

filled with red liquid. His voice was metallic and deep. "It's wonderful to see you after so long."

"If I knew the business was this good, I would have come back sooner, Arkady," Mimi replied.

"Come in, come in." Arkady gestured with his free hand. "All of you. Chef had refreshments set in my lounge. Your message was rather vague, and I confess it's had my mind stirring."

Kos' arm brushed Orinthia's as they followed their host down the hall. Orinthia watched him through the side of her eye. He stood at full height and squared his shoulders. She pinched her lips together to hide a grin. Though she was not attracted to the other man, she understood the appeal. No, she liked her men human and moderately unstable.

Thrutt must have noticed, as well. He chuckled and nudged Kos a little too hard, almost causing him to trip.

Kos looked at Thrutt then Orinthia and glared as they both straightened their faces. He let out a puff of air through his nose and relaxed his posture slightly.

THE VIEW from Arkady's penthouse was even more spectacular than from the entrance. There was nothing but clear views of the entire south side of the island and the ocean beyond it. A balcony surrounded the entertaining area on two sides and formed an L-shape. Attached was a separate platform with a two-person hover car parked atop.

"Please, sit down," Arkady said. He planted himself on an overstuffed white couch and set his empty glass on the table beside him.

Mimi sat on the other end of Arkady's couch. Thrutt

looked around at the too-small seats. Instead of sitting, he took a spot behind Kos, who had guided Orinthia to sit beside him on the settee.

Arkady took a tray stacked with sweet cakes and handed it to Mimi. "Now, why've you come all this way to see me? I'm always willing to play host, but any information I may be able to give could have been passed over the comm link."

Mimi took a white frosted pastry from the tray and bit into it. She ate half of it before speaking. "I'm working on a missing person's case. A source gave us the last known location, but the problem is, it's impossible they'd be there."

The smuggler crossed a leg over the other and leaned back in his seat.

"But you see," Mimi continued through the side of her mouth. "This source is never wrong. So, I'm starting to think this impossible place just might exist."

"What is this *place*?" Arkady asked. He leaned forward and took a treat from the tray. It was gone in two bites.

"Elendoras," Mimi said.

"Ah, I see why this was an in-person visit," Arkady said, rubbing his fingers together to dust off the powder. He gave long looks to the four across from him before saying, "Questions about Elendoras can get you killed."

Orinthia stiffened. His words sounded too much like a threat than a warning for her liking.

"Do you get many questions about Elendoras?" Kos asked.

Arkady rubbed his tongue against the inside of his cheek as he studied Kos. "One or two. But that's more than I'd like." He looked back to Mimi. "Who is your source?"

"That's confidential," Mimi said, wagging a finger at him. "If I start revealing my informants, then no one will work with me. Trust me though, the intel is good."

"Well, I'm sorry you came all this way," Arkady said. He patted his palms to his knees and stood. "The only information I have on Elendoras is that it's gone."

Orinthia's head hummed. She looked expectantly between Arkady and Mimi.

Kos placed a hand on her tight fists. Their eyes met. He gave her an almost unnoticeable head shake to say *not yet*.

As if roles were reversed and she was the true owner of the lavish loft, Mimi threw her arms on the back of the couch. "I've seen the maps. Someone erased Elendoras, but not from existence."

Arkady shifted his weight to his right leg and straightened the hem of his waistcoat. "The Mod Bleyers demolished the entire planet. It happened right in front of me."

Orinthia's mod hummed again. The skin around her ears warmed.

"Then why isn't there a debris field on the map?" Mimi questioned. "There would be evidence."

The man shrugged. "That's not my department. I was just a sailor, like you were, following orders and doing my job. What happened after that was none of my business."

Kos pressed harder on Orinthia's trembling hands. Her pulse was in her throat.

Mimi straightened herself but remained seated. Her calm was cracking. "Can you tell us what happened? I can't go back to my client empty-handed."

Arkady sighed and returned to his seat. He took a decanter of red liquid from the table and refilled his glass. In no hurry, he sipped the drink and rested on the couch. The other four people stared at him, waiting for him to answer Mimi's question.

"From what our investigation uncovered," Arkady began, "The Mod Bleyers had overrun the EC settlement and embedded charges into the planet's bedrock as a last line of defense. They had taken control of the planet, and the EC ordered us to take it back at all costs. Elendoras wasn't even a true planet. More like a terraformed asteroid caught in orbit. We fought for days until we began to gain ground. When they realized they were losing, they took action and hit the kill switch. It took everyone on the surface and half of our ships."

Orinthia's head hummed with every word. She broke free from Kos' grasp and threw out both her blades as she leaped over the table. The edges of her swords crossed on either side of Arkady's throat and pressed against his skin. The red drink from his cup splashed on her leg as he dropped it in surprise.

"Thia," Kos called out. He grabbed her shoulder and tugged her back.

"I'm tired of chasing my tail," Orinthia shouted. She placed all her weight onto her right foot and pushed Kos away with the other. "I've been shot, poisoned, arrested, and sentenced to death to get here. You will give me an answer, or I will take your head. This is non-negotiable."

Arkady examined her face. "Who are you looking for?"

"My father," Orinthia said. "Desidario Anton."

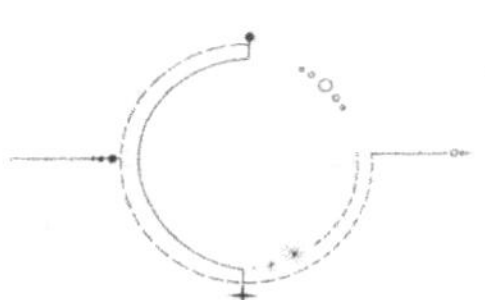

44

Thrutt grabbed Orinthia by the middle and hoisted her off Arkady. The edge of her black blade grazed his neck and a thin line of green fluid dripped from the cut. Arkady's eyes went wide, and he touched the wound. He said nothing, only watched the two men before him wrestle his attacker into a seat.

Arkady reached for his glass, refilled it, and took a sip. The green fingerprints left marks on the glass. He looked at Mimi who had not moved from her seat. "Is this your client?"

"And my source," Mimi said. "She has information from a sequencer."

Arkady's eyes narrowed toward Orinthia. "Elendoras was more than an EC base," he said, emptying the drink into his mouth in one go. "It was a prison camp. EC defectors and Mod Bleyers were held there. A riot broke out and the prisoners overran the compound. My fleet was sent to take it back. Nothing prepared us for what we saw. The smell, oh the smell…"

Arkady paused and stared out the window at the afternoon sky. He twirled the empty glass in his fingers. "I'm not sure how they were able to do any of it. Most of them were walking skeletons with skin. Their mods gave them the edge, I suppose. The EC used them as free labor and experiments. They were given half a meal a day and only enough water to keep them alive."

Kos shifted in his seat. His hand tightened over Orinthia's fists.

"The survivors were too busy burying their dead to attack us when we arrived," Arkady continued. "Men, women, and children were imprisoned there. My commander decided we were on the wrong side. He left my landing team behind to help while he returned to the ship. A plea for cease-fire was made. Our ship's captain agreed, but some of the others didn't. A fight broke out within the fleet."

Arkady took in a deep, shuddering breath. "We sacrificed our own in the name of peace."

Orinthia did not struggle anymore. Her body trembled with fury, but he was telling the truth. "But why does everyone think the planet is gone?"

"Our navigator erased all data on the planet from the maps," Arkady answered. His voice was low. The memory drained him. "The first story I told you is the official one we gave the EC. You tell a lie long enough, people believe you. And with the losses of our people, it worked."

The room was silent for several minutes. Kos' palm burned against Orinthia's skin.

Mimi broke the silence. "Why are the other planets missing? Why hasn't anyone gone to confirm your story?"

"We needed to make it look like everything was taken out so no one would go to the other planets and accidentally stumble upon Elendoras," Arkady said. "And even if they tried, there is a very active minefield that surrounds the sector."

"How do we get around it?" Kos asked. His hands were shaking almost as much as Orinthia's.

"What's in it for me?" Arkady asked.

"You get to keep your life," Orinthia said, making another unsuccessful attempt to break free from Thrutt.

"My people would kill you before you even make it out of the compound." Arkady waved his hand to dismiss her threat. "Let's make a deal. You do a delivery for me, and I'll tell you how to get through the mines."

"I'm not taking any more detours," Orinthia yelled. She restarted her struggle.

"It won't be a detour," Arkady said. "Part of keeping Elendoras a secret is the Mod Bleyers aren't allowed to leave. We smuggle goods in and out of there. We have trade routes between a few of the planets in the sector and the rest of the galaxy. This way they stay hidden while still flourishing."

Kos, who was not restricted by stone hands, moved to his feet. His fists were clenched, and his voice deepened as he spoke. "I am not supplying Mod Bleyers with anything."

Arkady did not react. He responded with soft words. "You still think the war was black and white. I see your tattoos. I understand the losses you've suffered. But it is so much more than us versus them. No one won the war. Do you feel like you've won? The EC signed away our peace, then sat back while we killed each other in their name. To be honest, I don't even know what we were fighting for."

"They perverted life and misused the tech they created," Kos said. His voice was strained, like he was in pain. "Turned people into things they should never have been allowed to be."

The base of Arkady's glass clanked against the table as he set it down to stand. He spoke every word slow and with intention. "And what did the Navy do to you?"

Orinthia looked at Kos. All fight left her body and was replaced with cold realization. She thought the same thing on occasion. Kos was burning alive from the number of modifications he was forced to take in. She did not agree with his reasoning, but Arkady was right. Her fingers moved to brush against Kos' hand.

Kos yanked it back and reeled to look at her. His pupils were wide and the embers behind them threatened to overtake him. "You can't be siding with him."

Orinthia tried to think of what she could say to help him understand. "Can we take a minute to talk about it?"

"Tell me about the shipment," Mimi said, standing up. She pulled Arkady aside.

Thrutt released Orinthia and moved back enough to give them their space. He did not go so far that he could not step in if needed, however.

Orinthia kept her hands in her lap and dared not touch Kos again. "I can't imagine what you're feeling right now. To hear everything you fought for, everything you did was built on a lie. I wasn't a soldier and I know nothing about the war, but I do know what the Navy did to you should never have been done. Kos, they took your soul. You married Mimi just to bypass their rules. They have no loyalty to you."

She paused and took a second to choose her words carefully. "I don't know anything about Mod Bleyers. That was my father's world and I wanted nothing to do with it. But I have to go there. This is the only way we can do it."

Kos closed his eyes to slits. He took in long breaths through his nose. His body was tense for a minute. Then he threw his head back and let out a long huff.

"I'm not siding with Arkady," Orinthia said. She risked reaching for him and ran her fingers down his forearm. "I'm on your side. I hate what the war did to you. The EC is no better than the Mod Bleyers as far as I'm concerned. If it's true that my father was a traitor, then my mods are Mod Bleyer tech. Do you hate me for it?"

Kos lowered his head and rolled it to face her. He let out a sigh. "Of course not."

Orinthia traced his tattoo down to the back of his hand and grasped it in hers. She lifted it to her cheek and rested her face against his palm. "We'll face our demons together, because I can't do this without you."

Kos' hand formed around her face, and he returned to sitting next to her. He stroked her skin with his thumb. "I don't like any of this."

"Neither do I. But we've run out of options. Elendoras holds too many answers. If there was any other way to get Uri back, I would do it. I need him as much as I need you."

They sat silently for a minute. Mimi and Arkady stood talking at the other end of the room. The sun cast warm light through the large windows. It would have been paradise if not for the circumstances.

"We'll take the shipment," Kos whispered.

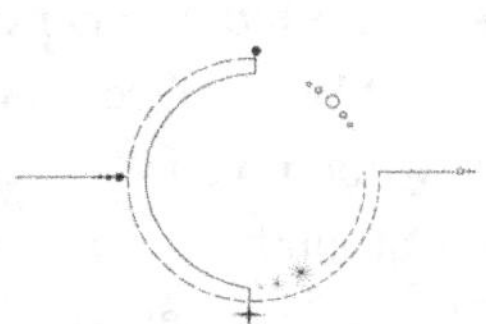

*a*rkady's men loaded the last of the fifty crates into *Freya's* hold. There were no labels other than sets of numbers to indicate what was inside. They were stacked five high in ten rows, each nearly touching the ceiling. Thrutt checked and double-checked every strap before allowing the smugglers to leave. Satisfied, he sealed the doors and recalled the ramp into the ship.

Kos, who had immediately gone down to the cockpit upon returning, called over the speakers. "The coordinates are set. Everyone get buckled in."

Orinthia, Mimi, and Thrutt did as they were told and moved to their seats. The ship rumbled to life. In a few seconds, gravity was pushing down on them as they propelled through the sky. The windows closed, blocking out the final view of Imjumi.

Hundreds of thoughts ran through Orinthia's head as they raced through the atmosphere toward open space. Everything they worked for was coming to a point. But more importantly, she would soon be face-to-face with the man she swore she would never talk to again. Not even the brief sensation of zero gravity shook it from her mind.

The others had disconnected their buckles once they leveled out. Orinthia took her time in following suit. By the time she went to the lower level, Mimi had returned to their room and closed the door. Thrutt's cabin door was open, and Orinthia made her way to him. Inside, instead of the rows of bunks like in her room, there were only two beds, one on either side of the room.

Thrutt stood by the larger bed. Beside him was a wall-mounted display of dozens of weapons. They ranged from blasters and grenades to swords and daggers. The display itself took up half the room and spanned the wall from floor to ceiling. Thrutt turned his head to look at her as she walked in. He had a greasy rag in one hand and a blaster in the other.

"I've been thinking," Orinthia said. She leaned against the wall just inside the room. Her eyes passed over the display as she spoke. "My swords are good in close combat, but I haven't had a blaster of my own since our first mission with the *Fera*. And even then, it didn't work."

Thrutt set down the gun and rag. "Are you asking for one of mine?"

Orinthia nodded. "Not to keep. Just in case I need it on Elendoras."

The stone man's face squished together, and he made a noise. "I'm not so sure it's a good idea."

Shocked, Orinthia jerked her head back. "Why not? You let me have one on Sarv'on."

"You're more than a little emotional right now," Thrutt said. "And seeing Desidario might make you more upset. I don't want you to do anything you might regret."

"You think I'm going to kill him the minute we get

there?" The skin around her ears went hot. Her cheeks burned. "I need him to fix Uri."

"And if he says no?"

"I'll make him." Orinthia was almost shouting.

"With a blaster?"

Orinthia pushed off the wall and stood straight. "I don't know. But what if we run into trouble? Anyone more than a few feet from me has the advantage. Or if there isn't enough room to call out my swords, I can at least stick a blaster in someone's gut if I have to."

"Rogue and I will be there with you," Thrutt said. He turned his whole body to face her.

"You can't guarantee that. We were supposed to have stayed together on Caytoo. But I was alone. I've lost the ability to use my mods three times in a very short amount of time. Celso tried to…" she let her words cut off. "I need a gun."

"Take one of mine, then," Kos said from the corridor.

Orinthia spun around, surprised to see him. She had not heard him walk up.

Kos touched one of his hips and the compartment opened. He pulled the golden blaster from it and held it by the barrel.

"I can't take yours." Orinthia looked at the gun then back to Kos. "It's part of you."

"If it would make you feel better, then you can keep it," Kos said, still holding out the blaster between them. "I promised I wouldn't let you face him alone. And I intend to keep that promise, but you're right. If we get separated, or something happens to me, then I need to know you're safe. So, take mine."

"I don't think—" Thrutt started to say.

"Thrutt, your opinion is always valued and taken into

consideration," Kos said, darting a shadowed look at his friend. His voice was rougher than Orinthia had ever heard it when speaking to Thrutt. "But we're going into completely unknown territory. She's never faced a Mod Bleyer before."

"Kos, I can't." Orinthia pushed the blaster back toward him, but he forced it into her hand.

"You will. I don't care what Arkady said. Mod Bleyers are not to be trusted. They are not victims, and they are not our friends."

Orinthia gave in and wrapped her fingers around the butt of the gun. It was heavy and warm in her hands.

Kos closed the compartment on his hip. "I'm pushing *Freya*'s warp drive as hard as I can. If she doesn't blow up first, we should be there in half a day-cycle. You both need to rest and collect yourselves before we arrive." He turned on his heel and left before Thrutt or Orinthia could respond.

A heavy feeling set on Orinthia, and she leaned out of the room and watched him walk to the galley. She stuffed the blaster in her belt and followed him. "Kos, wait."

He ignored her.

"We need to talk," she continued, catching up to him.

They stepped into the galley, and she closed the door behind her. Kos faced her and rested his backside on the edge of the table.

"You told me not to shut you out," Orinthia said. "Don't do it to me."

"I'm not mad at you," Kos answered. He placed his hands on either side of him and laid them flat on the table. "I'm mad at everything else."

"Then tell me", she said.

Kos let out a long sigh. "How can I tell you? If I share my ghosts, you'll never want to look at me again."

Orinthia closed the gap between them and stood with the toes of their shoes touching. "I've been looking at the real you since the moment you went back for me when I was shot on Rust Rock. I know you better than you think. If the Navy hadn't forced you to repay your father's debt, I think you still would have enlisted. The desire to save everyone drives you, but it's not for glory."

"They took your loyalty and morphed you into something unrecognizable," Orinthia continued. Her palms were cold, and she trembled as she spoke. "But you're still in there. I saw it when you stood up to Ahto. Mod Bleyers or not, you're no longer at war. Please stop living in it."

"They killed my mom, Thia," Kos said. His voice was above a whisper. "The Mod Bleyers are the ones who first created body modifications. Arkady can say the ones on Elendoras are innocents, but that doesn't negate the fact they started all of this. Every one of the hundreds of lives I took was for her. And to smuggle in supplies so they can continue to survive feels like a betrayal to not only her but everything I did."

"I'm sorry, Kos." Orinthia looked at the wall beside her. "I keep making you do things you don't want to do. First in leaving the *Fera* and now this."

Kos took her hands in his. "I don't regret leaving. Ahto would have dragged me down just as much as the EC did, if not more. I was drowning in my own self-loathing, believing I had no other choice. You showed me the way out. I only wish there was another way to get to Elendoras without taking these boxes."

"Once we get Uri back and I find out what really happened to my mom, we won't have to think about that place or Mod Bleyers again," Orinthia said. She looked at their hands. His bronzed skin was etched with pale scars from a lifetime of hard work. Hers were soft and pink, nurtured in a pseudo-stable home. Beneath their skin, they were the same. Both struggled to find a life outside of their past.

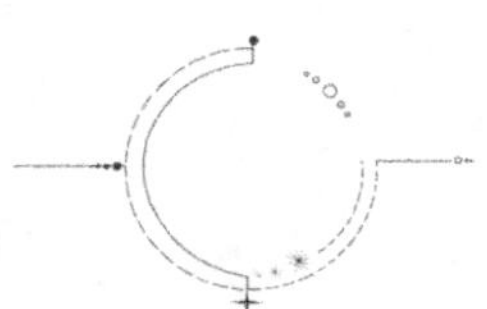

46

The air in Orinthia's shared room was chemically sweet when she returned. Mimi sat on her bed in the far corner with her PortTab propped up on pillows. She alternated between scrolling through what was on the screen and adding another layer of color to her nails. With a glance up, Mimi smiled and said, "You should have come to me for a blaster. Thrutt has the best intentions, but sometimes he's overprotective."

Orinthia's face flushed. She tossed the golden blaster on her mattress, moved to Mimi's bed, and sat on the foot. "How much did you hear?"

"Enough to know who you really are." Mimi capped the paint and leaned the bottle against the screen of her tablet. "I've been watching you, trying to figure out what is making them do all of this. But I see it now."

"Excuse me?" Orinthia grew defensive.

"No, don't get me wrong," Mimi said. She held a hand out with her palm toward Orinthia. "It's always been the two of them. The rest of us come and go, but they stay together. Rogue is self-destructive because he feels like he doesn't deserve better. Thrutt will follow that man to the edges of peril. And here you are, giving them purpose again. You think they saved you, but really, you're saving them."

Orinthia could not see how she was saving anyone. The number of times they were almost blown up or thrown into prison was astonishing for such a short period of time. She said so to Mimi.

"They would have found ways to do that on their own anyway," Mimi said waving her hand. "What I mean is they are actually happy. Do you know how many times I've seen Rogue smile? Maybe a handful and most of them have been more recently."

Orinthia thought back to all the times she caught Mimi staring at her.

"I'm sure by now you know we were married and why. Don't confuse my concern for jealousy. I wouldn't be here if I thought you were a danger to them. It's why I didn't join Ahto."

Her last statement bordered a threat, but Orinthia left it alone. She understood where Mimi was coming from. Thrutt and Kos deserved every good thing in life.

"Why are you telling me all this?" Orinthia asked.

"Because I'm going back to my life once the job is done. I want to be sure they're going to be taken care of. We were prepared to die for each other a long time ago. That bond doesn't end because the contract did."

"Thanks for trusting me. I think," Orinthia said. It was endearing that Mimi cared about her friends, but hearing someone's open judgment was not one of her favorite activities. They sat in silence for a minute. Orinthia kicked her heel on the ground and looked around the room trying to find something else to say. "So, how'd you become a bounty hunter anyway?"

Mimi collected her things and set them in a case on the floor. The bottles of paint clacked together as they fell. "My ex-boyfriend, Tomislaw. We met shortly after I stopped doing security for Arkady. He was a retired Marine. When I met him, he'd been out for a little over four years."

She bit her bottom lip and looked out past the ship. A loaded smile crossed her face. "He was the most gorgeous cyborg I'd ever seen. Unlike your brother, he opted to show his mechanisms."

Orinthia blushed as the thought of Mimi looking at Uri that way crossed her mind.

"Anyway," Mimi continued, returning from her memory, "He taught me how to find contracts and decipher what was worth the money and what wasn't. We worked together and dated for three years. Until I discovered he liked his chems. He was spending all our credits chasing relief. Like many of us, he was fighting against his mind. I'd been getting help for my own darkness and I begged him to come with me. He refused, saying there was no going back for him. Then one day he staggered out of the house and never returned."

Orinthia could feel the air move in and out of her mouth. The tale took a direction she had not expected, and Mimi's candid words left her stunned. "Did you look for him?"

Mimi twisted her face and tilted her head. "Of course I did. But he made his way to a memory-eraser. By the time I got to him, he had no idea who I was."

"I'm so sorry," Orinthia said in a whisper.

"I've come to terms with it. There's a home for vets like him. He's finally getting the help he needs, and I check on him every now and then. But he doesn't remember me from before the eraser."

Kos and his mile-long gaze came to Orinthia's mind. *Would it ever get so bad that he'd choose to forget me, too?*

Between the four of them, it started to look like her childhood was moderate compared to the other's adult lives.

"We're coming out of warp," Kos called over the speakers. "I want everyone up here."

Mimi reached for a case under the bed and set it in front of her. She opened it and pulled out a black leather holster. "Strap this to your belt. That blaster will be easier to use if you can get to it quicker." It flew a few feet as Mimi tossed it at Orinthia and left the room without saying anything further.

Orinthia waited a few extra minutes to be sure they were actually out of the warp. She stood and adjusted her belt to fit the holster. When it was secured, she grabbed the blaster she had tossed on her bunk and added it to her hip. Instinctively, she moved to Uri and hovered around him, checking his restraints one last time.

There was a knock on the door before it opened. "Everything okay?" Kos asked.

Orinthia nodded and ran her fingers through Uri's hair. She left the room with Kos to join the others. From the corridor, she could see mines dot the void. As she stepped inside the cockpit, the view spanned beyond the width of the windshield.

"Scan complete, captain," Freya announced.

"Upload to my data then pull it up on the screen, please," Kos said, taking his place in front of his seat.

A three-dimensional image of the minefield on the window replaced the real thing. Several rows of mines were highlighted in red. Their path curved and went from one edge to the other.

"It looks like that should be the way to get through." Kos pointed at the line of mines. "These are reading as deactivated. Everything else is magnetically charged and will ignite if we get too close."

"I still don't like this," Thrutt said. "Thia's mod said Arkady was telling the truth, but it still feels off."

Mimi stepped up and said, "I've been thinking about that. Since this was my intel, I'm going to take the skiff through to show it's safe."

"The skiff does have a hyperdrive on it," Kos said, disconnecting his seat from the floor to open the compartment below. Thrutt opened the hatch door while Kos moved the chair out of the way. "It's not built for long-distance but should be able to get you to Elendoras without much trouble."

"That your handiwork, Rogue?" Mimi teased. "Fine. Once I'm through I'll run recon on Elendoras until you get down there. See if I can find where Desidario is holed up."

"You're going now?" Orinthia asked as Mimi moved to the hatch.

"Why not?" Mimi answered. "There's no point in waiting around."

"The sooner she gets through, the sooner we can, too," Kos said. None of them looked phased by the sudden decision to jump ship and fly into a minefield. Orinthia could not wrap her mind around the pace they were moving.

"It'll be fine," Mimi said. She swung a leg over the hole and placed it on the first rung of the ladder. "This was exactly what I did during the war. I'm not ashamed to say I kinda missed it."

"You two are going to let her do this?" Orinthia looked between Kos and Thrutt as she spoke. "Neither of you are certain the mines are safe and you're okay with Mimi going through them?"

Kos held up his hands at his chest with the palms out. "The skiff is too small to activate the mines. Even if they were live, she'd still be safe. This way she can run a closer diagnostic and make sure there aren't any other traps out there."

"Even so," Mimi said shrugging her shoulders. "If anything happens, I've had a good run. No one lives forever." She tossed a glance at Thrutt. "Well, most of us don't."

"Very funny," Thrutt said wagging his head toward her. "Get going already. I think I grew another six inches waiting for you to leave."

They both exchanged mocked offended faces before Mimi continued to climb down.

"Wait," Orinthia said. The others might have been okay with the plan, but she did not want anyone else to get hurt because of her. She gained everyone's attention. There was nothing to *wait* for, only to stall Mimi from going for a little longer. "Be careful when you get down there."

"I'm glad somebody cares." Mimi winked. "See you all on the other side. Wherever that may be." With that, she descended into the dim compartment space and disappeared out of sight.

In reverse action, Thrutt closed the hatch and Kos secured his captain's chair. There was a dull thud below deck. A light blinked on the dash. After a slight shake, the light stopped. Orinthia moved to the other side of the cockpit and watched through the open space beside the map. A craft half the size of Celso's ship emerged from under *Freya*. Within seconds, it reached the edge of the mines. Without hesitation, the skiff moved through the first row and safely on to the next.

"Now we wait," Kos said, closing the image on the window.

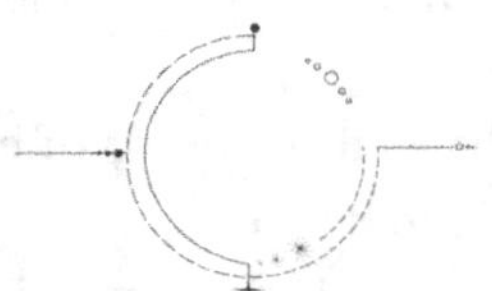

47

Time after Mimi left ticked by slowly. Orinthia watched the skiff grow smaller until it disappeared. The cockpit was quiet, save for the usual background noises the ship made while idling in open space. Everything was as it should be, except nothing about waiting outside a minefield was normal.

Kos moved from his captain's chair to stand beside Orinthia. He held a hand over the console and leaned his head toward hers. "See that bright dot? That's Elendoras."

Orinthia strained her eyes to follow Kos' finger. A tiny light, slightly brighter than the stars past it, shone directly in front of them. She tried to picture what Elendoras would look like once they landed. Rust Rock was the first place she saw after joining them on the *Fera*. It had been a thriving city built onto an asteroid until the rust virus destroyed everything. Rust Rock's inhabitants were trapped, like the Mod Bleyers on Elendoras. The similarities did not allow her to imagine the two entities as separate.

"It's so far away," Orinthia said. "But too close for warp, right?"

"Yes," Kos answered. "But *Freya's* warp drive isn't standard for a ship this size. I added it after I took command. We'll have to use the ordinary hyperdrive she came with."

Orinthia chuckled to herself and thought about the mismatched hostess droid from his restaurant. Like the droid, *Freya* was a unique fusion of parts customized solely for Kos' needs. She leaned her head on Kos' shoulder. "Can Uri and I stay when this is all done?"

"What do you mean?" Kos asked, pressing his cheek to the top of her head. "Where?"

"Here. On *Freya*."

Kos jostled with laughter. "I had no plans on letting you leave. If he wants to stay, he's more than welcome to. I'm trying to build a life with you, and that includes blending our wild extended families. Though I'm seriously going to have to rearrange the living quarters. It's getting cramped down here."

Orinthia enjoyed the sound of his words. *I'm trying to build a life with you*, she repeated in her head. A smile formed over her lips. They were so close to the end. Everything would be different in a few hours, but she could work with different. She had already adjusted to a new life once; another change would be a small price to pay to have everything she wanted.

A red light on the dash caught her eye. Orinthia straightened to get a better look. Kos did the same. Neither of them needed Freya to announce what it meant.

"The *Fera* is attempting to hail, captain," Freya said.

Kos pulled Orinthia to the entrance of the cockpit and said, "Get Thrutt and stay hidden."

"Why? He already knows I'm here."

"I need to try to talk him down," Kos said, pushing her

away. "Maybe if he doesn't see you, I can break his focus. Either way, I don't want you seen."

"Captain?" Freya said.

"Go." Kos pointed behind Orinthia, with his nostrils flared and lips pressed together.

As she walked away, Orinthia could hear Kos say, "Freya, strengthen our shields to full capacity and charge the cannon. We don't need surprises."

She opened Thrutt's door and rushed in to find him on his bed reading. The contrast of rooms was almost comical if it had not been for the fact they were in the range of a malfunctioning AI war machine's cannons.

Thrutt did not wait for her to say anything before he tossed the book down and jumped off the bed. "Mimi?"

"Ahto." Orinthia shook her head.

Without further explanation, Thrutt dashed across the room and passed Orinthia. Alone, Orinthia placed herself inside his room and moved her head out far enough to see the cockpit.

The view outside the window was masked by an image of Ahto. His ghostly grey skin had a shimmer to it, mimicking the metal plating of his alternate form. Thin black lines replaced his pupils, and his abnormally straight teeth were sharp and curved inward. He was a terrifying mix of his two selves.

"We don't have to be enemies," Kos said. "If he is down there, I can get Anton to fix you."

Orinthia had missed the pleasantries while talking to Thrutt. His door was closer to the cockpit than her room's, but she still had to strain to listen clearly.

"I am not accepting negotiations, Rogue," Ahto said. His voice scratched as it left his throat. "You've led me to him. I will get him on my own."

"There is no way you can navigate through the minefield," Kos said. He leaned forward and pressed his palms to the console. "Deactivate your weapons and I will board the *Fera* to show you the way."

Orinthia bit her lip to avoid yelling out. Her mod had not hummed.

Ahto tilted his head and curved it closer to the screen. He studied his former quartermaster for several seconds. With a snap, he turned to look at something off-screen. His fangs appeared between parted lips as he gave a devilish grin. "Your assistance is not necessary. We will simply follow the skiff that has already gone through."

Kos curled his fingers into fists. "I won't let you get near her."

"Ah, so it is Anton's daughter on the skiff," Ahto said. "Are you willing to die for her?"

"Without hesitation," Kos answered. He moved back from the console and clasped his hands behind his back.

"Oh." Ahto turned his face and looked down with his narrow eyes. "I see. It was really *my* code you were worried about breaking. You were trying to get a piece of—"

"We left because you are falling apart." Kos interrupted with a loud voice. "I am done blindly following orders of those who wish to use me as cannon fodder."

"That is what you were remade for." Ahto's face turned completely snakelike, but his body stayed the same. He thrashed his head around until it snapped back to its previous form. "But now it is time to die. I will bid farewell to Thia for you."

Kos slammed his hand down on a button across from him. The image disappeared. "Freya, fire at the *Fera*," he shouted. "Thrutt, do you have them in your sights?"

The ship jostled to the side as the cannon fired.

"Two missiles inbound," Thrutt responded.

"Use the chaff and flare, then return fire." He tapped his temple and called his visor. "Freya, raise the helm and take us in. Stay as close to the edge of the path as possible."

"Aye, captain."

Orinthia moved from the door to the viewport of Kos and Thrutt's room. A dozen bright lights erupted from the back of the ship. *Freya* moved forward, leaving just before the missiles met with the flares. Each detonated upon contact. Shrapnel plinked against the hull.

"Thia, get in here," Kos yelled.

Leaving the window, Orinthia ran from the room to the cockpit. The space between them and the mines was almost gone.

"Close the door and strap in," Kos ordered.

"Brace," Thrutt shouted.

Orinthia gripped the doorframe and smashed her eyes closed. The ship rattled from an impact. Sweat built up on her palms and her grip slipped from the wall. She stumbled back but managed to stay standing. Once the shaking stopped, she did as she was told and jumped into the seat beside Kos.

They moved through the first row of mines. From this close, Orinthia could see they were not spread as far apart as she had believed them to be. *Freya* weaved through the path.

A red dot flashed behind them on the radar. The *Fera* was not too far behind.

Thrutt grunted and Orinthia turned to see him press down on the turret's triggers.

"Keep them at a distance," Kos said. "I need to try and disrupt Mimi's trail so they can't follow."

A second and third impact hit the ship, one immediately after the other.

"What about our trail?" Orinthia asked, facing Kos again. "Won't they see the way we're going and just do the same?"

Kos' shoulders stiffened. "That's the plan."

Orinthia did not understand what he meant. *It's the plan to have them follow us safely?* she thought.

"I can't get a lock through the mines," Thrutt said. "They're causing too much interference."

Mortars continued to beat against the ship. Each hit made the walls groan. The sound was almost deafening.

Kos let out a long stream of air. "Freya, are the shields at full strength?"

"Aye, captain." Her mechanical voice was tense. "I can draw auxiliary power when necessary."

"Be ready to hyperjump the moment we exit the field," Kos said. He took one hand off the helm and swiped at his armor tattoo. Once covered he turned to look at Orinthia. "Do you trust me?" His voice was muffled.

The pieces fell into place. "Absolutely," she said.

Focusing back on what was in front of them, Kos said, "Thrutt, switch to the pulse cannon. I'm going to roll into the mines, and I need you to keep them off us."

Thrutt waited several seconds before replying. "Understood."

Orinthia could not see what Kos saw on his visor to know how close they were to the live mines. She gripped the arms of her seat. As Kos pulled to the right, the ship spun around her. Everything outside of the ship moved in a blur. Orinthia's stomach lurched. She squinted her eyes and tried to focus on the radar.

They continued to barrel roll for half a minute before Kos leveled out and dove two rows down from their original plane. The mines in their immediate vicinity flew apart in all directions. Almost in slow motion, a wave of energy erupted in a flash of orange. The edges of the blast caught more mines, igniting them one after the other.

"Push the boosters, Freya," Kos ordered.

Orinthia watched the red dot fall behind. Though they were putting distance between the two ships, the *Fera* continued to fire. The ship shook and pounded from everywhere.

Kos moved through the detonating mines with such force, it took his whole body to steer. Every explosion rocked the ship. Alarms blared, joining the banging. The entire window filled with orange, making the cockpit's temperature shoot up.

A scream ripped through Orinthia, shredding her throat like knives. She squeezed her eyes and waited for heat to overtake them.

Then, as fast as it had come, the room cooled again.

Orinthia risked an eye open.

Kos had pressed the helm into a dive, and they neared the end of the minefield. A blue hue grew around the ship. *Four rows to the edge.* The stars shimmered ahead of them. *Two rows.* A high whistling sound crescendo from somewhere in the ship. As they moved by the last mine, the blackness of space brightened to aqua. With a punch, the ship shot forward.

For several heart-pounding minutes, Orinthia could not draw in full breaths. The cockpit swam as a dark ring formed around the edges of her vision. She leaned forward and put her head between her knees. Her vision cleared, but breathing was still difficult. It took all her strength not to pass out.

With a jolt that felt like a punch to the chest, *Freya* came out of the hyperjump. The light in the cockpit returned to normal. Alarms continued to blare at different pitches. Every indicator on the console was lit, but they were alive.

Outside the window was Elendoras.

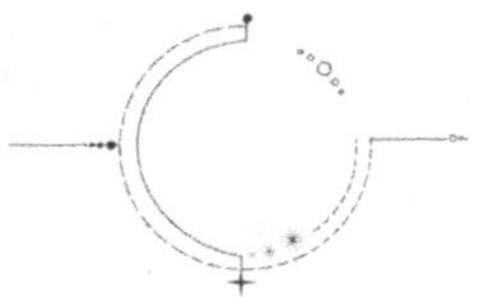

*K*os pulled on the helm to try to slow their descent. Every rivet rattled like hail against the hull. The window darkened to shield against the blinding white heat. The air in the cockpit warmed.

"Freya, apply airbrakes," Kos said through his visor. His voice was strained and muffled. "Reverse the thrusters. We're still going too fast."

"I'm trying, captain," Freya said. "Some of the flaps are damaged and will not engage."

Orinthia gripped the arms of her seat so tightly that she could hardly feel her fingers anymore. Her seat vibrated with such force she thought the post would snap any minute. Shaking made it difficult to see clearly. She held her teeth clenched and took in quick bursts of air through her nose.

Thrutt had turned his chair to face the window. He glanced over at her every few minutes. His eyebrows were crushed together, and his mouth pinched tight. He held his hand over the latch of his buckle.

"All flaps open," Freya announced. "Two working at capacity, two at half."

Gradually, the ship slowed. It was unnoticeable at first, but Kos eased back on the helm. The rattling quieted. *Freya's* front window cleared to show land. It grew larger as they approached, and the ship leveled out to a more even descent instead of the free fall it had been in moments before.

In twenty minutes, the ship's landing gear thumped out from the belly, and they landed securely on the ground.

Kos fell into his seat. His arms hung over the sides. The alarms continued to sound, and lights flashed. But they were alive.

All three crew members stayed silent for the first few moments. Orinthia's hands trembled, and her body was light. She allowed herself to take in long breaths. Her lungs shook as they filled to capacity.

"Is everyone alright?" Kos asked. He sounded as breathless as Orinthia felt.

"I am," Thrutt replied, unbuckling and standing up.

"Me, too," Orinthia said. She thought about Uri in their room. Her hands fumbled with the seat restraint for a second before she was able to undo it. "I have to check on Uri."

"I'll do it," Thrutt said, putting a hand on her shoulder and forcing her back down. "Stay here. Things could have come loose or damaged during the battle."

Orinthia watched as Thrutt walked away. She tried to move her head to see inside her room better, but from her line of sight, she could only see the edge of the washroom door.

Kos' comm beeped, nearly masked by the rest of the alarms. He deactivated his armor and slid up to sit better. "Freya, turn off the alarms and run a complete diagnostic." He retrieved the comm from his side and clicked it on.

"What happened?" Mimi shouted over the speaker before Kos said anything. "I can see *Freya* smoking from here."

"Ahto," Kos said definitively.

There was a long pause. "I only saw your ship come down."

"We detonated the minefield with them inside," Kos said.

"Do you think they're—"

"I don't know." Kos cut her off. "We didn't stay around to find out. *Freya* hyper-jumped as soon as we were out of the blast."

"Well, I'm coming back," Mimi said. "It looks like you're on the far edge of the town, so it shouldn't take too long."

"Did you find what you were looking for?" Kos asked. He leaned forward and placed his elbows on his knees.

Orinthia's heart skipped a beat.

"I got some intel," Mimi replied. "I'll fill you in when I get there."

"Copy," Kos said. He closed the comm and tossed it onto the console. With a huff, he leaned back in his chair again and rolled his head to the side.

Orinthia opened her mouth to commend Kos on his flying, but Freya interrupted.

"Captain," Freya said. "I haven't finished the diagnostic, but my preliminary checks show there is a leak in the warp drive. If it is not repaired soon, we will not be able to leave this sector."

Kos did not answer. He rubbed his face and stood.

"What can I do to help?" Orinthia asked, joining him. Her legs were off balance, but she held to the side of her chair.

"I'll take care of it," Kos said. "As long as I can rig it well enough to stop the leak, we'll be fine." His voice was flat and there was no spark to his eyes. He was a man who neared his limit.

Orinthia wanted to push the issue, but she stayed quiet. She needed him to clear out what was in his head.

Without saying anything more, Kos left her alone in the

cockpit. He stopped by his room for a few minutes and then emerged with a bag of tools. Tossing the strap over his shoulder, he climbed up the ladder.

Thrutt came out of Orinthia's room and watched Kos go up. He looked at Orinthia and pointed to the top deck. "Where's he going?"

"The warp drive has a leak," she said, moving closer to him.

"I should go help him."

"No," Orinthia said, placing a hand on his stone arm. "I think he needs some space. How was Uri?"

"His restraints were a little loose, but no worse for wear," Thrutt said, tossing his head back to the room. "Everything else was a little disheveled, but I cleaned up what I could. Speaking of, we should check the crates, too."

Orinthia glanced at her brother. She could not bring herself to go into the room. They had made it to Elendoras. She wanted the next time she spoke to him to be when he could speak back.

Thrutt led the way up the ladder to the top deck. He was already checking the straps on the crates by the time she reached him.

"Did Arkady say what's inside?" she asked.

"No." Thrutt tugged on each of the restraints. Nothing moved or even wiggled. "And this far away from any type of port, I'm not sure how we're going to get them delivered. The skiff can fit maybe three or four boxes at a time, but that'll make for a lot of trips. That's time we don't have."

Orinthia thought through their options. "Could we drag them behind the skiff? Make a sled or something?"

"If we had the materials, sure. Even some scrap metal would be better than nothing. But we don't." Thrutt paused. "I'm going to have to ask Rogue what his plan is."

Orinthia followed Thrutt out of the ship. The sky of Elendoras was an inky blue, and darker than she had seen on earth. She could make out a handful of stars, as well. Her shadow was crisp and nearly as black as the void of space itself.

Freya's hull was pocked with dents. A few burns had stripped paint from the metal. Grey smoke hung around the ship like a cloud. The farther they moved down the side, the more damage Orinthia could see. Pieces of *Freya's* wings were missing. There were jagged cuts every few feet. She found several holes larger than her hand, as well. It was a miracle they landed as safely as they had.

The duo moved to the back of the ship where they found Kos strapped and hanging upside down in a harness beneath the retrofitted engine. His hair was pulled in a ponytail and hung down in a straight line from the top of his head. The tool in his hand made a clicking sound as he spun it in quarter-turns.

"What are we going to do with the crates?" Thrutt asked.

"Toss them." Kos did not look away from what he was working on.

"We brought them all this way," Orinthia said, shocked by his answer. "The people need them."

"Our agreement was to bring boxes. I didn't say I would deliver them."

Orinthia frowned. "We don't even know what's in the crates. It could be food or medical supplies."

"That's exactly my point," Kos said. He reached for the bag that hung across his chest and took out another tool. "We *don't* know what's inside. And I'm not going to scan them to find out, either. I can see the town from here. Someone will find them eventually."

She had not been disappointed in Kos since they were on

the *Fera*, but his attitude toward the supplies left a sore spot in her mind. "I'm going to open one, then."

"No," Kos said. With a toss of his legs, he moved upright and looked at her. "It doesn't matter what it is. Get them out of the ship."

Thrutt held up a hand to keep her from responding. "Fine. If that's what you want, we'll do it." He pulled Orinthia back to the hold and did not stop until they were on the ramp. "Let it go for now. When Mimi gets back, I'll work something out."

As if on command, the skiff crested a small hill. It took a few minutes for the vehicle to pull around and park beside Orinthia and Thrutt. Mimi opened the side door and stepped out. She tossed her head and ran a hand through her hair. "I found him," she said.

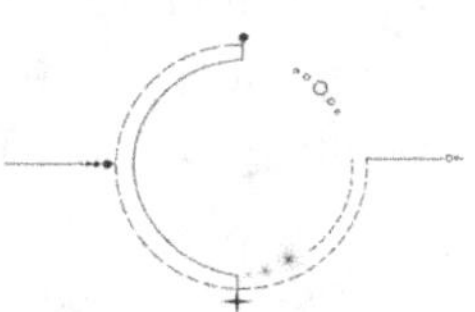

49

Mimi refused to share any information until they were all together. As they waited for Kos to finish the repairs to the drive, Thrutt and Orinthia retold the battle with the *Fera*. After ten minutes, Kos joined the group. He had black marks on his arms and hands. His pants were lined with grime.

"What did you find?" Kos asked Mimi. He stopped a foot away from the others and placed the back of his hands on his hips.

Mimi stared at Orinthia before answering. "There are definitely Mod Bleyers here. A lot more than I anticipated. Turns out, Arkady doesn't just smuggle in goods, but Mod Bleyers that are looking to start over."

Kos let out a puff of air from his nose and shook his head but said nothing.

"I asked around about Anton," Mimi continued. "No one has heard that name, but there is a doctor that set up shop in one of the old EC buildings. He showed up a few years ago and sometimes offers tech in exchange for labor."

"That sounds like him, then," Orinthia said.

"My thoughts exactly." Mimi gave Orinthia another long look. Her eyes ran down the sides of Orinthia's face.

"Why do you keep doing that?" Orinthia asked. She pulled her head back and gave Mimi a hard glare of her own.

"I'm working out a plan," Mimi replied. "But it will involve splitting the group."

"In what way?" Orinthia changed her posture. Her hands clenched together at her side. She could feel the weight of Kos' blaster hanging on her belt.

Mimi tilted her head and held up a palm. "Before you get upset, just listen. *Freya* is too damaged to fly all the way over there. Thrutt and I will stay and do what we can to get her flight-worthy. In the meantime, you and Kos will go to your dad and sort things out. If everything works out fine, we'll bring Uri in *Freya* when you're ready."

"*Freya* will draw too much attention if you fly her over," Kos said.

"We can't all fit in the skiff," Mimi said. "The three of us —" she pointed between herself, Orinthia, and Kos, "— maybe, but not everyone."

"Yes, I know. But you can take us to town. We'll walk the rest of the way. Then you come back and load Uri into the skiff. When we're ready, I'll contact Thrutt to bring him. Once he's fixed, you can pick us up in *Freya*. It won't matter how much attention she gets, since we'll be out of here before it becomes an issue."

Kos turned to Thrutt. "While we're gone, you unload the crates so we're ready to leave when we get back."

Thrutt made to respond but Kos shook his head. "I'm not arguing. Unless you want to walk each of the crates to town yourself, they are staying right here."

"Your plan is my plan with more steps," Mimi said.

"What does it matter if we draw attention? You've already done that."

The air on Elendoras was flat and almost stale. There was no noise made while they waited for Kos to respond. No birds chirped, no echoes came from the town, and not even a breeze brushed by.

"*Freya* doesn't have much left in her," Kos said, lowering his voice and his face. "I'm afraid if we move her too soon, we'll use up everything we have and that's it. We have to wait until the last possible minute to move her."

No one said anything for a moment. Orinthia stared at the mangled body of their ship. *Freya* had protected them through each encounter they had. She paid the price for them to be on Elendoras. Next, she looked at Kos. He had yet to raise his head and continued to focus on the ground. *Freya* was more than a ship to him. She was a treasure. He pieced her together himself, building her into what he needed. The ship was his home, and as she thought more, Orinthia's home, too.

"We'll do it Kos' way," Orinthia said, breaking the silence. "All of you have more experience in things like this than I do, but at the end of the day it's his ship, so it's his call. Now, can we do something? I'm about ready to drag Uri over there myself."

THE SUN NEARED the horizon by the time Orinthia, Mimi, and a freshly changed Kos climbed into the skiff. Bright stars, more than Orinthia had seen on Earth, twinkled in the violet sky. Sparse trees cast thick black shadows over the patchy dried grass. The skiff flew high enough off the ground not to kick up dust.

When Arkady had described Elendoras as a terraformed asteroid, Orinthia pictured lush green landscapes. In reality, it was nothing more than another desert. Dry, too warm, and hardly anything was alive. In the middle of the barren land were blocky, grey structures. Most stood only a few stories high. Orinthia could see posts where a fence had once been, but there were no signs of barriers left.

Mimi slowed the skiff and landed a few hundred feet from a tall building. She nodded her chin toward the window. "This is where I leave you. It's less busy on this side so you'll be able to slip in unnoticed." For a few more seconds, she looked between Kos and Orinthia. "You didn't tell her, did you?"

The skiff swayed as Kos fidgeted in his seat. He kept his face toward the front but did not respond.

"Tell me what?" Orinthia asked. The hair on her arms stood up as goosebumps rose.

"That you look like them," Mimi said. "Your hair and your eyes. Did no one ever ask if you were a Mod-Bleyer?"

Orinthia let out a nervous chuckle. "There are others in the NCR like me. Not many, but a few."

"Have you ever met one or was that what you were told?" Mimi asked.

Orinthia tried to picture people from back home. Even convicts she arrested. No one came to mind. *But I was* told *that*, she thought. *I would know if he was lying. My mod never gets it wrong. But lately it seems like everything I knew was wrong.*

When she did not respond, Mimi raised her eyebrows and shrugged her shoulder. "That's what I thought. Most people don't modify their children. But Mod Bleyers do, so no one will bat an eye in your direction. As long as Rogue keeps his coat on, you two should be fine."

Kos, who had frozen in his place, finally spoke up. "Get back to the ship and help Thrutt get things ready. We're wasting time sitting here." Before anyone could respond, he opened the hatch on his side and climbed out. Warm air flowed in from the opening. He pushed the back of his seat forward to make room for Orinthia to follow him.

"Follow the coordinates I gave you," Mimi said, leaning over to see them better. "I have nothing to reference whether or not it's him, but I'm willing to bet my shiny leg on it."

"If you don't hear anything in an hour, come find us," Kos said. He pulled his coat together and buttoned it closed. "And keep an eye out for the *Fera*. I don't like how quiet it's been."

"Will do," Mimi said, tipping her chin to her chest. "See you in a bit." With that, she moved back to sit upright and sealed the skiff with a press of a button. Dust spiraled in small clouds as the vehicle lifted and returned toward *Freya*.

The farther she moved away, the quieter the surrounding area became. It made Orinthia's ears ring as they strained to find something to listen to. They were only a few hundred feet from the back of a building, but no noise traveled to them.

"Come on," Kos said. He pulled the collar up and placed his hands in his pockets.

The pair walked in silence for half the way. Their steps were dull and muffled. It was uncomfortable and made the nerves in Orinthia's shoulders ache.

"You knew what we were going to find here," Orinthia said, partly to break the hush.

"Of course, I knew," Kos said after a scoff. "It's the

reason I was so defensive when we first met. I assumed you were a Mod Bleyer trying to go into hiding."

Their initial meeting ran through her mind. He had been rigid and short with her. He didn't relax around her until they had left Rust Rock for the second time. After she was forced to confess who her father was and what he had done to her.

She stopped and grabbed his forearm. "If you hate them so much, why do you want to be with me? I'm nothing but a reminder of that life."

Kos did not respond right away. He dug the heel of his boot into the coarse sand. "Because you're not one of them. I see past what you look like, though I like that a lot. You are more than what was done to you. Life handed you the same bad cards I was, but you keep playing. I want you because you refuse to exist in the box you were put in and it makes me realize I don't have to stay there either. You *are* a reminder, yes. But of who I want to be, not who I was."

Without thinking, Orinthia tugged his arm and pulled him closer. She placed her other hand behind his head and gripped the back of his hair. Trembling, her mouth found his. She kissed him with such force it hurt, but she did not stop. Kos' fingers dug into her back. They stood wrapped around each other until she could no longer take the heat from his skin.

"I don't know what I said, but if you could tell me so I can keep it in mind for later, that would be nice," Kos said with a crooked smile. He placed his forehead to hers.

"My whole life has been about what other people wanted from me," Orinthia said quietly, trying to catch her breath. "You expect nothing of me but who I am. I can be me without fear. Even with Uri, I had to hide parts of myself because it didn't fit the image he had of me. With you, I'm free."

Kos brushed his nose against hers and gave her a second, gentler kiss. "You don't have to change for anyone again."

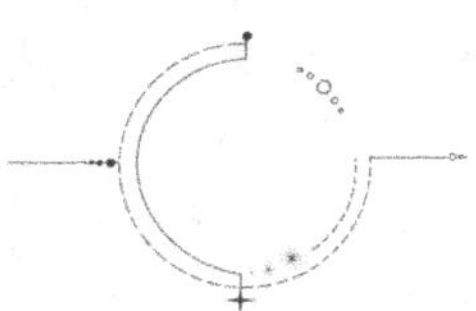

50

The first set of buildings appeared to be empty as Kos and Orinthia approached. Even at dusk none of the windows showed any light. Their steps made soft echoes as they crossed the cemented path. Each of the buildings was a copy of the last; two doors a quarter of the way in on either side of the long building, two windows for each section, a low-pitched roof, and tan walls. The only distinction they had was where the paint had chipped off.

"Generic military housing," Kos informed Orinthia. "Anyone who wasn't a ranking officer would have lived here while it was an active base."

They kept moving farther along the empty path for another five minutes. Light did not travel far on Elendoras, but as they moved closer, a dim glow showed between two buildings. Voices grew louder with each step. Laughter and talking filled the air. Kos stopped before they broke through the alley and put his hand out to keep Orinthia from going. He cocked his head around the side and looked around. Satisfied, he lowered his hand and nodded for her to follow again.

Orinthia tucked her chin into her chest, letting her hair

fan over the sides of her face, but kept her eyes up. They were on the edge of a courtyard surrounded by more buildings placed in a circle. A group of people walked toward them along their path. She missed a step and almost stumbled as the one in the middle caught her attention. The man had dark brown skin that contrasted strongly with his bright silver hair. The strands shimmered in the dull orange light of the street lamps. He glanced in her direction as they passed, but only for a second then continued with his conversion to his companions.

Across the way, beyond a dry fountain, were more than two dozen others. Half of them had the same hair coloring. Most of whom had exposed mechanics ranging from arm enhancements to entirely modified sections of their bodies. One man wore a grey helmet, but his eyes were covered by goggles. The skin around the helmet had grown over the metal and fused it in place. Orinthia tried to look away, but the closer they moved, the more she could see.

Kos tugged at his sleeves almost non-stop. He walked with stiff steps. His breathing was as if he had run the entire way from *Freya*.

A woman approached them. She had beautifully smooth, fawn skin. It looked as if it was brushed on. Her lower jaw was set with a solid grey steel replacement. It moved fluidly as if it were made of organic material. Lights flashed over the sides. As she came closer, Orinthia could see fine lines running from creases in the metal of her mouth to her violet eyes. A crown of silver hair sat braided around the top of her head. She held up a hand and stopped a foot from Orinthia and Kos. When she spoke, it was not in a language Orinthia could understand. The woman waited a second then tapped her chin and repeated her statement. This pattern continued five times.

Kos moved a hair in front of Orinthia and hovered his hand over his hip.

"You come down on that smoking ship?" The woman said in dialect Orinthia knew. Though, Orinthia had never heard words formed the way the woman spoke. They were elongated and the vowels were tight.

"Clipped a mine," Orinthia answered before Kos could react. "Almost didn't make it."

"Arkady's people are getting sloppy," the woman muttered and shook her head. "Either way, glad to have ya. I'm Tylira, the newcomer representative. We don't usually get transplants this late but suppose it's on account of your ship. Don't look worse for wear, so you're doing 'right."

Orinthia glanced at Kos then looked back to Tylira.

"First off, you'll need to get your translators updated," Tylira continued. "We've all come from scattered around, so it makes it easier."

"Actually," Orinthia said. Her heart was pulsing in her throat as she quickly built up a story. "We have a few friends who didn't make it as safely as we did. The ship only had a few restraints. Is there a doctor we can get to check them out?"

Tylira twitched her jaw and squinted her eyes a fraction. She looked between the two people standing before her. "We've got no doctor."

Orinthia's head hummed. "Please. I know we're new and it's a lot to ask right away, but is there anyone that can help?"

Half a minute passed before Tylira answered. "You don't tell him I sent you, got it? He doesn't like visitors."

"I understand, thank you."

Shaking her head, like she was about to make a decision she knew she would eventually regret, Tylira made a quarter turn and pointed a slender metal hand toward the edge of the courtyard. "Go beyond the square to the last set of houses. There will be torn-down buildings. Keep walking until you find the one with the fence. Looks abandoned, but if it has a gate, that's the right place."

Tylira lowered her hand and turned to face them again. "Don't make me regret this. I know Arkady vets us before coming, but I don't want to be the one who messed up. Just get help for your friends then come back to me for that update."

With a nod, Orinthia took Kos by the hand and guided him away. He held tight. They moved quickly through a few more groups of people but it did not take long to reach the other side. It was darker there. Kos activated his visor. Still holding Orinthia's hand, he moved to the front and led the way. Neither of them spoke. Orinthia was not sure she would be able to if she wanted to. Her mouth was dry and her throat tight. It was a struggle to breathe. A warm, sharp sensation built up in her belly. Her legs ached to turn and run back the way she came.

There were still piles of rubble from when the Mod Bleyers had overthrown the EC base. Collapsed buildings stood partially intact, but the majority were demolished. Only one building had each of its four walls up. The one with the gate. Orinthia could hardly make it out until they were feet from it. Elendoras had no moon to brighten the night. Only the last glow of twilight was left, and it faded by the second.

At the gate, Kos released Orinthia's hand and undid the latch. The hinges screeched as it swung open. Kos again took Orinthia's hand and led through. She could see nothing and relied on him solely. Rocks crunched beneath her feet. Other than her breathing and their steps, she could hear nothing else. It felt like minutes to cross the path. She ran into the back of Kos as he stopped.

"What is it?" Orinthia asked. Her imagination ran away with itself, and she could only picture every frightful creature in front of them.

"The front door," Kos whispered.

She didn't know how, but that scared her more than anything she had imagined. Beyond the door was Desidario. And he *was* worse than any danger she could think up.

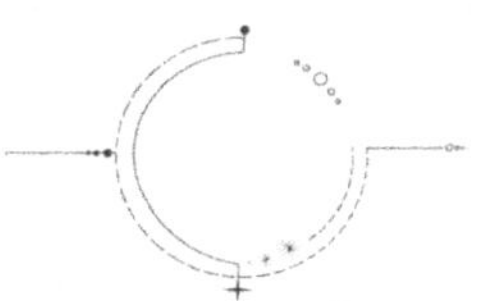

Kos and Orinthia stood in front of the door for a solid six minutes. This was only made known to Orinthia after Kos had asked her for a third time if she was ready to go inside. She would have rather waited another ten or fifteen minutes, perhaps even years to gather the courage to enter. But she knew that was not the time they had. If Tylira had seen the smoke from *Freya*, there was a chance others might go check it out and find the rest of their crew.

With a trembling breath, Orinthia said, "Let's go."

First, Kos tried the handle. It was no surprise when the knob did not turn. Orinthia could hear him shove something metallic against the dense door. Kos grunted a few times before saying, "Give me a second." He released Orinthia's hand. More scraping sounded, followed by a thud. A puff of cool air drifted out from somewhere in front of her. Kos' warm hand slipped back into hers and he pulled her forward.

The air around her was closer and she could feel the presence of something dense in the distance. Her steps were light, but the borrowed shoes tapped against what she guessed was a tiled floor.

"We're in some type of lobby," Kos explained in a hushed tone. "To the right is a door about twenty feet away. On the left is a hall that turns a corner. Which way do you want to go?"

It was not a decision she thought she would have to make. In her mind, they would just see Desidario and that would be it. After as much as she did to get there, she was still searching for him. "Left, I guess," Orinthia said. It did not matter either way. She would go through every room if she had to.

They only moved a few feet before Kos froze. He shoved Orinthia behind him and she heard the whirr of his blaster charging. A circle of light silhouetted Kos, casting a shadow behind them.

"Get out or I'll kill you right here," a man's gravelly voice said.

Orinthia swallowed the panic away. It was the voice of her nightmares. All sense of a plan evaporated from her mind. She did not know what to say or do and continued to cower against Kos.

"Are you Desidario Anton?" Kos asked. He did not sound like Orinthia felt. His words were clear and bold.

A blaster fire sparked on the wall near the door. "I didn't miss. Now get out."

Afraid for Kos' life, Orinthia stepped around him into the light. She held her hands up to show they were free of weapons.

There was a gasp from beyond the blinding light. Orinthia squinted and tried to make out the face of the man in front of her.

The flashlight tilted up, illuminating the hall. A thin, balding man stood near the turn. He had thick rounded lenses sealed over his eyes. His pale skin was wrinkled, and his cheeks sagged. In the center of his face sat a perpetually swollen nose. "What are you doing here? How did you find me?"

"I need your help," Orinthia said. Her arms shook as she spoke.

Desidario looked at Kos, who had not lowered his blaster, then back to Orinthia. "I came here to work and die. Whatever your problem is, find someone else to take care of it."

A fire burned through Orinthia, replacing any fear she may have had a second before. "I've flown across the galaxy to find you. You will help me."

Her father stepped closer. "I owe you nothing. I made you who you are. You owe me everything. Instead, you constantly choose to throw it away."

The weight of the blaster on her hip begged her to pick it up. She ignored it. "You experimented on me. It never stops. My head is killing me. Don't you understand what you've done to me?" Two years apart changed nothing. The argument they had in her apartment picked up exactly where it left off.

"It was for the greater good." Desidario wagged his head like he was trying to shake something free. "You never appreciated your role in our family. I depended on you. We were allies."

"I was a puppet. A child. This was never meant to be a burden for me to carry. You were the parent. You were supposed to protect us, not ruin us. Uri was the one who kept me alive. Now I need you to save him."

Desidario's eyes squinted behind the thick, pink-hued

glass. He took a moment to absorb the information tossed at him. "What do you mean?"

Orinthia took a steading draw of air. "Adora blew a hole through his chest, thanks to our well-adjusted sibling dynamic."

"Where is my son?" Orinthia detected a strain in Desidario's voice.

"With the rest of our crew on the other side of the compound," Kos said. He continued to hold his blaster over Orinthia's shoulder.

"So, you come to me and demand I fix him without so much as a 'hello?'" Desidario tilted his head back and looked down his fat nose at Orinthia.

"I would rather die than waste pleasantries on you," Orinthia said. Thick saliva built up in her mouth. "If I wasn't being framed for his murder, we'd be at the Moon's cyborg hospital."

"That wouldn't have worked anyway," Desidario said. "He's not a true cyborg."

All warmth rushed from Orinthia. "What?"

"I only ever said he was," Desidario continued. He stepped closer. "It was better and easier to explain."

Orinthia shook her head. "No, I would've known. You always said he was a cyborg. Even his scan shows his mechanisms." Her mind raced to recall any hint of humming from her childhood.

"You never listen." Desidario was halfway up the hall. The light shone brighter. "If someone believes a lie to be true, you won't detect it."

"Then what is he?" Orinthia locked her legs to keep standing.

He stopped in front of a door and opened it without

answering. The flashlight in his hand turned to illuminate the second room. He disappeared inside as he said, "Synthetic flesh over steel, programmed to age."

Orinthia dashed to follow him. Kos was on her heels, and they descended a set of stairs.

"There was nothing left to save," Desidario continued. "He and your mother were crushed. But I challenged myself to try anyway. The Irelad project was in full swing, and I took what I learned and reimagined him. As he grew, I had to replace parts and mechanics here and there, but he is my greatest creation."

Orinthia's stomach twisted. A cold sweat formed on her upper lip.

They reached the base of the stairs and were met by another hall. Desidario turned right and went to the third door. "I gave him every memory I had, every story I could think of. I taught the AI to be him. Even Uri doesn't know the difference." He pulled a set of keys from his slacks and unlocked the door.

There was not a single hum in Orinthia's head as he spoke. Nothing suggested he was lying. A thought struck her, twisting her stomach more.

"You could have brought both of them back," Orinthia said. Her breath quickened. "I grew up without a mother and you could have done the same thing with her."

Desidario turned to face Orinthia. His hand was still on the doorknob. "I was done with your mother. She betrayed me."

"Did you have her killed?" Orinthia's voice grew louder. "I've seen the list. I saw she was assassinated. Was it you?"

"No, but I can't say I was surprised when it happened. I only regret that my son was collateral damage." Desidario opened the door and stepped in. He thumbed on lights that blinked to life. The room was scattered with tech on the floor and projects over tables. A foul smell hung in the air.

Kos stiffened.

Orinthia pressed her arm to her nose as she followed her dad. "Why? Why was she killed?"

Desidario rotated his head over his shoulders. "She couldn't keep her opinions to herself. Always advocating for the war to end. Her No-Mod charity was the leading force behind regulating mods. Wars make money. Those who profit off wars don't like when people try to end them."

The room swayed around her. Orinthia ran her hand behind her and reached for Kos to brace herself.

"I didn't kill her," Desidario continued. "But with her out of the way, I was free to continue creating. And, as an added bonus, experimenting with Uri led me to perfecting the Irelad. I saved lives with the knowledge I gained and made the most efficient soldier ever to exist."

"You're disgusting," Orinthia yelled at him. She swallowed the bile that shot up her throat.

Desidario moved to his full height and threw up his hand.

Orinthia did not flinch but set her jaw and waited to be hit.

As he swung down, Kos came around Orinthia and caught his wrist.

"How dare you touch me," Desidario said through gritted teeth.

"I'd do more than that if she didn't need you. If you even think of hurting her again before you've fixed Uri, know I'm prepared to let her hate me forever if it means she'd be free of you."

Desidario jerked his arm and tried to break free. "She is my daughter, and I will do what I have to to keep her in line."

"She is my universe," Kos said. He leaned closer to Desidario and stood toe to toe with him. "She's the only thing that keeps me sane. I've seen the healed fractures on her bones. Trust me, I've killed for less, and this time I'll enjoy it."

With another yank, Desidario stumbled back as Kos let go. He glared at Kos and moved to a table in the center of the room. "I gave Uri memories of your mother. More than he would have had on his own. Part of her lived through him." He cleared papers from the table and patted it, facing Orinthia. "Have a seat."

The sudden order jarred her senses. "Why?"

"You don't think I'm going to fix him for free, do you?" Desidario asked. "I came to Elendoras to work. Help me and I'll help you."

"He is your son," Orinthia shouted.

"And this is my life's work." Desidario placed his hands behind his back. "Rebuilding Uri was my greatest milestone. Now you'll help me reach the next one. I couldn't work in the EC, but I've completed it here."

Orinthia shook her head. She wanted to lunge at him; to gut him with her sword. The smell slowly registered in her mind. It was the sick scent of death. "How many have you experimented on?"

"Enough to make it work," Desidario answered.

Kos asked, "What experiment?"

"The future of modification." Desidario lifted his head and looked as if he were posing for a photo. "After the EC banned weaponized tech, I fled here to continue my work. There were more than enough willing subjects to test on. Mod Bleyers are so easy to please as long as you offer them shiny new enhancements."

"And they all failed," Orinthia said. "You killed them."

"Sacrifices were made." Desidario waved a hand to

dismiss her accusation. "All paving stones on the path to glory."

"I won't be one of those paving stones," Orinthia said.

"Then I hope you've enjoyed the time with your brother."

Orinthia pulled the blaster from her holster. It was heavy in her hand, but she held it steady. "You don't have a choice."

Desidario chuckled. "Looks like the choice is yours. Kill me, you don't get Uri back. Don't help me and you still don't get Uri back. On second thought, it isn't that hard of a decision, is it?"

"I'll do it," Kos said. "Give me the mod."

"It will kill you," Orinthia said. She did not know how her body could handle any more stress. "You're already burning alive as it is."

"I'm not wasting my mod just for you to die," Desidario said. "That's happened enough. It has to be Orinthia or no one else. I always had it in mind for it to be hers. It's what I wanted you to help with before I left the NCR."

Orinthia lowered the blaster. "I hate you. Everything you've done to me has been a curse. The only good thing you've done was making Uri. He is the only reason you're still alive."

Kos put his hands on Orinthia's shoulders and pulled her back. "We will have to find another way."

"We both know there isn't one. There is nothing you can say to change my mind."

"I love you," Kos whispered. His voice was broken. "I need you. I'm afraid of who I am when you're not around."

With her free hand, Orinthia touched his cheek. She ran her thumb over his coarse beard. "As much as I don't like it, he would never hinge his life or reputation on something he wasn't certain about. I know his mod will work."

"Thank you for the faith in me," Desidario said. Pride oozed from his words.

Orinthia dropped her hand and faced him. "It's faith in your arrogance."

"If you fail," Kos said, "if anything goes wrong, know I will gladly turn this entire asteroid to rubble."

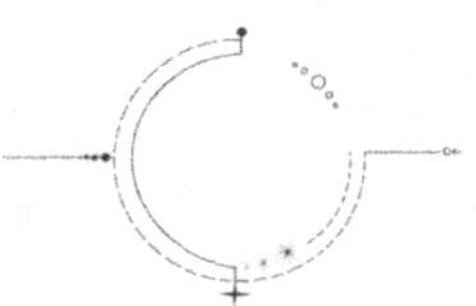

52

Orinthia stood beside the surgical table. She refused to sit until Desidario agreed to work on Uri at the same time as giving her the new mod. As Kos called Thrutt to join them, Desidario rolled a second table beside hers. He gathered needles, chemicals, wires, as well as different types of machines and set them within reach of the two tables.

"What did you tell Thrutt?" Orinthia asked when Kos rejoined her.

"Only that we were ready for him to bring Uri," Kos answered. He took off his coat and tossed it on the back of a chair. "I didn't want him to come in here guns blazing. He's not going to be happy."

"I'm not doing this willingly." Orinthia looked at Kos. "Just because I agreed doesn't mean I'm not being forced. You know that."

"I do." Kos pulled her against him and put his cheek on her head. "Thrutt will understand, too. We might have to talk him out of killing Desidario, however."

"You do know I can hear you, right?" Desidario said from

across the room. He connected two cords together and dropped them to the ground.

"We're not trying to hide it," Kos said. He kept his arm on Orinthia but straightened his head. "You're disgusting to do this at all, let alone to your children."

Desidario looked Kos up and down. "Don't pretend you're so much better than me. We've both taken lives for the greater good. Except my only master was progress."

"Where are your mods, then?" Kos asked.

"I have none," Desidario said with a sniff.

Kos let out a choked laugh. "Hypocrite. You make all this tech and won't even put any in yourself?"

"Modifications are meant as enhancements, which I am in no need of. Aside from my failing vision, that is."

"Stop it, Kos," Orinthia said. "He's taken enough, don't let him steal these last moments. I know I said I believe it will work, but I'm scared this might be the end."

A hush fell over the room. Even Desidario paused from his work for a moment.

"We have too much ahead of us for this to be the end." Kos turned her to face him. His eyes were dark, but the fire did not consume him. He was fighting the shadows, holding on to stay there for her. "The galaxy is waiting to be explored, remember? We're going to leave this life and forge a new path. I won't settle for anything less than to have you by my side."

Orinthia did not know how to respond. Dying was not something she could control. If this mod killed her as it did the others, then it was out of her hands. Instead, she looked to Desidario. "You never said what this mod does. What are you putting inside me?"

"Finally," Desidario said, clapping his hands together. "Being so far from people who understand the gravity of my work is excruciating. This will change the future of modification." He came around the tables and stood in front of the couple. His eyes were wide, and he tilted his chin up. "You will be remade on a cellular level, rewriting your DNA's replication code. Once complete, you'll be able to manipulate everything around you."

"Like telekinesis?" Orinthia asked. She tried to suppress a tremor that ran up her spine and hoped Kos did not notice.

"Yes. But it will no longer be limited to specific species. Before I came here, I studied the DNA of those who already have this ability. Their energy can tap into and match the frequencies of living and non-living things. What I have created is only a fraction of what is possible, but it is a feat nonetheless."

Orinthia wondered if she had made the right decision. Detecting lies was one thing, being rewritten was another. She wanted to save Uri but knew he would have forbidden her from going through with it. *But he's not here to stop me,* she thought. *And he never will be if I back out.*

In truth, she knew it was too late to do that. Thrutt was on his way and would be there any minute.

Kos pulled Orinthia a few feet toward the door, away from Desidario. "You can't do this," he said with a forced hush voice. "It isn't some tech we can remove once we get out of here."

Orinthia attempted to smile, to pretend like the description she was presented with did not freeze her to her core. "I think it could be interesting. The process doesn't sound that great, but maybe it won't be that bad."

Before Kos could respond, his comm chirped. He closed his eyes and flared his nostrils. Taking the comm from his pant pocket, he flicked it open. "You close?"

"I'm outside," Thrutt said. "But I got word from Naka-hara a few minutes ago. Two sloops came across the radar."

Kos eyed Orinthia. "Any chance they're Arkady's?"

"Not likely," Thrutt answered. "They weren't moving in a landing pattern."

"Get down here and we'll figure it out." The comm snapped closed. He pinched the bridge of his nose and let out a chest full of air.

"I'm not leaving without Uri fixed," Orinthia said without prompting. "This has gone on long enough. The next person to get in my way will taste my blade from the inside out."

Kos took half a step back. He held his hands loosely in front of him. "Okay, I won't make you leave. But the minute it gets hot out there, I'm pulling the plug."

"He's rewriting my DNA, Kos. I don't think that's going to be possible. We have to see this to the end. I'm sorry to put you in this position. This was never my intention. I don't know how I went from being a washed-up Marauder Hunter to fighting enemies on two fronts, but it's where our path led. Errol will probably have a stroke if he finds out about this."

"You're insane," Kos said, shaking his head.

"I know." Orinthia gave him a solemn smile. "Now, come on. I want to be ready for when Thrutt brings Uri."

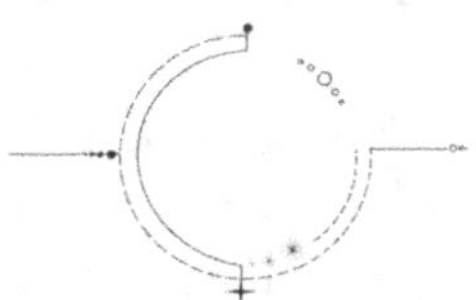

53

The metal table was cold, even through her pants. Orinthia swung her legs back and forth over the side and kept an eye on the entrance. The minutes she spent waiting for Thrutt to arrive felt like hours. Her nails drummed against the metal.

A thin tube ran from a needle in the crook of her arm to an unpowered machine behind her. Her skin smelled of disinfectant and stung her nose when she breathed. Swinging her legs was the only thing keeping her from having full convulsions. Her muscles ached and her heart raced faster than it had before. If she did not keep moving, the fear would take over.

The heavy pounding of Thrutt's feet sounded down the steps. He appeared from behind the door, carrying Uri over his shoulder. Thrutt moved closer and as he passed Orinthia kept his gaze glued to her.

She kept her face down and did not meet his eyes.

"Set him here," Desidario informed Thrutt, gesturing toward the second table. He glanced at the giant multiple times, then passed looks over Orinthia and Kos.

Orinthia wished she could hear what her father was thinking. Did he realize he was in a room with two deadly veterans who could easily end him? Who not only hated him for what his part was in the war, but what he had done to her. Did he know they cared more about her than their own lives? Despite the anxiety gripping her chest, she took a moment to appreciate the fact. It was short-lived, however, when Thrutt stood in front of her. *These men do love me more than their lives,* she thought. *And I'm going to hurt them doing this.*

"Hey, kid," Thrutt said, slowly. "What's this setup for?"

The trembling she fought to control rippled through her body. An icy sensation slithered up her spine. Hot tears pricked at her eyes and blurred her vision. "I have to do this," she whispered.

"No, you don't," Thrutt said. "I'm not sure what *this* is, but no."

"What would you trade to get your family back?" Orinthia lifted her head and blinked away tears.

"I can't get them back."

"But I can get Uri back," Orinthia said. "It's just a new mod. It'll be okay."

"You look terrified. Uri would not want this for you. How do you think he's going to react when he finds out you did this for him?"

"I won't care because if he reacts at all that means he's alive." Orinthia placed her hands on his diamond ones. "Thrutt, you three are my family. You told me we make sacrifices for each other. That's what I'm doing. If this goes bad, I want you to know that I had the best life since meeting you. There is not a thing I would change. Except maybe this moment, obviously."

Thrutt shook his head. "I should have left you in that bar. You would have been safer there."

"But I would never have known happiness," Orinthia said and gave him a half smile. "Besides, your life would be boring if you hadn't met me."

"Aye, that it is truth." Thrutt sighed. "Promise you'll be here when I get back?"

"It's Ahto, isn't it?"

"I believe so. But I'm going to keep them away from here for as long as I can."

"The skiff doesn't have weapons," Orinthia said.

"Let me worry about that, but I need to borrow Rogue for a moment."

Kos, who had not left Orinthia's side since she climbed onto the table, said, "I'm not leaving this spot."

"Go," Orinthia said. "He's already gotten me to do what he wants, nothing worse can happen. Probably."

With a huff, Kos followed Thrutt to the entrance. His fists were clenched at his side, and he moved quickly.

Mostly alone, Orinthia turned her focus to Uri. Desidario had undone Uri's shirt and exposed the hole in its entirety. It had been covered for so long that seeing it made Orinthia's stomach turn. The gears cranked slowly, slower than she remembered them to be. Their whirring was quieter, as well.

"How do you know Ahto?" Desidario asked. Metal tools clanked against the tray as he laid them in neat rows.

"Your Irelad was my captain, once upon a time," Orinthia answered. "Adora fired me from the GMH, so I became a marauder." She briefly retold how Ahto had sent her and her friends to find Errol and how their escapades eventually led to her sitting on a surgical table. "He's malfunctioning. The last time we saw him, it looked like he could no longer control his shifting."

"I did not design him to last forever." Desidario left Uri

and moved to Orinthia's table. "Though his longevity is a credit to my ingenuity."

Orinthia made a scratching sound in her throat. "Give it a rest. There's no one here to impress, least of all me. If I didn't need you, I would have told him exactly where you were, and he could do whatever he wanted with you."

"You disappoint me," Desidario said with tight lips. He placed his hands under the table and rolled out a black strap. In a quick motion, he attached it to Orinthia's wrist and tightened it until it dug into her skin.

Orinthia reached over to undo it, but Desidario slapped her hand out of the way.

"This is for your safety, believe it or not. I've seen grown men tear their skin apart during the process. Over time I've perfected it, but it will still be painful."

"What happened to the last one?" Orinthia asked. She drew shallow breaths through her nose. "How do you know this time will work if all the rest have died?"

Desidario moved to her other side and undid the second restraint. His thin fingers wrapped around her wrist and fixed the strap to her arm. "He didn't die at first. It took a few days. Before he died, however, he was able to do exactly what I intended him to do. The building next door was almost completely intact, and he pulled it down on top of himself. But it worked flawlessly."

Unsure of whether to gasp or scream, Orinthia sat with her mouth ajar. The muscles in her neck tightened. She pictured the destroyed buildings above her. Piles of rubble, potentially with a dead man buried beneath.

"It was not the mod that killed him," Desidario said, pointing a finger in her face. "Don't be stupid and pull down the walls of an unstable building while you're inside and you'll be fine."

"Do you even know his name?" Orinthia asked, coming back to her senses.

"Who?"

"The man before me? We were just talking about him."

"Progress is paved with nameless participants." Desidario drew himself back and tucked his arms behind himself. "My name is what matters."

"I lived with marauders who had more humanity than you." Orinthia curled her upper lip in disgust. She tugged at the restraints but could not break free. Once again, she was right where he wanted her, and she did not put up much of a fight to stop him. Desidario may have been a monster, but he knew how to play the game and win. He always won.

Kos emerged from behind the door and froze as his eyes fell upon a restrained Orinthia. "What is this?" He rushed to her and began to undo the straps.

Desidario shoved him aside. "Leave them. They are to keep her from hurting herself. That's what you want, isn't it? Now remove yourself from this spot while I work." He put a hand on her chest and the other behind her head, slowly guiding her down. It was the most gentle he had ever touched her.

A torrent of fear coursed through her. The metal clasps of the straps tapped against the table like rattles as she shook. Anticipation, adrenaline, terror, and regret rushed over her in drowning waves. A humming sound grew louder beside her. She turned her head to see Desidario activate the machine connected to her arm. A line of yellow fluid filled the clear tube and flowed toward her. Whimpers broke from her mouth.

A fire burned in her other hand, drawing her attention away from the machine. Kos gripped her tightly. His face had lost some color and was twisted. Lines creased in his forehead, creating deep channels.

The fluid reached her veins. It was cool in the tube that touched her skin. Her fingers chilled as it worked its way through her arm. An acidic taste filled her mouth. But that was it. She felt no pain other than the tugging of the tube under the tape. Orinthia let out long streams of air and tried to focus on what was going on beyond her.

Across from her, Desidario took a laser scalpel between his fingers and leaned closer to Uri. He ran a finger from his rib to the base of his neck and turned his head to the side. Flipping the scalpel on, he made a rectangular incision on the back of his neck. Lifting the flesh revealed exposed wires and servos.

Orinthia clenched her teeth together.

Desidario slid his index finger through a space between two rods and dug around for a moment. "His internal repair system was lowered to slightly above the average healing rate for a human," he explained to no one in particular. "I'll need to replace some of the mechanisms in his chest, but this will take care of the rest."

"I could have done that myself," Orinthia said. Her voice raised. "If I had known he was synthetic and that was the solution, I could have saved him a long time ago. I wouldn't need you."

Desidario looked over his shoulder to her. "But you did need me. The fix may have been simple, but without my knowledge, you never would have discovered it."

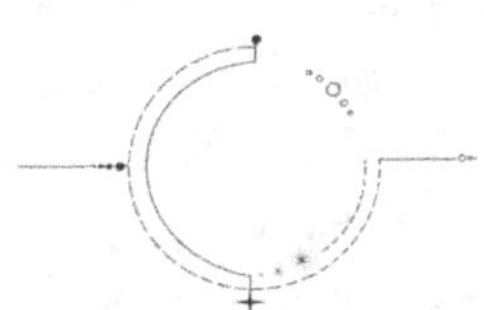

54

The air was thick and warm in the basement laboratory. Uri's newly replaced parts in his chest buzzed, but it was the only sound. No one had spoken in half an hour. Occasionally, Orinthia would feel a shock of electricity shoot through her, which lasted a few seconds at a time.

Kos sat beside her with his hand still in hers and stroked her hair each time she clenched in pain. When she was calm, he rested his head on his arm on the edge of the table. He never took his eyes off her.

Desidario sat on a rolling chair behind a desk. His hands were folded over his middle and his head leaned back. Soft snores came from his direction.

A faint beeping came from Kos' pocket. He lifted himself and retrieved the comm. "Thrutt?"

"We lost sight of the sloops," Mimi said over the line.

"The radar, too?" Kos asked. He stiffened.

Mimi was quiet for a moment. "*Freya*'s radar went dead a little bit ago. Thrutt was tracking them with the skiff, but they gave him the slip."

Kos muttered curses under his breath. "Why are you telling me and not him?"

"Easier than explaining it twice, I guess," Mimi responded. Irritation laced her voice. "It doesn't matter. I wanted to warn you so you can be ready if anyone shows up. Thrutt was heading back to you."

A stream of hot electricity raced through Orinthia. It lasted twice as long as the previous one. She dug her nails into her palms and her jaw muscles ached from clenching her teeth.

"Get *Freya* ready to fly," Kos ordered. He watched Orinthia with intent. His chest rose and fell quickly. "Have her turn off anything that isn't completely necessary. Lose anything we can to lighten the load. The food, everything. Keep enough for a few days but that's it. We'll have to leave the skiff, too."

The pain stopped.

"You're not serious," Mimi said.

"Very. She's in poor shape and I'll need all the help I can get to fly her out of here."

"You know her best, I guess. I'll do what I can in the meantime. Call me as soon as you're ready."

The line went dead, and Kos closed the comm again. He touched Orinthia's forehead. "That was the longest one so far."

"I know," Orinthia said. Her breath was rapid. "They're getting stronger, too. My skin feels like there are millions of hot pokers pressing against it."

"I wish I could take this for you," Kos said.

"This is how it was supposed to happen," Orinthia said. She paused as another wave of pain moved through her. A groan escaped from between her pinched lips. When it was over, she continued. "You have to be ready for Ahto. He's not going to be reasoned with when he gets here."

"I am already here," a raspy voice said from behind Kos.

Kos spun around and placed himself with his arms wide in a defensive stance. Through the gap, Orinthia could see the image of what used to be a man.

Ahto's skin shimmered. He walked crooked, like a drunk. His head was cocked at an angle and he held his slitted eyes wide. He no longer wore a human face, it was overtaken by the snake he was. Daggers for teeth snapped and a forked tongue licked the air.

White light blocked Orinthia's vision. She tried to fight through, but the pain blinded her. The blood in her body rushed loudly.

"Master, I've come home," Ahto said. He must have shouted because Orinthia could hear him over the noise in her body.

As fast as it came, the pain stopped, and her sight returned.

Desidario was no longer at his desk but stood near her head. She could hear his shoes tap against the floor as he shuffled his feet. "The time of the Irelad has passed," he said.

Orinthia realized she missed part of the conversation during her episode. For which she was about to lose more as another, longer pain went through her. She struggled to take in air. Her body flailed and convulsed.

Then stillness.

When she opened her eyes, Kos stood with his armor on. He held his blaster in one hand and dagger in the other. She searched for her father but could not find him. Uri lay still on his table, his eyes shut. The hole in his chest was much smaller than it had been before.

A loud clang sounded to her right and she tossed her head to the side in time to see Ahto slash at Kos with his bladed tail.

More fire and electricity rushed through her. She knew she screamed by the burning in her throat, but could not hear it. The restraints dug into her skin as she thrashed around.

The blinding light faded, and she gasped for air. Her palms were wet, though she could not see from what. She had enough strength to roll her head to the side before another rush of pain coursed through her.

The world around her faded into darkness. There was no sound, no air, no elements; only her.

LIKE COMING out of a deep pool, Orinthia filled her lungs with air. Her eyes flew open to see the blurry ceiling above her. Sweat clung to her skin. Her hands were wet. Every nerve tingled. Orinthia blinked to clear her vision.

From somewhere in the room, she heard a crash. Slowly, she moved her head toward the sound. Kos slid across the floor and his armored body slammed into the wall. A rush of anger whirled around her. She tried to move from the table, but the restraints held her down.

Ahto coiled around her father and hoisted him into the air. In a swift motion, he released the old man. As he fell, Ahto curved his tail and caught Desidario through the back, his blade pierced through his chest.

Desidario gasped for air and fumbled with the blade sticking through his middle. Blood dripped down Ahto's tail like crimson streams.

Orinthia's throat seared as a scream ripped through her. The straps on her wrists banged against the table, ringing around the room.

Ahto flicked his tail and tossed Desidario's body to the floor.

Time slowed. The metal snake curved himself to turn toward Kos, his head angled and mouth wide to strike with his teeth.

Her restraints fell off, freeing her to move. Before she was fully on her feet, Orinthia yanked out the needle from her arm and activated her blades. "Stay away from him," she shouted.

Ahto drifted into a hard turn and faced her. Without missing a beat, he charged at Orinthia, dragging Desidario's blood across his belly. He reared up four feet from Orinthia and poised to strike.

Orinthia slid her feet apart, angled her elbows at her hips, and swung in an upward motion. Sparks flew over her as her black blade slashed across his throat. His weight, still moving toward her, forced her to a knee. She managed to roll out of the path and jumped back to her feet to face her enemy.

Ahto, with a wide gash through his metallic skin, waved his head and hissed. He slunk back for a moment, readying for a second strike.

With deep breaths, Orinthia focused on what was around her. She could feel the ripples of energy flowing off Ahto. She found him in her mind and pictured the monster coming for her. As if on command, Ahto flew at her, mouth wide.

Orinthia planted her feet on the ground, and with a yell, threw her blades up. Ahto's upper jaw caught the full force. His body weight combined with momentum caused the blade to slide all the way through to the back of his head.

The massive beast collapsed on top of her, pinning her to

the floor, and trapping her arms inside his mouth. Orinthia lifted her legs and tried to push him off her but could not get a good angle. The pressure made her struggle for air. Strength left her and another blanket of darkness fell over her. She fought to stay conscious but lost.

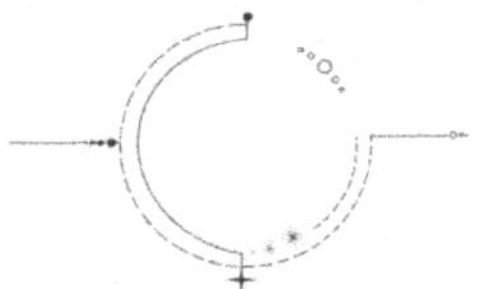

55

Orinthia did not know how long it was before footsteps drew her back to reality. Even in her half-aware state, she recognized Thrutt's heavy steps rushing toward her.

"Thia?" Worry oozed from the single word. Thrutt lifted Ahto off her, tossing his lifeless snake form aside.

Free, Orinthia drew in a full breath of air. Her throat burned, causing her to cough, which sent more slivers of pain through her esophagus. Her body was racked with pain, and she had no energy to move. It was only Thrutt's cold crystal hands on her face that kept her awake.

"Stay still," Thrutt said. "Rogue is still out, and I need him to scan you before I can move you."

"Uri?" Orinthia croaked.

"I haven't checked, yet. Let me take care of you first."

Orinthia did not have the strength of mind to argue. She rested her head on his hand and focused on staying awake.

"What happened?" Thrutt asked. "I couldn't get Rogue on the comm and decided to come looking. This was not what I was expecting to find."

"I don't know," Orinthia answered. "It happened so fast. My head hurts."

"Don't overdo it." Thrutt placed his palm on her forehead. "Stay here. I'm going to see if I can wake up Rogue." He stood up and bounded to the back wall where Orinthia had last seen Kos. Thrutt disappeared out of her view, and she tried to listen for movement.

Metal scraped across the floor, and she heard hushed voices from Thrutt's direction. She could hear Kos' armor fold away. A few seconds later, two sets of footsteps came back to her.

Kos held his side and knelt beside her. He had his visor pulled over his eyes. "Hi there," he said, wincing as he smiled. "We're going to take you back to *Freya*, okay?" After looking her up and down, he faced Thrutt. "I don't see anything that would be made worse from transport. She has a broken rib, though, so be gentle."

"Check Uri, please," Orinthia said.

Thrutt scooped her up.

Orinthia hissed in air through her teeth as a sharp pain tugged at her middle. She tried to place an arm over Thrutt's shoulder for better support but realized both were still active swords.

"Can you deactivate them?" Thrutt asked, apparently noticing her predicament.

"Sit me down somewhere and I'll try." The words were hard to speak. They moved softly to the table she had laid on earlier. Thrutt placed her upright and held her back for support. Orinthia concentrated on her arms and drew them close to her body. With a grunt, she threw them back and recalled her normal hands.

Across from her, Kos examined Uri. "He looks fine," he

announced. "He's breathing and the hole is gone. I'm not sure why he isn't up yet."

"We can't leave him," Orinthia said.

"You up for carrying her?" Thrutt asked in Kos' direction.

Kos turned and put up his visor. "I think so. Is Mimi on her way?"

"Should be," Thrutt answered. He slowly moved his hand from Orinthia's back and hovered near her for a few seconds. "I called her when I couldn't get ahold of you."

"See where she's at, then we can head topside."

Thrutt pulled the comm from his pocket and moved toward the door.

Orinthia tried to follow him with her head, but Kos put his hand on her cheek.

"Don't look that way," he said. "Promise me you'll keep your eyes shut when we walk out."

A sick feeling settled in her stomach. Her jaw quivered and her body went cold. "I hated him, but I didn't want him dead."

Kos leaned forward and kissed her forehead. "I know. We'll work through it after we're far away from here."

Dust fell from her hands as she rubbed them together. Orinthia looked down to see deep gashes in her palms where her nails had dug in. The open wounds tugged with each movement. Her wrists were raw and red, too. As clarity settled in, the more pain she felt. Fatigue hit her as well.

Thrutt returned and moved to Uri's table. He placed his arms around him and hoisted the unconscious man over his shoulder. "She's five minutes out."

Orinthia lifted her arms and wrapped them around Kos' neck. He slid one arm under the bend in her knees and the other supported her back. His face scrunched together, and he breathed in through his nose.

"I'll try to walk," Orinthia said, trying to push away from him so he'd set her down.

"No, I'm fine," Kos said.

Orinthia's head hummed. She shook her head.

"I can do it, let's go." Kos took a few shaky steps before finding his stride. He kept his back to the wall and pressed his forehead to hers, trying to block out what was around them.

Orinthia pinched her eyes closed. She had enough nightmares of seeing Desidario dead, she did not need to experience more of the real thing. A rusty scent hung in the air. Seconds later, the space around her felt more confined and she peeked to see they were in the stairway.

Kos took the steps one at a time, holding her tight and apologizing every time she winced. The top of the stairs came into view. Thrutt's feet pounded the wooden steps as he followed behind them. Dawn was breaking and a soft glow cut through the darkness as they moved through the empty lobby to outside. Stars blinked above in the cloudless lavender sky.

A few hundred feet away, beyond the fence, the mangled ship sat with the ramp down. Smoke hung around the rear. Mimi stood at the opening and waved them closer. Kos moved faster and half-jogged the rest of the way, holding Orinthia tightly to avoid jostling her too much.

Clean air rushed from the hold and washed over Orinthia's face. Kos set her down on the floor near the entrance and hurried to the ladder. Thrutt was next to walk in. He put Uri beside her and laid him on his back.

Orinthia looked at her brother. His chest moved in a steady rhythm as he breathed. She smiled. They were safe. Fatigue took over and she rested her head back on the wall. The world around her went black and she let it swallow her.

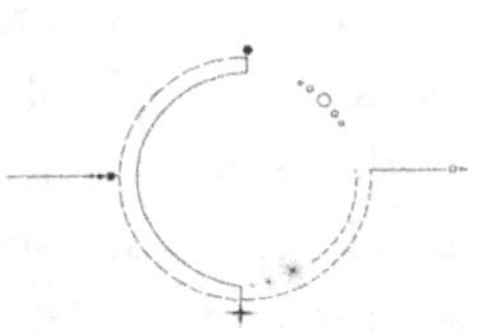

56

A cool breeze brushed hair across Orinthia's face, tickling her nose. She sneezed. Her stomach muscles tensed, and she gasped, sending her eyes flying open. After several shallow breaths, the pain subsided. She squinted her eyes to block out the light coming in from the window at the end of the bed. Orinthia tried to remember the last place she had been, but even in her haze, she realized she was not on a ship.

A curtain rustled, sending soft shadows across the blush-pink walls. Beside her was a table with a half-filled glass of water. She ran her tongue over her dry lips and reached for the cup. Her fingers were inches away from it, but she could not grab it. The glass wobbled for a second and fell back, spilling the contents on the wall. A staticky feeling danced around her hand and she pulled it back to herself, shaking the sensation away.

The sound of glass clicking together caught her attention. She looked to her right and found a door cracked open. Laughter, hearty deep laughter, filled the space on the other side. It was the sound of life.

Finding her strength, Orinthia slid out of bed. Every inch of her ached. Her legs felt like they were made of the same material as the bedsheets she sat on. She stiffened her muscles before forcing herself to stand. With her free hand, Orinthia braced herself on the wall and waited for her equilibrium to catch up to her movement. Her head was heavy, and her neck burned. Slowly, with her hand still on the wall, she moved toward the door. Winded, she took a pause to catch her breath. She reached out for the doorknob, and it moved toward her, opening fully.

The smell of freshly cooked food hit her before anything else. Warm spices and salted meat made her stomach grumble. She took a step out the door and moved down a narrow hall. Following the wall, she found an opening that led to a brightly lit kitchen. Light filtered in through a skylight in the ceiling, adding extra warmth to the space.

Mimi was the first to notice Orinthia enter the room. She flashed a wide smile. The others followed her gaze. Chairs scraped across the floor, but Orinthia did not see who stood. She focused on one face. Her heart raced. "Uri?"

His face was bright and rosy, and mismatched eyes wide. He stood and rushed to her, grabbing her elbow and shoulder. "Oh, my Thia."

Orinthia fell into his arms. Uri wrapped her tight and slowly rocked her back and forth. The pair held each other until Orinthia had no choice but to let go, or she felt like her body would snap.

Kos pulled a chair behind her, and she slid into it. He stood beside her, placing his fingertips on her shoulder.

Uri brought his chair and sat down in front of her in the middle of the kitchen.

Orinthia's mind raced to find the words to say. Thankfully, Uri spoke first.

"I told you that you were impulsive and made poor decisions," he said with a grin.

"I'm just glad to hear you say anything at all," Orinthia said. She soaked in the sound of his voice. It was better than any piece of music she had heard. "I've missed you so much."

"My sweet girl," Uri said, patting her knee. "Look at all you've done. I owe you everything."

"We owe them," Orinthia said, looking at the faces of her friends. "I couldn't have done it without any of them."

"That's not the story they tell," Uri said with a smirk. "But what do I know? I've been as good as dead for almost half a year."

Orinthia did not understand why she found his statement funny, but she let out an uncontrollable minute of laughter. Her sides pulled together, and she said "ow," in between laughs. The others looked on with half confusion and half amusement. For the first time in a long time, she was at peace. There was nowhere to go, no one to find, nothing left to do. She had everything.

"Let's get you back to bed and more comfortable and I'll bring you something to eat," Kos said.

Uri stood and took Orinthia by the elbow, drawing her to her feet.

"I'll check on you in a while," Thrutt told her. "Give you time to catch up."

Orinthia smiled at him. She wanted to keep them all around and not let any of them out of her sight. But she would settle for what she could get. She and Uri moved arm-in-arm back to the room she came from. Once inside and a little more clearheaded, Orinthia took a moment to inspect her surroundings.

There was a table at the foot of the bed lined with plants.

Lush, green, and alive. A soft beige carpet formed around her bare feet. The bedspread was white and had a delicate flower pattern. It was one of the most peaceful places she had been in. Nearly the opposite of her old apartment.

With Orinthia back in bed, Uri sat on the edge and put a knee up to face her better. After all the time she spent wanting to talk to him, she did not know what to say. She took long stares at him, moving from his face to his hands. Even with the new information about who he was, she could not picture him any differently. She wondered if anyone had told him yet, or what they talked about while she was out.

Kos walked in with a tray of food and juice. He set it on her lap and sat beside her with his back resting on the headboard.

The two men glanced at each other but said nothing. An uncomfortable sensation built up on Orinthia's body, like butterfly wings beating beneath her skin. She could feel Kos and Uri individually as if they were touching her, though they were far from her. With deep breaths, she pushed it from her mind and the feeling faded away.

"Kos owns a restaurant in the old part of District One," Orinthia said, trying to break the tension in the air. "We'll have to take you someday."

Kos cleared his throat and made a sniff. "We're not going anywhere for a while."

"I'm getting better," Orinthia said. "It doesn't have to be today; I'd like to stay in one place for a bit."

"*Freya* used up everything to get us here," Kos said. He lowered his head and rubbed his thumb against the back of his other hand. "She's going to need a lot more than just a patch-up. So, for now, we're stuck here."

Orinthia's heart sank. Not for being marooned, but for

Kos' loss. "I'm so sorry, Kos. What can I do to help? Maybe I can get a job to put credits towards new parts."

"That will be something to figure out later," Kos said, patting her arm. "For now, Mimi is letting us stay here with her until things get sorted. Thrutt and I already have work lined up. But you focus on healing. I still don't know how much your mod will affect you now that you're awake."

She chose not to tell them about the water cup and wanted to ignore her new mod altogether. The window was open, and it could have been nothing more than a natural reason for it to tip. There would be a time she would have to face reality, but not until she was ready. Everything was the way she wanted it to be, aside from *Freya*, and she was not willing to change it. "Those are beautiful plants," Orinthia said, awkwardly gesturing to the end table. She picked up the utensil and poked around the food Kos brought her.

"I didn't know what to do with myself while you were out," Kos said, sheepishly. "I felt so helpless standing around the house, waiting."

"The first day we were here, he and I took a walk to get to know each other a bit and fill me in with what's been going on," Uri interjected. "We passed a flower shop and I mentioned how much you loved things that grew."

"So, I bought you a plant," Kos said, pointing to the one at the very left of the table. "I wanted you to have something nice to wake up to. The next day, when waiting around got to be too much, I went back and bought you another. After a few days, it became my ritual. Now you have one plant for every day you've been out."

Orinthia looked at the foliage and counted eight, each different from the last. A warm feeling built in her chest. They were hers.

"And Kos fronted me the money," Uri said, leaning down

and pulling something from under the bed. "But I got you these." He held up a pair of black, ankle-high boots. "They said you were wearing mine."

She knew Kos deserved to hear it privately, but in that moment, she understood what love truly meant. It was about sacrifice, devotion, and selflessness. Orinthia loved the two men beside her in different ways—one was her brother, and the other was someone she wanted to spend her life with. They loved her back, and though things were about to change, she felt at peace. It was as if everything around her was shifting towards something better. In the quiet of that moment, she realized that with love, even the darkest nights can be transformed into a dawn of endless possibilities.

And though she was as homeless and jobless as she was when she first met her friends, everything was different. There were people who cared about her. People she would give her life to protect. Even though she had nothing, she had more than she needed. Her crew, her friends, were her family. They would help her navigate the new world she was thrust into, and she would never be alone again. Their bond was forged in blood and fire, and it was stronger than anything she ever knew.

ACKNOWLEDGMENTS

My husband has been the biggest supporter of my author dreams. Thank you, my love. You and our beautiful kids mean everything to me. Every 2am chat about my book has gotten us here. I could not have done this without you. You believe in me more than I do myself and for that I can never repay you. I hope I encourage you as much as you do me.

Thank you to my editor, Ayesha E. B. Your glowing review breathed life into my failing confidence. I was sure it was going to come back with every line marked out, but that was not the case. Your words have put a new spark in my heart and I can only hope the next book will receive as much praise as this has.

And lastly, thank you to all the indie authors I have met online. You all are so kind and I am grateful to get to know you, even if it is virtually. I hope I can inspire you all and encourage you, too! We got this.

ABOUT THE AUTHOR

Lorena Para (1990-present) was born in Southern California. Her parents moved to The Land of Enchantment (New Mexico, USA) in 1993, where she lived until high school graduation in 2008. She moved back to California for college, and while working on her bachelor's degree in Elementary Education, she met her husband. They live together in a small mountain town tucked away between Los Angeles and Fresno, along with their two children, dogs, chickens, ducks, and hobby homestead.

Lorena is a fan of writing science fiction and post-apocalyptic genres. She finished her first self-published series in 2020 and is currently working on an expansive space pirate series.

When she isn't writing, she is running a small handmade sticker business, homeschooling, her daughter, playing video games, and consuming all forms of Star Wars media.

Stay up to date by joining her newsletter crew:
TheShortWriter.com

The Lenore Monroe Series

Short Autumn Days

Last Winter Days

Cloudy Spring Days

Wavering Summer Days

Space Marauder Chronicles

The Fera

The Gravity of Elendoras